SHARP ENDS

Stories from the World of the First Law

JOE ABERCROMBIE

First published in Great Britain in 2016 by Gollancz
an imprint of the Orion Publishing Group Ltd
Carmelite House, 50 Victoria Embankment,
London EC4Y 0DZ

An Hachette UK Company

This anthology edited by Gillian Redfearn.

1 3 5 7 9 10 8 6 4 2

A CIP catalogue record for this book is available from the British Library

ISBN 978 0 575 10469 3

Typeset at The Spartan Press Ltd, Lymington, Hants

Printed and bound by CPI Group (UK) Ltd, Croydon, CR0 4YY

www.joeabercrombie.com
www.orionbooks.co.uk
www.gollancz.co.uk

For Mum and Dad,
Couldn't have done it without
Your genetic material.

Contents

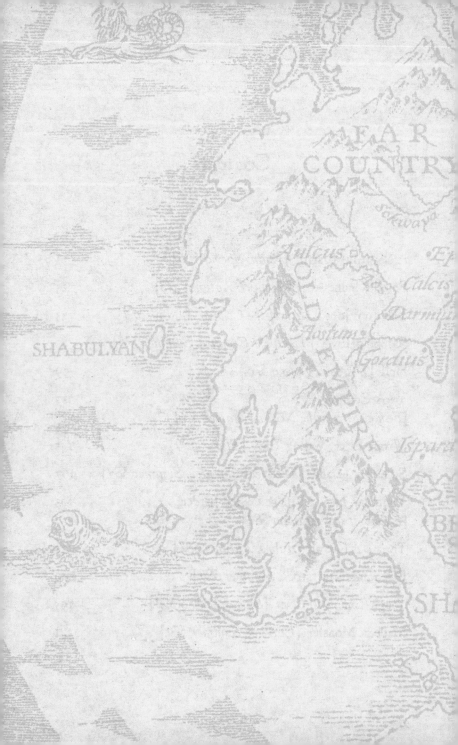

A
BEAUTIFUL
BASTARD

Kadir, Spring 566

'Yes!' shrieked Salem Rews, quartermaster of his August Majesty's First Regiment. 'Give 'em hell!'

Hell was what Colonel Glokta always gave his opponents, whether in the fencing circle, on the battlefield, or in the far more savage context of a social engagement.

His three hapless sparring partners lumbered after him as ineffectually as the cuckolded husbands, ignored creditors and spurned companions did wherever he passed. Glokta smirked as he danced around them, fully living up to his twin reputations as the Union's most celebrated swordsman and show-off. He pranced and prowled, switched and swaggered, nimble as a mayfly, unpredictable as a butterfly and, when he chose, vindictive as an offended wasp.

'Put some effort in!' he called, spinning clear of an inept lunge then administering a smart thwack across the buttocks of its perpetrator that made the crowd convulse with mocking laughter.

'Good show!' called Lord Marshal Varuz, rocking with enjoyment in his folding field chair.

'*Damn* good show!' snapped Colonel Kroy at his right hand.

'Excellent work!' chuckled Colonel Poulder, on the left, the two of them competing to agree the most with their commander.

Quite as if there could be no enterprise more noble than humiliating three recruits who had scarcely held a sword before in their lives.

Salem Rews, with outward delight and secret shame, cheered as loudly as any of them. But he couldn't prevent his eyes occasionally wandering from the fascinating, nauseating exhibition. Over to the valley, and the wretched example of military disorganisation it contained.

While its commanders sunned themselves up here on the ridge – quaffing wine, chortling away at Glokta's self-indulgent display, relishing the priceless luxury of a breath of breeze – down in the sun-baked crucible below, partly obscured in a choking fog of dust, the greater part of the Union army struggled on.

It had taken them all day to squeeze soldiers, horses and the steadily degrading wagons that carried their supplies over the narrow bridge, taunted by the trickle of water in the deep-cut creek below. Now the men were strung out in sluggish shreds and tatters, more sleepwalking than marching. Any hint of a road had long ago been stomped away and all semblance of shape, discipline or morale was a distant memory, red jackets, polished breastplates, drooping golden standards all turned the ubiquitous beige of the sun-parched Gurkish dust.

Rews hooked a finger into his collar and tried to get a little air onto his sweaty neck, wondering again if someone should be doing more to bring order to the chaos down there. Surely it would be a damned bad thing for them if the Gurkish turned up now? And the Gurkish had a habit of turning up at the worst moments.

But Rews was only a quartermaster. Among the officers of the First he was considered the lowest of the low and no one bothered to try and hide the fact, not even him. He shrugged his prickling shoulders and decided – as he so often did – that it was simply someone else's problem. He let his eyes be drawn back, as if by magnetic attraction, to the peerless athleticism of Colonel Glokta.

The man would, no doubt, have looked handsome in a portrait, but it was the way he stood, the way he grinned, sneered, cocked a mocking eyebrow, the way he *moved*, that truly set him apart. He had the poise of a dancer, the stance of a hero, the strength of a wrestler, the speed of a snake.

Two summers ago, in the considerably more civilised surroundings of Adua, Rews had watched Glokta win the Contest without conceding a single touch. He had watched from the cheap seats, of course, so high above the Circle that the fencers were tiny in the distance, but even so his heart had pounded and his hands twitched in time to their movements. Observing his idol at close quarters had only intensified his admiration. Honestly, it had intensified it beyond the point a reasonable judge would have called love. But it had also tempered that admiration with a bitter, spiteful and carefully concealed hatred.

Glokta had everything, and what he didn't have, no one could stop him from taking. Women adored him, men envied him. Women envied him and men adored him, for that matter. One would have thought, with all the good fortune showered upon him, he would have to be the most pleasant man alive.

But Glokta was an utter bastard. A beautiful, spiteful, masterful, horrible bastard, simultaneously the best and worst man in the Union. He was a tower of self-centred self-obsession. An impenetrable fortress of arrogance. His ability was exceeded only by his belief in his own ability. Other people were pieces to be played with, points to be scored, props to be arranged in the glorious tableaux of which he made himself the centrepiece.

Glokta was a veritable tornado of bastardy, leaving a trail of flattened friendships, crushed careers and mangled reputations in his heedless wake.

His ego was so powerful it shone from him like a strange light, distorting the personalities of everyone around him at least halfway into being bastards themselves. Superiors became snivelling accomplices. Experts deferred to his ignorance. Decent men were reduced to sycophantic shits. Ladies of judgement to giggling cyphers.

Rews once heard the most committed followers of the Gurkish religion were expected to make the pilgrimage to Sarkant. In the same way, the most committed bastards might be expected to make a pilgrimage to Glokta. Bastards swarmed to him like ants to a half-eaten pastry. He had acquired a constantly shifting coterie of bastards, a backstabbing gaggle, a self-aggrandising entourage. He had bastards streaming after him like the tail after a comet.

And Rews knew he was no better than the rest. When Glokta mocked others he laughed along, desperate to have his pandering collaboration noticed. When, with sick inevitability, Glokta's ruthless tongue was turned on him, he laughed even louder, delighted to receive even that much attention.

'Teach 'em a lesson!' he screeched as Glokta doubled one of his sparring partners up with a savage poke of the short steel in his gut. Even as he did it, Rews wondered what lesson they were supposed to be learning. That life was cruel, horrible and unfair, presumably.

Glokta caught a man's sword scraping on his long steel, in an instant sheathed his short and slapped him across the face, one way then the other, pushed him bleating over with a snort of derision. The civilians who had come to observe the progress of the war spluttered their admiration while the ladies who accompanied them cooed and swished their fans in the shade of their flapping awning. Rews stood in a paralysis of guilt and joy, only wishing he'd been the one slapped.

'Rews.' Lieutenant West pushed in beside him and wedged one dusty boot up on the fence.

West was one of the very few under Glokta's command who seemed immune to the bastardising effect, expressing unpopular dismay at his worst excesses. Paradoxically he was also one of the very few for whom Glokta appeared to have a genuine respect, in spite of his low birth. Rews saw this, even entirely understood it, but found himself unable to follow West's example. Perhaps it was because he was fat. Or perhaps he simply lacked the moral courage. He lacked every other kind of courage, after all.

'West,' Rews muttered from the side of his mouth, not wanting to miss a moment of the display.

'I've been over by the bridge.'

'Oh?'

'The rearguard are in a shambles. Insofar as there's a rearguard at all. Captain Lasky's laid out with that foot of his. They say he might lose it.'

'Been wrong-footed, has he?' Rews chuckled at his own joke, congratulating himself on it being just the sort of thing Glokta might have said.

'His company's a mess without him.'

'Well, I suppose that's their problem— Jab! Jab! Oooooh!' As Glokta neatly dodged, kicked a man's foot away and sent him rolling in the dirt.

'It could turn into everyone's problem pretty damn quickly,'

West was saying. 'The men are exhausted. Moving slowly. And the supply train's all tangled up—'

'The supply train's always tangled, it's practically a standing order for them— Oh!' Rews gasped with everyone else as Glokta dodged a thrust with consummate speed and kicked the man – he was hardly more than a boy, honestly – in the groin, folding him up with eyes bulging.

'But if the Gurkish come now . . .' West was saying, still frowning at the parched landscape beyond the river.

'The Gurkish are miles away. Honestly, West, you're always worried about something.'

'Someone needs to be—'

'Then complain to the Lord Marshal!' Rews nodded at Varuz, who was almost tipping from his folding chair, so engrossed was he in the heady combination of swordsmanship and bullying. 'I've no idea what you think I can do about it. Send in an order for more horse feed?'

There was a sharp snapping sound as Glokta caught the last man across the face with the flat of his sword and sent him reeling back with an agonised shriek, hand to his cheek.

'Is that really your best?' Glokta stepped forward and gave one of the others a resounding kick in the arse as he tried to get up, sending him face down in the dust to peels of merriment. Glokta soaked up the applause like some parasitic jungle flower absorbing the sap of its host, bowing, beaming, blowing kisses, and Rews smashed his palms together until they hurt.

What a bastard Colonel Glokta was. What a beautiful bastard.

As his three sparring partners hobbled from the enclosure, nursing injuries that would soon heal and humiliations that would accompany them to the grave, Glokta draped himself across the fence behind which the ladies were gathered. He gave particular attention to Lady Wetterlant – young, rich, beautiful if considerably over-powdered, and dressed in the elaborate height of fashion despite the heat. Recently married, but to an older husband kept in Adua by the politics of the Open Council. Rumour had it he fulfilled her financial needs but was otherwise not terribly interested in women.

Colonel Glokta's interest in women, on the other hand, was infamous.

'Might I borrow your handkerchief?' he asked.

Rews had observed a special manner he had when speaking to a woman who interested him. A slight roughening of the voice. A loitering just that fraction closer than was strictly appropriate. A tunnel-like attentiveness, as though his eyes were stuck to them with glue. It hardly needed to be said that the moment he got what he wanted from his conquests, their setting themselves on fire could not persuade him to glance their way again.

And yet new objects of affection fell over themselves to be incinerated by the flames of scandal with the breathless buzzing of moths around a candle, unable to resist the challenge of being the special one to buck the trend.

Lady Wetterlant raised one carefully plucked brow. 'Why ever not, Colonel?' And she reached to take the handkerchief from her bodice. 'I—'

She and her attendants gasped as, quick as lightning, Glokta flicked it from her dress with the blunted point of his long steel. The gauzy fabric floated gently through the air and straight into his waiting hand with all the assurance of a magic trick.

One of the ladies gave a croaky cough. Another fluttered her eyelashes. Lady Wetterlant was perfectly still, eyes wide, lips parted, hand frozen halfway to her chest. Perhaps they were wondering whether the colonel could have flicked the hooks and eyes of her bodice open as easily, had he so desired.

Rews never doubted that he could have.

'My thanks,' said Glokta, dabbing at his forehead.

'By all means keep it,' murmured Lady Wetterlant in a voice slightly hoarse. 'Consider it a gift.'

Glokta smiled as he slipped it into his shirt, a waft of purple fabric still showing. 'I shall keep it close to my heart.' Rews snorted. As if he had one. Glokta dropped his voice, though still perfectly audible to everyone present. 'And perhaps return it later?'

'Whenever you have a moment,' she whispered, and Rews was forced to wonder, once again, what was so damnably attractive about things that were obviously so very, very bad for you.

Glokta had already turned back to his audience, spreading his arms wide as though to give them all a crushing, dominating, loveless hug. 'Is there no one among you clumsy dogs who can give our visitors a better show?' Rews felt a breathless leaping in his chest as Glokta's eyes met his. 'Rews, how about you?'

There was a smattering of laughter and Rews joined in, loudest of all. 'Oh, I couldn't possibly!' he squeaked out. 'I'd hate to embarrass you!'

He instantly realised he had gone too far. Glokta's left eye faintly twitched. 'I'm embarrassed whenever I find myself in a room with you. You're supposed to be a soldier, aren't you? How the hell do you stay so fat when the food is so bloody awful?'

More laughter, and Rews swallowed, plastering the smile to his face and feeling sweat tickle his spine beneath his uniform. 'Well, sir, I've always been fat, I suppose. Even as a boy.' His words plummeted into the sudden silence with the awful finality of victims into a mass grave. 'Very ... fat. Hugely fat. I'm a very fat man.' He cleared his throat, praying that the ground would swallow him.

Glokta's eyes drifted on, seeking a worthier adversary. His face brightened. 'Lieutenant West!' he called, with a flashing flourish of his practice steel. 'How about you?'

West winced. 'Me?'

'Come now, you're probably the best swordsman in the whole damn regiment.' Glokta beamed even wider. 'The best but one, that is.'

West blinked about at what might easily have been several hundred expectant faces. 'But ... I have no blunted steel with me—'

'By all means use your battle steel.'

Lieutenant West looked down at the hilt of his sword. 'That could be rather dangerous.'

The edge on Colonel Glokta's smile was positively ferocious. 'Only if you touch me with it.' More laughter, more applause, a couple of whoops from the enlisted men, a couple of gasps from the ladies. When it came to making ladies gasp, Colonel Glokta was unmatched.

'West!' someone shouted. 'West!' And gradually it became a chant: 'West! West! West!' The ladies laughed as they joined in, clapping in time.

'Go on!' shouted Rews along with the others, a kind of bullying mania upon them all. 'Go on!'

If anyone thought this was a bad idea, they kept it to themselves. Some men you simply don't argue with. Some men you'd simply like to see run through. Glokta fell into both camps.

West took a long breath, then, to a smattering of applause, smoothly vaulted the fence, unbuttoned his jacket and draped it over the rail. With the faintest ringing of metal, and the faintest unhappy look, West drew his battle steel. It did not boast the jewelled quillons, gilded basketwork or engraved ricasso that many of the splendid young officers of his Majesty's First affected. No man there would have called it a beautiful sword.

And yet there was a beautiful economy in the way West presented it, a studied precision in his stance, an elegant control in the twitch of the wrist that brought the blade as perfectly level as the surface of a still pool, the sun glinting on a point polished to murderous sharpness.

A breathless silence settled on the crowd. Commoner he might have been, but even the most ignorant observer could have told that the young Lieutenant West was no bumpkin when it came to handling a sword.

'You've been practising,' said Glokta, tossing his short steel to his servant, Corporal Tunny, leaving him with just the long.

'Lord Marshal Varuz has been good enough to give me a few pointers,' said West.

Glokta raised a brow at his old fencing master. 'You never told me we were seeing other people, sir.'

The Lord Marshal smiled. 'You won a Contest already, Glokta. It is the tragedy of the fencing master that he must always find new pupils to lead to victory.'

'So nice that you're sniffing at my crown, West. But you may find I'm not quite ready to abdicate.' Glokta sprang forward with lightning quickness, jabbed, jabbed. West parried, steel scraping, flickering in the sun. He gave ground, but carefully, watchfully, eyes fixed on Glokta's. Again Glokta came on, cut, cut, thrust, almost too fast for Rews to follow. But West followed well enough, turning the slashes efficiently away, shuffling cautiously back, the crowd giving 'oohs' and 'aahs' with every contact.

Glokta grinned. 'You really have been practising. When will

you learn, West, that work is no substitute for talent!' And he laid into West faster and more ferociously than ever, steel ringing, clattering. He came close and dealt the young lieutenant a savage knee in the ribs, made him wince and stumble, but West found his balance instantly, parried once, twice, reeled away and was ready once more, breathing hard.

And Rews found himself wishing with a painful longing that West would stab Glokta right through his horrible, beautiful face, and make the ladies gasp for very different reasons.

'Hah!' Glokta sprang forward, jabbing, and West dodged the first but to everyone's surprise came on to meet the second, steered it aside with a shrieking of steel, stepped inside Glokta's guard and barged him heavily with his shoulder. For an instant Glokta lurched off balance and West growled, teeth bared, steel flashing as it darted out.

'Gah!' Glokta reeled back and Rews caught a delicious flash of his face stricken with shock. Glokta's practice steel tumbled from his hand and skittered in the dirt, and Rews found that he was bunching his fists painfully tight in delight.

West started forward at once. 'Are you all right, sir?'

Glokta touched one hand to his neck, stared down at his bloody fingertips in profound puzzlement. As if he could hardly believe that he could have been caught. As if he could hardly believe that, having been caught, he might bleed like other men.

'Fancy that,' he grunted.

'I'm so sorry, Colonel,' stammered West, lowering his steel.

'For what?' Glokta's twisted grin looked as if it took every grain of effort he possessed. 'A very fine touch. You've got a great deal better, West.'

And the crowd began to clap, and then to whoop, and Rews

noticed the muscles of Glokta's jaw working, and his left eye twitching, and he held out one hand and sharply snapped his fingers.

'Corporal Tunny, do you have my battle steel with you?'

The young corporal, promoted only the day before, blinked. 'Of course, sir.'

'Bring it here, would you?'

With shocking speed the atmosphere had turned decidedly ugly. The atmosphere around Glokta often did. Rews looked nervously for Varuz to put a stop to this deadly nonsense, but the Lord Marshal had left his seat and wandered off to stare down into the valley, Poulder and Kroy with him. There was to be no help from the grown-ups.

With eyes on the ground, West carefully sheathed his own sword. 'I think I've played with knives enough for one day, sir.'

'But you really must give me the chance to pay you back in kind. Honour demands it, West, really it does.' As if Glokta had the slightest idea what honour was, beyond a tool for manipulating people into doing stupid, dangerous things. 'Surely you understand that, nobleman or no?'

West's jaw tightened. 'Fighting one's friends with sharpened steels while there is an enemy to face seems foolish rather than honourable, sir.'

'Are you calling me a fool?' whispered Glokta, whipping his battle steel from the sheath with an angry hiss as Corporal Tunny nervously offered it out.

West stubbornly folded his arms. 'No, sir.'

The crowd were struck entirely silent, but there was some sort of hubbub rising just beyond them. Rews picked out muttered calls of, 'Over there,' and 'The bridge,' but was too fixed on the drama before him to pay much attention.

'I advise you to defend yourself, Lieutenant West,' snarled Glokta as he worked his heels into the dusty ground, baring his teeth and levelling his shining steel.

And at that moment there was an ear-splitting scream, guttering away into a ragged moan.

'She's fainted!' someone called.

'Get her some air!'

'Where from? I swear there isn't a breath of air in the whole bloody country,' followed by braying laughter.

Rews hastened over to the civilian's enclosure on the pretext of offering assistance. He knew even less about helping people from a faint than he did about being a quartermaster but there was always the possibility of catching a glimpse up the woman's skirts while she was insensible. It was a sad fact that Rews was rarely if ever offered glimpses up the skirts of conscious ladies.

But he froze before he came near the knot of well-wishers, the sight beyond them causing Rews the unpleasant sensation of his ample guts dropping right out of his arse. There, in the distant sweep of beige beyond the bridge, an infestation of black dots was gathering, plumes of dust rising from the swarm. He might not have been good for much, but Rews had always possessed an unerring sense for danger.

He lifted a trembling arm. 'The Gurkish!' he wailed.

'What?' Someone laughed uncertainly.

'There, to the west!'

'That's east, fool!'

'Wait, you're serious?'

'We'll be slaughtered in our beds!'

'We're not in our beds!'

'Silence!' roared Varuz. 'This isn't a damn finishing school.' The hubbub died, the officers brought instantly to guilty quiet.

'Major Mitterick, I want you to get down there now and hurry the men along.'

'Yes, sir.'

'Lieutenant Vallimir, would you be good enough to conduct the ladies and our civilian guests to safety?'

'Of course, sir.'

'A few men could hold them at that bridge,' Colonel Poulder was saying, tugging at his lustrous moustaches.

'A few heroes,' said Varuz.

'A few dead heroes,' said Colonel Kroy, under his breath.

'Do you have fresh men?' asked Varuz.

Poulder shrugged. 'Mine are blown.'

'Mine, too,' added Kroy. 'Even more so.' As though the whole war was a competition at exhausting your regiment.

Colonel Glokta slapped his battle steel back into its sheath. 'My men are fresh,' he said, and Rews felt the fear creeping out from his stomach to every extremity. 'They've been resting up after that last little jaunt of ours. Chomping at the bit to have at the enemy. I daresay his Majesty's First would be willing to hold that bridge long enough to get the men clear, Lord Marshal.'

'Chomping at the bit!' brayed one of Glokta's staff, clearly too drunk to realise what he was volunteering for.

Another, a little less drunk, blinked nervously towards the valley. Rews wondered how many men in his Majesty's First the colonel could be speaking of. The regiment's quartermaster was in no hurry to give his life for the greater good, of that he was absolutely positive.

But Lord Marshal Varuz had not become commander of the Union army by preventing people from sacrificing themselves to make up for his oversights. He slapped Glokta warmly on the arm. 'I knew I could rely on you, my friend!'

'Of course, sir.'

And Rews reflected, with mounting horror, that it was true. Glokta could always be relied upon to jump at the faintest hint of vainglorious showing off, regardless of how fatal it might be for those who followed him into the jaws of death.

Varuz and Glokta, commander and favoured officer, fencing master and finest pupil, and as big a pair of bastards as one could find in a year of searching, drew themselves up and gave each other a salute vibrating with feigned emotion. Then Varuz swept away, snapping orders to Poulder and Kroy and his own gaggle of bastards, presumably to hurry the army to safety and make the sacrifice of his Majesty's First worthwhile.

Because, Rews realised as he looked towards the gathering Gurkish storm on the far side of the bridge, this was most certainly going to be a sacrifice.

'This is suicide,' he whispered to himself.

'Corporal Tunny?' called Glokta, buttoning his jacket.

'Sir?' The keenest of young soldiers snapped out the keenest of salutes.

'Could you bring me my breastplate?'

'Of course, sir.' And off he ran to get it. There were a lot of people running to get things. Officers to get soldiers. Men to get horses. Civilians to get away, Lady Wetterlant with a dewy-eyed glance over her shoulder. Rews was quartermaster of the regiment, wasn't he? He should have some urgent business to be about. And yet he could only stand there, his own eyes very wide and more than a little dewy themselves, mouth and hands opening and closing to no purpose whatsoever.

Two very different kinds of courage were on display. Lieutenant

West was frowning towards the bridge, his face pale and his jaw clenched, determined to do his duty in spite of his very real fear. Colonel Glokta, meanwhile, smirked at death as though it were a jilted lover begging for more, entirely fearless in his certain knowledge that danger was something that applied only to the little people.

Three kinds of courage were on display, Rews realised, because he was there, too, displaying what a total lack of it looked like.

And, indeed, a fourth soon arrived in the form of young Corporal Tunny, sun gleaming on his highly polished strapping, Glokta's breastplate in his eager hands, eyes bright with the courage of untried youth desperate to prove itself.

'Thank you,' said Glokta as Tunny did up the buckles, his narrowed eyes focused on the gathering body of Gurkish cavalry beyond the river, more horses appearing with frightening speed. 'Now I'd like you to hop back to the tent and get my things squared away.'

Tunny's face was a picture of shocked disappointment. 'I was hoping to ride down there with you, sir—'

'Of course you were, and I'd like nothing better than to have you at my side. But if we both die down there, who'll take my personal effects back to Mother?'

The young corporal blinked away tears. 'But, sir—'

'Come, come.' And Glokta slapped him on the shoulder. 'I wouldn't wish to cut short a glittering career. I've no doubt you'll make Lord Marshal one of these days.' Glokta turned his back on the stunned corporal and hence dismissed him utterly from his mind. 'Captain Lackenhorm, would you mind going to the enlisted men and asking for volunteers?'

The prominent lump on the front of Lackenhorm's stringy neck bobbed uncertainly. 'Volunteers for what duty, Colonel?'

Though the duty was obvious enough, set out clearly before them all in the valley below, a vast melodrama slowly unfolding on a grand stage.

'Why, to clear the Gurkish from that bridge, you silly old goat. Quick now, and get them armed and ready, sharp as you like.'

The man gave a nervous smile and hurried away, partly tangled with his sword.

Glokta sprang up onto the fence, one boot on the lower rail and one on the upper. 'I plan to teach these Gurkish a little lesson today, my proud boys of his Majesty's First!'

The young officers crowded eagerly about him, just as though they were ducks and Glokta's heroic platitudes were crumbs.

'I won't order anyone to come – let the decision be on each man's conscience!' He curled his lip. 'How about you, Rews? Will you be waddling after us?'

Rews thought his conscience could probably bear the strain. 'I would like nothing better than to join the charge, Colonel, but my leg—'

Glokta snorted. 'I understand entirely, carrying that body of yours around is a challenge for any leg. I wouldn't want to inflict such a burden on some underserving horse.' Widespread laughter. 'Some men are made to do great things. Others to do . . . whatever it is you do. Of course you're excused, Rews. How could you not be?'

The crushing insult was altogether drowned in a giddy wave of relief. He who laughs last, after all, laughs loudest, and Rews doubted many of his tormentors would be laughing in an hour's time.

'Sir,' West was saying as the colonel swung from the fence into his saddle with the agility of an acrobat. 'Are you sure we have to do this?'

'Who else do you suppose is going to?' asked Glokta, jerking the reins and pulling his steed savagely about.

'A lot of men will surely die. Men with families.'

'Why, yes, I expect so. It is a *war*, Lieutenant.' A scattering of obsequious laughter from the other officers. 'That's what we're here for.'

'Of course, sir.' West swallowed. 'Corporal Tunny, would you be good enough to saddle my horse—'

'No, Lieutenant West,' said Glokta, 'I need you to stay here.'

'Sir?'

'When this is all over I'll require an officer or two who can tell his arse from a pair of melons.' He directed a withering glance at Rews, who hitched his wrinkled trousers up a little. 'Besides, I suspect that sister of yours will grow up to be quite a handful. Couldn't rob her of your sobering influence, could I?'

'But, Colonel, I should—'

'Won't hear of it, West. You'll stay and that's an order.'

West opened his mouth as if to speak, then smartly shut it, drew himself up and gave a rigid salute. Corporal Tunny did the same, the shimmering of a tear at the corner of his eye. Rews crept guiltily to follow suit, light-headed with horror and delight at the thought of a Glokta-less universe.

The colonel grinned at them, his full complement of perfect, brilliantly white teeth almost painful to look upon in the sun's bright glare.

'Come now, gentlemen, don't be maudlin. I'll be back before you know it!'

With a jerk on the reins he caused his horse to rear, frozen for an instant against the bright sky like one of those heroic statues, and Rews wondered if there could ever have been a more beautiful bastard.

Then the dust showered in his face as Glokta thundered down the hillside.

Down towards the bridge.

SMALL
KINDNESSES

Westport, Autumn 573

When Shev arrived to open up that morning, there were a pair of big, dirty, bare feet sticking out of the doorway of her Smoke House.

That might once have caused her quite the shock, but over the last couple of years Shev had come to consider herself past shocking.

'Oy!' she shouted, striding up with her fists clenched.

Whoever it was on their face in the doorway either chose not to move or was unable. She saw the long legs the feet were attached to, clad in trousers ripped and stained, then the ragged mess of a torn and filthy coat. Finally, wedged into the grubby corner against Shev's door, a tangle of long red hair, matted with twigs and dirt.

A big man, without a doubt. The one hand Shev could see was as long as her foot, netted with veins, filthy and scabbed across the knuckles. There was a strange shape to it, though. Slender.

'Oy!' She jabbed the toe of her boot into the coat around where she judged the man's arse to be. Still nothing.

She heard footsteps behind her. 'Morning, boss.' Severard turning up for the day. Never late, that boy. Not the most careful in his work but for punctuality you couldn't knock him. 'What's this you've caught?'

'A strange fish, all right, to wash up in my doorway.' Shev scraped some of the red hair back, wrinkled her nose as she realised it was clotted with blood.

'Is he drunk?'

'She.' It was a woman's face under there. Strong-jawed and strong-boned, pale skin crowded with enough black scab, red graze and purple bruise to make Shev wince, even if she rarely saw anyone who wasn't carrying a wound or two.

Severard gave a soft whistle. 'That's a lot of she.'

'And someone's given her a lot of a beating, too.' Shev leaned close to put her cheek near the woman's battered mouth, heard the faintest wheezing of breath. 'Alive, though.' Then she rocked away and squatted there, wrists on her knees and her hands dangling, wondering what to do. There'd been a time she just dived into whatever messes presented themselves without a backward glance, but somehow the consequences always lurked nearer to hand than they used to. She puffed her cheeks out and gave the weariest of sighs.

'Well, it happens,' said Severard.

'Sadly, yes.'

'Not our problem, is it?'

'Happily, no.'

'Want me to drag her into the street?'

'Yes, I want that quite a lot.' And Shev rolled her eyes skywards and gave another sigh, maybe even wearier than the last. 'But we'd best drag her inside, I reckon.'

'You sure, boss? You remember the last time we helped someone out—'

'Sure? No.' Shev didn't know, after all the shit that had been done to her, why she still felt the need to do small kindnesses. Maybe *because* of all the shit that had been done to her. Maybe there was some stubborn stone in her, like the stone in a date, that refused to let all the shit that had been done to her make her into shit. She turned the key and elbowed the door wobbling open. 'You get her feet.'

When you run a Smoke House you'd better get good at shifting limp bodies, but the latest recipient of Shev's half-arsed charity proved quite the challenge.

'Bloody hell,' grunted Severard, eyes popping as they manhandled the woman down the stale-smelling corridor, her backside scuffing the boards. 'What's she made of, anvils?'

'Anvils are lighter,' groaned Shev through her gritted teeth, waddling from side to side under the dead weight of her, bouncing off the peeling walls. She gasped as she kicked open the door to her office – or the broom-cupboard she called an office. She strained with every burning muscle as she hauled the woman up, knocked her limp head on the doorframe as she wrestled her through, then tripped on a mop and with a despairing squawk toppled back onto the cot with the woman on top of her.

In bed under a redhead was nothing to object to, but Shev preferred them at least partly conscious. Preferred them sweeter-smelling, too, at least when they got *into* bed. This one stank like sour sweat and rot and the very end of things.

'That's where kindness gets you,' said Severard, chuckling away to himself. 'Wedged under a mighty weight of trouble.'

'You going to giggle or help me out, you bastard?' snarled Shev, slack springs groaning as she struggled from underneath, then hauled the woman's legs onto the bed, feet dangling well off the end. It wasn't a big bed, but it looked like a child's with her on it. Her ragged coat had fallen open and the stained leather vest she wore beneath it had got dragged right up.

When Shev spent a year tumbling with that travelling show

there'd been a strongman called himself the Amazing Zaraquon, though his real name had been Runkin. Used to strip to the waist and oil himself up and lift all kinds of heavy things for the crowd, though once he was offstage and towelled down you couldn't get the lazy oaf to lift a thimble for you. His stomach had been all jutting knots of muscle as if beneath his tight-stretched skin he was made of wood rather than meat.

This woman's pale midriff reminded Shev of the Amazing Zaraquon's, but narrower, longer and even leaner. You could see all the little sinews in between her ribs shifting with each shallow breath. But instead of oil her stomach was covered in black and blue and purple bruises, plus a great red welt that looked like it had been left by a most unfriendly axe-handle.

Severard whistled softly. 'They really did give her a beating, didn't they?'

'Aye, they did.' Shev knew well enough what that felt like, and she winced as she twitched the woman's vest down, then dragged the blanket up and laid it over her. Tucked it in a little around her neck, though she felt a fool doing it, and the woman mumbled something and twisted onto her side, matted hair fluttering over her mouth as she started to snore.

'Sweet dreams,' Shev muttered, not that she ever got any herself. Wasn't as if she really needed a bed here, but when you've spent a few years with nowhere safe to sleep, you tend to make a bed in every halfway safe place you can find. She shook the memories off and herded Severard back into the corridor. 'Best get the doors open. We aren't pulling in so much business we can let it slip by.'

'Folk really after husk at this time in the morning?' asked Severard, trying to wipe a smear of the woman's blood off his hand.

'If you want to forget your troubles, why live with them till lunchtime?'

By daylight the smoking room was far from the alluring little cave of wonders Shev had dreamed of making when she bought the place. She planted her hands on her hips as she looked around and gave that weary sigh again. Fact was it bore more than a passing resemblance to an utter shit-hole. The boards were split and stained and riddled with splinters and the cushions greasy as a Baolish kitchen and one of the cheap hangings had come away to show the mould-blooming plaster behind. The Prayer Bells on the shelf were the only things that lent the faintest touch of class, and Shev gave the big one an affectionate stroke, then went up on tiptoe to pin the corner of that hanging back where it belonged, so at least the mould was hidden from her eyes even if her nose was still well aware of it, the smell of rotten onions all-pervasive.

Even a liar as practised as Shev couldn't have convinced a fool as gullible as Shev that it wasn't a shit-hole. But it was her shit-hole. And she had plans to improve it. She always had plans.

'You clean the pipes?' she asked as Severard stomped back from opening the doors, brushing the curtain aside.

'The folk who come here don't care about clean pipes, boss.'

Shev frowned. '*I* care. We may not have the biggest place, or the most comfortable, or the best husk –' she raised her brows at Severard's spotty face '– or the prettiest folk to light it for you, so what's our advantage over our competitors?'

'We're cheap?'

'No, no, no.' She thought about that. 'Well, yes. But what else?'

Severard sighed. 'Customer service?'

'Ding,' said Shev, flicking the biggest Prayer Bell and making it give off that heavenly song. 'So clean the pipes, you lazy shit, and get some coals lit.'

Severard puffed out his cheeks, patched with the kind of downy beard that's meant to make a boy look manly but actually makes him look all the more boyish. 'Yes, boss.'

As he went out the back Shev heard footsteps coming in the front, and she propped her hands on the counter – or the hacked-up piece of butcher's block she'd salvaged off a rubbish heap and polished smooth – and put on her professional manner. She'd copied it from Gusman the carpet-seller, who was the best damn merchant she knew. He had a way of looking like a carpet was sure to be the answer to all your problems.

The professional manner slid off straight away when Shev saw who came strutting into her place.

'Carcolf,' she breathed.

God, Carcolf was trouble. Tall, blonde, beautiful trouble. Sweet-smelling, sweet-smiling, quick-thinking, quick-fingered trouble as subtle as the rain and as trustworthy as the wind. Shev looked her up and down. Her eyes didn't give her much choice in the matter. 'Well, my day's looking better,' she muttered.

'Mine, too,' said Carcolf, brushing past the curtain so the sunlight shone through her hair from behind. 'It's been too long, Shevedieh.'

The room looked vastly improved with Carcolf in it. You wouldn't find a better ornament than her in any bazaar in Westport. Her clothes weren't tight but they stuck in all the right places, and she had this way of cocking her hips. God, those hips. They went all over the place, like they weren't attached to a spine like everyone else's. Shev heard she'd been a dancer. The day she quit had been a loss to dancing and a gain to fraud, without a doubt.

'Come for a smoke?' asked Shev.

Carcolf smiled. 'I like to keep a clear head. How can you enjoy life otherwise?'

'Guess it depends whether your life's enjoyable or not.'

'Mine is,' she said, prancing around the place like it was hers and Shev was a valued guest. 'What do you think of Talins?'

'Never liked it,' muttered Shev.

'I've got a job there.'

'Always loved the place.'

'I need a partner.' The Prayer Bells weren't all that low down. Even so, Carcolf bent over to get a good look at them. Entirely innocently, it would appear. But Shev doubted Carcolf ever did an innocent thing in her life. Especially bend over. 'I need someone I can trust. Someone to watch my arse.'

Shev's voice came hoarse. 'If that's what you want you've come to the right girl, but...' And she tore her eyes away as her mind came knocking like an unwelcome visitor. 'That's not all you're after, is it? I daresay it wouldn't hurt if this partner of yours could pick a lock or a pocket, either.'

Carcolf grinned as if the idea had only just come to her. 'It wouldn't *hurt*. Be good if she could keep her mouth shut, too.' And she drifted over to Shev, looking down at her, since she was a good few inches taller. Most people were. 'Except when I wanted her mouth open, of course...'

'I'm not an idiot.'

'You'd be no use to me if you were.'

'I go with you I'll likely end up abandoned in some alley with nothing but the clothes I'm standing in.'

Carcolf leaned even closer to whisper, Shev's head full of the scent of her, which was a far stretch more appealing than rotten onions or sweaty redhead. 'I'm thinking of you lying down. And without your clothes.'

Shev made a squeak like a rusty hinge. But she forced herself not to grab hold of Carcolf like a drowning girl to a beautiful, beautiful log. She'd been thinking between her legs too long. Time to think between her ears.

'I don't do that kind of work any more. I've got this place to worry about. And Severard to look after, I guess...'

'Still trying to set the world to rights, eh?'

'Not all of it. Just the bit at my elbow.'

'You can't make every stray your problem, Shevedieh.'

'Not every stray. Just this one.' She thought of the great big woman in her bed. 'Just a couple of 'em...'

'You know he's in love with you.'

'All I did was help him out.'

'That's why he's in love with you. No one else ever has.' Carcolf reached out and gently brushed a stray strand of hair out of Shev's face with a fingertip, and gave a sigh. 'Is that boy knocking at the wrong gate, poor thing.'

Shev caught her wrist and guided it away. Being small didn't mean you could let folk just walk all over you. 'He's not the only one.' She held Carcolf's eye, made her voice calm and level. 'I enjoy the act. God knows I enjoy it, but I'd rather you stopped. If you want me just for me, my door's always open and my legs shortly after. If you want me so you can squeeze me out like a lemon and toss my empty skin aside in Talins, well, no offence but I'd rather not.'

Carcolf winced down at the floor. Not so pretty as the smile, but a lot more honest. 'Not sure you'd like me without the act.'

'Why don't we try it and see?'

'Too much to lose,' muttered Carcolf, and she twisted her hand free, and when she looked up the act was on again. 'Well. If you change your mind . . . it'll be too late.' And with a smile over her shoulder deadly as a knife blade, Carcolf walked out. God, that walk she had. Flowing like syrup on a warm day. How did she get it? Did she practise in front of a mirror? Hours every day, more than likely.

The door shut, and the spell was broken, and Shev let go that weary sigh again.

'Was that Carcolf?' asked Severard.

'It was,' murmured Shev, all wistful, a trace of that heavenly scent still battling the mould in her nostrils.

'I don't trust that bitch.'

Shev snorted. 'Fuck no.'

'How do you know her?'

'From around.' From all around Shev's bed and never quite in it.

'The two o' you seem close,' said Severard.

'Not half as close as I'd like to be,' she muttered. 'You clean the pipes?'

'Aye.'

Shev heard the door again, turned with a smile stuck halfway between carpet-seller and needy lover. Maybe it was Carcolf come back, decided she wanted Shev just for Shev—

'Oh, God,' she muttered, face falling. Usually took her at least a little longer than that to regret a decision.

'Morning, Shevedieh,' said Crandall. He was trouble of an altogether less pleasant variety. A rat-faced little nothing, thin at the shoulders and slender in the wits, pink at the eyes and runny at the nose, but he was Horald the Finger's son, and that made him a whole lot of something in this town. A rat-faced little nothing with power he hadn't earned, which made him tetchy, brutal, and prickly spiteful, and jealous of anything anyone had that he didn't. And everyone had something he didn't, even if it was just talent, or looks, or a shred of self-respect.

Shev hitched that professional smile back up though it was hard to think of anyone she wanted less in her place. 'Morning, Crandall. Morning, Mason.'

Mason ducked in just behind his boss. Or his boss's son, anyway. He was one of Horald's boys from way back, broad face criss-crossed with scars, ears all cauliflowered up and a nose so often broken it was shapeless as a turnip. He was as hard a bastard as you'd find anywhere in Westport, where hard bastards were in plentiful supply. He looked over at Shev, still stooping on account of his towering frame and the low ceiling, and gave an apologetic twitch of the mouth. As if to say, *Sorry, but none of this is up to me. It's up to this fool.*

The fool in question was peering at Shev's Prayer Bells, and without bending down, mouth all twisted with contempt. 'What's these? Bells?'

'Prayer Bells,' said Shev. 'From Thond.' She tried to keep her voice calm as three more men crowded past Mason into her place, trying to look dangerous but finding the room too tight for anything but uncomfortable. One had a face all pocked from old boils and eyes bulging right out, another had a leather coat far too big for him, got tangled with a curtain and near tore it down thrashing it away, and the last had his hands shoved deep in his pockets and a look that said he had knives in there. No doubt he did.

Shev doubted she'd ever had so many folk in her place at once. Sadly, they weren't paying. She glanced at Severard, saw him shifting nervously, licking his lips, held out her palm to say, *Calm, calm,* though she had to admit she wasn't feeling too calm herself.

'Didn't think you'd be much for prayer,' said Crandall, wrinkling his nose at the bells.

'I'm not,' said Shev. 'I just like the bells. They lend the place a spiritual quality. You want a smoke?'

'No, and if I did I wouldn't come to a shit-hole like this.'

There was a silence, then the pock-faced one leaned towards her. 'He said it's a shit-hole!'

'I heard him,' said Shev. 'Sound carries in a room small as this one. And I'm well aware it's a shit-hole. I've got plans to improve it.'

Crandall smiled. 'You've always got plans, Shev. They never come to nothing.'

True enough, and mostly on account of bastards like this. 'Maybe my luck'll change,' said Shev. 'What do you want?'

'I want something stolen. Why else would I come to a thief?'

'I'm not a thief any more.'

'Course you are. You're just a thief playing at running a shit-hole Smoke House. And you owe me.'

'What do I owe you for?'

Crandall's face twisted in a vicious grin. 'For every day you don't have a pair o' broken legs.' Shev swallowed. Seemed he'd somehow managed to become more of a bastard than ever.

Mason's deep voice rumbled out, soft and calming. 'It's just a waste is what it is. Westport has lost a hell of a thief and gained a very average husk-seller. How old are you? Nineteen?'

'Twenty-one.' Though she sometimes felt a hundred. 'I'm blessed with a youthful glow.'

'Still far too young to retire.'

'I'm about the right age,' said Shev. 'Still alive.'

'That could change,' said Crandall, stepping close. As close to Shev as Carcolf had been and a very great deal less welcome.

'Give the lady some room,' said Severard, lip stuck out defiantly.

Crandall snorted. 'Lady? Are you fucking serious, boy?'

Shev saw Severard had that stick of hers behind his back. Nice length of wood, it was, just the right weight for knocking someone on the head. But the very last thing she needed was him swinging that stick at Crandall. He'd be carrying it up his arse by the time Mason was through with him.

'Why don't you go out back and sweep the yard?' said Shev.

Severard looked at her, jaw all set for action, the fool. God, maybe he was in love with her. 'I don't want—'

'Go out back. I'll be fine.'

He swallowed, shot the heavies one more glance, then slid out.

Shev gave a sharp whistle, brought all the hard eyes back to her. She knew well enough what having no choice looked like. 'This thing you want. If I steal it, is that the last of it?'

Crandall shrugged. 'Maybe it is. Maybe it isn't. Depends whether I want something stolen again, don't it?'

'Whether your daddy does, you mean.'

Crandall's eye twitched. He didn't like being reminded he was just a little prick in his daddy's big shadow. But Shev was always saying the wrong thing. Or the right thing at the wrong time. Or the right thing at the right time to the wrong person, maybe.

'You'll do as you're told, you little gash-licking bitch,' he spat in her face, 'or I'll burn your shit-hole down with you in it. And your fucking Prayer Bells, too!'

Mason gave a disgusted sigh, scarred cheeks puffed out. As if to say, *He's a rat-faced little nothing, but what can I do?*

Shev stared at Crandall. Damn, but she wanted to butt him in the face. Wanted to with all her being. She'd had bastards like this kicking her around her whole life. Almost be worth it to kick back just once. But she knew all she could do was smile. If she hurt Crandall, Mason would hurt her ten times as bad. He wouldn't like it, but he'd do it. He made a living doing things he didn't like. Didn't they all?

Shev swallowed. Tried to make her fury look like fear. The deck was always stacked against folk like her.

'Guess I haven't got a choice.'

Crandall blasted her with shitty breath as he smiled. 'Who does?'

Never consider the ground, that's the trick to it.

Shev straddled the slimy angle of the roof, broken tiles jabbing her in the groin as she inched along, thinking about how much she'd rather be straddling Carcolf. Down in the busy street to her right some drunk idiots were haw-hawing way too loud over a joke, someone else blabbering in Suljuk which Shev didn't understand more than one word in thirty of. Down in the empty alleyway on her left it seemed quiet, though.

She inched to the chimney, keeping low, just a shadow in the darkness, slipped the loop of her rope over it. Looked solid enough but she gave a good heave to check. Varini used to tell her she weighed two-thirds of nothing but even so she'd almost dragged a chimney clean off once and would've taken a tumble into the street with half a ton of masonry on her head if not for a luckily placed windowsill.

Careful, careful, that's the trick, but a healthy streak of good luck doesn't hurt, either.

Her heart was pounding now and she took a long breath and tried to settle it. Out of practice was all. She was the best thief in Westport, that was well known. That was why they wouldn't let her stop. Why *she* wouldn't let her stop. That was her blessing and her curse.

'Best thief in Westport,' she muttered to herself and slid down the rope to the edge of the roof, peering over. She could see the two guards flanking the doorway, lamplight gleaming on their helmets.

About the right time, and she heard the whores' voices, shrill and angry. Saw the guards' heads turn. More shrieking, and she caught the briefest glimpse of the women struggling before they went down in the gutter. The guards were drifting down the alleyway to watch and Shev smiled to herself. Those girls put on a hell of a show for a couple of silvers.

Seize your moment, that's the trick to it.

In a twinkling she swung over the eaves, down the rope and in through the window. It had only taken a few coppers to get the maid to leave the shutters off the latch. She pulled them to as she dropped onto the other side. Someone was on their way down the stairs, a light tread, unhurried, but Shev was taking no chances. She nipped to the candle and pinched it out with her gloved fingers, sank the corridor into comfortable darkness.

The rope would still be dangling but there wasn't much to do about that. Couldn't afford a partner to hoist it back up. Have to hope she was long gone by the time they noticed.

In and out quick, that's the trick to it.

She could still hear the whores screeching in the street, no doubt having attracted quite the crowd by now, folk betting on the outcome and everything. There's something about women fighting that men can never seem to take their eyes away from. Specially if the women in question aren't wearing much. Shev hooked a finger in her collar and dragged a bit of air in, squashing a stray instinct to go and take a peek herself, and padded softly down the corridor to the third door, already slipping out her picks.

It was a damn good lock. Most thieves wouldn't have even bothered with it. Would've moved along to something easier. But Shev wasn't most thieves. She shut her eyes, and touched the tip of her tongue to her top lip, and slid her picks inside, and started to work the lock. It only took her a few moments to tease out the innards of it, to tickle the tumblers her way. It gave a little metal gasp as it opened up for her, and Shev slipped her tongue and her picks away, eased the knob around – though she was a lot less interested in knobs than locks, being honest – worked the door open a crack and slipped through just as she heard the boots on the stairs, and felt herself grinning in the darkness.

She hadn't wanted to admit it, least of all to herself, but God, she'd missed this. The fear. The excitement. The stakes. The thrill of taking what wasn't hers. The thrill of knowing how damn good she was at it.

'Best fucking thief in Westport,' she mouthed and eased over to the table. The satchel was where Crandall had said it'd be, and she slipped the strap over her shoulder in blissful, velvet silence. Everything just the way she'd planned.

Shev turned back towards the door and a board creaked under her heel.

A woman sat bolt upright in the bed. A woman in a pale nightdress, staring straight at her.

There wasn't supposed to be anyone in here.

Shev raised her gloved hand. 'This is nothing like it looks—'

The woman let go the most piercing scream Shev ever heard in her life.

Cleverness, caution and plans will only get a thief so far. Then luck's a treacherous bitch and won't always play along, so boldness will have to take you the rest of the way. Shev raced to the window, raised her black boot and gave the shutters an almighty kick, splintering the latch, and sent them shuddering open as the woman heaved in a whooping breath.

A square of night sky. The second storey of the buildings across the way. She caught a glimpse of a man with his head in his hands through the window directly opposite. She thought about how far down it was and made herself stop. You can't think about the ground. The woman let blast another bladder-loosening scream. Shev heard the door wrenched wide, guards yelling. She jumped through.

Wind tugged, flapped at her clothes, that lurching in her stomach as she started to fall. Like doing the high drop when she was tumbling with that travelling show, hands straining to catch Varini's. The reassuring smack of her palms into his and the puff of chalk as he whisked her up to safety. Every time. Every time but that last time when he'd had a drink too many and the ground had caught her instead.

She let it happen. Once you're falling, you can't fight it. There's an urge to flail and struggle but the air won't help you. No one will. No one ever will, in her experience.

With a teeth-rattling thud she dropped straight into the wagon of fleeces she'd paid Jens to leave under the window. He looked suitably amazed to see her floundering out from his cargo, dragging the satchel after her and scurrying across the street, weaving between the people and into the darkness between the ale-shop and the ostler's, the shouting fading behind her.

She reeled against the wall, gripping at her side, growling with each breath and trying not to cry out. Rim of the cart had caught her in the ribs and from the sick pain and the way her head was spinning she reckoned at least one was broken, probably a few more.

'Fucking ouch,' she forced through gritted teeth. She glanced back towards the building as Jens shouted to his mule and the wagon rolled off, a guard leaning out of the open window, pointing wildly across the street towards her. She saw someone slip out of a side door and gently push it closed. Someone tall, and slim, a strand of blonde hair falling from a black hat and a satchel over her shoulder. Someone with a hell of a walk, hips swaying as she drifted quietly into the shadows.

The guard roared something and Shev turned, stumbled on down the alley, squeezed through the little crack in the wall and away.

Now she remembered why she'd wanted to stop and run a Smoke House instead.

Most thieves don't last long. Not even the good ones.

'You're hurt,' said Severard.

Shev really was hurt, but she'd learned to keep her hurts as hidden as she could. In her experience, people were like sharks, blood in the water only made them hungry. So she shook her head, tried to smile, tried to look not-hurt with her face twisted up and sweaty and her hand clamped to her ribs. 'It's nothing. We got customers?'

'Just Berrick.'

He nodded towards the old husk-head, sprawled out on the greasy cushions with eyes closed and mouth open, spent pipe beside him.

'When did he smoke?'

'Couple of hours past.'

Shev gripped her side tight as she knelt beside him, touched him gently on the cheek. 'Berrick? Best wake up, now.'

His eyes fluttered open, and he saw Shev, and his lined face suddenly crushed up. 'She's dead,' he whispered. 'Keep remembering it fresh. She's dead.' And he closed his eyes and squeezed tears down his pale cheeks.

'I know,' said Shev. 'I know and I'm sorry. I'd usually let you stay long as you need, and I hate to do this, but you got to get up, Berrick. Might be trouble. You can come back later. See him home, eh, Severard?'

'I should stay here, I can watch your back—'

More likely he'd do something stupid and get the pair of them killed. 'I been watching my own back long as I can remember. Go feed your birds.'

'Fed 'em already.'

'Feed 'em again, then. Just promise me you'll stay out till Crandall's come and gone.'

Severard worked his spotty jaw, sullen. Shit, the boy really was in love with her. 'I promise.' And he slipped an arm under Berrick's and helped him stagger out of the door. Two less little worries, but still the big one to negotiate. Shev stared about, wondering how she could be ready for Crandall's visit. Routes of escape, hidden weapons, backup plans in case something went wrong.

The coals they used to light the pipes were smouldering away in the tin bowl on their stand. Shev picked up the water jug, thinking to douse them, then reckoned maybe she could fling them in someone's face if she had to and moved the stand back against the wall in easy reach instead, coals sliding and popping as she set it down.

'Evening, Shev.' She spun about, trying not to wince at the

stab of pain in her side. For a big, big man, Mason sure had a light tread when he felt the need.

Crandall ducked into the Smoke House, looking even more sour than usual. She watched two of his thugs crowd in behind him. Big-Coat with his big coat on and Hands-in-Pockets with his hands still stuffed in his pockets.

The door to the yard creaked open and Pock-Face sidled through and shouldered it shut. So much for the escape route. Shev swallowed. Just say as little as possible, do nothing to rile them and get them out quick as she could. That was the trick to it.

'Black suits you,' said Mason, looking her up and down.

'That's why I wear it,' she said, trying to come across relaxed but only managing queasy. 'That and the thieving.'

'Got it?' snapped Crandall.

Shev slipped the satchel from under the counter and tossed it to him, strap flapping.

'Good girl,' he said as he caught it. 'Did you open it?'

'None of my business.'

Crandall pulled the satchel open. He poked around inside. He looked up at her with far from the satisfied-customer expression she'd been hoping for. 'This a fucking joke?'

'Why would it be?'

'It's not here.'

'What's not?'

'What was supposed to be in here!' Crandall shook the satchel at her and the frowns his men wore grew a little bit harder.

Shev swallowed again, a sinking feeling in her gut like she was standing at a cliff edge and could feel the earth crumbling at her feet. 'You didn't say there'd be anything in it. You didn't say there'd be some champion screamer in the room, either. You said get the satchel, and I got it!'

Crandall flung the empty satchel on the floor. 'Thought you'd fucking sell it to someone else, didn't you?'

'What? I don't even know what *it* is! And if I'd screwed you I wouldn't be standing here waiting with nothing but a smile, would I?'

'Take me for a fool, do you? Think I didn't see Carcolf leaving here earlier?'

'Carcolf? She just came cause she had a job… in Talins…' Shev trailed off with that same feeling she'd felt when her hands slipped from Varini's and she'd seen the ground flying up to greet her. Crandall's men shifted, Pock-Face pulling a jagged-edged knife out, and Mason gave a grimace even bigger'n usual, and slowly shook his head.

Oh, God. Carcolf had finally fucked her. But not in a good way. Not in a good way at all.

Shev held her hands up, calming, trying to give herself time to think of something. 'Look! You said get the satchel and I got it.' She hated the whine in her voice. Knew there was no point begging but couldn't help herself. Looked to the doors, the thugs slowly closing on her, knew the only question left was how bad they'd hurt her. Crandall stepped towards her, face twisting.

'Look!' she screeched, and he punched her in the side. Far from the hardest punch she'd ever taken, but as bad luck had it his fist landed right where the wagon had, there was a flash of pain through her guts and straight away she doubled up and puked all down his trousers.

'Oh, that's *it*, you fucking little bitch! Hold her.'

The one with the pocked face caught her left arm, and the one with the stupid coat her right, and stuck his forearm in her throat and pinned her against the wall, both of them grinning like it was a while since they'd had so much fun. Shev could've been enjoying herself more as Pock-Face waved his knife in her face, her mouth acrid with sick and her side on fire and her eyes crossed as she stared at the bright point.

Crandall snapped his fingers at Mason. 'Give me your axe.'

Mason puffed his cheeks out. 'More'n likely it's that bitch Carcolf behind all this. Nothing Shevedieh could've done. We kill her she can't help us find what we're after, eh?'

'It's past business now,' said Crandall, the little rat-faced nothing, 'and on to teaching a lesson.'

'What lesson will this teach? And to who?'

'Just give me your fucking axe!'

Mason didn't like it, but he made a living doing things he didn't like. Wasn't as if this crossed some line. His expression said, *I'm real sorry*, but he pulled out his hatchet and slapped the polished handle into Crandall's palm anyway, turning away in disgust.

Shev twisted like a worm cut in half but could hardly breathe for the pain in her ribs, and the two bastards had her fast. Crandall leaned closer, caught a fistful of her shirt and twisted it. 'I would say it's been nice knowing you, but it fucking hasn't.'

'Try not to spatter me this time, boss,' said Pock-Face, closing the bulging eye nearest to her so he didn't get her brains in it.

Shev gave a stupid whimper, squeezing her eyes shut as Crandall raised the axe.

So that was it, then, was it? That was her life? A shit one, when you thought about it. A few good moments shared with halfway decent folk. A few small kindnesses done. A few little victories clawed from all those defeats. She'd always supposed the good stuff was coming. The good stuff she'd be given. The good stuff she'd give. Turned out this was all there was.

'It is a long time since I last saw Prayer Bells.'

Shev opened her eyes again. The red-haired woman she'd dragged into her bed that morning and forgotten all about was standing larger than life in Shev's smoking room in that ripped leather vest, peering at the bells on the shelf.

'This is a very fine one.' And she brushed the bronze with her scabbed fingertips. 'Second Dynasty.'

'Who's this fucking joker?' snarled Crandall, weighing the hatchet in his hand.

Her eyes shifted lazily over to him. Or the one eye Shev could see did, tangled red hair hanging across the other. That hard-boned face was spattered with bruises, the nose cut and swollen and crusted with blood, the lips split and bloated. But she had this look in that one bloodshot eye as it flickered across Crandall and his four thugs, lingered on Mason a moment, then away. An easy contempt. As though she'd taken their whole measure in that single glance, and wasn't troubled by it one bit.

'I am Javre,' said the woman Shev found unconscious in her doorway. She had some strange kind of an accent. From up north somewhere, maybe. 'Lioness of Hoskopp and, far from being a joker, I am in fact often told I have a poor sense of humour. Who put me to bed?'

Pinned against the wall by three men, the most Shev could do was raise one finger.

Javre nodded. 'That was a kindness I will not forget. Do you have my sword?'

'Sword?' Shev managed to croak, the forearm across her throat easing off as its owner turned to sneer at the new arrival.

Javre hissed through her teeth. 'It could be very dangerous

if it fell into the wrong hands. It is forged from the metal of a fallen star.'

'She's mad,' said Crandall.

'Fucking loon,' grunted Hands-in-Pockets.

'Lioness of Hoskopp,' said Big Coat, and gave a little giggle.

'I will have to steal it back,' she was musing. 'Do any of you know a decent thief?'

There was a pause, then Shev raised that one finger again.

'Ah!' Javre's blood-clotted brow went up. 'It is said the Goddess places the right people in each other's paths.' She frowned as though she was only just making sense of the situation. 'Are these men inconveniencing you?'

'A little,' Shev whispered, grimacing at the dull ache that had spread from her side right to the tips of her fingers.

'Best to check. You never can tell what people enjoy.' Javre slowly worked her bare shoulders. They reminded Shev of the Amazing Zaraquon's, too, woody hard and split into a hundred little fluttering shreds of muscle. 'I will ask you once to put the dark-skinned girl down and leave.'

Crandall snorted. 'And if we don't?'

That one eye narrowed slightly. 'Then long after we are gone to the Goddess, the grandchildren of the grandchildren of those who witness will whisper fearful stories of the way I broke you.'

Hands-in-Pockets shoved his hands down further still. 'You ain't even got a weapon,' he snarled.

But Javre only smiled. 'My friend, I am the weapon.'

Crandall jerked his head towards her. 'Put this bitch out o' my misery.'

Pock-Face and Big-Coat let go of Shev, which was a blessing, but closed in towards Javre, which didn't seem to be. Big-Coat pulled a stick from his coat, which was a little disappointing since he had ample room for a greatsword in there. Pock-Face spun his jagged-edged dagger around in his fingers and stuck out his tongue, which was uglier than the blade, if anything.

Javre just stood, hands on her hips. 'Well? Do you await a written invitation?'

Pock-Face lunged at her but his knife caught nothing. She dodged with a speed even Shev could hardly follow and her white hand flashed out and chopped him across the side of the neck with a sound like a cleaver chopping meat. He dropped as if he had no bones in him at all, knife bouncing from his hand, flopping and thrashing on the floor like a landed fish, spitting and gurgling and his eyes popping out further than ever.

Big-Coat hit her in the side with his stick. If he'd hit a pillar, that was the sound of it. Javre hardly even flinched. Muscle bulged in her arm as she sank her fist into his gut and he bent right over with a breathy wheeze. Javre caught him by the hair with her big right fist and smashed his head into Shev's butcher-block counter, blood spattering the cheap hangings.

'Shit,' breathed Crandall, the hand he was holding Shev with going limp.

Javre looked over at the one with his hands rammed in his pockets, whose mouth had just dropped open. 'No need to feel embarrassed,' she said. 'If I had a cock I would play with it all the time, too.'

He jerked his hands out and flung a knife. Shev saw the metal flicker, heard the blade twitter.

Javre caught it. She made no big show of it, like the jugglers in that travelling show used to. She simply plucked it from the air as easily as you might catch a coin you'd tossed yourself.

'Thank you,' she said. She tossed it back and it thudded into the man's thigh. He gave a great spitty screech as he staggered back through the doorway and into the street.

Mason had just pulled his own knife out, a monster of a thing you could've called a sword without much fear of correction. Javre planted her hands on her hips again. 'Are you sure this is the way you want it?'

'Can't say I want it,' said Mason, drifting into a fighting crouch. 'But there's no other way for it to be.'

'I know.' Javre shook her shoulders again and raised those big empty hands. 'But it is always worth asking.'

He sprang at her, knife a blur, and she whipped out of the way. He slashed at her and she dodged again, watching as he lumbered towards the door, tearing the curtain from its hooks. He lunged at her, feathers spewing up in a fountain as he hacked a cushion open, splinters flying as he smashed the counter over with his flailing boot, cloth ripping as he slashed one of the hangings in half.

Mason gave a bellow like a hurt bull and charged at her once more. Javre caught his wrist as the knife blade flashed towards her, big vein popping from her arm as she held it, straining, the trembling point just a finger's width from her forehead.

'Got you now!' Mason sprayed spit through his clenched teeth as he caught Javre by her thick neck, forced her back a step—

She snatched the big Prayer Bell from the shelf and smashed him over the head with it, the almighty clang so loud it rattled the teeth in Shev's head. Javre hit him again, twisting free of his clutching hand, and he gave a groan and dropped to his knees, blood pouring down his face. Javre raised her arm high and smashed him onto his back, bell breaking from handle and clattering away into the corner, the ringing echoes gradually fading.

Javre looked up at Crandall, her face all spotted with Mason's blood. 'Did you hear that?' She raised her red brows. 'Time for you to pray.'

'Oh, hell,' croaked Crandall. He let the hatchet clatter to the boards and held his open palms up high. 'Now look here,' he stammered out, 'I'm Horald's son. Horald the Finger!'

Javre shrugged as she stepped over Mason's body. 'I am new in town. One name strikes me no harder than another.'

'My father runs things here! He gives the orders!'

Javre grinned as she stepped over Big-Coat's corpse. 'He does not give me orders.'

'He'll pay you! More money than you can count!'

Javre poked Pock-Face's fallen knife aside with the toe of her boot. 'I do not want it. I have simple tastes.'

Crandall's voice grew shriller as he shrank away from her. 'If you hurt me, he'll catch up to you!'

Javre shrugged again as she took another step. 'We can hope so. It would be his last mistake.'

'Just... please!' Crandall cringed. 'Please! I'm begging you!'

'It really is not me you have to beg,' said Javre, nodding over his shoulder.

Shev whistled and Crandall turned around, surprised. He looked even more surprised when she buried the blade of Mason's hatchet in his forehead with a sharp crack.

'Bwurgh,' he said, tongue hanging out, then he toppled backwards, his limp hand catching the stand and knocking it and the tin bowl flying, showering hot coals across the wall.

'Shit,' said Shev as flames shot up the flimsy hangings. She grabbed the water jug but its meagre contents made scarcely any difference. Fire had already spread to the next curtain, shreds of burning ash fluttering down.

'Best vacate the premises,' said Javre, and she took Shev under the arm with a grip that was not to be resisted and marched her smartly out through the door, leaving four dead men scattered about the burning room.

The one who'd had his hands in his pockets was leaning against the wall in the street, clutching at his own knife stuck in his thigh.

'Wait—' he said as Javre caught him by the collar, and with a flick of her wrist sent him reeling across the street to crash head first into a wall.

Severard was running up, staring at the building, flames already licking around the doorframe. Javre caught him and guided him away. 'Nothing to be done. Bad choice of décor in a place with naked flames.' As if to underscore the point, the window shattered, fire gouting into the street, and Severard ducked with his hands over his head.

'What the hell happened?' he moaned.

'Went bad,' whispered Shev, clutching at her side. 'Went bad.'

'You call that bad?' Javre scraped the dirty red hair out of her battered face and grinned at the ruin of Shev's hopes as though it looked a good enough day's work to her. 'I say it could have been far worse!'

'How?' snapped Shev. 'How could it be fucking worse?'

'We might both be dead.' She gave a sharp little laugh. 'Come out alive, it is a victory.'

'This is what happens,' said Severard, his eyes shining with reflected fire as the building burned brighter. 'This is what happens when you do a kindness.'

'Ah, stop crying, boy. Kindness brings kindness in the long run. The Goddess holds our just rewards in trust! I am Javre, by the way.' And she clapped him on the shoulder and near knocked him over. 'Do you have an older brother, by any chance? Fighting always gets me in the mood.'

'What?'

'Brothers, maybe?'

Shev clutched at her head. Felt like it was going to burst. 'I killed Crandall,' she whispered. 'I bloody killed him. They'll come after me now! They'll never stop coming!'

'Pffffft.' Javre put one great, muscled, bruised arm around Shev's shoulders. Strangely reassuring and smothering at once. 'You should see the bastards coming after me. Now, about stealing back this sword of mine...'

THE FOOL
JOBS

East of the Crinna,
Autumn 574

Craw chewed the hard skin around his nails, just like he always did. They hurt, just like they always did. He thought to himself that he really had to stop doing that. Just like he always did.

'Why is it,' he muttered under his breath, and with some bitterness too, 'I always get stuck with the fool jobs?'

The village squatted in the fork of the river, a clutch of damp thatch roofs, scratty as an idiot's hair, a man-high fence of rough-cut logs ringing it. Round wattle huts and three long halls dumped in the muck, ends of the curving wooden uprights on the biggest badly carved like dragons' heads, or wolves' heads, or something that was meant to make men scared but only made Craw nostalgic for decent carpentry. Smoke limped up from chimneys in muddy smears. Half-bare trees still shook browning leaves. In the distance the reedy sunlight glimmered on the rotten fens, like a thousand mirrors stretching off to the horizon. But without the romance.

Wonderful stopped scratching at the long scar through her shaved-stubble hair long enough to make a contribution. 'Looks to me,' she said, 'like a confirmed shit-hole.'

'We're way out east of the Crinna, no?' Craw worked a speck of skin between teeth and tongue and spat it out, wincing at the pink mark left beside his nail, way more painful than it had any right to be. 'Nothing but hundreds of miles of shit-hole in every direction. You sure this is the place, Raubin?'

'I'm sure. She was most specifical.'

Craw frowned. He weren't sure if he'd taken such a pronounced dislike to Raubin 'cause he was the one that brought the jobs and the jobs were usually cracked, or if he'd taken such a pronounced dislike to Raubin 'cause the man was a weasel-faced arsehole. Bit of both, maybe. 'The word is "specific", half-head.'

'Got my meaning, no? Village in a fork in the river, she said, south o' the fens, three halls, biggest one with uprights carved like fox heads.'

'Aaaah.' Craw snapped his fingers. 'They're meant to be foxes.'

'Fox Clan, these crowd.'

'Are they?'

'So she said.'

'And this thing we've got to bring her. What sort of a thing is it, exactly?'

'Well, it's a thing,' said Raubin.

'That much we know.'

'Sort of... this long, I guess. She didn't say, precisely.'

'Unspecifical, was she?' asked Wonderful, grinning with every tooth.

'She said it'd have a kind of a light about it.'

'A light?' asked Craw. 'What? Like a magic bloody candle?'

All Raubin could do was shrug, which weren't a scrap of use to no one. 'I don't know. She said you'd know it when you saw it.'

'Oh, nice.' Craw hadn't thought his mood could drop much lower. Now he knew better. 'That's real nice. So you want me to bet my life, and the lives o' my crew, on knowing it when I see it?' He shoved himself back off the rocks on his belly, out of sight of the village, clambered up and brushed the dirt from his coat, muttering darkly to himself since it was a new one and he'd been taking some trouble to keep it clean. Should've known that'd be a waste of effort, what with the shitty jobs he always ended up in to his neck. He started back down the slope, shaking his head, striding through the trees towards the others. A good, confident stride. A leader's stride. It was important, Craw reckoned, for a chief to walk like he knew where he was going.

Especially when he didn't.

Raubin hurried after him, whiny voice picking at his back. 'She didn't precisely say. About the thing, you know. I mean, she don't, always. She just looks at you, with those eyes . . .' He gave a shudder. 'And says, fetch me this thing, and where from. And what with the paint, and that voice o' hers, and that sweat o' bloody fear you get when she looks at you . . .' Another shudder, hard enough to rattle his rotten teeth. 'I ain't asking no questions, I can tell you that. I'm just looking to run out fast so I don't piss myself on the spot. Run out fast, and fetch whatever thing she's after—'

'Well, that's real sweet for you,' said Craw, 'except insofar as actually getting this thing goes.'

'As far as getting the thing goes,' mused Wonderful, splashes of light and shadow swimming across her bony face as she looked up into the branches, 'the lack of detail presents serious difficulties. All manner of things in a village that size. Which one, though? Which thing, is the question.' Seemed she was in a thoughtful mood. 'One might say the voice, and the paint, and the aura of fear are, in the present case . . . self-defeating.'

'Oh no,' said Craw. 'Self-defeating would be if she was the one who ended up way out past the Crinna with her throat cut, on account of some blurry details on the minor point of the actual job we're bloody here to do.' And he gave Raubin a hard glare as he strode out of the trees and into the clearing.

Scorry was sitting sharpening his knives, eight blades neatly laid out on the patchy grass in front of his crossed legs, from a little pricker no longer'n Craw's thumb to a hefty carver just this side of a short-sword. The ninth he had in his hands, whetstone working at steel, squick, scrick, marking the rhythm to his soft, high singing. He had a wonder of a singing voice, did Scorry Tiptoe. No doubt he would've been a bard in a happier age, but there was a steadier living in sneaking up and knifing folk these days. A sad fact, Craw reckoned, but those were the times.

Brack-i-Dayn was sat beside Scorry, lips curled back, nibbling at a stripped rabbit bone like a sheep nibbling at grass. A huge, very dangerous sheep. The little thing looked like a toothpick in his great tattooed blue lump of a fist. Jolly Yon frowned down at him as if he was a great heap of shit, which Brack might've been upset by if it hadn't been Yon's confirmed habit to look at everything and everyone that way. He properly looked like the least jolly man in all the North at that moment. It was how he'd come by the name, after all.

Whirrun of Bligh was kneeling on his own on the other side of the clearing, in front of his great long sword, leaned up against a tree for the purpose. He had his hands clasped in front of his chin, hood drawn down over his head, just the sharp end of his nose showing. Praying, by the look of him. Craw had always been a bit worried by men who prayed to gods, let alone swords. But those were the times, he guessed. In bloody days, swords were worth more than gods. They certainly had 'em outnumbered. Besides, Whirrun was a valley-man, from way out north and west, across the mountains near the White Sea, where it snowed in summer and no one with the slightest sense would ever choose to live. Who knew how he thought?

'Told you it was a real piss-stain of a village, didn't I?' Never was in the midst of stringing his bow. He had that grin he tended to have, like he'd made a joke on everyone else and no one but him had got it. Craw would've liked to know what it was, he could've done with a laugh. The joke was on all of 'em, far as he could see.

'Reckon you had the right of it,' said Wonderful as she strutted past into the clearing. 'Piss. Stain.'

'Well, we didn't come to settle down,' said Craw, 'we came to get a thing.'

Jolly Yon achieved what many might've thought impossible by frowning deeper, black eyes grim as graves, dragging his thick fingers through his thick tangle of a beard. 'What sort of a thing, exactly?'

Craw gave Raubin another look. 'You want to dig that one over?' The fixer only spread his hands, helpless. 'I hear we'll know it when we see it.'

'Know it when we see it? What kind of a—'

'Tell it to the trees, Yon, the task is the task.'

'And we're here now, aren't we?' said Raubin.

Craw sucked his teeth at him. 'Brilliant fucking observation. Like all the best ones, it's true whenever you say it. Yes, we're here.'

'We're here,' sang Brack-i-Dayn in his up-and-down Hillman accent, sucking the last shred o' grease from his bone and flicking it into the bushes. 'East of the Crinna where the moon don't shine, a hundred miles from a clean place to shit and with wild, crazy bastards dancing all around think it's a good idea to put bones through their own faces.' Which was a little rich, considering he was so covered in tattoos he was more blue than white. There's no style of contempt like the stuff one kind of savage has for another, Craw guessed.

'Can't deny they've got some funny ideas east of the Crinna.' Raubin shrugged. 'But here's where the thing is, and here's where we are, so why don't we just get the fucking thing and back fucking home?'

'Why don't you get the fucking thing, Raubin?' growled Jolly Yon.

''Cause it's my fucking job to fucking tell you to get the fucking thing is why, Yon fucking Cumber.'

There was a long, ugly pause. Uglier than the child of a man and a sheep, as the Hillmen have it. Then Yon talked in his quiet voice, the one that still gave Craw prickles up his arms, even after all these years. 'I hope I'm wrong. By the dead, I hope I'm wrong. But I'm getting this feeling...' He shifted forward, and it was awfully clear all of a sudden just how many axes he was carrying, 'like I'm being disrespected.'

'No, no, not at all, I didn't mean—'

'*Respect*, Raubin. That shit costs nothing, but it can spare a man from trying to hold his brains in all the way back home. Am I clear enough?'

'Course you are, Yon, course you are. I'm over the line. I'm all over it on both sides of it, and I'm sorry. Didn't mean no disrespect. Lot o' pressure, is all. Lot o' pressure for everyone. It's my neck on the block, just like yours. Not down there, maybe, but back home, you can be sure o' that, if she don't get her way...' Raubin shuddered again, worse'n ever.

'A touch of respect don't seem too much to ask—'

'Enough.' Craw waved the pair of 'em down. 'We're all sinking on the same leaky bloody skiff, there's no help arguing about it. We need every man to a bucket, and every woman, too.'

'I'm always helpful,' said Wonderful, all innocence.

'If only.' Craw squatted, pulling out a blade and starting to scratch a map of the village in the dirt. The way Threetrees used to do a long, low time ago. 'We might not know exactly what this thing is, but we know where it is, at least.' Knife scraped through earth as the others gathered, kneeling, sitting, squatting, looking on. 'A big hall in the middle, with uprights on it carved like foxes' heads. They're dragons, you ask me, but, you know, that's another story. There's a fence around the outside, two gates, north and south. Houses and huts over here. A pigpen there, I think. That's a forge, maybe.'

'How many do we reckon might be down there?' asked Yon.

Wonderful rubbed at the scar on her scalp, face twisted as she glanced up towards the pale sky. 'Could be fifty, sixty fighting men? A few elders, few dozen women and children, too. Some o' those might hold a blade.'

'Women fighting.' Never grinned. 'A disgrace, is that.'

Wonderful bared her teeth back at him. 'Get those bitches to the cook-fire, eh?'

'Oh, the cook-fire...' Brack stared up into the cloudy sky like it was packed with happy memories.

'Sixty warriors? And we're but seven – plus the baggage.' Jolly Yon curled his tongue and blew spit over Raubin's boots in a neat arc. 'Shit on that. We need more men.'

'Wouldn't be enough food then.' Brack-i-Dayn laid a sad hand on his belly. 'There's hardly enough as it—'

Craw cut him off. 'Maybe we should stick to plans using the number we've got, eh? Plain as plain, sixty's way too many to fight fair.' Not that anyone had joined his crew for a fair fight, of course. 'We need to draw some off.'

Never winced. 'Any point asking why you're looking at me?'

'Because ugly men hate nothing worse than handsome men, pretty boy.'

'It's a fact I can't deny.' Never sighed, flicking his long hair back. 'I'm cursed with a fine face.'

'Your curse my blessing.' Craw jabbed at the north end of his dirt-plan, where a wooden bridge crossed a stream. 'You'll take your unmatched beauty in towards the bridge. They'll have guards posted, no doubt. Mount a diversion.'

'Shoot one of 'em, you mean?'

'Shoot near 'em, maybe. Let's not kill anyone we don't have to, eh? They might be nice enough folks under different circumstances.'

Never sent up a dubious eyebrow. 'You reckon?'

Craw didn't, particularly, but he'd no desire to weight his conscience down any further. It didn't float too well as it was. 'Just lead 'em a little dance, that's all.'

Wonderful clapped a hand to her chest. 'I'm so sorry I'll miss it. No one dances prettier than our Never when the music gets going.'

Never grinned at her. 'Don't worry, sweetness, I'll dance for you later.'

'Promises, promises.'

'Yes, yes.' Craw shut the pair of 'em up with another wave. 'You can make us all laugh when this fool job's done with, if we're still breathing.'

'Maybe we'll make you laugh, too, eh, Whirrun?' said Wonderful.

The valley-man sat cross-legged, sword across his knees, and shrugged. 'Maybe.'

'We're a tight little group, us lot, we like things friendly.'

Whirrun's eyes slid across to Jolly Yon's black frown, and back. 'I see that.'

'We're like brothers,' said Brack, grinning all over his tattooed face. 'We share the risks, we share the food, we share the rewards, and from time to time we even share a laugh.'

'Never got on too well with my brothers,' said Whirrun.

Wonderful snorted. 'Well, aren't you blessed, boy? You've been given a second chance at a loving family. You last long enough, you'll learn how it works.'

The shadow of Whirrun's hood crept up and down his face as he slowly nodded. 'Every day should be a new lesson.'

'Good advice,' said Craw. 'Ears open, then, one and all. Soon as Never's drawn a few off, we creep in at the south gate.' And he put a cross in the dirt to show where it was. 'Two groups, one each side o' the main hall there, where the thing is. Where the thing's meant to be, leastways. Me, Yon and Whirrun on the left.' Yon spat again, Whirrun gave the slightest nod. 'Wonderful, take Brack and Scorry down the right.'

'Right y'are, Chief,' said Wonderful.

'Right for us,' sang Brack.

'So, so, so,' said Scorry, which Craw took for a yes.

He stabbed at each of 'em with one chewed-to-bugger finger-nail. 'And all on your best behaviour, you hear? Quiet as a spring breeze. No tripping over the pots this time, eh, Brack?'

'I'll mind my boots, Chief.'

'Good enough.'

'We got a backup plan?' asked Wonderful. 'In case the

impossible happens and things don't work out quite according to the scheme?'

'The usual. Grab the thing if we can, then run like fuck. You,' and Craw gave Raubin a look.

His eyes went wide as two cook-pots. 'What, me?'

'Stay here and mind the gear.' Raubin gave a long sigh of relief and Craw felt his lip curl. He didn't blame the man for being a hell of a coward, most men were. Craw was one himself. But he blamed him for letting it show. 'Don't get too comfortable, though, eh? If the rest of us come to grief these Fox fuckers'll track you down before our blood's dry and more'n likely cut your fruits off.'

Raubin's sigh rattled to a quick stop.

'Cut your head off,' whispered Never, eyes all scary-wide.

'Pull your guts out and cook 'em,' growled Jolly Yon.

'Skin your face off and wear it as a mask,' rumbled Brack.

'Use your cock for a spoon,' said Wonderful.

They all thought about that for a moment.

'Right, then,' said Craw. 'Nice and careful, and let's get in that hall without no one noticing and find us that thing. Above all . . .' And he swept the lot of 'em with his sternest look, a half-circle of dirt-smeared, scar-pocked, bright-eyed, beard-fuzzed faces. His crew. His family. 'Nobody die, eh? Weapons.'

Quick sharp, and with no grumbling now the work was at their feet, Craw's crew got ready for action, each one smooth and practised with their gear as a weaver with his loom, weapons neat as their clothes were ragged, bright and clean as their faces were dirty. Belts, straps and bootlaces hissed tight, metal scraped, rattled and rang, and all the while Scorry's song floated out soft and high.

Craw's hands moved by themselves through the old routines,

mind wandering across the years to other times he'd done it, other places, other faces around him, a lot of 'em gone back to the mud long ago. A few he'd buried with his own hands. He hoped none of these folk died today, and became nothing but dirt and worn-out memories. He checked his shield, grip bound in leather all tight and sturdy, straps firm. He checked his knife, his backup knife, and his backup backup knife, all tight in their sheaths. You can never have too many knives, someone once told him, and it was solid advice, provided you were careful how you stowed 'em and didn't fall over and get your own blade in your fruits.

Everyone had their work to be about. Except Whirrun. He just bowed his head as he lifted his sword gently from the tree-trunk, holding it under the crosspiece by its stained leather scabbard, sheathed blade longer'n one of his own long legs. Then he pushed his hood back, scrubbed his dirty fingernails through his flattened hair and stood watching the others, head on one side.

'That the only blade you carry?' asked Craw as he stowed his own sword at his hip, hoping to draw the tall man in, start to build some trust with him. Tight crew like this was, a bit of trust might save your life. Might save everyone's.

Whirrun's eyes swivelled to him. 'This is the Father of Swords, and men have a hundred names for it. Dawn Razor. Grave-Maker. Blood Harvest. Highest and Lowest. *Scac-ang-Gaioc* in the valley tongue, which means the Splitting of the World, the Battle that was fought at the start of time and will be fought again at its end.' For a moment he had Craw wondering if he'd list the whole bloody hundred but thankfully he stopped there, frowning at the hilt, wound with dull grey wire. 'This is my reward and my punishment both. This is the only blade I need.'

'Bit long for eating with, no?' asked Wonderful, strutting up from the other side.

Whirrun bared his teeth at her. 'That's what these are for.'

'Don't you ever sharpen it?' asked Craw.

'It sharpens me.'

'Right. Right y'are.' He hoped Whirrun was as good with that great big blade as he was supposed to be, 'cause he surely brought nothing to the table as a conversationalist.

'Besides, to sharpen it you'd have to draw it,' said Wonderful, winking at Craw with the eye Whirrun couldn't see.

'True.' Whirrun's eyes slid up to her face. 'And once the Father of Swords is drawn, it cannot be sheathed without—'

'Being blooded?' she finished for him. Didn't take skill with the runes to see that coming, Whirrun must've said the same words a dozen times since they left Carleon. Enough for everyone to get somewhat tired of it.

'Blooded,' echoed Whirrun, voice full of portent.

Wonderful gave Craw a look. 'You ever think, Whirrun of Bligh, you might take yourself a touch too serious?'

He tipped his head back and stared up into the sky. 'I'll laugh when I hear something funny.'

Craw felt Yon's hand on his shoulder. 'A word, Chief?'

'Course,' with a grin that took some effort.

He guided Craw away from the others a few steps and spoke soft, the same words he always did before a fight. 'If I die down there—'

'No one's dying today,' snapped Craw, the same words he always used in reply.

'So you said last time, 'fore we buried Jutlan.' That drove Craw's mood another rung down the ladder into the bog. 'No one's fault, we do a dangerous style o' work and all know it. Chances are good I'll live through, but all I'm saying is, if I don't—'

66

'I'll stop by your children, and take 'em your share, and tell them what you were.'

'That's right. And?'

'And I won't dress it up any.'

'Right, then.' Jolly Yon didn't smile, of course. Craw had known him years and hadn't seen him smile more'n a dozen times, and even then when it was least expected. But he nodded, satisfied. 'Right. No man I'd rather give the task to.'

Craw nodded back. 'Good. Great.' No task he wanted less. As Yon walked off, he muttered to himself. 'Always the fool jobs...'

It went pretty much just like Craw planned. He wouldn't have called it the first time ever, but it was a pleasant surprise, that was sure. The six of them lay still and silent on the rise, followed the little movements of leaf and branch that marked Never creeping towards that crap-arse of a village. It looked no better the closer you got to it. Things rarely did, in Craw's experience. He chewed at his nails some more, saw Never kneel in the bushes across the stream from the north gate, nocking an arrow and drawing the string. It was hard to tell from this range, but it looked like he still had that knowing little grin even now.

He loosed his shaft and Craw thought it clicked into one of the logs that made the fence. Faint shouting drifted on the wind. A couple of arrows wobbled back the other way, vanished into the trees as Never turned and scuttled off, lost in the brush. Craw heard some kind of a drum beating, more shouting, then men started to hurry out across that bridge, weapons of rough iron clutched in their hands, some dragging furs or boots on still. Perhaps three dozen, all told. A neat piece of work. Provided Never got away, of course.

Yon shook his head as he watched a good chunk of the Fox

Clan shambling over their bridge and into the trees. 'Amazing, ain't it? I never quite get used to just how fucking stupid people are.'

'Always a mistake to overestimate the bastards,' whispered Craw. 'Good thing we're the cleverest crew in the Circle of the World, eh? So could we have no fuck-ups today, if you please?'

'I won't if you won't, Chief,' muttered Wonderful.

'Huh.' If only he could make that promise. Craw tapped Scorry on his shoulder and pointed down into the village. The little man winked back, then slid over the rise on his belly and down through the undergrowth, nimble as a tadpole through a pond.

Craw worked his dry tongue around his dry mouth. Always ran out of spit at a time like this, and however often he did it, it never got any better. He glanced out the corner of his eye at the others, none of 'em showing much sign of a weak nerve. He wondered if they were bubbling up with worry on the inside, just like he was, and putting a stern face on the wreckage, just like he was. Or if it was only him scared. But in the end it didn't make much difference. The best you could do with fear was act like you had none.

He held his fist up, pleased to see his hand didn't shake, then pointed after Scorry, and they all set off. Down towards the south gate – if you could use the phrase about a gap in a rotten fence under a kind of arch made from crooked branches, skull of some animal unlucky enough to have a fearsome pair of horns mounted in the middle of it. Made Craw wonder if they had a straight piece of wood within a hundred bloody miles.

The one guard left stood under that skull, leaning on his spear, staring at nothing, tangle-haired and fur-clad. He picked his nose and held one finger up to look at the results. He flicked it away.

He stretched and reached around to scratch his arse. Scorry's knife thudded into the side of his neck and chopped his throat out, quick and simple as a fisher gutting a salmon. Craw winced, just for a moment, but he knew there'd been no dodging it. They'd be lucky if that was the only man lost his life so they could get this fool job done. Scorry held him a moment while blood showered from his slit neck, caught him as he fell, guided his twitching body soundless to the side of the gate, out of sight of any curious eyes inside.

No more noise than the breeze in the brush, Craw and the rest hurried up the bank, bent double, weapons in hand. Scorry was waiting, knife already wiped, peering around the side of the gatepost with one palm up behind him to say wait. Craw frowned down at the dead man's bloody face, mouth a bit open as though he was about to ask a question. A potter makes pots. A baker makes bread. And this is what Craw made. All he'd made his whole life, pretty much.

It was hard to feel much pride at the sight, however neatly the work had been done. It was still a man murdered just for guarding his own village. Because they were men, these, with hopes and sorrows and all the rest, even if they lived out here past the Crinna and didn't wash too often. But what could one man do? Craw took a long breath in and let it out slow. Just get the task done without any of his own people killed. In hard times, soft thoughts can kill you quicker than the plague.

He looked at Wonderful and jerked his head into the village, and she slid around the gatepost and in, slipping across to the right-hand track, shaved head swivelling carefully left and right. Scorry followed at her heels and Brack crept after, silent for all his great bulk.

Craw took a long breath, then crept across to the left-hand

track, wincing as he tried to find the hardest, quietest bits of the rutted muck to plant his feet on. He heard the hissing of Yon's careful breath behind him, knew Whirrun was there, too, though he moved quiet as a cat. Craw could hear something clicking. A spinning wheel, maybe. He heard someone laugh, not sure if he was imagining it. His head was jerked this way and that by every trace of a sound, like he had a hook through his nose. The whole thing seemed horribly bright and obvious, right then. Maybe they should've waited for darkness, but Craw had never liked working at night. Not since that fucking disaster at Gurndrift where Pale-as-Snow's boys ended up fighting Littlebone's on an accident and more'n fifty men dead without an enemy within ten miles. Too much to go wrong at night.

But then Craw had seen plenty of men die in the day, too.

He slid along beside a wattle wall, and he had that sweat of fear on him. That prickling sweat that comes with death right at your shoulder. Everything was picked out sharper than sharp. Every stick in the wattle, every pebble in the dirt. The way the leather binding the grip of his sword dug at his palm when he shifted his fingers. The way each in-breath gave the tiniest whistle when it got three-quarters into his aching lungs. The way the sole of his foot stuck to the inside of his boot through the hole in his sock with every careful step. Stuck to it and peeled away.

He needed to get him some new socks, is what he needed. Well, first he needed to live out the day, then socks. Maybe even those ones he'd seen in Uffrith last time he was there, dyed red. They'd all laughed at that. Him, and Yon, and Wonderful, and poor dead Jutlan. Laughed at the madness of it. But afterwards he'd thought to himself – there's luxury, that a man could afford to have his socks dyed, and cast a wistful glance over his shoulder at that fine cloth. Maybe he'd go back after this fool job was done with and get himself a pair of red socks. Maybe he'd get himself two pairs. Wear 'em on the outside of his boots just to show folk what a big man he was. Maybe they'd take to calling him Curnden Red Socks. He felt a smile in spite of himself. Red socks, that was the first step on the road to ruin if ever he'd—

The door to a hovel on their left wobbled open and three men walked out of it, all laughing. The one at the front turned his shaggy head, big smile still plastered across his face, yellow teeth sticking out of it. He looked straight at Craw, and Yon, and Whirrun, stuck frozen against the side of a longhouse with their mouths open like three children caught nicking biscuits. Everyone stared at each other.

Craw felt time slow to a weird crawl, that way it did before blood spilled. Enough time to take in silly things. To wonder whether it was a chicken bone in one of their ears. To count the nails through one of their clubs. Eight and a half. Enough time to think it was funny he wasn't thinking something more useful. It was like he stood outside himself, wondering what he'd do but feeling it probably weren't up to him. And the oddest thing of all was that it had happened so often to him now, that feeling, he could recognise it when it came. That frozen, baffled moment before the world comes apart.

Shit. Here I am again—

He felt the cold wind kiss the side of his face as Whirrun swung his sword in a great reaping circle. The man at the front didn't even have time to duck. The flat of the sheathed blade hit him on the side of the head, whipped him off his feet, turned him head over heels in the air and sent him crashing into the wall of the shack beside them upside down. Craw's hand lifted his sword without being told. Whirrun darted forward, arm lancing out, smashing the pommel of his sword into the second man's mouth, sending teeth and bits of teeth flying.

While he was toppling back like a felled tree, arms spread wide, the third tried to raise a club. Craw hacked him in the side, steel biting through fur and flesh with a wet thud, spots of blood showering out of him. The man opened his mouth and gave a great high shriek, tottering forward, bent over, eyes bulging. Craw split his skull wide open, sword-grip jolting in his hand, the scream choked off in a surprised yip. The body sprawled, blood pouring from broken head and all over Craw's boots. Looked like he'd come out of this with red socks after all. So much for no more dead, and so much for quiet as a spring breeze, too.

'Fuck,' said Craw.

By then time was moving way too fast for comfort. The world jerked and wobbled, full of flying dirt as he ran. Screams rang and metal clashed, his own breath and his own heart roaring and surging in his ears. He snatched a glance over his shoulder, saw Yon barge a mace away with his shield and roar as he hacked a man down. As Craw turned back, an arrow came from the dead knew where and clicked into the mud wall just in front of him, almost made him fall over backwards with shock. Whirrun went into his arse and knocked him sprawling, gave him a mouthful of mud. When he struggled up, a man was charging right at him, a flash of screaming face and wild hair smeared across his sight. Craw was twisting around behind his shield when Scorry slid out from nowhere and knifed the running bastard in the side, made him shriek and stumble. Craw took the side of his head off, blade pinging as it chopped through bone then thumped into the ground, nearly jerking from his raw fist.

'Move!' he shouted, not sure who at, trying to wrench his blade free of the earth. Jolly Yon rushed past, head of his axe dashed with red, teeth bared in a mad snarl. Craw followed, Whirrun behind him, face slack, eyes darting from one hut to another, sword still sheathed in one hand. Around the corner of a hovel and into a wide stretch of muck scattered with ground-up straw. Pigs were honking and squirming in a pen at one side. The hall with the carved uprights stood at the other, steps up to a wide doorway, only darkness inside.

A red-haired man pounded across the ground in front of them, a wood-axe in his fist. Wonderful calmly put an arrow through his cheek at six strides distant and he came up short, clapping a hand to his face, still stumbling towards her. She stepped to meet him with a fighting scream, swept her sword out and around and took his head right off. It spun into the air, showering blood, and dropped in the pigpen. Craw wondered for a moment if the poor bastard still knew what was going on.

Then he saw the heavy door of the hall being swung shut, a pale face at the edge. 'Door!' he bellowed and ran for it, pounding across squelching mud and up the wooden steps, making the boards rattle. He shoved one bloody, muddy boot in the gap just as the door was slammed and gave a howl, eyes bulging, pain lancing up his leg. 'My foot! Fuck!'

There were a dozen Fox Clan or more crowded around the end of the yard now, growling and grunting louder and uglier than the hogs. They waved jagged swords, axes, rough clubs in their fists, a few with shields, too, one at the front with a rusted chain hauberk on, tattered at the hem, straggling hair tangled with rings of rough-forged silver.

'Back.' Whirrun stood tall in front of them, holding out his sword at long arm's length, hilt up, like it was some magic charm to ward off evil. 'Back, and you needn't die today.'

The one in mail spat, then snarled at him in broken Northern. 'Show us your iron, thief!'

'Then I will. Look upon the Father of Swords, and look your last.' And Whirrun drew it from the sheath.

Men might've had a hundred names for it – Dawn Razor, Grave-Maker, Blood Harvest, Highest and Lowest, *Scac-ang-Gaioc* in the valley tongue which means the Splitting of the World, and so on, and so on – but Craw had to admit it was a disappointing length of metal. There was no flame, no golden light, no distant trumpets or mirrored steel. Just the gentle scrape as long blade came free of stained leather, the flat grey of damp slate, no shine or ornament about it except for the gleam of something engraved down near the plain, dull crosspiece.

But Craw had other worries than that Whirrun's sword weren't worth all the songs. 'Door!' he squealed at Yon, scrabbling at the edge of it with his left hand, all tangled up with his shield, shoving his sword through the gap and waving it about to no effect. 'My fucking foot!'

Yon roared as he pounded up the steps and rammed into the door with his shoulder. It gave all of a sudden, tearing from its hinges and crushing some fool underneath. Him and Craw burst stumbling into the room beyond, dim as twilight, hazy with scratchy-sweet smoke. A shape came at Craw and he whipped his shield up on an instinct, felt something thud into it, splinters flying in his face. He reeled off balance, crashed into something else, metal clattering, pottery shattering. Someone loomed up, a ghostly face, a necklace of rattling teeth. Craw lashed at him with his sword, and again, and again, and he went down, white-painted face spattered with red.

Craw coughed, retched, coughed, blinking into the reeking gloom, sword ready to swing. He heard Yon roaring, heard the thud of an axe in flesh and someone squeal. The smoke was clearing now, enough for Craw to get some sense of the hall. Coals glowed in a fire-pit, lighting a spider's web of carved rafters in sooty red and orange, casting shifting shadows on each other, tricking his eyes. The place was hot as hell and smelled like hell besides. Old hangings around the walls, tattered canvas daubed with painted marks. A block of black stone at the far end, a rough statue standing over it, and at its feet the glint of gold. A cup, Craw thought. A goblet. He took a step towards it, trying to waft the murk away from his face with his shield.

'Yon?' he shouted.

'Craw, where you at?'

Some strange kind of song was coming from somewhere, words Craw didn't know but didn't like the sound of. Not one bit. 'Yon?' And a figure sprang up suddenly from behind that block of stone. Craw's eyes went wide and he almost fell in the fire-pit as he stumbled back.

He wore a tattered red robe, long, sinewy arms sticking from it, spread wide, smeared with paint and beaded up with sweat, the skull of some animal drawn down over his face, black horns curling from it so he looked in the shifting light like a devil bursting straight up from hell. Craw knew it was a mask, but looming up like that out of the smoke, strange song echoing from that skull, he felt suddenly rooted to the spot with fear. So much he couldn't even lift his sword. Just stood there trembling, every muscle turned to water. He'd never been a hero, that was true, but he'd never felt fear like this. Not even at Ineward when he'd seen the Bloody-Nine coming for him, snarling madman's face all dashed with other men's blood. He stood helpless.

'Fuh . . . fuh . . . fuh . . .'

The priest came forward, lifting one long arm. He had a thing gripped in painted fingers. A twisted piece of wood, the faintest pale glow about it.

The thing. The thing they'd come for.

Light flared from it brighter and brighter, so bright it burned its twisted shape fizzing into Craw's eyes, the sound of the song filling his ears until he couldn't hear anything else, couldn't think anything else, couldn't see nothing but that thing, searing bright as the sun, stealing his breath, crushing his will, stopping his breath, cutting his—

Crack. Jolly Yon's axe split the animal skull in half and chopped into the face underneath it. Blood sprayed, hissed in the coals of the fire-pit. Craw felt spots on his face, blinked and shook his head, loosed all of a sudden from the freezing grip of fear. The priest lurched sideways, song turned to a guttering gurgle, mask split in half and blood squirting from under it. Craw snarled as he swung his sword, chopped into the sorcerer's chest and knocked him over on his back. The thing bounced from his hand and spun away across the rough plank floor, the blinding light faded to the faintest glimmer.

'Fucking sorcerers,' snarled Yon, curling his tongue and blowing spit onto the corpse. 'Why do they bother? How long does it take to learn all that jabber and it never does you half the good a decent knife...' He frowned. 'Uh-oh.'

The priest had fallen in the fire-pit, scattering glowing coals across the floor. A couple had skittered as far as the ragged hem of one of the hangings.

'Shit.' Craw took a step on shaky legs to kick it away. Before he got there, flame sputtered around the old cloth. 'Shit.' He tried to stamp it out, but his head was still a touch spinny and he only got embers scattered against his trouser leg, had to hop around, slapping them off. The flames spread, licking up faster'n the plague. Too much flame to put out, spurting higher than a man. 'Shit!' Craw stumbled back, feeling the heat on his face, red shadows dancing among the rafters. 'Get the thing and let's go!'

Yon was already fumbling with the straps on his leather pack. 'Right y'are, Chief, right y'are! Backup plan!'

Craw left him and hurried to the doorway, not sure who'd be alive still on the other side. He burst out into the day, light stabbing at his eyes after the gloom.

Wonderful was standing there, mouth hanging wide open. She'd an arrow nocked to her half-drawn bow, but it was pointed at the ground, hands slack. Craw couldn't remember the last time he'd seen her surprised.

'What is it?' he snapped, getting his sword tangled up on the doorframe then snarling as he wrenched it free. 'You hurt?' He squinted into the sun, shading his eyes with his shield. 'What's the...' And he stopped on the steps and stared. 'By the dead.'

Whirrun had hardly moved, the Father of Swords still gripped in his fist, long, dull blade pointing to the ground. Only now he was spotted and spattered head to toe in blood, and the twisted and hacked, split and ruined corpses of the dozen Fox Clan who'd faced him were scattered around his boots in a wide half-circle, a few bits that used to be attached to them scattered wider still.

'He killed the whole lot.' Brack's face was all crinkled up with confusion. 'Just like that. I never even lifted my hammer.'

'Damndest thing,' muttered Wonderful. 'Damndest thing.' She wrinkled her nose. 'Can I smell smoke?'

Yon burst from the hall, stumbled into Craw's back and nearly sent the pair of them tumbling down the steps. 'Did you get the thing?' snapped Craw.

'I think I...' Yon blinked at Whirrun, standing tall in his circle of slaughter. 'By the dead, though.'

Whirrun started to back towards them, twisted himself sideways as an arrow looped over and stuck wobbling into the side of the hall. He waved his free hand. 'Maybe we better—'

'Run!' roared Craw. Perhaps a good leader should wait until everyone else gets clear. First man to arrive in a fight and the last to leave. That was how Threetrees used to do it. But Craw weren't Threetrees, it hardly needed to be said, and he was off like a rabbit with its tail on fire. Leading by example, he'd have called it. He heard bowstrings behind him. An arrow zipped past, just wide of his flailing arm, stuck wobbling into one of the hovels. Then another. His squashed foot was aching like fury but he limped on, waving his shield-arm. Pounding towards the jerking, wobbling archway with the animal's skull above it. 'Go! Go!'

Wonderful tore past, feet flying, flicking mud in Craw's face. He saw Scorry flit between two huts up ahead, then swift as a lizard around one of the gateposts and out of the village. He hurled himself after, under the arch of branches. Jumped down the bank, caught his hurt foot, body jolting, teeth snapping together and catching his tongue. He took one more wobbling step then went flying, crashed into the boggy bracken, rolled over his shield with just enough thought left to keep his sword from cutting his own nose off. He struggled to his feet, laboured on up the slope, legs burning, lungs burning, through the trees, trousers soaked to the knee with marsh-water. He could hear Brack lumbering along at his shoulder, grunting with the effort, and behind him Yon's growl, 'Bloody... shit... bloody... running... bloody... shit...'

He tore through the brush and wobbled into the clearing where they'd made their plans. Plans that hadn't flown too smoothly, as it went. Raubin was standing by the gear. Wonderful near him with her hands on her hips. Never was kneeling on the far side of the clearing, arrow nocked to his bow. He grinned as he saw Craw. 'You made it, then, Chief?'

'Shit.' Craw stood bent over, head spinning, dragging in air. 'Shit.' He straightened, staring at the sky, face on fire, not able to think of another word, and without the breath to say one if he could have.

Brack looked even more shot than Craw, if it was possible, crouched over, hands on knees and knees wobbling, big chest heaving, big face red as a slapped arse around his tattoos. Yon tottered up and leaned against a tree, cheeks puffed out, skin shining with sweat.

Wonderful was hardly out of breath. 'By the dead, the state o' you fat old men.' She slapped Never on the arm. 'That was some nice work down there at the village. Thought they'd catch you and skin you sure.'

'You hoped, you mean,' said Never, 'but you should've known better. I'm the best damn runner-away in the North.'

'That is a fact.'

'Where's Scorry?' gasped Craw, enough breath in him now to worry.

Never jerked his thumb. 'Circled around to check no one's coming for us.'

Whirrun ambled back into the clearing, hood drawn up again and the Father of Swords sheathed across his shoulders like a milkmaid's yoke, one hand on the grip, the other dangling over the blade.

'I take it they're not following?' asked Wonderful, one eyebrow raised.

Whirrun shook his head. 'Nope.'

'Can't say I blame the poor bastards. I take back what I said about you taking yourself too serious. You're one serious fucker with that sword.'

'You get the thing?' asked Raubin, face all pale with worry.

'That's right, Raubin, we saved your skin.' Craw wiped his mouth, blood on the back of his hand from his bitten tongue. They'd done it, and his sense of humour was starting to leak back in. 'Hah. Could you imagine if we'd left the bastard thing behind?'

'Never fear,' said Yon, flipping open his pack. 'Jolly Yon Cumber, once more the fucking hero.' And he delved his hand inside and pulled it out.

Craw blinked. Then he frowned. Then he stared. Gold glinted in the fading light and he felt his heart sink lower than it had all day. 'That ain't fucking it, Yon!'

'It's not?'

'That's a cup! It was the *thing* we wanted!' He stuck his sword point-down in the ground and waved one hand about. 'The bloody thing with the kind of bloody light about it!'

Yon stared back at him. 'No one told me it had a bloody light!'

There was silence for a moment then, while they all thought about it. No sound but the wind rustling the old leaves, making the black branches creak. Then Whirrun tipped his head back and roared with laughter. A couple of crows took off startled from a branch, it was that loud, flapping up sluggish into the grey sky.

'Why the hell are you laughing?' snapped Wonderful.

Inside his hood, Whirrun's twisted face was glistening with happy tears. 'I told you I'd laugh when I heard something funny!' And he was off again, spine arching like a full-drawn bow, whole body shaking.

'You'll have to go back,' said Raubin.

'Back?' muttered Wonderful, her dirt-streaked face a picture of disbelief. 'Back, you mad fucker?'

'You know the hall caught fire, don't you?' snapped Brack, one big, trembling arm pointed down towards the thickening column of smoke wafting up from the village.

'It what?' asked Raubin as Whirrun blasted a fresh shriek at the sky, hacking, gurgling, only just keeping on his feet.

'Oh, aye, burned down, more'n likely with the damn thing in it.'

'Well . . . I don't know . . . you'll just have to pick through the ashes!'

'How about we pick through *your* fucking ashes?' snarled Yon, throwing the cup down on the ground.

Craw gave a long sigh, rubbed at his eyes, then winced down towards that shit-hole of a village. Behind him, Whirrun's laughter sawed throaty at the dusk. 'Always,' he muttered, under his breath. 'Why do I always get stuck with the fool jobs?'

FAR
COUNTRY

WHITE SEA

ANGLAND

Ostenhor

Holsthe

New
Keln

Sewaya

Rostod

MIDDER

Aulcus

Epedra

STARKLAND

Ad

Keln

Calcus

Nos

Stark

CIRCLE

Darmum

Aostum

Gordius

Dagosk

Ul

OLD EMPIRE

Ispania

GULF

Daleppa

KADIR

Al-Khatif

OF

BRIGHT
SEA

Alubat

GURKHU

Shaffa

Bizurt

Ul

SHAMIR

GURKHU

Sarkant

SKIPPING
TOWN

The Near Country,
Summer 575

'**M**aybe we should skip town.' said Javre.

'Oh no, no, no, not this time,' Shev snapped back at her. 'You can't just career through life leaving the wreckage of your mistakes behind you.'

A silence as they hurried on through the shadows, Shev having to half-jog to keep up as Javre ploughed ahead with immense strides, brow furrowed in thought.

'What is it that we have been doing this past year, then?'

'Well . . . we've . . .' Shev thought about it. 'That's just my point! We can't *keep* doing it.'

'I see. So we give Tumnor his jewel, we collect the promised money, we pay our gambling debts—'

'*Your* gambling debts.'

'Then what? We put down roots here?' Javre raised one red brow at the crumbling buildings, the rubbish-strewn street, a fish-stinking beggar hacking out diseased coughs in a doorway.

'Well, no. We move on.'

'And what we left behind us tonight?' Javre jerked her head the way they'd come. 'Would you call that wreckage?'

'I would call that . . .' Shev wondered how much this particular truth would stretch before it tore to bits. 'A series of mishaps.'

'It looked like wreckage to me. Once the front of the mansion collapsed, you would have to call that wreckage, no?'

Shev glanced quickly over her shoulder yet again to make sure no one was following. 'I suppose an uncharitable speaker could describe it so.'

'Then explain to me, if you would, Shevedieh, how your way differs from mine, except that we leave town with less money?'

'We leave with less enemies as well! I tire of leaving a new score in every shit-hole we pass through like a rabbit leaves droppings! Sooner or later I might need a good shit-hole to pass through again. All the damn *enemies*. I wake up sweating, you know, in the night!'

'That is all that spicy food,' said Javre. 'I do not know how often I have warned you about your diet. And enemies are a good thing. Enemies show you make . . . an *impression*.'

'Oh, you make an impression, all right, that I would never deny. You made a hell of an impression on those boys tonight.'

Javre grinned a mass of white teeth as she punched one scabbed fist into one calloused palm with a smack like a door slamming. 'I certainly did.'

'But I'm a thief, Javre, not . . . whatever you are. I'm supposed to keep a low profile.'

'Ah!' Javre raised that same red brow again as she glanced sideways. 'Hence all the black.'

'And it does look rather well on me, I think you'd have to agree.'

'You certainly are a shadowy and seductive corruptor of innocent maidenhood!' Javre playfully jogged Shev in the ribs with an elbow and nearly sent her careering into the nearest wall, then caught her by the hand and dragged her into a crushing embrace, her cheek squashed into Javre's armpit. 'We shall do it your way, then, Shevedieh, my friend! Straight and true and morally upright, just as a thief should be! We shall pay your debts, then get drunk and find some men.'

Shev was still struggling to get a breath in after that elbow. 'What is it exactly that you think I'd do with them?'

Javre grinned. 'The men would be for me. I am a woman of Thond and have grand appetites. You can keep watch.'

'My towering thanks for the immensity of that honour,' said Shev, slipping from under the weight of Javre's mightily muscled arm.

'It is the least I could do. You have been a fine sidekick so far.'

'I thought this was an equal partnership.'

'All the best sidekicks think that,' said Javre, striding towards the front door of the Weeping Slaver, its sign hanging precariously from a rusting pole by one loop.

Shev caught Javre's arm and, by hanging off it with all her weight and digging her heels into the mud, managed to stop her taking the next step. 'I have a feeling Tumnor will be expecting us.'

'That was the arrangement.' Javre looked down at her, puzzled.

'Given that he was less than entirely forthcoming about the job, it may be that he'll try to double-cross us.'

Javre frowned. 'You think he might break the agreement?'

'He didn't mention the traps, did he?' asked Shev, still heaving at Javre's arm. 'Or the long drop? Or the wall? Or the dogs? And he said two guards, not twelve.'

Muscles worked as Javre clenched her jaw. 'He said nothing about that sorcerer, either.'

'Exactly,' Shev managed to gasp, every sinew trembling with effort.

'Breath of the Mother, you're right.'

Shev breathed a sigh of relief and slowly stood, patting Javre's arm as she released it. 'I'll sneak in around the back and make sure that—'

Javre gave her a huge smile. 'The Lioness of Hoskopp never uses the back door!' And she sprang up the steps, raised one boot, kicked the front door splintering from its hinges and strode inside, the filthy tails of her once-white coat flapping after.

Shevedieh gave brief but serious consideration to sprinting off down the street, then sighed and crept up the steps after her.

The Weeping Slaver wasn't the most auspicious of settings, though Shev had to admit she'd been in worse. Indeed, she'd spent most of the last few years in worse.

Size it had, big as a barn with a balcony at first-floor level, ill-lit by a vast circular chandelier with smoking candles in stained glass cups. The floor was covered in dirty straw and a mismatched jumble of chairs and tables, a warped counter down one side with the cheapest spirits of a dozen dozen cultures stacked on shelves behind.

The place smelled of smoke and sweat, of spilled drinks and sprayed vomit, of desperation and wasted chances, and was very much as it had been three nights ago when they took the job, just before Javre lost half their promised earnings at dice. There was one clear difference, however. That night it had overflowed with scum of every kind. Tonight there appeared to be just the one patron.

Tumnor sat at a table in the middle of the room, a fixed grin on his plump face and a sheen of sweat across his forehead. He looked extremely nervous, even for a man perpetrating a

double-cross on a pair of notorious thieves. He looked in immin-
ent fear of his life.

'It's a trap,' he grunted through his clenched teeth, without
moving his hands from the tabletop.

'That we had gathered, fiend!' said Javre.

'No,' he grunted, eyes swivelling wildly sideways, then back to
them, then sideways again. 'A *trap.*'

That was when Shev noticed his hands were nailed to the table.
She followed his glance, past a large brown stain on the floor that
looked suspiciously like blood and into the shadows. She saw a
figure there. The glint of eyes. The glimmer of steel. A man poised
and ready. Now she took in other telltale gleams in the dark
corners of the inn – an axeman wedged behind a drinks cabinet,
the nose of a flatbowman peeking into the light on the balcony
above, a pair of boots sticking out from the door to the cellar
which she deduced must still be attached to the dead legs of one
of Tumnor's hired men. Her heart sank. She hated fighting, and
she had the strong feeling she was going to be fighting very soon.

'It would appear,' murmured Shev, leaning towards Javre, 'that
the scum who double-crossed us have been double-crossed by
some other scum.'

'Yes,' whispered Javre. Her whispers were louder than the usual
speaking voice of most people. 'I find myself conflicted. Who to
kill first?'

'Perhaps we could talk our way out?' Shev ventured hopefully.
It was important to stay hopeful.

'Shevedieh, we must face the possibility that there will be
violence.'

'Your prescience is uncanny.'

'When things get underway, I would be ever so grateful if you
could attend to the flatbowman on the balcony just there?'

'Understood,' muttered Shev.

'Most of the rest you can probably leave to me.'

'Too kind.'

And now the unmistakable tread of heavy boots and jingling metal echoed from the back of the inn, and Tumnor's face grew even more drawn, beads of sweat rolling down his cheeks.

Javre narrowed her eyes. 'And the villain is revealed.'

'Villains tend to love a bit of theatre, though, don't they?' muttered Shev.

When she emerged into the shifting candlelight, she was lean and very tall. Almost as tall as Javre, perhaps, her black hair chopped short, one sinewy arm bare and covered in blue tattoos and the other with plates of battered steel, a gauntlet like a claw at the end, curving nails of sharpened metal clicking as she walked. Her green, green eyes glinted as she smiled towards them.

'It has been a while, Javre.'

Javre pushed her lips out. 'Oh, arse of the Goddess,' she said. 'Well met, Weylen. Or badly met, at least.'

'You know her?' muttered Shev.

Javre winced. 'I must admit she is not an entire stranger to me. She was Thirteenth of the Fifteen.'

'I am Tenth now,' said Weylen. 'Since you killed Hanama and Birke.'

'I offered them the same choice I will soon offer you.' Javre shrugged. 'They chose death.'

'Er . . .' Shev held up one gloved finger. 'If I may ask . . . What the hell are we talking about?'

The woman's emerald-green eyes moved across to her. 'She did not tell you?'

'Tell me what?'

Javre winced even more. 'Those friends of mine I mentioned, from the temple.'

'The temple in Thond?'

'Yes. They're not so much friends.'

'So . . . neutral towards you, then?' Shev ventured hopefully. It was important to stay hopeful.

'More enemies,' said Javre.

'I see.'

'The fifteen Knights Templar of the Golden Order are forbidden to leave the temple except on the orders of the High Priestess. On pain of death.'

'And I'm guessing you had no such permission to go?' asked Shevedieh, looking around at all the sharpened steel on display.

'Not in so many words.'

'Not in so many?'

'Not in any.'

'Her life is forfeit,' said Weylen. 'As is the life of anyone who offers her succour.' And she extended her steel-taloned forefinger and drove it into the top of Tumnor's head. He made a sound like a fart, then dropped forward, blood bubbling from the neat wound in his pate.

Shev held her empty palms up. 'Well, I've offered no succour, that I promise you. I like a succouring just as much as the next girl, if not a good deal more, but Javre?' She worked her hand gently, making sure the mechanism was engaged, hoping that it looked like nothing more than an expressive gesture. 'No offence to her, I daresay she'll make several men a wonderful husband some day, but she's not my type at all.' Shev raised her brows at Weylen who, it had to be said, was much closer to her type, those eyes of hers really were something. 'And, you know, not wanting to blow my own horn, but once I *offer* succour? I generally get all the succouring one woman can—'

'She means help,' said Javre.

'Eh?'

'Succour. It is not a sexual thing.'

'Oh.'

'Kill them,' said Weylen.

The flatbowman raised his weapon, candlelight glinting on the sharpened tip of the loaded bolt, as several other thugs burst from the shadows brandishing a selection of unpleasant-looking weapons. Though what weapons look pleasant, Shev reflected, when brandished at you?

Shev twisted her wrist and the throwing knife sprang into her hand. Unfortunately, the spring was wound too tight, and it shot straight through her clutching fingers and thudded into the ceiling, neatly cutting the rope that held the chandelier. Pulleys whirred and the huge thing began to plummet towards them.

The flatbowman smiled as he squeezed the trigger, aiming straight at Shev's heart. A thug raised a huge axe above his head. Then a great weight of wood, glass and wax crashed down upon him, crushing him flat, the flatbow bolt shuddering into the side of the chandelier an instant before it hit the ground with a shattering impact, taking two more thugs with it and sending dust, splinters, shards and candles flying.

'Shit,' whispered Shev, stunned and blinking as the echoes faded. She and Javre stood together in the centre of the chandelier's circular wreckage, apparently entirely unhurt.

Shev gave a whoop of triumph which turned, as many of her triumphant whoops did, into a gurgle of horror as an uncrushed thug sprang over the ruins of the chandelier with his sword a blur of hard-swung steel. She leaped back, tripped over a table, fell over a chair, rolled, saw a blade flash past, scrambled under another table, dust filtering around her as someone beat it with an axe. She heard crashes, clashes, loud swearing and all the familiar noise of a fight in an inn.

Bloody hell, Shev hated fights. *Hated* them. Considering how much she hated them, she got into a lot of them. Partnering up with Javre had not helped her record in that regard or, at a brief assay, any other. She slid out from under the table, sprang up, was punched in the face and sprawled painfully against the counter, spluttering and wobbling and trying to blink the tears from her eyes.

A snarling thug came at her overhand with a knife and she jerked back at the waist, steel flashing by her and thunking into the counter. She jerked forward and butted him in the face, knocked him staggering with his hands to his nose, snatched his knife from the wood and sent it whirling through the air in one smooth motion, burying itself in the flatbowman's forehead as he levelled his reloaded weapon. His eyes rolled up and he toppled off the balcony and onto a table below, sending bottles and glasses flying.

'What a knife-thrower,' Shev muttered to herself, 'I could have— Urgh!' Her smugness was knocked out of her along with her breath as a man cannoned into her side and sent her reeling.

He was a big man of surpassing ugliness, swinging this way and that with a mace almost as big and ugly as he was, smashing glasses and furniture, filling the air with splinters. Shev whimpered every curse she could think of as she weaved and dodged, scrambling and jumping desperately, not even getting the chance to look for an opening, running steadily out of space and time as she was herded towards a corner.

He raised his mace to strike, broad face twisted with rage.

'Wait!' she wailed, pointing over his shoulder.

It was amazing how often that worked. He jerked his head to look, pausing just long enough for her to knee him in the fruits with all her strength. He gasped, tottered, dropped to his knees, and she whipped out her dagger and stabbed him sharply at the meeting of his neck and his shoulder. He groaned, tried to stand, then sprawled on his face, welling blood.

'Sorry,' said Shev. 'Damn it, I'm sorry.' And she was, just as she always was. But it was better to be sorry than dead. Just as it always was. That lesson she had learned long ago.

No further fights presented themselves. Javre stood by the chandelier's wreckage, her dirty white coat spotted with blood and the twisted bodies of a dozen thugs scattered about her. She had another bent over with his head wedged in the crook of one arm, and yet another pinned against a table by his neck at arm's length, kicking and struggling to absolutely no effect.

'Things must be going downhill.' And with a twitch of her face and a flex of her muscular arm she snapped the first man's neck and let his body flop to the floor. 'The temple used to stretch to a better class of thug.' She dipped her shoulder and flung the other one bodily through a window and into the street, tearing the shutters free, his despairing squeal cut off as his head tore a chunk from a supporting pillar with him.

'The best I could find at short notice,' said Weylen, reaching behind her back. 'But it was always going to come to this.' And she drew a curved sword, the long blade looking to Shev's eye to be made of a writhing black smoke.

'It need not,' said Javre. 'You have two choices, just as Hanama and Birke did. You can go back to Thond. Go back to the High Priestess and tell her I will be no one's slave. Not ever. Tell her I am free.'

'Free? Ha! Do you suppose the High Priestess will accept that answer?'

Javre shrugged. 'Tell her you could not find me. Tell her whatever you please.'

Weylen's mouth bitterly twisted. 'And what would be my other—'

'I show you the sword.' There was a popping of joints as Javre shifted her shoulders, boots scraping into a wider stance, and from inside her coat she drew a bundle, long and slender, a thing of bandages and rags, but near the end Shev caught the glint of gold.

Weylen lifted her chin, and did not so much smile as show her teeth. 'You know there is no choice for us.'

Javre gave a nod. 'I know. Shevedieh?'

'Yes?' croaked Shev.

'Close your eyes.'

She jammed them shut as Weylen sprang over a table with a fighting scream, high, harsh and horrible. She heard quick footsteps on the boards, rushing up with inhuman speed.

There was a ringing of metal and Shev flinched as a sudden bright light shone pink through her lids. A scraping, and a croaking gasp, and the light was gone.

'Shevedieh.'

'Yes?' she croaked.

'You can open them now.'

Javre still held the bundle in one hand, torn rags flapping about it. With the other she held Weylen up, her limp arms flopping back, steel-cased knuckles scraping the floor. There was a red stain on her chest, but she looked peaceful. Aside from the black blood pouring from her back to spatter on the boards in spurts and dashes.

'They will find you, Javre,' she whispered, blood specking her lips.

'I know,' said Javre. 'And they each will have their choice.' She lowered Weylen to the boards, into the spreading pool of her blood, and gently brushed her eyelids closed over her green, green eyes. 'May the Goddess have mercy on you,' she murmured.

'May she have mercy on us first,' muttered Shevedieh, wiping the blood from under her throbbing nose as she approached the counter, dagger at the ready, and peered over. The inn's owner was cowering behind and cringed even further as he saw her. 'Don't kill me! Please don't kill me!'

'I won't.' She hid the dagger behind her back and showed him her open palm. 'No one will. It's all right, they've ...' She wanted to say 'gone' but, glancing around the wreckage of the inn, was forced to say, rather croakily, 'died. You can get up.'

He slowly stood, peered over the counter, and his jaw dropped open. 'By the—'

'I must apologise for the damage,' said Javre. 'It looks worse than it is.'

Part of the far wall, riddled with cracks, chose that moment to collapse into the street, sending up a cloud of stone dust and making Shev step back, coughing.

Javre pushed her lips out and put one considering fingertip against them. 'Perhaps it is exactly as bad as it looks.'

Shev heaved up an aching sigh. Not the first she'd given in the company of Javre, Lioness of Hoskopp, and she doubted it would be the last. She pulled the pouch from her shirt, undid the strings and let the jewel roll onto the split counter, where it sat glinting.

'For your trouble,' she said to the gawping innkeeper. Then she wiped her dagger on the jacket of the nearest corpse and slid it back into its sheath, turned without another word, stepped over the splintered remains of the door and out into the street.

Dawn was coming, the sun bringing the faintest grey smudge to the eastern sky above the ramshackle roofs. Shev took a long breath and shook her head at it. 'Damn it, Shevedieh,' she whispered to herself, 'but a conscience is a hell of an encumbrance to a thief.'

She heard Javre's heavy footsteps behind, felt her looming presence at her shoulder, heard her deep voice as she leaned to speak in Shev's ear.

'Would you like to skip town now?'

Shev nodded. 'Yes, I think we'd better.'

FAR
COUNTRY

Sakwaya

Aulcus

OLD EMPIRE

Kos

Calcis

Darmin

Acstum

Gordius

SHABULYAN

Ispar

SH

HELL

Dagoska, Spring 576

Temple ran.

It was hardly the first time. He had spent half his life running away from things and most of the rest running back towards them. But he had never run like this. He ran as though hell yawned at his back. It did.

The ground shook again. Light flared in the night, at the corner of Temple's eye, and he flinched. A moment later came the thunderous boom, so loud it made his ears ring. Fire shot up above the buildings to his left, mad arms of it, reaching out and scattering liquid flame across the Upper City. A piece of stone the size of a man's head thudded into the road just in front of him, bounced across his path and smashed through a wall in a cloud of dust. Smaller stones rained down, pinging and rattling.

Temple ran on, heedless. If Gurkish fire plunged from the heavens and ripped him to specks that could never be found, there was nothing he could do. Precious few would mourn him. One little drip in an ocean of tragedy. He could only hope God had chosen him for saving, even if he could not think of one good reason why.

There was not much he was certain of, but he knew he did not want to die.

He reeled to a stop against a wall, caught by a sudden coughing fit, his chest raw from breathing smoke. From days of breathing smoke. His eyes ran with tears. From the dust. From the fear. He looked back the way he had come. The walls of the Upper City, broken battlements cut out black against the fire. Men struggled there, tiny figures lit red.

It was hopeless. It had been hopeless for days. But still they fought. Perhaps to protect what was theirs. Their property, their family, their way of life. Perhaps they fought out of love. Perhaps out of hate. Perhaps there was nothing else left.

Temple had no idea what could make a man fight. He had never been much of a fighter.

He scuttled down a rubbish-strewn side street, tripped on a fallen beam and skinned his knees, staggered to the corner, one hand up as a feeble shield against the heat of a burning building, flames crackling, smoke roiling skywards into the night.

Fire, fire everywhere. *I have seen hell*, Verturio said, *and it is a great city under siege.* Dagoska had been like hell for weeks. Temple never doubted that he deserved to be there. He just didn't remember dying.

He saw figures crowding about a door, a man swinging an axe, the sound of wood splintering. Gurkish troops somehow broken through the wall already? Or looters taking their chance to snatch something while there was something still to snatch? Temple supposed he could hardly blame them. He'd snatched plenty in his time. And what did blame mean now, anyway?

When there is no law, there is no crime.

He scurried on, keeping low, torn sleeve across his mouth. You would never have known that his acolyte's robe had been pure white. It was as frayed and filthy now as the beggar's rags he had worn before, stained with ash and dirt and blood, his own and that of those he had tried to help. Those he had failed to help.

Hell

Temple had lived in Dagoska all his life. Grown up on these streets. Known them like a child knows his mother's face. But now he hardly recognised them. Houses were blackened shells, bare beams showing like the ribs of desert carcasses, trees scorched stumps, heaps of rubble spilled across the cracked roadways. He kept the rock ahead of him, the lights of the Citadel perched at its top, caught a glimpse of one of the Great Temple's slender spires above a fallen roof, and hurried on.

Fire raged all across the city, but no more fell from the sky. That only made Temple more fearful. When the fire stopped falling, the soldiers came. Always he was running from soldiers. Before the Gurkish it had been the Union, before the Union it had been the Dagoskans themselves. Give a man a sword and he always acts the same, whatever the colour of his skin.

There had been a market here, where rich folk had bought meat. Only a few blackened arches of it remained. He had begged here, as a boy, hands stretching out. Older, he had stolen from a merchant. Older still, had kissed a girl at night beside a fountain. Now the fountain was cracked, choked with ashes. The girl? Who could say?

It had been a beautiful place. A proud street in a proud city. All gone, and for what?

'Is this your plan?' he whispered at the sky.

But God rarely speaks to beggar-boys. Even those educated at the Great Temple.

'Help me,' came a hissing voice. 'Help me.'

A woman lay in the rubble beside him. He had almost stepped on her as he ran past. A fragment from a Gurkish bomb had struck her, or perhaps from a burning building. Her neck was scorched and blistered, some of her hair burned away. Her shoulder was a ruin, arm twisted behind her. He could not tell what was torn cloth and what torn flesh. She smelled like cooking meat. A smell that made Temple's empty stomach growl and then made him want to be sick a moment later. Her throat clicked with every breath and something bubbled in her chest. Her eyes were wide and dark in her black-spattered face.

'Oh, God,' whispered Temple. He did not know where to begin. There was nowhere to begin.

'Help me,' she whispered again, clutching at him, her eyes on his.

'There's nothing I can do,' croaked Temple. 'I'm sorry.'

'No, no, please—'

'I'm sorry.' He peeled her fingers away, tried not to look into her eyes. 'God have mercy on you.' Though it seemed plain that He had none. 'I'm sorry!' Temple stood. He turned away. He went on.

As her cries faded behind him, he tried to tell himself that this was not just the easy thing, but the right thing. There was nothing he could have done for her. She would not have lived. The Gurkish were too close. He could not outrun them carrying her. He had to warn the others, it was his duty. He could not save her. He could only save himself. Better one of them die than both, surely? God would understand that, wouldn't he? God was made of understanding.

Times like these reveal a man for what he truly is. For a while Temple had convinced himself he was a righteous man, but it is easy to be virtuous before your virtue is put to the test. Like a camel turd baked in the sun, beneath the pious crust he was the same stinking, self-serving coward he had always been.

Conscience is that piece of Himself that God puts into everyone, Kahdia would have said. *A splinter of the divine. There is always a choice.*

Hell

He came to an uncertain halt, staring down at the bloody smears her fingers had made on his sleeve. Should he go back? He stood trembling, breathing hard, trapped between right and wrong, between sense and stupidity, between life and death.

Kahdia once told him he thought too much to be a good man.

He looked over his shoulder, back the way he had come. Flames, and buildings lit in the garish colours of flames, and against the flames he saw black shapes moving. The slender shadows of swords and spears, the tall helmets of Gurkish soldiers. And was it a trick of the shimmering haze, or could he see another figure there? A woman's shape, tall and thin, swaggering forward in white armour, a glimpse of golden hair shining. Fear clutched at Temple's throat and he fell, scrambled up, ran. The mindless impulse of the child grown up on the streets. Of the rabbit that sees the hawk's shadow. He hardly knew what there was to live for, but he knew he did not want to die.

Wheezing, coughing, legs burning, he struggled up the cracked steps to the Great Temple. He felt a moment of relief as the familiar façade came into view, even though he knew it would not be long until Gurkish soldiers flooded into this square. Gurkish soldiers . . . or worse.

He hurried across to the looming gates, ashes whirling past, burning papers fluttering down on the hot wind, thumped at the door until his fist hurt, called out his name until his throat was raw. A small door within the door was pulled suddenly open and he scrambled through, the bar swung down behind him with a reassuring finality.

Safety. Even if only for a few moments. A man in the desert must take such water as he is offered, after all.

The first time Temple entered that glorious space and gazed upon the sparkling mosaics, and the filigree stonework, and the light pouring in through the star-shaped windows and making gleam the gilded letters of scripture written man-high upon the walls, he had felt the hand of God upon his shoulder.

He did not feel the presence of God now. Only a few lamps lit the vastness, the shadows of flames beyond the windows flickering across the ceiling. It stank of fear and death, echoed with the whimpers of the wounded, the endless low murmuring of hopeless prayers. Even the mosaic faces of the prophets which had once seemed moved by heavenly ecstacy seemed fixed in terror now.

The place was crowded with people – men and women, young and old, all filthy and desperate. Temple shouldered his way through the press, trying to swallow his fear, trying to think of nothing but finding Kahdia, finally saw him on the dais where the pulpit had once stood. One sleeve of his white robe he had torn off at the shoulder to make bandages. The other was blood-spotted to the elbow from working on the wounded. His eyes were sunken, cheeks hollow, but the more desperate the situation became, the calmer he appeared to grow.

What mighty strength must it take, Temple wondered, to carry the burden of all these people's lives?

There were Union soldiers gathered about him and Temple hung back nervously on old instincts. A dozen of them, perhaps, swords sheathed out of respect for the holy ground but hands twitching always towards the hilts. General Vissbruck was among them, a long smear of ash down his sunburned face. He had been a plump man before the siege, but his uniform hung loose from him now. They all were thinner than they had been, in Dagoska.

'Gurkish soldiers have flooded through the North Gate and into the Upper City.' He spoke in the Union tongue, of course, but Temple understood it as well as any native of Midderland. 'It will not be long until the wall is lost. We suspect treachery.'

Hell

'You suspect Nicomo Cosca?' asked Kahdia.

'I have suspected him for some time, but – whatever else he is – Cosca is no fool. If he meant to sell the city he would have done it while there was still a good price to be had.'

'What about his life?' snapped the soldier with the sling.

Vissbruck snorted. 'One thing on which he has never placed the slightest value. The man is an entire stranger to fear.'

Gods, what a blessing that must be. Temple's fears had been his closest companions since before he could remember.

'It makes no difference now, in any case,' Vissbruck was saying. 'Whether Cosca betrayed us or not, whether alive or dead, he is surely in hell now. Just like the rest of us. We are pulling back to the Citadel, Haddish. You should come with us.'

'And when the Gurkish follow, where will you pull back to?'

Vissbruck swallowed, the sharp knobble bobbing in his throat, and spoke on as if Kahdia had said nothing. Something the people of the Union had proved themselves expert at ever since they came to Dagoska. 'You have been a courageous leader and a true friend to the Union. You have earned a place in the Citadel.'

Kahdia gave a weary smile. 'If I have earned any place it is here, in my temple, among my people. I am proud to take it.'

'I knew you would say so. But I had to ask.'

Kahdia held out his hand. 'It has been an honour.'

'The honour is mine.' The general started forward and embraced the priest. The Union man and the Dagoskan. The white-skinned and the dark. A strange sight. 'I am sorry,' he said, eyes shining with tears, 'that I did not understand you until it was too late.'

'It is never too late,' said Kahdia. 'I believe we may meet in heaven.'

'Then I hope once again that your beliefs are true, and not

mine.' Vissbruck let Kahdia go, turned on his heel, and stopped. He looked back.

'Superior Glokta warned me that a man might be better off killing himself than becoming a prisoner of the Gurkish,' said Vissbruck. Kahdia blinked, and said nothing. 'Whatever one thinks of our erstwhile leader, when it comes to being a prisoner of the Gurkish he must be considered an unchallengeable expert.' Again, the Haddish did not speak. 'Do you have any opinion on that matter?'

'To kill oneself is reckoned an offence against God.' Kahdia shrugged. 'But at times like these, who can say what is right?'

Vissbruck slowly nodded. 'We are cut loose. From the Union. From our families. From God. We all must find our own way now.' And he marched swiftly towards the temple's back entrance, his boot heels clicking against the marble as the press parted to let him and his soldiers through.

Temple started forward, grabbing Kahdia by the arm. 'Haddish, you must go with them!'

Kahdia gently peeled Temple's fingers from his wrist. Just as Temple had peeled away the fingers of the dying woman. 'I am glad you are still alive, Temple. I was worried about you. But you are bleeding—'

'It's nothing! You must go to the Citadel.'

'Must? We always have a choice, Temple.'

'They are coming. The Gurkish are coming.' He swallowed. Even now, he could not bring himself to raise his voice when he spoke the words. 'The Eaters are coming.'

'I know. That is why I must stay.'

Temple gritted his teeth. The old man's calm was making him furious, and he knew why. Not for Kahdia's sake, but for his own. He wanted the priest to run so that he could run with him. Even though there was no place safe from the Eaters. Nowhere in all the world, and certainly not in Dagoska. Even though taking refuge in the Citadel could only buy him days, and probably not that many.

The Haddish smiled. As though he saw it all. Saw it all, and forgave him even so.

'I must stay,' he said. 'But you should go, Temple. If you feel you need my permission, I give it gladly.'

Temple cursed. He had been forgiven too often. He wanted to be raged at, to be blamed, to be beaten. He wanted a reason to take the easy way and run, but Kahdia would not let him take the easy way. It was why Temple had always loved him. There were tears in his eyes. He cursed. But he stayed.

'What do we do?' croaked Temple.

'We care for the wounded. We give comfort to the weak. We bury the dead. We pray.'

He did not say fight, but that was clearly on some minds. Five acolytes had gathered uncertainly beside one wall, shifty as children about some secret game. Temple saw the glint of a blade. An axe hanging in the fold of a robe.

'Set down those weapons!' called Kahdia, striding over to them. 'This is a temple!'

'Do you think the Gurkish will respect our holy ground?' one of them screeched, a madness of fear in his eyes. 'Do you think they'll put aside their weapons?'

Kahdia was calm as still water. 'God will judge them for their crimes. He will judge us for ours. Set down your weapons.'

The men glanced at each other, shifted their weight uncertainly, but armed though they were, none of them had the courage to meet Kahdia's unwavering eye. One by one they set their weapons down.

The Haddish put his hand on the shoulder of the man who had challenged him. 'You are on the wrong side as soon as you pick one, my son. We must act as we would want to act. We must act as we would want others to act. Now more than ever.'

'How will that help us?' Temple found he had muttered.

'In the end, what else is there?' And Kahdia looked towards the great doors, and drew himself up, and set his shoulders.

Temple realised that a silence had fallen outside. In the square that had once echoed with the priests' calls to prayer. Then with the merchants' calls to buy. Then with the cries of the wounded, and the orphaned, and the helpless. Silence could only mean one thing.

They were here.

'Do you remember what you were when we first met?' asked Kahdia.

'A thief.' Temple swallowed. 'A fool. A boy with no code and no purpose.'

'And see what you have become!'

He hardly felt any different than he had. 'What will I become now, without you?'

Kahdia smiled and set his hand on Temple's shoulder. 'That is in your hands. And in the hands of God.' He came a little closer, to whisper. 'Do nothing foolish, do you understand? You must live.'

'Why?'

'Like a storm, like a plague, like a swarm of locusts, the Gurkish will pass. When they do, Dagoska will have need of good men.'

Temple was about to point out that he was no better than the next thief when there was a booming blow on the gates. The great doors shook, dust filtering down as the lamps wildly flickered. A gasp went through the people and they shrank back, back into the shadows at the far end of the temple.

Another blow, and the doors, and the crowd, and Temple all shuddered at it.

Then a word was spoken. Spoken in a voice of thunder, impossibly, deafeningly loud, mighty as the tolling of a great bell. Temple did not know the tongue and yet he saw the letters of it burned into the door in blinding light. The heavy gate burst apart in a cloud of splinters, chunks of wood tumbling across the marble floor and scattering wide.

A figure stepped between the twisted hinges. A figure in white armour, marked with letters of gold, a smile upon his face, a face as perfect as if it was cast from dark glass.

'Greetings from the Prophet Khalul!' he called out, warm and friendly, and the people whimpered and crowded back further.

The letters of fire were still written across Temple's swimming sight in the darkness, holy letters, unholy letters, his ears still humming with their echoes. A girl whimpered beside him, hands over her face. And Temple put his on her shoulder, clutched at it, trying to calm her, trying to calm himself. More figures sauntered into the temple. Figures in white armour.

They were only five but the crowd shrank back as though they were sheep and these were wolves, crushing each other in their fear. Close to Temple came a woman, beautiful, awful, tall and thin as a spear, a light to her pale face like the glistening of a pearl, golden hair floating as if she carried her own breeze with her.

'Hello, my pretties.' She smiled wide at Temple and ran the tip of a long, pointed tongue down one long, pointed tooth, then shut her mouth with a snap and winked at him. His guts were water.

There was a cry. Someone jumped from the crowd. One of the acolytes. Temple saw a flash of metal in the darkness, was jerked sideways by another sudden ripple of fear through the crowd.

'No!' shouted Kahdia.

Too late. One of the Eaters moved. As fast as lightning and just as deadly. She caught the man's wrist, snatched him from his feet, whirled him around with impossible strength and flung him flailing through the air across the full width of the temple, as a sulking child might fling away a broken doll, his fallen dagger skittering across the tiles.

His scream was cut off as he crunched into the wall perhaps ten strides up, flopped bonelessly to the ground in a shower of blood and cracked marble. His head was flattened, twisted all the way around, his face thankfully turned to the wall.

'God,' whispered Temple. 'Oh, God.'

'Still, all of you!' called Kahdia, one arm out.

'You are their leader?' asked the foremost of the Eaters, raising one brow. His dark face was young, and smooth, and beautiful, but his eyes were old.

'I am Kahdia, Haddish of this temple.'

'A priest, then. A man of the book. Dagoska has been the birthplace of many holy men. Of revered philosophers, admired theologists. Men who heard the voice of God. Are you one such, Haddish Kahdia?'

Temple did not know how, but Kahdia showed no fear. He spoke as he might to one of his congregation. Even this devil born of hell, this eater of the flesh of men, he treated as if he was no lesser or greater than himself. 'I am but a man. I struggle to be righteous.'

'Believe it or not, so do we all.' The Eater frowned down at his hand, and made a fist of it, and let the fingers slowly open again as if allowing sand to drain from his palm. 'And here is where the road to righteousness has led me. Do you know who I am?' There was no mocking triumph in his perfect face. Only a sadness.

'You are Mamun,' said Haddish Kahdia. 'The fruit of the desert. Thrice Blessed and Thrice Cursed.'

'Yes. Though with every year the curses weigh heavier, and the blessings seem more dust.'

'You have only yourself to blame,' said Kahdia, calmly. 'You broke God's law and ate the flesh of men.'

'And of women, and of children, and of everything that breathes.' Mamun frowned over towards the acolyte's ruined corpse. One of the Eaters had squatted beside the body, and she put one finger in the pooling blood and began to smear it on her blandly smiling face. 'If only I had known then what I know now things might have been different.' He gave a sad smile. 'But it is easy to speak of the past, impossible to go there. I am powerful in ways you can only dream, yet I am still a prisoner of what I have done. I can never escape the cell I have made for myself. Things are what they are.'

'We always have a choice,' said Kahdia.

Mamun smiled at him. A strange smile, it was. Almost . . . hopeful. 'Do you think so?'

'God tells us so.'

'Then I offer you yours. We can take them.' He glanced towards the crowd, and as his glassy eyes passed over Temple he felt the hairs rise on his neck. 'We can take all of them, but you will be spared.'

The Eater with the golden hair winked at Temple again, and he felt the girl beside him trembling, and he felt himself trembling, too.

'Or we can take you,' said Mamun, 'and they will be spared.'

'All of them?' asked Kahdia.

'All of them.'

That was the time to step forward, Temple knew. To act as he would want to act. As he would want others to act. That was the moment for courage, for selflessness, for solidarity with the man who had saved his life, who had shown him mercy, who had given him a chance he did not deserve. To step forward, and offer himself in Kahdia's place. Now was the time.

Temple did not move.

No one did.

The Haddish gave a smile, though. 'You drive a poor bargain, Eater. I would happily have given my life for any one of them.'

The blonde woman raised her long arms, let her head fall back and began to sing. High and dazzlingly pure, her voice soared in the great spaces above, more beautiful than any music Temple had ever heard.

Mamun fell to his knees before Kahdia and pressed one hand to his heart. 'All heaven rejoices in the finding of one righteous man. Wash him. Give him food and water. Convey him with honour to the Prophet's table.'

'God be with you,' murmured Kahdia over his shoulder, the smile still on his face. 'God be with you all.' And he walked from the temple, an Eater on either side, their heads respectfully bowed as his was held high.

'Shame,' said the Eater with the blood-daubed face, her lips pushed out in a pout. She took the acolyte's corpse by one ankle and dragged it after her, swaggering to the doors and leaving a bloody trail across the floor.

Mamun paused for a moment in the broken doorway. 'The rest of you are free. Free from us, at least. From yourselves, there is no escape.'

Hell

How long did they stand in that sweating press, after the Eaters were gone? How long did they stand silent, staring towards the ruined gate? Frozen with terror. Rooted with guilt. Minutes? Hours? While outside, faintly, they heard the burning, the clash of steel, the screams, the sound of the sack of Dagoska. The sound of the end of the world.

Finally the girl beside Temple leaned close and asked in a broken whisper, 'What do we do?'

Temple swallowed. 'We care for the wounded. We give comfort to the weak. We bury the dead. We pray.'

God, it sounded hollow. But what else was there?

TWO'S
COMPANY

Somewhere in the North, Summer 576

'This is hell,' muttered Shev, peering over the brink of the canyon. 'Hell.' Rock shiny-dark with wet disappeared into the mist below, water rushing somewhere, a long way down. 'God, I hate the North.'

'Somehow,' answered Javre, pushing back hair turned lank brown by the eternal damp, 'I do not think God is listening.'

'Oh, I'm abundantly aware of that. No one's bloody listening.'

'I am.' Javre turned away from the edge and headed on down the rutted goat-track beside it with her usual mighty strides, head back, heedless of the rain, soaked cloak flapping at her muddy calves. 'And, what is more, I am intensely bored by what I am hearing.'

'Don't toy with me, Javre.' Shev hurried to catch her up, trying to find the least boggy patches to hop between. 'I've had about as much of this as I can take!'

'So you keep saying. And yet the next day you take some more.'

'I'm bloody furious!'

'I believe you.'

'I mean it!'

'If you have to tell someone you are furious, and then, further-more, that you mean it, your fury has failed to achieve its desired effect.'

'I hate the bloody North!' Shev stamped at the ground, as though she could hurt anything but herself, succeeding only in showering wet dirt up her leg. Not that she could have made herself much wetter or dirtier. 'The whole place is made of *shit*!'

Javre shrugged. 'Everything is, in the end.'

'How can anyone stand this cold?'

'It is bracing. Do not sulk. Would you like to ride on my shoulders?'

Shev would have, in fact, very much, but her bruised pride insisted that she continue to squelch along on foot. 'What am I, a bloody child?'

Javre raised her red brows. 'Were you never told only to ask questions you truly want the answer to? Do you want the answer?'

'Not if you're going to try to be funny.'

'Oh, come now, Shevedieh!' Javre bent down to snake one huge arm about her shoulders and gave her a bone-crushing squeeze. 'Where is that happy-go-lucky rascal I fell in love with back in Westport, always facing her indignities with a laugh, a caper and a twinkle in her eye?' And her wriggling fingers crept towards Shev's stomach.

Shev held up a knife. 'Tickle me and I will fucking stab you.'

Javre puffed out her cheeks, took her arm away and squelched on down the track. 'Do not be so overdramatic. It is exhausting. We just need to get you dry and find some pretty little farmgirl for you to curl up with and it will all feel better by morning.'

'There are no pretty farmgirls out here! There are no girls! There are no farms!' She held out her arms to the endless murk, mud and blasted rock. 'There isn't even any bloody morning!'

'There is a bridge,' said Javre, pointing into the gloom. 'See? Things are looking up!'

'I never felt so encouraged,' muttered Shev.

It was a tangle of fraying rope strung from ancient posts carved with runes and streaked with bird-droppings, rotten-looking slats tied to make a precarious walkway. It sagged deep as Shev's spirits as it vanished into the vertiginous unknown above the canyon and shifted alarmingly in the wind, planks rattling.

'Bloody North,' said Shev as she picked her way towards it and had a tentative drag at the ropes. 'Even their bridges are shit.'

'Their men are good,' said Javre, clattering out with no fear whatsoever. 'Far from subtle, but enthusiastic.'

'Great,' said Shev as she edged after, exchanging a mutually suspicious glance with a crow perched atop one of the posts. 'Men. The one thing that interests me not at all.'

'You should try them.'

'I did. Once. Bloody useless. Like trying to have a conversation with someone who doesn't even speak your language, let alone understand the topic.'

'Some are certainly more horizontally fluent than others.'

'No. Just *no*. The hairiness, and the lumpiness, and the great big fumbling fingers and ... *balls*. I mean, *balls*. What's *that* about? That is one singularly unattractive piece of anatomy. That is just ... that is bad design, is what that is.'

Javre sighed. 'It is the great shame of creation that we cannot all be so perfectly formed as you, Shevedieh, springy little string of sinew that you are.'

'There'd be more bloody meat on me if we weren't living on high hopes and the odd rabbit. I may not be perfect but I don't have a sock of bloody gravel swinging around my knees, you'd have to give me ... Hold on.' They had reached the sagging middle of the bridge now, and Shev could see neither rock face. Only the ropes fading up into the grey in both directions.

'What?' muttered Javre, clattering to a stop.

The bridge kept on bouncing. A heavy tread, and coming towards them.

'There's someone heading the other way,' muttered Shev, twisting her wrist and letting the dagger drop from her sleeve into her waiting palm. A fight was the last thing she ever wanted, but she'd reluctantly come to find there was no downside to having a good knife ready. It made a fine conversation point, if nothing else.

A figure started to form. At first just a shadow, shifting as the wind drove the fog in front of them. First a short man, then a tall one. Then a man with a rake over his shoulder. Then a half-naked man with a huge sword over his shoulder.

Shev squinted around Javre's elbow, waiting for it to resolve itself into something that made better sense. It did not.

'That is . . . unusual,' said Javre.

'Bloody North,' muttered Shev. 'Nothing up here would surprise me.'

The man stopped perhaps two strides off, smiling. But a smile more of madness than good humour. He wore trousers, thankfully, made of some ill-cured pelt, and boots with absurd fur tops. Otherwise he was bare, and his pale torso was knotted with muscle, criss-crossed with scars and beaded with dew. That sword looked even bigger close up, as if forged by an optimist for the use of giants. It was nearly as tall as its owner, and he was not short by any means, for he looked Javre more or less in the eye.

'Someone's compensating for something,' muttered Shev, under her breath.

'Greetings, ladies,' said the man, in a thick accent. 'Lovely day.'

'It's fucking not,' grumbled Shev.

'Well, it's all in how you look at it, isn't it, though?' He raised his brows expectantly, but when neither of them answered, continued, 'I am Whirrun of Bligh. Some folk call me Cracknut Whirrun.'

'Congratulations,' said Shev.

He looked pleased. 'You've heard of me, then?'

'No. Where the hell's Bligh?'

He winced. 'Honestly, I couldn't say.'

'I am Javre,' said Javre, puffing up her considerable chest, 'Lioness of Hoskopp.' Shev rolled her eyes. God – warriors, and their bloody titles, and their bloody introductions, and their bloody chest-puffing. 'We are crossing this bridge.'

'Ah! Me too!'

Shev ground her teeth. 'What is this, a stating-the-obvious competition? We've met in the middle of it, haven't we?'

'Yes.' Whirrun heaved in a great breath through his nose and let it sigh happily away. 'Yes, we have.'

'That is quite a sword,' said Javre.

'It is the Father of Swords, and men have a hundred names for it. Dawn Razor. Grave-Maker. Blood Harvest. Highest and Lowest. *Scac-ang-Gaioc* in the valley tongue which means the Splitting of the World, the Battle that was fought at the start of time and will be fought again at its end. Some say it is God's sword, fallen from the heavens.'

'Huh.' Javre held up the roughly sword-shaped bundle of rags she carried with her. 'My sword was forged from a fallen star.'

'It looks like a sword-shaped bundle of rags.'

Javre narrowed her eyes. 'I have to keep it wrapped up.'

'Why?'

'Lest its brilliance blind you.'

'Ooooooooh,' said Whirrun. 'The funny thing about that is,

now I really want to see it. Would I get a good look *before* I was blinded, or—'

'Are you two done with the pissing contest?' asked Shev.

'I would not get into a pissing contest with a man.' Javre pushed her hips forward, stuck her hand in her groin and indicated the probable arc with a pointed finger. 'I have tried it before and you can say what you like about cocks but they just get far more distance. Far more. What?' she asked, frowning over her shoulder. 'It simply cannot be done, no matter how much you drink. Now, if *you* want a pissing contest—'

'I don't!' snapped Shev. 'Right now all I want is somewhere dry to kill myself!'

'You are so overdramatic,' said Javre, shaking her head. 'She is so overdramatic. It is exhausting.'

Whirrun shrugged. 'It's a fine line between too much drama and too little, isn't it, though?'

'True,' mused Javre. 'True.'

There was a pause, while the bridge creaked faintly.

'Well,' said Shev, 'this has been lovely, but we are being pursued by agents of the Great Temple in Thond and some fellows hired by Horald the Finger, so, if you don't mind—'

'In fact I do. I, too, am pursued, by agents of the King of the Northmen, Bethod. You'd think he'd have better things to do, what with this mad war against the Union, but Bethod, well, like him or no, you have to admit he's persistent.'

'Persistently a shit,' said Shev.

'I won't disagree,' lamented Whirrun. 'The greater a man's power swells, the smaller his good qualities shrivel.'

'True,' mused Javre. 'True.'

Another long silence, and the wind blew up and made the

bridge sway alarmingly. Javre and Whirrun frowned at one another.

'Step aside,' said Javre, 'and we shall be on our way.'

'I do not care to step aside. Especially on a bridge as narrow as this one.' Whirrun's eyes narrowed slightly. 'And your tone somewhat offends me.'

'Then your delicate feelings will be even worse wounded by my boot up your arse. Step aside.'

Whirrun swung the Father of Swords from his shoulder and set it point-down on the bridge. 'I fear you will have to show me that blade after all, woman.'

'My pleasure—'

'Wait!' snapped Shev, ducking around Javre to hold up a calming palm. 'Just wait a moment! You can murder each other with my blessing but if you set to swinging your hugely impressive swords on this bridge, the chances are good you'll cut one of the ropes, and then you'll kill not just each other but me, too, and that you very much do not have my blessing for.'

Whirrun raised his brows. 'She has a point.'

'Shevedieh can be a deep thinker,' said Javre, nodding. She gestured back the way they had come. 'Let us return to our end to fight.'

Shev gave a gasp. 'So you wouldn't step aside to let him past but you'll happily plod all the way back to fight?'

Javre looked baffled. 'Of course. That is only good manners.'

'Exactly!' said Whirrun. 'Manners are everything to a good-mannered person. That is why we must go to my end of the bridge to fight.'

It was Javre's turn to narrow her eyes. She was almost as dangerous an eye-narrower as she was a fighter, which was saying something. 'It must be my end.'

'My end,' growled Whirrun. 'I insist.'

Shev rubbed at her temples. The past few years, it was a wonder she hadn't worn them right through. 'Are you two idiots really going to fight over where you fight? We were going this way! He's offering to let us go this way! Let's just go this way!'

Javre narrowed her eyes still further. Blue slits, they were. 'All right. But don't think you're talking us out of fighting, Shevedieh.'

Shev gave her very weariest sigh. 'Far be it from me to prevent bloodshed.'

Whirrun wedged his great sword point-down into a crack in the rocks and left it gently wobbling. 'Let's put our blades aside. The Father of Swords cannot be drawn without being blooded.'

Javre snorted. 'Afraid?'

'No. The witch Shoglig told me the time and place of my death, and it is not here, and it is not now.'

'Huh.' Javre set her own sword down and began, one by one, to explosively crack her knuckles. 'Did she tell you the time of me kicking you so hard you shit yourself?'

Whirrun's face took on a contemplative look. 'She did predict my shitting myself, but that was because of a rancid stew and, anyway, that happened already. Last year, near Uffrith. That is why I have these new trousers.' He bent over to smile proudly upon them, then frowned towards Shev. 'I trust your servant will stay out of this?'

'Servant?' snapped Shev.

'Shevedieh is not my servant,' said Javre.

'Thank you.'

'She is at least a henchman. Possibly even a sidekick.'

Shev planted her hands on her hips. 'We're partners! A duo!'

Javre laughed. 'No. Duo? No, no, no.'

'Whatever she is,' said Whirrun, 'she looks sneaky. I don't want her stabbing me in the back.'

'Don't *bloody* worry about that!' snapped Shev. 'Believe me when I say I want less than no part of this stupidity. As for sneaking, I tried to get out of that business and open a Smoke House, but *my partner* burned it down!'

'Sidekick at best,' said Javre. 'And as I recall it was you who knocked the coals over. Honestly, Shevedieh, you are always looking for someone to blame. If you want to ever be half of a duo you must learn to take responsibility.'

'Smoke House?' asked Whirrun. 'You like fish?'

'No, no,' said Shev. 'Well, yes, but not that kind of Smoke House, you . . . Forget it.' And she dropped down on a rock and propped her chin on her fists.

'Since we are making rules . . .' Javre winced as she hitched up her bust. 'Can we say no strikes to the tits? Men never realise how much that hurts.'

'Fine.' Whirrun lifted one leg to rearrange his groin. 'If you avoid the fruits. Bloody things can get in the way.'

'It's poor design,' said Shev. 'Didn't I say it? Poor design.'

Javre shrugged her coat off and tossed it over Shev's head.

'Thanks,' she snapped as she dragged it off her damp hair and around her damp shoulders.

Javre raised her fists and Whirrun gave an approving nod as the sinews popped from her arms. 'You are without doubt an impressive figure of a woman.' He put up his own fists, woody muscle flexing. 'But I will take no mercy on you because of that.'

'Good. Except around the chest area?'

'As agreed.' Whirrun grinned. 'This may be a battle for the songs.'

'You will have trouble singing them without your teeth.'

They traded blows, lightning quick. Whirrun's fist sank into Javre's ribs with a thud but she barely seemed to notice, letting go three quick punches and catching him full on the jaw with the last. He did not waver, only took a quick step back, already set and watchful.

'You are strong,' he said. 'For a woman.'

'I will show you how strong.'

She lunged at him with a vicious flurry of blows but caught only air as he jerked this way and that, slippery as a fish in the river for all his size. Meat slapped as Javre caught his counters on her forearms, growling through gritted teeth, shrugged off a cuff on her forehead and caught Whirrun's arm. In a flash she dropped to one knee, heaved him over her head and into the air, but he tucked himself up neat as Shev used to when she tumbled in that travelling show, hit the turf with his shoulder, rolled and came up on his feet, still smiling.

'Every day should be a new lesson,' he said.

'You are quick,' said Javre. 'For a man.'

'I will show you how quick.'

He came at her, feinted high, ducked under her raking heel and caught her other calf, lifting her effortlessly to fling her down. But Javre had already hooked her leg around the back of his neck and dragged him down with her. They tumbled in a tangle of limbs to the muddy ground, rolling about with scant dignity, squirming and snapping, punching and kneeing, spitting and snarling.

'This is hell.' Shev gave a long groan and looked off into the mist. 'This is . . .' She paused, heart sinking even lower. 'You two,' she muttered, slowly standing. 'You two!'

'We are . . .' snarled Javre as she kneed Whirrun in the ribs.

'A little . . .' snarled Whirrun as he butted her in the mouth.

'Busy!' snarled Javre as they rolled struggling through a puddle.

'You may want to stop,' growled Shev. Figures were emerging from the mist. First three. Then five. Now seven men, one of them on a horse. 'I think perhaps Bethod's agents have arrived.'

'Arse!' Whirrun scrambled free of Javre, hurrying over to his sword and striking a suitably impressive pose with his hand on the hilt, only slightly spoiled by his whole bare side being smeared with mud. Shev swallowed and let the dagger drop into her hand once again. It spent a lot more time there than she'd like.

The first to take full shape from the mist was a nervous-looking boy, couldn't have been more than fifteen, who half-drew his bow with somewhat wobbly hands, arrow pointed roughly in Whirrun's direction. Next came a selection of Northmen, impressively bearded if you liked that kind of thing, which Shev didn't, and even more impressively armed, if you liked *that* kind of thing, which Shev didn't either.

'Evening, Flood,' said Whirrun, dabbing some blood from his split lip.

'Whirrun,' said the one who Shev presumed to be the leader, leaning on his spear as if he'd walked a long way.

Whirrun began to conspicuously count the Northmen with a wagging finger, his lips silently moving.

'There are seven,' said Shev.

'Ah!' said Whirrun. 'You're right, she's a quick thinker. Seven! I'm touched Bethod can spare so many, just for me. Thought he'd need every man, what with this war against the Southerners. I mean to say, they call me mad, but this war? Now *that's* mad.'

'Can't say I disagree,' said Flood, combing at his beard with his dirty fingers, 'but I don't make the choices.'

'Some men don't have the bones to make the choices.'

'And some men are just tired of their choices always turning out the wrong ones. I know being difficult comes natural to you, Whirrun, but could you try not to be just for a little while? Bethod's King of the Northmen, now. He can't have people just going their own way.'

'I am Whirrun of Bligh,' said Whirrun, puffing up his considerable chest. 'My way is the only way I go.'

'Oh, God,' muttered Shev. 'He's the male Javre. He's the male you, Javre!'

'He is certainly in the neighbourhood,' said Javre, with a note of grudging appreciation, flicking away some sheep's droppings which had become stuck in her hair in the struggle. 'Why does only one of you have a horse?'

The Northmen glanced at each other as though this was the source of some friction between them.

'There's a war on,' grunted one with shitty teeth. 'Not that many horses about.'

Shev snorted. 'Don't I know it. You think I'd be walking if I didn't have to?'

'It's my horse,' said Flood. 'But Kerric's got a bad leg so I said he could borrow it.'

'We've all got bad legs,' grunted a big one with an entirely excessive beard and an axe even more so.

'Now is probably not the time to reopen discussion of who gets the horse,' snapped Flood. 'The dead know we've argued over that particular issue enough, don't you bloody think?' With a gesture, he started the men spreading out to the right and left. 'Who the hell are the women anyway, Whirrun?'

Shev rolled her eyes as Javre did her own puffing up. 'I am Javre, Lioness of Hoskopp.'

Flood raised one brow. 'And your servant?'

Shev gave a weary groan. 'Oh, for—'

'She's not a servant, she's a henchman,' said Whirrun. 'Or...
henchwoman? Is that a word?'

'Partner!' snapped Shev.

'No, no.' Javre shook her head. 'Partner? No.'

'It really doesn't matter,' said Flood, starting to become impatient. 'The point is Bethod wants to talk to you, Whirrun, and
you'll be coming with us even if we have to hurt you—'

'One moment.' Javre held up her big hand. 'This man and I
are in the midst of resolving a previous disagreement. You can
hurt whatever is left of him when I am done.'

'By the dead.' Flood pressed thumb and forefinger into his eyes
and rubbed them fiercely. 'Nothing's ever easy. Why is nothing
ever easy?'

'Believe me,' said Shev, tightening her grip on her knife, 'I feel
your pain. You were going to fight him for nothing, now you're
going to fight *for* him for nothing?'

'We stand where the Goddess puts us,' growled Javre, knuckles
whitening where she gripped her sword.

Flood gave an exasperated sigh. 'Whirrun, there's no call for
bloodshed here—'

'I'm with him,' said Shev, holding up a finger.

'—but you're really not giving me much of a choice. Bethod
wants you in front of Skarling's chair, alive or dead.'

Whirrun grinned. 'Shoglig told me the time of my death, and
it is not here, and it is not—'

A bowstring went. It was that boy with the wobbly hands,
looking as surprised he'd let fly as anyone. Whirrun caught the
arrow. Just snatched it from the air, neat as you like.

'Wait!' roared Flood, but it was too late. The man with the
big beard rushed at Whirrun, roaring, spraying spit, swinging
his axe. At the last moment, Whirrun calmly stepped around the

Father of Swords so the axe-haft clanged into its sheathed blade and stabbed the bearded man in the neck with the arrow. He dropped spluttering.

By then everyone was shouting.

For someone who hated fights, Shev surely ended up in a lot of the bastards, and if she'd learned one thing it was that you've got to commit. Try your damndest to negotiate, to compromise, to put it off, but when the time comes to fight, you've got to commit. So she flung her knife.

If she'd thought about it, Shev might have figured that she didn't want to weigh down her conscience any more than she had to, and killing a horse wasn't as bad as killing a man. If she'd thought about it more, she might have considered that the man had chosen to be there while the horse hadn't, so probably deserved it more. But if she'd thought about it even more, she might have considered that the man probably hadn't chosen to be there in any meaningful sense any more than Shev had herself, but had been rolled along through life like a stone on the riverbed according to his situation, acquaintances, character and bad luck without too much chance of changing anything.

But folk who spend a lot of time thinking in fights don't tend to live through them, so Shev left the thinking for later and threw at the easiest target to hit.

The knife stuck into the horse's hindquarters and its eyes bulged. It reared, stumbled, bucked and tottered, and Shev had to scramble out of the way while the rider tore desperately at the reins. The horse plunged and kicked, the saddle-girth tore and the saddle slid from the horse's back as it toppled sideways, rolled over its rider, bringing his despairing wail to a sharp end, then slipped thrashing over the rocky verge of the canyon and out of sight.

So Shev ended up with horse *and* rider on her conscience. But the sad fact was, only the winners got to regret what they did in a fight, and right now Shev had other worries. Namely, a man with the shittiest teeth she ever saw and a hell of an intimidating mace. Why was he grinning? God, if she had those teeth, you'd have needed a crowbar to get her lips apart.

'Come here,' he snarled at her.

'I'd rather not,' Shev hissed back.

She scrambled out of the way, damp stones scattering from her heels, the screech, crash and clatter of combat almost forgotten in the background. Scrambling, always scrambling, from one disaster to another. Often at the edge of an unknowable canyon, at least a metaphorical one. And, as always, she could never quite get away.

The shitty-toothed maceman caught her collar with his free hand, jerking it so half the buttons ripped off and driving her back so her head cracked on rock. She stabbed at him with her other knife but the blade only scraped his mail and twisted out of her hand. A moment later, his fist sank into her gut and drove her breath out in a shuddering wheeze.

'Got yer,' he growled in her face, his breath alone almost enough to make her lose consciousness. He lifted his mace.

She raised one finger to point over his shoulder. 'Behind you . . .'

'You think I'm falling for—'

There was a loud thudding sound and the Father of Swords split him from his shoulder down to his guts, gore spraying in Shev's face as if it had been flung from a bucket.

'Urrgh!' She slithered from under the man's carcass, desperately trying to kick free of the slaughterhouse slops that had been suddenly dumped in her lap. 'God,' she whimpered, struggling up, trembling and spitting, clothes soaked with blood, hair dripping with blood, mouth, eyes, nose full of blood. 'Oh, God.'

'Look on the sunny side,' said Whirrun. 'At least it's not your own.'

Bethod's men were scattered about the muddy grass, hacked, twisted, leaking. The only one still standing was Flood.

'Now, look,' he said, licking his lips, spear levelled as Javre stalked towards him. 'I didn't want things to go this way—'

She whipped her sword from its scabbard and Shev flinched, two blinding smears left across her sight. The top part of Flood's spear dropped off, then the bottom, leaving him holding a stick about the length of Shev's foot. He swallowed, then tossed it on the ground and held up his hands.

'Get you gone back to your master, Flood,' said Whirrun, 'and thank the dead for your good luck with every step. Tell him Whirrun of Bligh dances to his own tune.'

With wide eyes Flood nodded, and began to back away.

'And if you see Curnden Craw over there, tell him I haven't forgotten he owes me three chickens!'

'Chickens?' muttered Javre.

'A debt is a debt,' said Whirrun, leaning nonchalantly on the Father of Swords, his bare white body now spattered with blood as well as mud. 'Talking of which, we still have business between us.'

'We do.' She looked Whirrun slowly up and down with lips thoughtfully pursed. It was a look Shev had seen before, and she felt her heart sink even lower, if that was possible. 'But another way of settling it now occurs to me.'

'Uh ... uh ... uh ...'

Shev knelt shivering beside a puddle of muddy rainwater, muttering every curse she knew, which was many, struggling to mop the gore from between her tits with a rag torn from a dead man's shirt, and trying desperately not to notice Javre's throaty grunting coming from behind the rock. It was like trying not to notice someone hammering nails into your head.

'Uh... uh... uh...'

'This is hell,' she whimpered, staring at her bedraggled reflection in the muddy, bloody puddle. 'This is hell.'

What had she done to deserve being there? Marooned in this loveless, sunless, cultureless, comfortless place. A place salted by the tears of the righteous, as her mother used to say. Her hair plastered to her clammy head like bloody seaweed to a rotting boat. Her chafed skin on which the gooseflesh could hardly be told from the scaly chill-rash. Her nose endlessly running, rimmed with sore pink from the wiping. Her sunken stomach growling, her bruised neck throbbing, her blistered feet aching, her withered dreams crumbling, her—

'Uh... uh... uh...' Javre's grunting was mounting in volume, and added to it now was a long, steady growling from Whirrun. 'Rrrrrrrrrrrrrrr...'

Shev found herself wondering what exactly they were up to, slapped the side of her head as though she could knock the thought out. She should be concentrating on feeling sorry for herself! Think of all she'd lost!

The Smoke House. Well, that hadn't been so great. Her friends in Westport. Well, she'd never had any she'd have trusted with a copper. Severard. No doubt he'd be far better off with his mother in Adua, however upset he'd been about it. Carcolf. Carcolf had betrayed her, damn it! God, those hips, though. How could you stay angry at someone with hips like that?

'Uh... uh... uh...'

'Rrrrrrrrrrrrrrr...'

She slithered back into her shirt, which her efforts at washing had turned from simply bloody to bloody, filthy and clinging with freezing water. She shuddered with disgust as she wiped blood out of her ear, out of her nose, out of her eyebrows.

She'd tried to do small kindnesses where she could, hadn't she? Coppers to beggars when she could afford it, and so on? And, for the rest, she'd had good reasons, hadn't she? Or had she just made good excuses?

'Oh, God,' she muttered to herself, pushing the greasy-chill hair out of her face.

The horrible fact was, she'd got no worse than she deserved. Quite possibly better. If this was hell, she'd earned every bit of it. She took a deep breath and blew it out so her lips flapped.

'Uh ... uh ... uh!'

'Rrrrrrrrrrr!'

Shev hunched her shoulders, staring back towards the bridge. She paused, heart sinking even lower than before. Right into her blistered feet.

'You two,' muttered Shev, slowly standing, fumbling with her shirt-buttons. 'You two!'

'We are ...' came Javre's strangled voice.

'A little ...' groaned Whirrun.

'Busy!'

'You may want to fucking stop!' screeched Shev, sliding out a knife and hiding it behind her arm. She realised she'd got her buttons in the wrong holes, a great tail of flapping-wet shirt plastered to her leg. But it was a little late to smarten up. Once again, there were figures coming from the mist. From the direction of the bridge. First one. Then two. Then three women.

Tall women who walked with that same easy swagger Javre had. That swagger that said they ruled the ground they walked on. All three wore swords. All three wore sneers. All three, Shev didn't doubt, were Templars of the Golden Order, come for Javre in the name of the High Priestess of Thond.

The first had dark hair coiled into a long braid bound with golden wire, and old eyes in a young face. The second had a great burn mark across her cheek and through her scalp, one ear missing. The third had short red hair and eyes slyly narrowed as she looked Shev up and down. 'You're very . . . *wet*,' she said.

Shev swallowed. 'It's the North. Everything's a bit damp.'

'Bloody North.' The scarred one spat. 'No horses to be had anywhere.'

'Not for love nor money,' sang the red-haired one, 'and believe me, I've tried both.'

'Probably the war,' said the dark-haired one.

'It's the North. There's always a war.'

Whirrun gave a heavy sigh as he clambered from behind the rock, fastening his belt. ''Tis a humbling indictment of our way of life, but one I find I can't deny.' And he hefted the Father of Swords over his shoulder and came to stand beside Shev.

'You aren't nearly as funny as you think you are,' said the scarred one.

'Few of us indeed,' said Shev, 'are as funny as we think we are.'

Javre stepped out from behind the rock, and the three women all shifted nervously at the sight of her. Sneers became frowns. Hands crept towards weapons. Shev could feel the violence coming, sure as the grass grows, and she clung tight to that entirely inadequate knife of hers. All the fights she got into, she really should learn to use a sword. Or maybe a spear. She might look taller with a spear. But then you've got to carry the bastard around. Something with a chain, maybe, that coiled up small?

'Javre,' said the one with the braid.

'Yes.' Javre gave the women that fighter's glance of hers. That careless glance that seemed to say she had taken all their measure in a moment and was not impressed by it.

'You're here, then.'

'Where else would I be but where I am?'

The dark-haired woman raised her sharp chin. 'Why don't you introduce everyone?'

'It feels like a lot of effort, when you will be gone so soon.'

'Indulge me.'

Javre sighed. 'This is Golyin, Fourth of the Fifteen. Once a good friend to me.'

'Still a good friend, I like to think.'

Shev snorted. 'Would a good friend chase another clear across the Circle of the World?' Under her breath, she added, 'Not to mention her good friend's partner.'

Golyin's eyes shifted to Shev's, and there was a sadness in them. 'If a good friend had sworn to. In the quiet times, perhaps, she would cry that the world was this way, and wring her hands, and ask the Goddess for guidance, but...' She gave a heavy sigh. 'She would do it. You must have known we would catch you eventually, Javre.'

Javre shrugged, sinews in her shoulders twitching. 'I have never been hard to catch. It is once you catch me that your problems begin.' She nodded towards the scarred one, who was slowly, smoothly, silently easing her way around the top of the canyon to their right. 'She is Ahum, Eleventh of the Fifteen. Is the scar still sore?'

'I have a soothing lotion for it,' she said, curling her lip. 'And I am Ninth now.'

'Nothingth soon.' Javre raised a brow at the red-haired one, working her way around them on the left. 'Her I do not know.'

'I am Sarabin Shin, Fourteenth of the Fifteen, and men call me—'

'No one cares,' said Javre. 'I give you all the same two choices I gave Hanama and Birke and Weylen and the others. Go back to the High Priestess and tell her I will be no one's slave. Not ever. Or I show you the sword.'

There was that familiar popping of joints as Javre shifted her shoulders, scraping into a wider stance and lifting the sword-shaped bundle in her left hand.

Golyin sucked her teeth. 'You always were so overdramatic, Javre. We would rather take you back than kill you.'

Whirrun gave a little snort of laughter. 'I could swear we just had this exact conversation.'

'We did,' said Javre, 'and this one will end the same way.'

'This woman is a murderer, an oathbreaker, a fugitive,' said Golyin.

'Meh.' Whirrun shrugged. 'Who isn't?'

'There is no need for you to die here, man,' said Sarabin Shin, finding her own fighting crouch.

Whirrun shrugged again. 'One place is as good for dying as another, and these ladies helped me with an unpleasant situation.' He pointed out the six corpses scattered across the muddy ground with the pommel of his sword. 'And my friend Curnden Craw always says it's poor manners not to return a favour.'

'You may find this situation of a different order of unpleasant-ness,' said the scarred one, drawing her sword. The blade smoked in a deeply unnatural and worrying way, a frosty glitter to the white metal.

Whirrun only smiled as he shrugged his huge sword off his shoulder. 'I have a tune for every occasion.'

The other two women drew their swords. Golyin's curved blade appeared to be made of black shadow, curling and twisting so its shape was never sure. Sarabin Shin smiled at Shev and raised her own sword, long, and thin, and smouldering like a blade just drawn from the forge. Shev hated swords, especially ones pointed at her, but she rarely saw one she liked the look of less than that.

She held up the hand that didn't have the knife in. 'Please, girls.' She wasn't above begging. 'Please! There really is no upside to this. If we fight, someone will die. They will lose everything. Those who win will be no better off than now.'

'She is a pretty little thing,' said the scarred one.

Shev tidied a bloody strand of hair behind her ear. 'Well, that's nice to—'

'But she talks too much,' said Golyin. 'Kill them.'

Shev flung her knife. Sarabin Shin swept out her sword and swatted it twittering away into the mist as she charged screaming forward.

Shev rolled, scrambled, ducked, dodged, dived while that smouldering blade carved the air around her, feeling the terrible heat of it on her skin. She tumbled more impressively than she ever had with that travelling show, the flashes of Javre's sword at the corner of her eye as she fought Golyin, the ringing of metal crashing on her ears as Whirrun and Ahum traded blows.

Shev flung all the knives at her disposal, which was maybe six, then when those were done started snatching up anything to hand, which, after the last fight, was a considerable range of fallen weapons, armour and gear.

Sarabin Shin dodged a hastily flung mace, then an axe, then carved a water-flask in half with a hissing of steam, then stepped around a flapping boot with a hissing of contempt.

The one hit Shev scored was with a Northman's cloven helmet, which bounced off Shin's brow opening a little cut, and only appeared to make her more intent on Shev's destruction than ever.

She ended up using the fallen saddle as a shield, desperately fending off blows while the snarling woman carved smoking chunks from it, leaving her holding an ever smaller lump of leather until, with a final swing, Shin chopped it into two flaming fist-sized pieces and caught Shev by her collar, dragging her close with an almost unbelievable strength, the smoking blade levelled at her face.

'No more running!' she snarled through her gritted teeth, pulling back her sword for a thrust.

Shev squeezed her eyes shut, hoping, for the second time that day, that against all odds and the run of luck she would find a way to creep into heaven.

'Get off my *partner*!' came Javre's furious shriek.

Even through her lids she saw a blinding flash and Shev jerked away, gasping. There was a hiss and something hot brushed gently against Shev's face. Then the hand on her collar fell away, and she heard something heavy thump against the ground.

'Well, that is that,' said Whirrun.

Shev prised one eye open, peered down at herself through the glittering smear Javre's sword had left across her sight. The headless body of Sarabin Shin lay beside her.

'God,' she whimpered, standing stiff with horror, clothes soaked with blood, hair dripping with blood, mouth, eyes, nose full of blood. Again. 'Oh, God.'

'Look on the sunny side,' said Javre, her sword already sheathed in its ragged scabbard. 'At least it is not—'

'Fuck the sunny side!' screamed Shev. 'And fuck the North, and fuck you pair of rutting lunatics!'

Whirrun shrugged. 'That I'm mad is no revelation, I'm known

for it. They call me Cracknut because my nut is cracked and that's a fact.' With the toe of his boot he poked at the corpse of Ahum, face down beside him, leaking blood. 'Still, even I can reckon out that these Templars of the Silver Order—'

'Golden,' said Javre.

'Whatever they call themselves, they are not going to stop until they catch you.'

Javre nodded as she looked about at the King of the Northmen's dead agents. 'You are right. No more than Bethod will stop pursuing you.'

'I have nothing pressing,' said Whirrun. 'Perhaps we could help each other with our enemies?'

'Two swords are better than one.' Javre tapped a forefinger thoughtfully against her lips. 'And we could fuck some more.'

'The thought had occurred,' said Whirrun, grinning. 'That was just starting to get interesting.'

'Wonderful.' Shev winced as she tried to blow the blood from her nose. 'Do I get a vote?'

'Henchpeople don't vote,' said Javre.

'And even if you did,' added Whirrun, giving an apologetic shrug, 'there are three of us. You'd be outvoted.'

Shev tipped her head back to look up at the careless, iron-grey sky. 'There's the trouble with fucking democracy.'

'So it's decided!' Whirrun clapped his hands and gave a boyish caper of enthusiasm. 'Shall we fuck now, or . . . ?'

'Let us make a start while there is still some daylight.' Javre stared over the fallen corpse of her old friend Golyin, off towards the west. 'It is a long way to Carleon.'

Whirrun frowned. 'To Thond first, so I can pay my debt to you.'

Javre puffed up her chest as she turned to face him. 'I will not hear of it. We deal with Bethod first.'

With a sigh of infinite weariness, Shev sank down beside the puddle, took up the bloody rag she had used earlier and wrung it out.

'I must insist,' growled Whirrun.

'As must I,' growled Javre.

As though by mutual agreement they seized hold of each other, tumbled wrestling to the ground, snapping, hissing, punching, writhing.

'This is hell.' Shev put her head in her hands. 'This is hell.'

WRONG PLACE, WRONG TIME

Westport, Spring 580

Canto Silvine finished his morning slice of bread and honey, licked his finger, used it to sweep up the crumbs from the plate, and smiled as he sucked it clean. The quiet joy of routine. It was something Mauthis was very keen on, routine. Canto tried to be keen on the same things powerful people were. He thought, perhaps, that might one day make him like them. He had no other ideas how to achieve it, anyway.

He frowned at a honey spot on his sleeve. 'Damn it!' Mauthis would be less keen on that, presentation being key, but any more time dithering and he would be late. And if Mauthis hated one quality above all others in a clerk, it was tardiness. He stood, trying desperately to make no noise, but the legs of his chair caught on the uneven boards and made an awful grinding.

'Cantolarus!' hissed Mimi's voice from the other room, and Canto winced. Only his mother used his full name. Only his mother, and his wife when she meant to give him a lecture. As she padded into the room with their son in her arms she had her serious eyes out, that slight wrinkle between the brows that he'd loved to see before he married her, but which had steadily lost its appeal over the months since. To begin with, that wrinkle had come when she told him how their life would be when they were married. Now it came when she told him how far their actual life fell short of what they had agreed.

'Yes, my love?' he said, in a tone that tried to laugh her off and reassure her both at once, and achieved neither.

'How long do you expect us to stay here?'

'Well, certainly until I get back from work!' He gave a nervous titter.

She did not. Rather, that wrinkle deepened. There was a loud bang on the ceiling, followed by the burble of raised voices from above, and Mimi's eyes rolled up towards it. Damn bad timing, for those bastards to start arguing just then. If Canto was half a man he would have gone up there and had a stern word with them about it. So Mimi told him. But Canto was not half a man. Mimi told him that, too.

'This was supposed to be temporary,' she said, and their son gave a quivering stretch as though attempting to pile more guilt on Canto's sagging shoulders.

'I know, and it is, it is! But ... we can't afford anything better quite yet. My pay won't cover it—'

'Then either your pay must rise or you must find a better-paying position.' That wrinkling grew harder. 'You're a father now, Canto-larus. You have to demand your due. You have to be a *man* about it.'

'I *am* a man!' he snapped, in the most peevish and effeminate way possible. He forced his voice deeper. 'I'm due a promotion. Mauthis said so.'

'He did?'

'I just said so, didn't I?' In fact, Mauthis had not spoken to him directly for three months, and that had been to bloodlessly correct him over a minor error in one of his calculations.

Mimi's angry frown had turned into a suspicious frown, however, and Canto counted that a victory, however it was managed.

'He's said it before,' she grumbled, hitching their son up a little. He truly was an enormous baby. 'It hasn't happened.'

'It will happen this time, my love. Trust me.' That's what he said every time. But it was easier to lie than to have the hard conversation. Much easier. Fortunately, their son chose that moment to give a mew and tug at his mother's nightshirt. Canto seized his chance. 'I have to go. I'm late as it is.'

She tipped her face towards him, probably expecting a kiss, but he did not have it in him, and fortunately their son was struggling now, eager to be fed. So instead he flashed a watery smile, and stepped out into the mouldy hallway, and pulled the door rattling to.

A problem left behind was just the same as a problem solved. Wasn't it?

Canto flung his ledger shut and started up from his desk, wriggling between a well-heeled merchant and her bodyguard and across the crowded banking floor. 'Sir! Sir, might I—'

Mauthis's cold stare flickered over him like a pawnbroker's over a dead man's chattels. 'Yes, Silvine?'

'Er . . .' Canto was wrong-footed, if not to say somewhat flushed with pleasure, at the mere fact of Mauthis knowing who he was. And it was so damned hot in the banking hall today that he found himself quite flustered. His mouth ran away with him. 'You know my name, sir—?'

'I know the names of every man and woman employed by the Banking House of Valint and Balk in Styria. Their names, and their roles, and their salaries.' He narrowed his eyes a fraction. 'I dislike changes to any of them. What can I do for you?'

Canto swallowed. 'Well, sir, the thing is . . .' Sounds seemed to be echoing at him in a most distracting way. The scratching of clerks' pens on paper and their rattling in inkwells; the hushed burbling of numbers, terms and rates; the clomp of a ledger being heaved shut felt loud as a door slamming. Nerves, was all, just nerves. He heard Mimi's voice. *You have to be a man about it.* Everyone was looking at him, though, the senior clerks with their books held close, and two fur-trimmed merchants who Canto now realised he had interrupted. *Have to be a man.* He tugged at his collar, trying to get some air in. 'The thing is—'

'Time is money, Silvine,' said Mauthis. 'I should not have to explain to you that the Banking House of Valint and Balk does not look kindly upon wasted money.'

'The thing is . . .' His tongue felt suddenly twice its usual size. His mouth tasted strange.

'Give him some air!' somebody shouted, over in the corner, and Mauthis's brows drew in, puzzled. Then almost pained.

'The thing . . .'

And Mauthis doubled up as though punched in the stomach. Canto took a sharp step back, and for some reason his knee almost gave way. So hot in the banking hall. Like that foundry he once visited with his father.

'Turn him over!' came echoing from the back of the hall. Everyone was staring. Faces swimming, fascinated, afraid.

'Sir? Sir?' One of the senior clerks had caught his master's elbow, was guiding him to the floor. Mauthis raised one quivering arm, one bony finger pointing, staring towards a woman in the press. A pale woman whose eyes burned bright behind black hair.

'Muh,' he mouthed. 'Muh . . .'

He started to flop wildly about on the floor. Canto was troubled by the thought that, plainly, this was not routine. Mauthis had always been such a stickler for routine. Then he was bent over by a sudden and deeply unpleasant coughing fit.

'Help!'

'Some air, I said!'

But there was no air. No air in the room at all. Canto sank slowly to his knees, tearing at his collar. Too tight. He could hardly catch a proper breath.

Mauthis lay still, pink foam bubbling from his mouth, his wide eyes staring up unseeing at the black-haired woman while she stared back. Who would Canto talk to now about a raise? But perhaps that was the wrong thing to be worrying about?

'Plague!' somebody shouted. A desk crashed over. People were charging this way and that. Canto clawed at someone for help but his fingers would hardly work. A flying knee caught him in the back and he was flung down, face crunching against the tiles, mouth filling with salty blood.

He tried to get up but he could hardly move, everything rigid, shaking, as if he was one enormous cramp. He thought the time had probably come now to cry out, but all that came was a bubbling gurgle. Mimi was right. Even now, he was half a man.

He saw feet stamping, shuffling. A woman screamed as she fell beside him, and the sound seemed to echo from the end of a long tunnel.

Everything was growing blurry.

He found, to his great dismay, that he could not breathe.

Sipani, Spring 580

'Don't much like the look of these,' muttered Onna, frowning as the entertainers strutted, danced, slouched into the courtyard of Cardotti's House of Leisure.

Do this job a while, you get a sense when someone's not

right. When they've a slant towards violence. You still can't avoid unpleasant surprises, of course. There are few worse jobs for unpleasant surprises. But you listen to your gut, if you're sensible, and Onna's gut was twitching now.

They might all be in gilded masks and merry motley but there was just something *off* about each and every one. A jaw muscle twitching on the stubbled side of a face. A set of eyes sliding suspiciously sideways through the eyeholes of a mask. A hand with scarred knuckles clenching and unclenching and clenching, over and over.

Onna shook her head. 'Don't like the look of these at all.'

Merilee blew out a plume of foul-smelling chagga smoke and sucked at her teeth. 'If you want men you like the look of, you might want to pick a profession other than whoring.'

Jirry took a break from filing her nails to give that little titter of hers, grinning with those pointy teeth. She was a great one for tittering, Jirry.

'We're supposed to call ourselves hostesses,' said Onna.

'Course we are.' Merilee could make her voice ooze so much sarcasm it was almost painful on the ears. 'Hostesses who fuck.'

Jirry tittered again and Onna sighed. 'You don't have to be ugly about it.'

'Don't have to be.' Merilee took another pull at her pipe and let the smoke curl from her nose. 'But I find it helps. You're too bloody nice for your own good. Read your book if you want pretty.'

Onna winced down at it. She was making slow progress, it had to be admitted. An overblown romance about a beautiful but bullied scullery girl she was reasonably sure would end up whisked away to a life of ease by the duke's handsome younger son. You'd have thought the uglier life got, the more you'd crave pretty fantasies, but maybe Merilee was right, and pretty lies just made the ugly truth feel all the worse. Either way, she was too nice to argue. Always had been. Too nice for her own good.

'Who are those two?' asked Jirry, nodding over towards a pair of women Onna hadn't seen before, slipping quietly indoors, already masked and dressed for entertaining. There was a set to the jaw of the dark-haired one that made Onna nervous, somehow. That, and when her leg slid out from her skirts, it looked like there was a long, red scar all the way up her thigh.

You need to be careful of strange hostesses. Strange hostesses attract strange guests. Onna shook her head. 'Don't like the looks of them, either.'

Merilee took the pipe from between her teeth long enough to snarl, 'Fucking save us,' at the sky.

'Ladies.' A fellow with waxed whiskers and a tall hat flicked out a bright handkerchief and gave a flourishing bow. There was a glint in his eye behind a mask sparkling with crystals. An ugly glint indeed. 'A most profound honour.' And he swaggered past, just the slightest bit trembly. A drinker, Onna reckoned.

'Silly old cock,' Merilee muttered out of the corner of her mouth in Northern, before wedging her pipe back between her teeth.

Onna gave her mask a little tweak, then plucked at her bodice under the armpits, trying to wriggle it up. However tight she asked one of the other girls to pull the laces, the damn thing always kept slipping. She was getting a little chafed from it, and cast an envious glance towards Bellit, who had the unimaginable luxury of straps on her dress. Straps, was that too much to ask? But off-the-shoulder was the fashion.

'Fuck,' hissed Jirry through gritted teeth, turning her back on the candlelit room, letting her smile slip to show a grimace of pain as she twisted her hips and tried to pluck her clinging skirts away. 'I'm like fucking raw beef down there.'

'How often have I told you to put some olive oil on it?' snapped Bellit, grabbing her wrist and shoving a little vial into her hand.

'Chance'd be a fine thing! I haven't had time to piss since we opened the doors. You didn't say there'd be half this many!'

'Twice the guests means twice the money. Get some oil on it then stand up and smile.'

Twice the guests meant twice the worry, far as Onna was concerned. There was a mad sense to Cardotti's tonight. Even worse than usual. Way overcrowded and with a feel on the edge of bloodthirsty. Voices shrill and crazy, braying boasts and hacking laughter. Maybe it was all the masks, made folk act even more like animals. Maybe it was that horrible screeching music, or the flame-lit darkness, or the high stakes at the gaming tables. Maybe it was all the drink, and the chagga, and the husk, and the pearl dust going round. Maybe it was the demented entertainments – fire and blades and danger. Onna didn't like it. Didn't like it one bit. Her gut was twitching worse than ever.

Felt like trouble coming, but what could she do? If she didn't need the money, she wouldn't be there in the first place, as Merilee was always telling her. So she stood, awkward, trying to strike a pose alluring enough to satisfy Bellit while at the same time fading into the many shadows and catching no one's eye. Sadly, an impossible compromise.

She jumped as Bellit leaned close to hiss in her ear. 'This one's yours.'

Onna glanced over to the door and felt her gut twitch worse than ever. He looked like a clenched fist, this bastard. Great bull shoulders and no neck at all, close-cropped ram of a head leaned forward, veins and tendons standing stark from the backs of his thick hands. Hands that looked meant for beating people with. Most men had to give up weapons at the gate but he had a sword at his hip and a polished breastplate, and that made him some rich man's guard, which made him a man used to doing violence and to facing no consequences. Beside his mask of plain, hard metal, the jaw muscles squirmed as he ground his teeth.

'I don't like the looks of that one,' she muttered, almost taking a step away.

'You don't like the fucking looks of anything!' hissed Bellit furiously through her fixed smile, catching her by the elbow and dragging her towards him. 'You think a baker likes the looks of the dough she kneads? Milk him and get on to the next!'

Onna had no idea why Bellit hated her. She tried to be nice. While Merilee was the biggest bitch in Styria and got her own way every time. It was like her mother said – nice comes last. But Onna just never had much nasty in her.

'All right,' she muttered, 'all right.' She wriggled her bodice up again. 'Just saying.' And she plastered the smile over her profound misgivings and swayed towards her mark. Her guest.

They were meant to call them guests, now.

'What's your name?' she asked as she reluctantly turned the key in the lock, reluctantly turned back into the room.

'Bremer.' For such a big man he had the strangest high, girlish little voice. He grimaced as he spoke, as if the sound of it hurt him. 'What's your name?'

She smiled as she sat beside him on the bed and brushed his jaw with a fingertip. She didn't much want to, and she got the feeling he didn't much want her to, but she felt if she was gentle maybe she could keep him gentle. Nice had to be worth something, didn't it? She tried to keep her voice soft, with no fear in it. 'You can call me whatever you want.'

He looked at her then. Eyes a little dewy behind his mask, maybe with emotion, maybe just with drink. Either one could be dangerous. 'I'll call you Fin, then.'

Onna swallowed. Here was a crossroads. Play along, pretend to be this Fin person, maybe calm him down? Maybe get away with wanking him off? Or at least going on top? Her skin was prickling at the thought of being trapped helpless under all that weight of muscle. Like being buried.

But what if this Fin was some lover who'd jilted him, or an ex-wife had an affair with his best friend, or his hated half-sister who'd got all his mother's love, someone he'd a burning desire to hurt? It was a gamble, and Onna had never been much of a gambler. Whoring was all a matter of pretending, though, wasn't it? Pretending to like them, pretending to enjoy it, pretending you were somewhere else. Pretending to be someone else was no great stretch.

'Whatever you want,' she said.

He was drunk. She could smell it on his breath. She wished she was. Felt like she was the only one in the whole place sober. A woman gave a gurgling giggle in the corridor. Laughter bubbled up from the courtyard outside. The horrible music had stopped, which was something of a mercy, except the violin had started hacking out a single sawing note made her more tense than ever.

She tried to breathe easy, and smile. Act like you're in charge, Merilee always said, and you're most of the way to being there. Never let them see you're scared.

'Whatever you want,' she said again, softly, and she brushed the cold metal of his breastplate with the backs of her fingers, sliding them down towards—

He caught her by the wrist, and for a moment she felt the terrible strength in his grip, and she thought the guts might drop right out of her. Then he let go, staring down at the floor. 'Do you mind if . . . we just . . . sit?'

He leaned towards her, but he didn't put his hands on her. Just clenched his fists against his breastplate with a faint clatter of metal, and hunched up in a ball, and rolled into her lap with his back against her, a great, dense weight across her thighs, his sword sticking out behind him and scraping at her side.

'Maybe you could hold me?' he squeaked in that high little voice.

Onna blinked. Whoring was a hell of a job for surprises, but pleasant ones were a sorry rarity. She slipped her arms around him. 'Whatever you want.'

They sat in silence while men whooped and metal scraped and clanged outside. Some show fight going on, she thought. Men love to watch a fight. Bloody foolishness, but she supposed it could be worse. They could be fighting for real. There was a crashing sound, like glass breaking. A shadow flickered across the window.

She realised her mark's great shoulders were shaking slightly. She raised her brows. Then she leaned down over him, pressing herself against his back, rocking him gently. Like she used to rock her little sister when she couldn't sleep, long ago.

'Shhhh,' she whispered softly in his ear. And he gripped hold of her arms, sobbing and blubbering. Awkward, no doubt, but being honest she was a lot happier playing the role of mother than the one she'd been expecting. 'Shhhh.'

She frowned towards the window. It sounded like a proper

fight out there now. No one was cheering any more, only screams that sounded worryingly like rage and pain and very genuine terror. The odd flash and flare of fire had become a constant, flickering glare through the distorting glass, brighter and brighter.

Her mark's head jerked up. 'What's going on out there?' he grunted, shoving her over with a clumsy hand as he rose and stumbled to the window. Onna had a worse feeling than ever as he fumbled with the latch and shoved it wide. Mad, horrible sounds spilled through. As if there was a battle being fought in the middle of Cardotti's.

'The king!' he hooted, spinning around and bouncing off the high cabinet, nearly falling on top of her. He fumbled his sword from its sheath and she shrank back. 'The king!'

He charged past, bounced from the locked door, cursed, then lifted his boot and shattered the lock with a kick, ducking out coughing into the corridor. Smoke curled in under the lintel after him, and not earthy husk or sweet chagga smoke, but woodsmoke, harsh and smothering.

What had happened? Onna slowly stood from the bed, knees weak, edged to the window and peered out.

Down in the yard bodies heaved, metal flashed by mad firelight. The dry ivy up the side of the building was burning right to the roof. Folk screamed, fought, wrestled with one another, dragged at the locked gates in a snarling crowd, crushed up against the bars. She saw blades swung. She saw bodies crushed and crumpled.

She jerked back, breath whimpering with fear, scratching and wheezing in her throat. She ran to the door, twisted her ankle in her high shoes and fell against the frame. She stumbled into the corridor, dim at the best of times, dark with smoke now.

Someone clutched at her, coughing, threatening to drag her right over. 'Help me!' she croaked. 'Help!'

Merilee, her mask all skewed, eyes all mad and wide inside, a great dead weight on her arm.

'Get off me, fucker!' Onna punched her in the face, and again, knocked her squealing through the doorway. Blood on her buzzing knuckles. Seemed enough fire would find the nasty in anyone.

Shattering glass tinkled. Burning wood popped and burst. Shouts of pain and fury came muffled through the choking murk. Flames flickered from under a door. Onna clapped a hand over her mouth, tottered a few steps. Someone clattered past, caught her with an elbow and knocked her into the wall.

She sank to her knees, coughing, retching, spitting. She couldn't see for the smoke. Couldn't breathe for the smoke. Someone was shouting. 'The king! The king!'

'Help,' she croaked.

But no one heard.

Ospria, Summer 580

'Can I get a surcoat?' asked Predo.

Three months in and he'd decided soldiering was the life for him. He'd tried a lot of other things and they hadn't worked out so good. He'd cut purses in Etrisani 'til he nearly got caught, then he'd held a mirror for a gambler in Musselia 'til he nearly got caught, then he'd looked out for a gang of footpads in Etrea 'til they did all get caught and hanged – apart from him, on account of he hadn't been looking out too thoroughly. But mostly he'd sucked cocks. Worked in a brothel in Talins for a while, which had been grand, but he'd had to sleep under the stairs then got thrown out for fighting with one of the girls. Girls were a lot more popular, in the main, which had always seemed upside down to Predo. If you wanted someone who really knew their way around a cock, you'd surely pick someone who had a cock themselves. Simple good sense, no? Go to an expert. But it seemed to Predo that very few people had good sense, and a lot of things were upside down. Just life, ain't it? You make the best of what you're offered.

He'd been thrown out of the whorehouse, and when he looked up from the gutter a recruiting sergeant was over on the other side of the street promising good food and glory for any man who'd fight for Grand Duke Orso and Predo had thought, *I'll try me some of that on for size.* And here he was, three months later, sat around a campfire on a hillside near bloody Ospria, of all places. You couldn't make it up.

'Surcoats are for veterans,' said Franchi, rubbing gently at the names of the battles stitched into his in gold and silver thread, around the edge of the white cross of Talins. A lifetime of victories. The more stitches a man had, the more respect he got. Predo wanted some respect. Wanted to feel part of a family. He'd never had a family. Or respect, for that matter.

Sculia slapped him on the shoulder, nearly made him spill his soup. 'Might be you'll get a surcoat after the battle.'

Predo gave a little shudder at that. Soldiering might be the profession for him but he had to admit he wasn't much looking forward to the actual *fighting* part. 'So there's sure to be a battle . . . is there?'

'There is.' The firelight picked out the scar through Sergeant Mazarine's grizzled beard as he leaned forwards. If anyone knew when there was going to be a battle, it was Mazarine. Had more stitching on his weather-stained surcoat than anyone except old Volfier, and it was only the names of forgotten battles that were keeping Volfier's surcoat together. 'The Duke of Delay's got nowhere to withdraw to any more. We've herded him right back to his own walls.'

'Won't he just stay behind 'em?' asked Predo, trying not to sound too hopeful.

'If he stays behind 'em we'll only starve him out, and he knows he's got no help coming.' Mazarine had a way of laying every word down heavy and solid like a stone in a wall, so you couldn't possibly think otherwise. Made Predo feel brave to hear it. 'No. Time's come for Rogont to fight, and he knows it. He's no fool.'

Franchi snorted as he licked his fingers and smoothed the feather on that silly little hat of his. 'No fool. Just a coward.' And Sculia gave a grim grunt of agreement.

Mazarine only shrugged, though. 'I'd rather fight a brave idiot than a clever coward. Far, far rather.'

'He's got Murcatto with him, though, no?' Predo shuffled forward, voice dropping quiet, like he was scared the Butcher of Caprile might hear her name and come dashing from the darkness with two swords in each hand. 'She's brave *and* clever.'

Franchi and Sculia exchanged a worried glance, but Mazarine was a solid rock of indifference. 'And quick and ruthless as a scorpion, too, but Murcatto's just one person, and battles ain't won by one person.' He sounded so sure and steady it made Predo feel sure and steady, as well. 'We got the numbers. That's the fact.'

'And right on our side!' said Predo, getting a little carried away now.

Mazarine shrugged. 'Not sure what that's worth, but we got the numbers.'

'And battles ain't so bad, lad!' Sculia clapped Predo on the shoulder again and this time actually did spill his soup, just a bit. 'Long as you're on the winning side, of course.'

'And we've been on the winning side for a long, long time,' said

Mazarine, and the others nodded. 'It gets to be a habit. Mop up Rogont and the job's done. The League of Eight's finished, and Orso will be King of Styria.'

'Bless his eternal Majesty,' said Franchi, with a smile up towards the star-dusted night sky.

That gave Predo a stab of nerves. He didn't fancy being kicked out of the army like he'd been kicked out of the whorehouse. 'But . . . won't Orso be getting rid of his soldiers, once he's won?'

Mazarine split a lined smile. 'Orso didn't get where he is by throwing his sword in the river. No, he'll keep us close to hand, don't worry about that.'

Sculia gave a grunt of agreement. 'He who prepares for peace prepares for defeat, Verturio said.'

'Who's he?' asked Predo.

'A very clever man,' said Franchi.

'There'll be a place for us still, I reckon.' And Mazarine leaned over and clapped Predo on the knee with his great scarred hand. 'And if there's a place for me, there'll be a place for all of you. Plague took my wife and my daughter, but the Fates sent me a new family, and I don't plan on losing that one.'

'A family.' Made Predo feel warm all over, that did, to have someone looking out for him. Someone so tough and solid. Never had anyone looking out for him before. 'Soldiering's a good life, I reckon.' He glanced nervously into the darkness beyond the firelight, towards the faint lights of Ospria. Towards the fords of the Sulva where they'd fight tomorrow. 'Apart from the battles, maybe.'

'Battles ain't so bad,' said Franchi.

Mazarine leaned back onto one elbow, grinning. 'Long as you're on the winning side.'

*

'It hurts,' snarled Sculia through his red teeth. 'Shit, it hurts.'

'What do I do?' There was blood everywhere. Blood all over Predo's hands. Blood bubbling from around the shaft of the bolt and from the joints in Sculia's armour and washing off in the frothing river. The white cross of Talins on his surcoat had turned red with it.

'What the hell do I do?' Predo screeched, but no one was listening, even if he could've been heard.

The noise was deafening. The sound of hell. Everyone shouting over each other. All questions and no answers. Howling, hardly like people at all. Men floundering past through the river, showering water over each other, falling, getting up, wounded screaming as they were dragged back the other way, arrows and bolts flitting from the blue sky without warning. Predo could see men sitting above the crowd. Riders. Metal twinkling as they hacked from their saddles with sword and axe. Predo wasn't sure whether they were friends or enemies. Didn't look like things could possibly be going to plan. Didn't look like there could be a plan.

He knelt there, icy water babbling around his legs, soaked with spray as men splashed past, just staring. Sculia wasn't saying it hurt any more. He wasn't saying anything.

'What do I do?' Predo whispered, and he felt someone grab him under the arm.

'He's dead.' Sergeant Mazarine, calm and steady as ever, a rock in this storm-tossed sea of men, pointing the way with his spear. 'Forward!' he roared over his shoulder. 'Forward!' Dragging Predo after him, sloshing in the cold river. Good thing he knew which way forward was, 'cause Predo had no notion, the breath wheezing and rattling in his throat as he scrambled on. Over the top of the blur of struggling men and mounts Ospria jerked and wobbled on its hill.

Something spattered in his face and he gasped. Touched his cheek, stared at his trembling hand. Blood, red-black on his water-wrinkled fingertips. A horse reared and kicked and sent a man flopping into Predo's side, nearly knocked him over.

Mazarine was up ahead, wading forward with his spear in his fists. Predo staggered back as a horse fell near him, pitching its rider down into the river. An axe rose and fell. Metal shrieked. Men screamed. He scraped the wet hair out of his eyes and blinked. He saw a woman crouched in the river ahead. A woman in bright armour with black hair plastered across her pale face.

It had to be her. Murcatto. The Butcher of Caprile. Smaller than he'd imagined, but who else could it be?

She swung at someone with a mace but missed, staggered after it. It was Franchi, and he shoved her with his shield, knocked her off balance, lifting his sword. As he stepped close, someone stepped close to him from behind. A great big bastard, stripped to the waist. A Northman, maybe, all blood-speckled head to toe like some death-drunk madman from a story. He swung his axe whistling down before Franchi could swing his sword and it thudded deep into his shoulder, cleaved him open like a butcher might cleave a side of beef.

Franchi made a hideous squeal, blood spraying out of him and into the woman's face. She reeled back, spitting, blinded, and Mazarine was on her, growling with fury. He stabbed at her with his spear and it shrieked down her breastplate, sending her toppling back into the water with a cry.

Predo started forward to help but his boot caught on something on the riverbed and he fell, coughed out a mouthful of water as he struggled up. A fallen battle flag. White cross on black cloth.

He raised his head to see Murcatto floundering to her knees as Mazarine raised his spear over her. She twisted around, a flash of metal as she drove a knife into the side of his leg and he bent forward, eyes bulging.

'No,' whispered Predo, tearing the clutching cloth from his ankle, but too late.

He saw the woman's teeth gritted through her tangle of bloody hair as she burst up, swinging the mace in a spray of shining water. There was a fountain of blood and teeth as it crunched into Mazarine's jaw and sent him tottering back.

She snarled as she lifted her mace high and clubbed him in the throat, knocked him limp on his back in the river and fell across him, rolled hissing and snapping through the water and up.

Predo stared numbly around, sword limp in his hand, half-expecting that someone would be charging at him with murder in their eyes, but all of a sudden the fighting seemed to be done. Men stood and stared, just like he did. They sank into the river, clutching at wounds. They reeled about in confusion. Then a rider not far away stood tall in his stirrups, ripping off his helmet, and screamed out, 'Victory!'

Sergeant Mazarine lay over a rock, arms spread wide. He was dead. They were all dead. Battles aren't so bad. Long as you're on the winning side.

Others began to cheer, and others. Osprians, clearly. Predo stared at the woman. She took a tottering step forward and flopped into the arms of the half-naked monster, her mace-head, still sticky with Sergeant Mazarine's blood, dangling against his bare back.

They were no more than three paces off in an exhausted embrace, and Predo was quick. He could've charged up and split the back of her head with his sword. Right then, he could've put an end to the infamous Serpent of Talins.

But at that moment the Northman looked right at him, and

Predo felt a great weight of icy fear settle on him. There was a mighty scar across his blood-dotted face, and in the midst of it a bright ball of dead metal, glinting with wet as the sun broke through the clouds.

That was the moment Predo decided soldiering weren't really the life for him. He swallowed, then thrust his sword up high in the air.

'Victory!' he screamed out, along with everyone else.

It was all chaos down there, after all, and there was nothing to show whether he stood with Talins or Ospria. Just another lad in a leather jerkin. Just one of the lucky ones who'd lived through it.

'Victory!' he shouted again in a cracking voice, trying to make out they were tears of happiness on his cheeks as he looked down at Sergeant Mazarine's broken corpse, draped over a rock with the river foaming around it.

Just life, ain't it? You make the best of what you're offered.

Seemed a lucky chance now he didn't have a surcoat.

SOME
DESPERADO

The Near Country,
Summer 584

S hy gave the horse her heels, its forelegs buckled and, before she had a notion what was happening, she and her saddle had bid each other a sad farewell.

She was offered a flailing instant aloft to consider the situation. Not a good one at a brief assay, and the impending earth allowed no time for a longer. She did her best to roll with the fall – as she tried to do with most of her many misfortunes – but the ground soon uncurled her, gave her a fair roughing up and tossed her flopping into a patch of sun-shrivelled scrub.

Dust settled.

She stole a moment just to get some breath in. Then one to groan while the world stopped rolling. Then another to shift gingerly an arm and a leg, waiting for that sick jolt of pain that meant something was broke and her miserable shadow of a life would soon be lost in the dusk. She would've welcomed it, if it meant she could stretch out and not have to run no more. But the pain didn't come. Not outside of the usual compass, leastways. As far as her miserable shadow of a life went, she was still awaiting judgement.

Shy dragged herself up, scratched and scuffed, caked in dust and spitting out grit. She'd taken too many mouthfuls of sand the last few months but she'd a dismal premonition there'd be more. Her horse lay a few strides distant, one foamed-up flank heaving, forelegs black with blood. Neary's arrow had snagged it in the shoulder, not deep enough to kill or even slow it right off, but deep enough to make it bleed at a good pace. With her hard riding, that had killed it just as dead as a shaft in the heart.

There'd been a time Shy had got attached to horses. A time – despite reckoning herself hard with people and being mostly right – she'd been uncommon soft about animals. But that time was a long time gone. There wasn't much soft on Shy these days, body or mind. So she left her mount to its final red-frothed breaths without the solace of her calming hand and ran for the town, tottering some at first but quickly warming to the exercise. At running she'd a heap of practice.

Town was perhaps an overstatement. It was six buildings and calling them buildings was being generous to two or three. All rough lumber and an entire stranger to straight angles, sun-baked, rain-peeled and dust-blasted, huddled about a dirt square and a crumbling well.

The biggest building had the look of tavern or brothel or trading post or more likely all three amalgamated. A rickety sign still clung to the boards above the doorway but the name had been rubbed by the wind to just a few pale streaks in the grain. *Nothing, nowhere*, was all its proclamation now. Up the steps two by two, bare feet making the old boards wheeze, thoughts boiling away at how she'd play it when she got inside, what truths she'd season with what lies for the most likely recipe.

There's men chasing me! Gulping breath in the doorway and doing her best to look beyond desperate – no mighty effort of acting at that moment, or any occupying the last twelve months, indeed.

Three of the bastards! Then – provided no one recognised her from all the bills for her arrest – *They tried to rob me!* A fact. No need to add she'd good and robbed the money herself from the new bank in Hommenaw in the company of those three worthies plus another since caught and hanged by the authorities.

They killed my brother! They're drunk on blood! Her brother was safe at home where she wished she was and if her pursuers were drunk it would likely be on cheap spirits, as usual, but she'd shriek it with that little warble in her throat. Shy could do quite a warble when she needed one, she'd practised it 'til it was something to hear. She pictured the patrons springing to their feet in their eagerness to aid a woman in distress. *They shot my horse!* She had to admit it didn't seem overpowering likely that anyone hardbitten enough to live out here would be getting into a sweat of chivalry but maybe fate would deal her a winning hand for once.

It had been known.

She blundered through the tavern's door, opening her mouth to serve up the tale, and stopped cold.

The place was empty.

Not just no one there but nothing, and for damn sure no winning hand. Not a twig of furniture in the bare common room. A narrow stairway and a balcony running across the left-hand wall, doorways yawning empty upstairs. Chinks of light scattered where the rising sun was seeking out the many gaps in the splitting carpentry. Maybe just a lizard skittering away into the shadows – of which there was no shortage – and a bumper harvest of dust, greying every surface, drifted into every corner. Shy stood there a moment, just blinking, then dashed back out, along the rickety stoop and to the next building. When she shoved the door it dropped right off its rusted hinges.

This one hadn't even a roof. Hadn't even a floor. Just bare rafters with the careless, pinking sky above, and bare joists with a stretch of dirt below every bit as desolate as the miles of dirt outside.

She saw it now, as she stepped back into the street with vision unhindered by hope. No glass in the windows, or wax-paper even. No rope by the crumbling well. No animals to be seen – aside from her own dead horse, that was, which only served to prove the point.

It was a dried-out corpse of a town, long since expired.

Shy stood in that forsaken place, up on the balls of her bare feet as though she was about to sprint off somewhere but lacked the destination, hugging herself with one arm while the fingers of the other hand fluttered and twitched at nothing, biting on her lip and sucking air fast and rasping through the little gap between her front teeth.

Even by recent standards, it was a low moment. But if she'd learned anything the last few months it was that things can always get lower. Looking back the way she'd come, Shy saw the dust rising. Three little grey trails in the shimmer off the grey land.

'Oh, hell,' she whispered, and bit her lip harder. She pulled her eating knife from her belt and wiped the little splinter of metal on her dirty shirt, as though cleaning it might somehow settle the odds. Shy had been told she was blessed with a fertile imagination, but even so it was hard to picture a more feeble weapon. She'd have laughed if she hadn't been on the verge of weeping. She'd spent way too much time on the verge of weeping the last few months, now she thought about it.

How had it come to this?

Some Desperado

A question for some jilted girl rather than an outlaw with four thousand marks offered, but still a question she was never done asking. Some desperado. She'd grown expert on the desperate part but the rest remained a mystery. The sorry truth was she knew full well how it came to this – the same way as always. One disaster following so hard on another she just bounced between 'em, pinging about like a moth in a lantern. The second usual question followed hard on the first.

What the fuck now?

She sucked in her stomach – not that there was much to suck in these days – and dragged the bag out by the drawstrings, coins inside clicking together with that special sound only money makes. Two thousand marks in silver, give or take. You'd think a bank would hold a lot more – they told depositors they always had fifty thousand on hand – but it turns out you can't trust banks any more than bandits.

She dug her hand in, dragged free a fistful of coins and tossed money across the street, leaving it gleaming in the dust. She did it like she did most things these days – hardly knowing why. Maybe she valued her life a lot higher'n two thousand marks, even if no one else did. Maybe she hoped they'd just take the silver and leave her be, though what she'd do once she was left be in this corpse town – no horse, no food, no weapon – she hadn't thought out. Clearly she hadn't fixed up a whole plan, or not one that would hold too much water, leastways. Leaky planning had always been a problem of hers.

She sprinkled silver as if she was tossing seed on her mother's farm, miles and years and a dozen violent deaths away. Whoever would've thought she'd miss the place? Miss the bone-poor house and the broke-down barn and the fences that always needed mending. The stubborn cow that never gave milk and the stubborn well that never gave water and the stubborn soil that only weeds would thrive in. Her stubborn little sister and brother, too. Even big, scarred, soft-headed Lamb. What Shy would've given now to hear her mother's shrill voice curse her out again. She sniffed hard, her nose hurting, her eyes stinging, and wiped 'em on the back of her frayed cuff. No time for tearful reminiscences. She could see three dark spots of riders now beneath those three inevitable dust trails. She flung the empty bag away, ran back to the tavern and—

'Ah!' She hopped over the threshold, bare sole of her foot torn on a loose nailhead. The world's nothing but a mean bully, that's a fact. Even when you've big misfortunes threatening to drop on your head, small ones still take every chance to prick your toes. How she wished she'd got the chance to grab her boots. Just to keep a shred of dignity. But she had what she had, and neither boots nor dignity were on the list, and a hundred big wishes weren't worth one little fact – as Lamb used boringly to drone at her whenever she cursed him and her mother and her lot in life and swore she'd be gone in the morning.

Shy remembered how she'd been, then, and wished she had the chance now to punch her earlier self in the face. But she could punch herself in the face when she got out of this.

She'd a procession of other willing fists to weather first.

She hurried up the stairs, limping a little and cursing a lot. When she reached the top she saw she'd left bloody toe-prints on every other one. She was working up to feeling pretty damn low about that glistening trail leading right to the end of her leg when something like an idea came trickling through the panic.

She paced down the balcony, making sure to press her bloody foot firm to the boards, and turned into an abandoned room at the end. Then she held her foot up, gripping it hard with one hand to stop the bleeding, and hopped back the way she'd come and through the first doorway, near the top of the steps, pressing herself into the shadows inside.

A pitiful effort, doubtless. As pitiful as her bare feet and her eating knife and her two-thousand-mark haul and her big dream of making it back home to the shit-hole she'd had the big dream of leaving. Small chance those three bastards would fall for that, even stupid as they were. But what else could she do?

When you're down to small stakes you have to play long odds.

Her own breath was her only company, echoing in the emptiness, hard on the out, ragged on the in, almost painful down her throat. The breath of someone scared near the point of involuntary shitting and all out of ideas. She just couldn't see her way to the other side of this. She ever made it back to that farm she'd jump out of bed every morning she woke alive and do a little dance, and give her mother a kiss for every cuss, and never snap at her sister or mock Lamb again for being a coward. She promised it, then wished she was the sort who kept promises.

She heard horses outside, crept to the one window with half a view of the street and peered down as gingerly as if she was peering into a bucket of scorpions.

They were here.

Neary wore that dirty old blanket cinched in at the waist with twine, his greasy hair sticking up at all angles, reins in one hand and the bow he'd shot Shy's horse with in the other, blade of the heavy axe hanging at his belt as carefully cleaned as the rest of his repugnant person was beyond neglect. Dodd had his battered hat pulled low, sitting his saddle with that round-shouldered cringe he always had around his brother, like a puppy expecting a slap. Shy would have liked to give the faithless fool a slap right then. A slap for starters. Then there was Jeg, sitting up tall as a lord in that long red coat of his, dirt-fringed tails spread out over his big horse's rump, hungry sneer on his face as he scanned the buildings, that tall hat which he thought made him look quite the personage poking off his head slightly crooked, like the chimney from a burned-out farmstead.

Dodd pointed to the coins scattered across the dirt around the well, a couple of 'em winking with the sun. 'She left the money.'

'Seems so,' said Jeg, voice hard as his brother's was soft.

She watched them get down and hitch their mounts. No hurry to it. Like they were dusting themselves off after a jaunt of a ride and looking forward to a nice little evening among cultured company. They'd no need to hurry. They knew she was here, and they knew she was going nowhere, and they knew she was getting no help, and so did she.

'Bastards,' Shy whispered, cursing the day she ever took up with them. But you have to take up with someone, don't you? And you can only pick from what's on offer.

Jeg stretched his back, took a long sniff and a comfortable spit, then drew his sword. That curved cavalry sword he was so proud of with the clever-arsed basketwork, which he said he'd won in a duel with a Union officer but Shy knew he'd stolen, along with the best part of everything else he'd ever owned. How she'd mocked him about that stupid sword. She wouldn't have minded the feel of the hilt in her hand now, though, and him with only her eating knife.

'Smoke!' bellowed Jeg, and Shy winced. She'd no idea who thought that name up for her. Some wag had lettered it on the bills for her arrest and now everyone used it. On account of her tendency to vanish like smoke, maybe. Though it could also have been on account of her tendencies to stink like it, stick in folks' throats and drift with the wind.

'Get out here, Smoke!' Jeg's voice clapped off the dead fronts of the buildings and Shy shrank a little further into the darkness. 'Get out here and we won't hurt you too bad!'

So much for taking the money and going. They wanted the price on her, too. She pressed her tongue into the gap between her teeth and mouthed, 'Cocksuckers.' There's a certain kind of man, the more you give him, the more he'll take.

'We'll have to go and get her,' she heard Neary say in the stillness.

'Aye,' said Jeg.

'I told you we'd have to go and get her.'

'You must be pissing your pants with joy over the outcome, then, eh?'

'Said we'd have to get her.'

'So stop pointing it out and get it done.'

Dodd's wheedling voice. 'Look, the money's here, we could just scrape this up and get off, there ain't no need to—'

'Did you and I really spring from between the same set o' legs?' sneered Jeg. 'You are the stupidest bastard.'

'Stupidest,' said Neary.

'You think I'm leaving four thousand marks for the crows?' said Jeg. 'You scrape that up, Dodd, we'll break the mare.'

'Where do you reckon she is?' asked Neary.

'I thought you was the big tracker?'

'Out in the wild, but we ain't in the wild.'

Jeg cocked an eyebrow at the empty shacks. 'You'd call this the highest extent of civilisation, would you?'

They looked at each other a moment, dust blowing up around their legs, then settling again.

'She's here somewhere,' said Neary.

'You think? Good thing I got the self-described sharpest eyes west of the mountains with me so I don't miss her dead horse ten fucking strides away. Yes, she's here somewhere.'

'Where, do you reckon?' asked Neary.

'Where would you be?'

Neary looked about the buildings and Shy jerked out of the way as his narrowed eyes darted over the tavern.

'In that one, I reckon, but I ain't her.'

'Course you ain't fucking her. You know how I can tell? You got bigger tits and less sense. If you was her I wouldn't have to fucking look for her now, would I?'

Another silence, another dusty gust.

'Guess not,' said Neary.

Jeg took his tall hat off, scrubbed at his sweaty hair with his fingernails, and jammed it back on at an angle. 'You look in there, I'll try the one next to it, but don't kill the bitch, eh? That'll halve the reward.'

Shy eased back into the shadows, feeling the sweat tickling under her shirt. To be caught in this worthless arsehole of a place. By these worthless bastards. In bare feet. She didn't deserve this. All she'd wanted was to be somebody worth speaking of. To not be nothing, forgotten the day of her death. Now she saw that there's a sharp balance between too little excitement and a huge helping too much. But like most of her lame-legged epiphanies, it had dawned a year too late.

She sucked air through the little gap between her teeth as she heard Neary creaking across the boards in the common room, maybe just the metal rattle of that big axe. She was shivering all over. Felt so weak of a sudden she could hardly hold the knife, let alone imagine swinging it. Maybe it was time to give up. Toss the blade out the doorway and say, 'I'm coming out! I'll be no trouble! You win!' Smile and nod and thank 'em for their betrayal and their kind consideration when they kicked the shit out of her or horsewhipped her or broke her legs and whatever else amused them on the way to her hanging.

She'd seen her share of those and never relished the spectacle. Standing there tied while they read your name and your crime, hoping for some last reprieve that wouldn't come while the noose was drawn tight, sobbing for mercy or hurling your curses and neither making the slightest hair of difference. Kicking at nothing, tongue stuck out while you shat yourself for the amusement of scum no better'n you. She pictured Jeg and Neary, up front in the grinning crowd as they watched her do the thief's dance at rope's end. Probably arrayed in even more ridiculous clothes secured with the reward money.

'*Fuck* them,' she mouthed at the darkness, lips curling back in a snarl as she heard Neary's foot on the bottom step.

She had a hell of a contrary streak, did Shy. From when she was a tot, when someone told her how things would be, she started thinking on how she'd make 'em otherwise. Her mother had always called her mule-stubborn and blamed it on her Ghost blood. 'That's your damn Ghost blood,' as though being born quarter savage was Shy's own choice rather than on account of her mother picking a half-Ghost wanderer to lie with, who turned out – no crashing surprise – to be a no-good drunk.

Shy would be fighting. No doubt she'd be losing, but she'd be fighting. She'd make those bastards kill her, and at least rob 'em of half the reward. Might not expect such thoughts as those to steady your hand, but they did hers. The little knife still shook, but now from how hard she was gripping it.

For a man who proclaimed himself the great tracker, Neary had some trouble keeping quiet. She heard the breath in his nose as he paused at the top of the steps, close enough to touch if it hadn't been for the plank wall between them.

A board groaned as he shifted his weight and Shy's whole body tensed, every hair twitching up. Then she saw him – not darting through the doorway at her, axe in his fist and murder in his eyes – but creeping off down the balcony after the bait of bloody footsteps, drawn bow pointed exactly the wrong the way.

When she was given a gift, Shy had always believed in grabbing it with both hands rather than thinking on how to say thank you. She dashed at Neary's back, teeth bared and the low growl ripping at her throat. His head whipped around, whites of his eyes showing and the bow following after, head of the arrow glinting with such light as strayed into that abandoned place.

She ducked low and caught him around the legs, shoulder driving hard into his thigh and making him grunt, her hand finding her wrist and clamping tight under Neary's arse, her nose suddenly full of the horse and sour sweat stink of him. The bowstring went but Shy was already straightening, snarling, screaming, bursting up and – big man though he was – she hoisted Neary right over the rail as neat as she used to hoist a sack of grain on her mother's farm.

He hung in the air a moment, mouth and eyes wide with shock, then he plummeted with a breathy whoop and crashed through the boards down below.

Shy blinked, hardly able to believe it. Her scalp was burning and she touched a finger to it, half-expecting to feel the arrow stuck right in her brains, but she turned and saw it was in the wall behind her, a considerably happier outcome from her standpoint. Blood, though, sticky in her hair, tickling at her forehead. Maybe the lath of the bow scratched her. Get that bow, she'd have a chance. She made a step towards the stairs, then stopped dead.

Jeg was in the doorway, his sword a long, black curve against the sun-glare street.

'Smoke!' he roared, and she was off down the balcony like a rabbit, following her own trail of bloody footprints to nowhere, hearing Jeg's heavy boots clomping towards the stairs. She hit the door at the end full tilt with her shoulder and burst into the light, out onto another balcony behind the building. Up onto the low rail with one bare foot – better to just go with her contrary streak and hope it somehow carried her through than to pause for thought – and she jumped. Flung herself writhing at a ramshackle balcony on the building across the narrow lane, as if flapping her hands and feet like she was having a fit might carry her further.

She caught the rail, wood smashing her in the ribs, slipped down, moaning, clawing for a grip, fought desperately to drag herself up and over, felt something give—

And with a groan of tortured wood the whole weather-blasted thing tore from the side of the building.

Again, Shy was offered a flailing instant aloft to consider the situation. Again not good, at a brief assay. She was just starting to wail when her old enemy the ground caught up with her – as the ground always will – folded her left leg, spun her over then smashed her in the side and drove her wind right out.

Shy coughed, then moaned, then spat more grit. That she'd been right about her earlier sandy mouth not being her last was scant comfort. She saw Jeg standing on the balcony where she'd jumped. He pushed his hat back and gave a chuckle, then ducked inside.

She still had a piece of the rail in her fist, well-rotted through. A little like her hopes. She tossed it away as she rolled over, waiting again for that sick pain that told her she was done. Again it didn't come. She could move. She worked her feet around and guessed she could stand. But she thought she might leave that for now. Chances were she'd only get to do it one more time.

She floundered clear of the tangle of broken wood against the wall, her shadow stretching out towards the doorway, groaning with pain as she heard Jeg's heavy footsteps inside. She started wriggling back on her arse and her elbows, dragging one leg after, the little knife blade hidden up behind her wrist, her other fist clutching at the dirt.

'Where are you off to?' Jeg ducked under the low lintel and into the lane. He was a big man, but he looked a giant right then. Half a head taller than Shy, even if she'd been standing, and probably not much short of twice her weight, even if she'd eaten that day. He strutted over, tongue wedged into his lower lip so it bulged out, heavy sword loose in his hand, relishing his big moment.

'Pulled a neat trick on Neary, eh?' He pushed the brim of his hat up a little to show the tan mark across his forehead. 'You're stronger'n you look. That boy's so dumb he could've fallen without the help, though. You'll be pulling no tricks on me.'

They'd see about that, but she'd let her knife say it for her. Even a little knife can be a damned eloquent piece of metal if you stick it in the right place. She scrambled back, kicking up dust, making it look like she was trying to push herself to her feet then sagging with a whimper as her left leg took her weight. Looking badly hurt was taking no great effort of acting. She could feel blood creeping from her hair and tickling her forehead. Jeg stepped out of the shadow and the low sun shone in his face, making him squint. Just the way she wanted it.

'Still remember the day I first put eyes on you,' he went on, loving the sound of his own bleating. 'Dodd come to me, all excited, and said he met Smoke, her whose killer's face is on all them bills up near Rostod, four thousand marks offered for her capture. The tales they tell on you!' He gave a whoop and she scrambled back again, moving that left leg underneath her, making sure it'd work when she needed it. 'You'd think you was a demon with two swords to a hand the way they breathe your name. Picture my fucking *disappointment* when I find you ain't naught but a scared girl with gappy teeth and a powerful smell o' piss about her.' As if Jeg smelled of summer meadows. He took another step forward, reaching out for her with one big hand. 'Now don't scratch, you're worth more to me alive. I don't want to—'

She flung the dirt with her left hand as she shoved up hard with her right, coming onto her feet. He twisted his head away, snarling as the dust showered across his face. He swung blind as she darted at him low and the sword whipped over her head, wind of it snatching at her hair, weight of it turning him sideways. She caught his flapping coat-tail in her left hand and sank her eating knife into his sword-shoulder with the other.

He gave a strangled grunt as she pulled the knife clear and stabbed at him again, blade ripping open the sleeve of his coat and the arm inside it, too, almost cutting into her own leg. She was bringing up the knife again when his fist crunched into the side of her mouth and sent her reeling, bare feet wrestling with the dirt. She caught hold of the corner of the building and hung there for a moment, trying to shake the light from her skull. She saw Jeg a pace or two off, bared teeth frothy with spit as he tried to fumble the sword from his dangling right hand into his left, fingers tangled with the fancy brass basketwork.

When things were moving fast, Shy had a knack for just doing, without thoughts of mercy, or thoughts of outcomes, or thoughts of much at all. That was what had kept her alive through all this shit. And what had landed her in it in the first place, for that matter. Ain't many blessings aren't mixed blessings once you have to live with them, and she'd a curse for thinking too much after the action, but that was another story. If Jeg got a good grip on that sword she was dead, simple as that, so before she'd quite stopped the street spinning she charged at him again. He tried to free an arm but she managed to catch it with her clawing left hand, pressing up against him, holding herself steady by his coat as she punched wildly with the knife – in his gut, in his ribs, in his ribs again, her snarling at him and him grunting at her with every thump of the blade, the grip slippery in her aching hand.

He grabbed her shirt, stitches tearing as the sleeve half-ripped off, tried to shove her away as she stabbed him again but there was no strength in it, only sent her back a step. Her head was clearing now and she kept her balance but Jeg stumbled and dropped on one knee. She lifted the knife up high in both hands and drove it right down on that stupid hat, squashing it flat, leaving the blade buried to the handle in the top of Jeg's head.

She staggered back, expecting him just to pitch on his face. Instead he lurched up suddenly like a camel she'd once seen at a fair, brim of his hat jammed down over his eyes to the bridge of his nose and the knife-handle jutting straight up.

'Where you gone?' The words all mangled as if his mouth was full of gravel. 'Smoke?' He lurched one way then the other. 'Smoke?' He shuffled at her, kicking up dust, sword dangling from his bloody right hand, point scratching grooves in the dust around his feet. He raised his left, fingers all stretched out stiff but the wrist all floppy, started prodding at his hat like he had something in his eye and wanted to wipe it clear.

'Shmoke?' One side of his face was twitching, shuddering, fluttering in a most unnatural way. Or maybe it was natural enough for a man with a knife lodged through his brains. 'Thmoke?' There was blood dripping from the bent brim of his hat, leaving red streaks down his cheek, shirt halfway soaked with it, but he kept coming, bloody right arm jerking, hilt of his sword rattling against his leg. 'Thmoe?' She backed away, staring, her own hands limp and all her skin prickling, until she hit the wall behind her. 'Thoe?'

'Shut your mouth!' And she dived at him with both palms, shoving him over backwards, sword bouncing from his hand, bloody hat still pinned to his head with her knife. He slowly rolled over, onto his face, right arm flopping. He slid his other hand underneath his shoulder as though he'd push himself up.

'Oh,' he muttered into the dust. Then he was still.

Shy slowly turned her head and spat blood. Too many mouthfuls of blood the last few months. Her eyes were wet and she wiped them on the back of her trembling hand. Couldn't believe what had happened. Hardly felt like she'd had any part in it. A nightmare she was due to wake from. She pressed her eyes shut, and opened them, and there he still lay.

She snatched in a breath and blew it out hard, dashed spit from her lip, blood from her forehead, caught another breath and forced it free. Then she gathered up Jeg's sword, gritting her teeth against the urge to spew rising in waves along with the thumping pain in the side of her face. Shit but she wanted to sit down. Just stop. But she made herself turn away. Forced herself up to the back door of the tavern. The one Jeg had come through, still alive, a few moments before. Takes a lifetime of hard work to make a man. Only takes a few moments to end one.

Neary had dragged himself out of the hole his fall had put through the floorboards, clutching at his bloody trouser leg and looking quite put out about it. 'Did you catch that fucking bitch?' he asked, squinting towards the doorway.

'Oh, no doubt.'

His eyes went wide and he tried to drag himself towards his bow, not far out of reach, whimpering all the way. She hefted Jeg's big sword as she got close and Neary turned over, eyes wide with terror, holding up one desperate arm. She hit it full-blooded with the flat of the sword and he moaned, clutching it to his chest. Then she hit him across the side of the head and rolled him over, blubbering into the boards. Then she padded past him, sliding the sword through her belt, picked up the bow and dragged some arrows from his quiver. She made for the door, stringing one as she went, and peered out into the street.

Dodd was still scraping coins from the dust and into the bag, working his way towards the well. Insensible to the fates of his two companions. Not as surprising as you might suppose. If one word summed up Dodd, it was insensible.

She padded down the steps of the tavern, near to their edges where they were less likely to give a warning creak, drawing the bow halfway and taking a good aim on Dodd, bent over in the dust with his back to her, dark sweat patch down the middle of his shirt. She gave some long, hard consideration to making that sweat patch the bull's eye and shooting him in the back right there. But killing a man isn't easy, especially after hard considera-tion. She watched him pick up the last coin and drop it in the bag, then stand, pulling the drawstrings, then turn, smiling. 'I got the—'

They stayed there a while. He with the bag of silver in one hand, uncertain smile lit up in the sun, but his eyes looking decidedly scared in the shadow of his cheap hat. She on the bottom step of the tavern – bloody bare feet, bloody split mouth, bloody hair plastered across her bloody forehead – but the bow good and steady.

He licked his lips, swallowed, then licked them again. 'Where's Neary?'

'In a bad way.' She was surprised by the iron in her voice. Sounded like someone she didn't even know. Smoke's voice, maybe.

'Where's my brother?'

'In a worse.'

Dodd swallowed, sweaty neck shifting, starting to ease gently backwards. 'You kill him?'

'Forget about them two and stop still.'

'Look, Shy, you ain't going to shoot me, are you? Not after all we been through. You ain't going to shoot. Not me. Are you?' His voice was rising higher and higher, but he kept edging back towards the well. 'I didn't want this. It weren't my idea!'

'Course not. You need to think to have an idea and you ain't up to it. You just went along. Even if it happened to mean me getting hanged.'

'Now look, Shy—'

'Stop still, I said.' She drew the bow all the way, string cutting tight into her bloody fingers. 'You fucking deaf, boy?'

'Look, Shy, let's just talk this out, eh? Just talk.' He held his trembly palm up like that might stop an arrow, his pale blue eyes were fixed on her, and suddenly she got a memory rise up of the first time she met him, leaning back against the livery, smiling free and easy, none too clever but plenty of fun. She'd had a profound lack of fun in her life since she'd left home. You'd never have thought she left home to find it.

'I know I done wrong, but . . . I'm an idiot.' And he tried out a smile, no steadier than his palm. He'd been worth a smile or two,

Dodd, at least to begin with, and though no artist of a lover had kept the bed warm, which was something, and made her feel as if she weren't on her own on one side with the whole rest of the world on the other, which was something more.

'Stop still,' she said, but more softly now.

'You ain't going to shoot me.' He kept on edging back towards the well. 'It's me, right? Me. Dodd. Just don't shoot me, now. What I'm going to do is—'

She shot him.

It's a strange thing about a bow. Stringing it, and drawing it, and nocking the arrow, and taking your aim – all that takes effort, and skill, and a decision. Letting go the string is nothing. You just stop holding it. In fact, once you've got it drawn and aimed it's easier to let fly than not to.

Dodd was no more than a dozen strides distant, and the shaft flitted across the space between them, missed his hand by a whisker and stuck silently into his chest. Surprised her, the lack of a sound. But then flesh is soft. Specially in comparison to an arrowhead. Dodd took one more wobbly pace, like he hadn't quite caught up with being arrow-stuck yet, his eyes going very wide. Then he blinked down at the shaft.

'You shot me,' he whispered, and he sank to his knees, blood already spreading out into his shirt in a dark oval.

'Didn't I bloody warn you!' She flung the bow down, suddenly furious with him and with the bow, too.

He stared at her. 'But I didn't think you'd do it.'

She stared back. 'Neither did I.' A silent moment, and the wind blew up one more time and stirred the dust around them. 'Sorry.'

'Sorry?' he croaked.

Might've been the stupidest thing she'd ever said, and that with some fierce competition, but what else could she say? No words were going to take that arrow out. She gave half a shrug. 'I guess.'

Dodd winced, hefting the silver in one hand, turning towards the well. Shy's mouth dropped open and she took off running as he toppled sideways, hauling the bag into the air. It turned over and over, curving up and starting to fall, drawstrings flapping, Shy's clutching hand straining for it as she sprinted, lunged, fell . . .

She grunted as her sore ribs slammed into the wall around the well, right arm darting down into the darkness. For a moment she thought she was going in after the bag – which would prob-ably have been a fitting conclusion – then her knees hit the dirt outside.

She had it by one of the bottom corners, loose canvas clutched by broken nails, drawstrings dangling as dirt and bits of loose stone filtered down around it.

Shy smiled. For the first time that day. That month, maybe.

Then the bag came open.

Coins tumbled into the darkness in a twinkling shower, silver pinging and rattling from the earthy walls, disappearing into the inky nothingness, and silence.

She straightened up, numb.

She backed away slowly from the well, hugging herself with one hand while the empty bag hung from the other.

She looked over at Dodd, lying on his back with the arrow sticking straight up from his chest, his wet eyes fixed on her, his ribs going fast. She heard his shallow breaths slow, then stop.

Shy stood there a moment, then doubled over and blew puke onto the ground. Not much of it, since she'd eaten nothing that day, but her guts clenched hard and made sure she retched up what there was. She shook so bad she thought she was going to fall, hands on her knees, sniffing bile from her nose and spluttering it out.

Damn but her ribs hurt. Her arm. Her leg. Her face. So many scrapes, twists and bruises she could hardly tell one from another, her whole body was one overpowering fucking throb.

Her eyes crawled over to Dodd's corpse. She felt another wave of sickness and forced them away, over to the horizon, fixing them on that shimmering line of nothing.

Not nothing.

There was dust rising in the distance. She wiped her face on her ripped sleeve one more time, so filthy now that it was as like to make her dirtier as cleaner. She straightened, squinting into the haze, hardly able to believe it. Riders. No doubt. A good way off, but as many as a dozen.

'Oh, hell,' she whispered, and bit her lip. Things kept going this way she'd soon have chewed right through the bloody thing. 'Oh, hell!' And Shy put her hands over her eyes and squeezed them shut and hid in self-inflicted darkness in the desperate hope she might have somehow been mistaken. Would hardly be her first mistake, would it?

But when she took her hands away the dust was still there. The world's a mean bully, all right, and the lower down you are the more it delights in kicking you. Shy put her hands on her hips, arched her back and screamed up at the sky, the word drawn out as long as her sore lungs would allow.

'Fuck!'

The echoes clapped from the buildings and died a quick death. No answer came. Perhaps the faint droning of a fly already showing some interest in Dodd. Neary's horse eyed her for a moment then looked away, profoundly unimpressed. Now Shy had a sore throat to add to her woes. She was obliged to ask herself the usual questions.

What the fuck now?

She clenched her teeth as she hauled Dodd's boots off and sat in the dust beside him to pull them on. Not the first time they'd stretched out together in the dirt, him and her. First time with him dead, though. His boots were way too loose on her, but a long stride better than no boots at all. She clomped back into the tavern in them.

Neary was making some pitiable groans as he struggled to get up. Shy kicked him in the face and down onto his back, plucked the rest of the arrows from his quiver and took his heavy belt-knife, too. Out into the sun again and she picked up the bow, jammed Dodd's hat onto her head, also somewhat on the roomy side but at least offering a bit of shade as the sun got up. Then she dragged the three horses together and roped them into a string – quite a ticklish operation since Jeg's big stallion was a mean bastard and looked determined to kick her brains out.

When she'd got it done she frowned off towards those dust trails. They were headed for the town all right, and fast. With a closer look she reckoned on about nine or ten, which was two or three better than twelve but still an almighty inconvenience.

Bank agents after the stolen money. Bounty hunters looking to collect her price. Other outlaws got wind of a score. A score that was currently in the bottom of a well, as it went. Could be anyone. Shy had an uncanny knack for making enemies. She found she'd looked over at Dodd, face down in the dust with his bare feet limp behind him. The only thing she had worse luck with was friends.

How had it come to this?

She shook her head, spat through the little gap between her

front teeth and hauled herself up into the saddle of Dodd's horse. She faced it away from those impending dust clouds, towards which quarter of the compass she knew not.

Shy gave the horse her heels.

YESTERDAY, NEAR A VILLAGE CALLED BARDEN...

Near Barden, Autumn 584

Tinder stood in his doorway, and watched the Union ruin his crop.

No pleasant pastime, just standing there and watching hours, and days, and months of your dawn-to-dusk hard work and hard worry crushed into the mud. But what were his choices? Charge out there with his pitchfork swinging and chase off the Union on his own? Tinder let out a bitter snort. Black Dow and all his War Chiefs and every Carl and Named Man in the wide and barren North were giving that their best effort and having little enough success. Tinder weren't the fighter he used to be, and he'd never been the hardest around.

So he stood in his doorway, and watched the Union ruin his crop.

First had come the scouts, hooves pounding. Then the soldiers, row upon row of 'em, boots tramping. Then the wagons, creaking and groaning like the dead in hell, wheels ripping up Tinder's land. Dozens. Hundreds. They'd churned the track to knee-deep slop, then they'd spilled off it and onto the verge and churned that to slop, then they'd spilled off that and into his crops and made slop of an ever-widening strip of them, too.

There's war for you. You start with something worth something, you end up with slop.

The morning after the first scouts passed through they'd come for his chickens, a dozen jumpy Union soldiers and a Northman to make 'em understood. Tinder understood well enough without words. He knew when he was being robbed. The Northman had looked sorry about it, but a sorry look was all he'd got in trade. What could you do, though? Tinder was no hero. He'd been to war, and he'd seen no heroes there, either.

He gave a long, rough sigh. Probably he deserved it, for the misdeeds of his youth, but deserving it made the thought of a hungry winter no sweeter. He shook his head and spat out into the yard. Bloody Union. Though it was no worse'n when Ironhead and Golden had their last little disagreement, and both came through here robbing whatever they could get their fat hands on. Put a few men with swords together, even men with usually pleasant manners, and it's never long before they're all acting like animals. It was like old Threetrees always said – a sword's a shitty thing to give a man. Shitty for him, and shitty for everyone around him.

'Are they gone yet?' asked Riam, creeping up close beside him to peer out, sunlight turning one half of her face white while the other was in shadow. She looked more like her mother with every day.

'I'll tell you when they're gone!' he growled at her, blocking the door with his body. He'd been on that march, down through Angland with Bethod. He'd done things, and he'd seen things done. Tinder knew how narrow the line was between folk in their house just minding their business and black bones in a burned-out shell. Tinder knew every moment those Union men were at the bottom of his field, him and his children were only just on the right side of that line. 'Stay inside!' he called after her as she made sulkily for the back room. 'And keep the shutters closed!'

When he looked outside again, Cowan was coming around the side of the house, milking pail in one hand, plain as day, just like it was any old morning.

'You soft in the head, boy?' Tinder snapped at him as he slipped through the doorway. 'Thought I told you to stay out o' sight?'

'You didn't say how. They're crawling everywhere. If they see me creeping they'll just think we've got something to hide.'

'We *have* got something to hide! You want 'em to take the goat as well?'

Cowan hung his head. 'She ain't giving much.'

Now Tinder felt guilty as well as scared. He reached out and ruffled his son's hair. 'No one's giving much right now. There's a war on. You just need to keep low and move quick, you hear?'

'Aye.'

Tinder took the pail from Cowan and put it down beside the door. 'Get back there with your sister, eh?' Then he snatched a quick peek around the frame and cursed under his breath.

A Union man was walking up to the house, and one Tinder liked the look of even less than most. Big, with too little neck and too much armour, a long sword sheathed on one side and a shorter on the other. Tinder might not have been the hardest, but he'd seen enough to spot a killer in a crowd, and something in the set of this big man got the back of his neck to tingling.

'What is it?' asked Cowan.

'Just get inside like I told you!' Tinder slid the hatchet from the table and let it fall down behind his leg, working his fist around the cool, smooth handle, mouth suddenly dry.

He might not be the fighter he once was, and he might never have been the hardest, but a man's no man who won't die for his children.

Tinder had been half-expecting the neckless bastard to draw one of those swords and kick the door right down and Tinder along with it. But all he did was take two slow steps up to the porch, Tinder's poor carpentry creaking under his big boots, and smile. An unconvincing, almost sorry-looking smile, slow to come, like doing it took an effort. Like he was smiling in spite of some burning wound.

'Hello,' he said, in Northern. Tinder felt his brows go up. He'd never heard such a strange, high little voice on a man, 'specially one big as this. Closer up his eyes were sad, not fierce. He had a satchel over his shoulder, a golden sun stamped into it.

'Hello.' Tinder tried to keep his face slack. Not angry. Not scared. Nothing and nobody. Certainly nobody who needed killing.

'My name is Gorst.' Tinder didn't see a need to reply to that. Like anything else, a name's a thing you share when you need to. Silence stretched out. An ugly, dangerous silence with the faint bad-tempered calls of men and animals floating over from the bottom of the field. 'Did I see your son with milk?'

Tinder narrowed his eyes. Here was a tester. Deny what this Gorst had already seen and risk riling him up, maybe put Tinder and his children in deeper danger? Or admit it and risk losing his goat along with all the rest? The Union man shifted in the doorway and the light caught the pommel of one of his swords, brought a steely glint to it.

'Aye,' croaked Tinder. 'A little.'

Gorst reached into his satchel, Tinder's eye following that big hand all the way, and came out with a wooden cup. 'Might I trouble you for some?'

Tinder had to put the axe down so he could pick up the bucket, but he didn't see much choice. Never seemed to have any choice these days, no more'n a leaf on the wind can pick its path. That's what it is to be ordinary folk with a war at the doorstep, he guessed.

The Union man dipped his cup, held it so a couple of drips fell, then looked up. They looked at each other for a long moment. No anger in the big man's eyes, or spite, or even much of anything. Tired eyes, and slow, and Tinder swallowed, sure he was looking his death in its face, and far from a pretty face, too. But in the end Gorst only nodded his balding rock of a head towards the trees, where a little smoke from the forge was smudging the iron-grey sky. 'Can you tell me the name of that village?'

'It's called Barden.' Tinder cleared his croaky throat, desperate to get his hand on the axe again but not sure how he could do it without the big man noticing. 'Ain't much there, though.'

'I was not planning a visit. But thank you.' The big man looked at him, mouth half-open as though he'd say something more. Then he turned and trudged off, shoulders hunched like he had a great weight on him. Greater even than all the weight of steel he was wearing. He sat down on the stump of that old fir Tinder had a bastard of a time cutting down in the spring. The one that nearly fell on him when he finally got through the trunk.

'What did he want?' came Riam's voice in his ear.

'By the dead, can't you stay out of sight?' Tinder nearly puked on the words, his throat was so tight, struggling to bundle his daughter away from the door with one arm.

But the big man showed no sign of ordering Tinder's goat seized, or his children, either. He pulled some papers from his satchel, placed them on the wood between his legs, uncorked a bottle of ink, dipped a pen in and wrote something. He took a sip of his milk – or Tinder's milk, in fact – frowned over towards the trees, then up at the sky, then towards the scarcely moving column of horses and carts, dipped his pen again and wrote something else.

'What's he doing?' whispered Riam.

'Writing.' Tinder worked his mouth and spat. It galled him a little, for no good reason, to have some big, sparrow-voiced Union bastard sitting on his stump, writing. What the hell was the use of writing when the world was so full of problems to be solved? But no doubt there was far worse he might be doing. And what could Tinder do about it anyway?

So he stood there, the mostly empty milking pail still gripped pale-knuckle tight in his fist, and watched the Union ruin his crop.

'Colonel Gorst?'

'Yes?'

There was absolutely no getting used to that voice, however much one might admire the man. It was like a lost little girl's.

'I'm Lieutenant Kerns. I was on the same ship as you coming over, was it . . . the *Indomitable*? The *Invincible*? The *Insomething*, anyway.' Gorst sat in silence, a few sheets of paper spread out on the tree-stump between his legs, ink bottle open beside them, pen held with strange delicacy in one ham of a hand and what looked to be a small cup in the other. 'I saw you training, more than once, on deck, in the mornings.' Many of the men had gathered to watch. None of them had ever seen anything like it. 'A most impressive spectacle. We spoke a little . . . at one point.' Kerns supposed that was true in the strictest sense, though it had, in fact, been him who had done virtually all of the speaking.

It was the same routine this time around. Gorst stared up in stony silence all the while, deep-set eyes appraisingly narrowed, and that caused Kerns to start to blather, words coming faster and faster while he said less and less. 'We talked about the reasons for the conflict, and so forth, and who was along, and who was in the right and wrong of it, and the whys and wherefores, you know.' By the Fates, why couldn't he shut up? 'And how Marshal Kroy would handle the campaign, and which division would fight where, and so forth, you know. I think then, perhaps, we discussed the virtues of Styrian steel as opposed to Union mixtures, for blades and armour, and so on. Then it started to rain, so I retired below decks.'

'Yes.'

How Kerns wished he could retire below decks now. He cleared his throat. 'I'm in charge of the guards on this section of the supply column.' Gorst swept the column with his glare, causing Kerns to cough ashamedly. For all his hard work, its order was hardly something a sensible man would take pride in. 'Well, I and Lieutenant Pendel are in charge of them, and I saw you here writing, and I thought I might reintroduce myself... I say, is that a letter to the king?'

Gorst frowned. Which was to say, he frowned even more deeply, and shifted his mass of armoured body as if to conceal his papers. 'Yes.'

'It's quite a thing, to think, you know, his Majesty, and all, reading those very words, along with his breakfast, or possibly his lunch. Can't imagine what his Majesty has for lunch—'

'It varies.'

Kerns cleared his throat. 'Of course. Of course it does. I was wondering, if it wouldn't be too much of an imposition, if it might be possible for me to borrow from you a sheet of paper? I received a letter from my wife this morning and I'm terribly keen to reply. Our first child was born just before we left, you see.'

'Congratulations.'

'Indeed. He's beautiful.' From what Kerns could remember, he had thought his son remarkably ugly, fat and prone to screaming, but fathers always said their children were beautiful, so he resolved to follow suit, and had practised that faraway smile you were supposed to make along with it. He flashed it now. 'A beautiful, beautiful boy. Anyway, if I could—'

Gorst thrust a sheet of paper at him.

'Yes. Exactly. Thank you so much. I will make sure to replace it in due course. Wouldn't dream of—'

'Forget it,' grunted Gorst, hunching his heavy shoulders as he turned back to his own letter.

'Yes.' Kerns cleared his throat again. 'Yes, of course.'

'Enough of this bloody nonsense.' Pendel pulled the shovel from the side of the cart and set off through the flattened crops, wet earth squelching under his feet each step.

'What are you doing?' came Kerns's niggling squawk. That voice was starting to scrape at Pendel's nerves like a blunt razor at a sore neck. And always with the stupidest damn questions.

'What do you think I'm doing?' Pendel waved the shovel at him. 'I'm going to dig a tunnel back to Adua!' He turned towards the trees, adding under his breath, 'You bloody moron.'

'You sure you should be going over there?' Kerns shouted after him, waving, for some reason, a sheet of paper. 'What if—'

'You can manage without me for a minute, I'm sure!' And Pendel added a quiet, 'You bloody moron,' to that, too. Probably he could've excused himself for the whole day and found the column no more than a few strides advanced for all of Kerns's silly fretting. It was always the same way with new officers. Rulebook, duty, honour, rulebook. If Pendel had wanted to be beaten over the head with the rules he could have stayed at headquarters and had Colonel bloody Felnigg belabour his undeserving skull with them every morning. Well, he could have stayed if it hadn't been for that little oversight of his and the subsequent disciplinary action, but that was beside the point. The fact was he needed to crap, and he wasn't going to do it with dozens of men and animals watching. Who wants to crap with an audience?

'What if there are Northmen near the—'

'Then I'll bloody crap on them!' And he left Kerns to kiss Gorst's great big useless squeaking royal observer arse and first trotted, and then, when the trotting made him short of breath, strolled through the crops towards the welcoming darkness of the trees.

'There they are.'

'Oh, aye,' muttered Pale-as-Snow around his pellet of chagga. 'No doubt.'

You couldn't very well miss the bastards. Dozens of carts and wagons, stretched out through the trampled wreckage that had once been some poor fool's crops, some cargoes covered under canvas, but quite a few without even that much care taken. Bare hay bales waiting invitingly for a passing torch. Bundles of flatbow bolts practically begging to be carried off and shot back at their owners later. All kinds of things to steal and things to break. Not much movement down there. Way too much gear and nowhere near enough road, the story of the Union invasion of the North, far as Pale-as-Snow could tell. Horses shifted and pawed. Drivers slumped bored in their places. Not many guards, though, and those there were struck him as more ready for a nap than a fight.

'Looks good, Chief,' whispered Ripjack.

Pale-as-Snow glanced sideways at his Second, narrow-eyed. 'Don't put the curse on it, eh?' Plenty were the times he'd come more'n a little unstuck in a good-looking situation. There was no such thing as too careful, even when it was the Union you were trying to creep up on.

Pale-as-Snow long ago lost count of the raids he'd had charge of. A lifetime of 'em, and he was still waiting for one that went exactly as he'd hoped. Still waiting for that perfect raid. However careful his planning, there was always some little splinter of bad luck. Some overeager fool on his side, or some over-watchful stickler on the other, a loose strap, or testy horse, or some wrinkle of the weather or the light, or a bloody dry twig in the wrong place. But that's war, Pale-as-Snow supposed. You get luck of all kinds, and the winner's the one who makes the best of his share.

But who knew? As he took in that flat field full of trampled crops with its one little house and its one little shed, and the great mass of unready, unruly men and supplies at the end of it, he started to get the tickly, eager feeling in the palms of his hands that this could be the day, and the corner of his mouth slowly twitched up.

Then he could go back and tell Scale that it had been a real beauty of a raid. A peach. His men all laughing and showing off their booty and telling ever less believable lies about their high deeds on the day. Scale clapping him on the back instead of giving him another rage to wince his way through. Honestly, Pale-as-Snow was getting a little sick of being raged at. He was a leader you could respect, was Scale. Just as long as he didn't open his mouth.

Pale-as-Snow gave his chagga a long, slow chew as he scanned the field again, then he nodded. A good fighter has to be careful, but sooner or later he has to fight. The moment comes up smiling and offers its hand, you got to grab it.

'All right. Let's get the boys ready.' He turned and started giving signals to the others, open hand pointing left and right through the trees to start 'em moving to where he wanted 'em, quicker at talking with his hands than he was with his mouth. Bows close to the treeline, Carls in two wedges to deal with the guards, Thralls in the centre, ready to rush the column and do as much damage as men could in the time it took for more guards to arrive. You'd be surprised how much damage men could do in that time, if they were good and ready for it. Just a little more of the right kind of luck and this might be the raid they measured all future raids against. A real beauty. A real—

'Chief,' hissed Ripjack.

'Uh?'

The Named Man held a finger over his mouth for quiet, his eyes all big and round, then shifted that finger to point off through the undergrowth.

Pale-as-Snow felt his heart sinking. There was someone coming across the field towards 'em. A Union man, his polished helmet gleaming, a shovel over his shoulder, not a care in the world. Pale-as-Snow twisted around, hissing hard between his teeth to get the lads' attention, then waving 'em frantically down. All together they dropped into the bushes, behind trees, found boulders, and like a trick of sorcery in a moment left the woods peaceful quiet and empty-looking.

The Southerner hadn't stopped, though. He ducked under the branches and crashed through the undergrowth a few steps, coming straight at them, whistling tunelessly to himself like he was on his way to market rather'n wrapped up in a war. They were bloody idiots, these Union men. Bloody idiots, but if he kept on walking he'd see 'em sure, and soon, however much of an idiot he was.

'Always something,' mouthed Pale-as-Snow, putting his hand

on his sword, the other one flat out behind him, palm up, to keep the rest of the lads quiet. Beside him he felt Ripjack very slowly slide out his knife, the blade of it gleaming murder in the shadows. Pale-as-Snow watched the Southerner come closer, a little itch making his eyelid twitch, his muscles tensing up all tight and ready to sweep his sword out and set to—

The Southerner stopped no more'n four strides away, dug his shovel down in the earth, took his helmet off and tossed it on the ground beside him, wiped his forehead on the back of his arm, turned around, then started undoing his belt.

Pale-as-Snow felt himself smile. He looked at Ripjack, took his hand gently from his sword, put his forefinger gently to his lips to say quiet, pointed it at the squatting Southerner busy getting his trousers down, then drew it gently across his throat.

Ripjack winced and pointed at his chest.

Pale-as-Snow grinned wider and nodded.

Ripjack winced more, then shrugged, then started to ease ever so very gently forward through the brush, twisting himself around the plants, eyes darting over the ground for anything might give him away. Pale-as-Snow settled back, watching. They'd sort this little piece of business, then they'd get the lads in place and everything ready, then they'd make a raid about which songs would be sung for a hundred years. Or they'd have a stab at it, anyway.

You get luck of all kinds in a war. The winner's the one who makes the best of his share.

Pendel wriggled down into his heels, trying to get comfortable, one hand on the shovel and the other on his knee. He grunted, gritted his teeth. That was the bloody army life for you, always too hard or too runny, never a happy medium. There was no happy medium in war. He sighed and was shifting his weight for another effort when he felt a sharp pain across his backside.

'Ah!' He twisted around, cursing. One of those monstrous bloody nettles they had up here had leaned in, as if on purpose, and stung his left buttock, damn it.

'Bloody North,' he hissed, rubbing furiously at the affected area and making it sting all the worse. 'Damn this fucking country.' They'd been marching for what felt like months and he'd yet to see an acre of the place that was worth one man's snot, let alone hundreds of lives, and he very much doubted—

Beyond the nettle, no more than a couple of strides away, a man was kneeling in the brush, staring at him.

A Northman.

A Northman with a knife in his hand.

Not a big knife. No more than average-sized.

But certainly big enough.

They stared at each other for what felt like a very long moment, Pendel squatting with his trousers around his ankles, the North-man squatting with trousers up but jaw down.

They moved together, as if on a signal firmly agreed and long prepared for. The Northman leaped forward, knife going up. Without conscious thought Pendel spun around, swinging the shovel, and its flat caught the Northman crisply on the side of the head with a metallic ping and sent blood, Northman and shovel all flying through the air.

With a girlish whoop, Pendel staggered away in the direction he'd come from, tripped, heard what he thought might be an arrow swish through the air beside him, rolled through a great patch of nettles and lurched to his feet, struggling to run, scream and pull his trousers up all at once with death breathing on his bare arse.

*

My darling wife Silyne,
I was overjoyed to receive your letter and the news of our son,
though it took three weeks to reach me. Damn army post,
you know. Glad to hear your mother is better. I wanted to
tell you

Kerns leaned back, staring wistfully off across the field. Wanted to tell her what? It was ever this way. Desperate to write, but when he sat down, no words. None worth a damn, anyway. He was not really even sure he wanted to write, just felt that he *should* want to. His wife would be left with the most bland and uninteresting collection of waste paper if he was ever to die in battle, that was certain. No poetic professions of his deep love, no sage advice to his infant son on how to be a man, no secrets of his innermost self. He was, in all honestly, unsure that he had an innermost self. Certainly not one with any profound revelations to make.

It was hardly as though anything of the faintest interest ever happened here, anyway. They barely moved, let alone fought. Kerns did not want to be a hero, just to do his part. To test his mettle against an enemy rather than fighting mud, horses and Pendel's incompetence every day. He had volunteered for *action*, not tedium. To distinguish himself. To win honour on the battlefield. To be celebrated, rewarded, toasted, admired. All right, he wanted to be a hero. And here he was, among the baggage, where the bravest deed done was greasing an axle.

He gave a long, tired sigh, frowned at his empty page and then over at Colonel Gorst, perhaps hoping to find inspiration there. But the colonel had put his pen down and was staring towards the trees with the most striking intensity. Kerns thought he heard a faint cry, high with a note of panic. It came again, louder, and Gorst shot to his feet, cup tumbling from his hand, milk spilling. Kerns looked towards the trees, his mouth dropping open. Pendel was there, bounding back through the crops towards them, trying to run and hold his open trousers up and shout all at the same time.

He managed to yell one audible word, voice shrill with terror. 'Northmen!'

As if to add drama to his exclamation, an arrow looped over from behind him, narrowly missing his shoulder and vanishing into the crops. Kerns felt his face go hot. Time seemed perceptibly to slow. He stood as if in a dream, his limbs heavy, his mind sluggishly struggling to catch up with reality. He gawped at Pendel. He gawped at the column. He gawped at Gorst, who was already rushing forwards, drawing his heavy steels. He gawped at the treeline, from which men had now started to appear, running, shrill cries echoing over the silent field.

'Bloody hell,' Kerns whispered, flinging his pen away and tearing at his sword hilt. Bloody thing wouldn't come free. He realised the securing thong was looped over the grip, started fumbling with it, failed, ripped his gloves off in a fury, fumbled again, finally loosening the hilt. He looked up. Northmen, undoubtedly Northmen, some of them with painted shields on their arms, bright weapons in their fists, whooping and shouting as they bounded towards the largely unguarded wagons.

He cast about for his helmet, knocking his ink bottle over and sending a spray of black across his banal fragment of a letter. Probably should've had his helmet on all the time but his men had mocked him mercilessly, and when he found it filled with dung that morning it had been the final straw. If he ever discovered who—

As he finally got his sword drawn and looked up, he realised it hardly mattered now. There were things moving in the air. Arrows. Arrows from kneeling Northmen, before the trees, bows raised. His wide eyes darted over the dark background of the woods, drawn by flickers of movement. He ducked uselessly, the arrows whispering past him and dropping among the carts. He saw one thud into wood and lodge there, quivering. Another stuck into a horse's flank and it reared up, screaming.

'With me!' he bellowed, no idea who he was bellowing at, not bothering to check if anyone was with him or not, doing his best to lift his feet over the barley as he floundered on, all the silly frustrations of being assigned supply duty suddenly banished. Action! Here was action!

Gorst was up ahead in combat with two Northmen. His long steel hit a shield with a loud crack and sent one stumbling back. Gorst dodged a two-handed axe-blow, the heavy blade missing him by a terrifying whisker. Even as it thudded into the earth Gorst was spinning around, swift as lightning in spite of his bulk, long steel feathering the crops. It took the axeman's right leg off cleanly at the knee and snatched the other out from under him, sending the unfortunate man cartwheeling in a spray of blood. His friend was just struggling to get up when Gorst's long steel left a great dent in the front of his helmet and knocked him back, mouth silently gaping, arms spread, sword tumbling from one nerveless hand.

Kerns felt a shock run through him as he realised that he had seen two men killed before his eyes. Shock, and disbelief, and breathless excitement. Here was most definitely action! To stand alongside Colonel Gorst, a man who had been the king's First Guard! To be smilingly acknowledged by him after the engagement, to be clapped on the shoulder and greeted as a brother! It was everything Kerns had dreamed of when he first tried on the uniform. Three more Northmen were jumping through the crops towards Gorst now, and Kerns hurried up to his side, raising his sword.

'Colonel Gorst!'

He saw a flash of movement at the corner of his eye, jerked his head away on an instinct, and—

Gorst felt his long steel crunch into something at the very end of his swing, twisting the grip in his fist as the Northman before him toppled back, blood squirting from his neatly slit throat. But he had no time to think on it. *I have other business.*

Namely a short man in tarnished chain mail, ageing and running somewhat to fat, roaring as lustily as he could after a charge through the crops, ruddy cheeks full of broken veins. *Those cheeks.* They surprised Gorst with a stray memory of his father, shortly before his death when he had been confined to his bed, unable to speak properly and eternally surprised by the animal noises that emerged from his twisted mouth. Fussing with the tassels on his nightgown, shrivelled to a ghostly prune of his former self. *A ghostly prune with prune-coloured cheeks.*

How many years did I put up with that old fool's disappointment, and his rebukes, and his jokes about ladies' voices, and smile and nod like a dutiful son? Gorst's lips curled back in an animal snarl. A passing resemblance to a close relative was not about to break his stride. Rather it urged him on. *After all, Father, I never could shut you up in life...*

The Northman swung his sword in an overhead arc as Gorst came close, a clumsy motion, easily anticipated. *One would think these fools had never drawn a sword before. Not really my job to show them how it's done, but....* Gorst deflected it effortlessly with his long steel, blades scraping, closed and stabbed once with his short, getting it tangled with the rim of the painted shield. There was enough force behind it to twist its prune-faced owner sideways, though. Gorst stabbed again and felt the blade slide through mail and into flesh, the man's mouth opening wide to scream. *Quiet, now, Father.* Gorst stabbed once more and cut that scream off in a last twisted gurgle. He shouldered the Northman away and chopped one ruddy cheek wide open with a swing of the long steel, showering blood and making another man check in his charge, check enough that Gorst could split his head, too, on the backswing and snatch him off his feet before he had time to remind Gorst of any other dead relatives.

No more enemies in easy reach, he spun about. There was fighting near the column. He saw a guard running, throwing his spear away as a wild-haired Northman bounded after him. Another was on his knees with an arrow in his shoulder. Dark shapes darted between the wagons. Someone had tossed a lit torch into a cart full of hay and quickly turned the cargo into a hearty fireball, rolls of oily smoke pouring up into the grey sky, horses screaming and plunging, harnesses tangling, dragging carts over in their terror.

'The horses!' Gorst squealed, not even bothering to deepen his voice. 'The horses!' *Not that I really give a damn about horses. Or anything else.* And he sprang over one of the corpses he had made and charged back towards the column, eager to make more.

Wrongside had never actually killed a man. Strange thing for a Thrall six years in the black business to take pride in, perhaps, and it wasn't like he was advertising the fact, but take pride in it he did. More'n once he'd had an arrow nocked and beaded on an enemy, or a side or back turned to him in a fight, and it had come to him at that moment what his mother's face would've looked like when he told her. She was long dead, o' course, plague took her a dozen winters since, but still. That same look she'd had when he'd got up to some mischief or other, all hurt. Wrongside didn't want to let his mother down. So he was proud he could say he'd never killed a man, even if he was only saying it to himself. Pale-as-Snow had said kill the horses, though, and when his Chief said a thing, Wrongside tried to do it.

So he squeezed his face into a wince and sank his spear into the nearest flank, keeping well clear of the thrashing hooves. Nothing the poor horse could do about it, harnessed as it was to three others. He dragged his spear clear as it fell and moved on to the next. Shit business, killing horses. But war's a steady stream of shit business, and Wrongside always did have bad luck with his jobs. Ended up on the wrong side of every case, hence the name. Was only a week ago he'd taken part in another of Pale-as-Snow's raids, just as the sun was going down and in the pissing rain, and a right bloody mess it had become, as usual. He'd ended up getting all turned around, splashing across a stream and well and truly onto the wrong side, with Union scouts crashing about everywhere looking for him.

Was only yesterday he'd finally found his way back to the rest of Scale's boys, talked 'em into believing that he hadn't run off on purpose and had been trying to get back best he could, so they didn't hang him and burn him, as Black Dow was in the habit o' doing to deserters. Then the very next day, another raid. How was that for shitty luck? Felt like he'd only just heard Pale-as-Snow's bloody peach of a raid speech and he was listening to it again. Wrongside hated fighting. Far as he could tell, it was the one major drawback of the soldiering life. Apart from the hunger. And the cold. And the threat of hanging and burning. The soldiering life had a lot of drawbacks, in fact, now he came to consider the case. But now wasn't the time for considering cases.

He gritted his teeth and stabbed another horse in its belly, his ears full of the screaming, crying, whinnying of dying animals. Sounded like children. They weren't children. They weren't, but it was still a bloody shame. He'd never seen such big, strong, beautiful beasts as these. Hurt his heart to think of what these lovely glossy horses might've fetched back at the market in his village. How the farmers' jaws would've dropped just to see 'em in the rough-carved pen. How it might've changed the lives of his old mum and dad to have a horse like one of these to drag the plough and pull the haycart, and show off on festival days. How proud they'd have been to own just one. And here he was making mud out of a dozen. Made his heart hurt, it did.

But war's a heart-hurting sort of an exercise, one way and another.

He dragged his blood-daubed spear from another horse, leaving it tottering sideways in its harness, neck arching. He turned for the next wagon and found himself staring, at reasonably close quarters, straight into the face of a Union man. A strange-looking one, unarmed, holding up his trousers with one hand while the broken buckle on his belt clinked at his knees.

Wrongside could tell from one glance at his eyes that he'd no more interest in fighting than Wrongside did. Not a word said, they made an agreement. Each man took a step back, circling gently away. Then another. Then they parted in good humour, more'n likely never to boast of or, indeed, mention it at all, but neither man the worse off for their meeting, which Wrongside felt was about the best that could be hoped for from two enemies on a battlefield.

He hurried away between two wagons, no wish to loiter, the

air sticky and his nose tickly with the tang of burning now. He ducked some flying hooves, saw old Racket lifting an axe, eyes wide, then he heard a high screech and a sword came down and split Racket's grey-haired head wide open, knees crumpling like he was made of leaves.

Wrongside didn't see who'd swung that blade, and he didn't wait to find out. Just turned right around and ran. He slipped in some horse-blood, caught his knee against the corner of a tipped-over cart and grabbed at it, stumbling sideways, stifling a groan of pain. 'Fuck, fuck, fuck.' Rubbing at his kneecap, then limping on, fast as he could. Had to get back across the field but there was a burning wagon on his right, a tower of flame and smoke, dead horses hitched to it and a living one plunging, flank dark with blood, eyes rolling with terror as it tried to get away and only dragged the fireball further into the midst of the column. Wrongside turned the other way, heard a scream and a clash of metal, decided swiftly against, took a deep breath and dived from the muddy track straight into the undergrowth, slithering down behind a tree, peering through the bracken and brambles, heart battering at his ribs.

'Oh, hell,' he whispered. Stuck in the woods, again, the enemy all around, again, covered head to toe in horse-blood... Well, this was the first time for that. But the rest was starting to become an uncomfortable pattern and no mistake. He wondered if old Pale-as-Snow would take his word for it this time around, when he finally stumbled back into camp after five days' cold and hungry creeping through the brush. If he made it back to camp.

'Oh, hell.' By the dead, his knee hurt. War's a knee-hurting sort of an exercise, one way and another.

*

So much for a peach of a raid.

Pale-as-Snow gave a sigh, licked the chagga juice from his front teeth, worked his tongue around and sourly spat into the undergrowth. He used to be a great man, didn't he? One of Bethod's four War Chiefs. He'd led the storming party at Uffrith. He'd shattered the Union line in the mist near the Cumnur. He'd been a man everyone had to respect, or at least show respect to and keep their contrary opinions to themselves. Hard to believe, now. Back to camp, and another of Scale's bloody rages.

Still, nothing to be gained by hanging on here. Wasn't as if everything would suddenly come out right. Surprise is like virginity. You only get the one chance at using it, and that normally turns out a crushing disappointment. Pale-as-Snow frowned towards the confused mess at the bottom of the field, then at Ripjack, squatting in the brush looking greatly sorry for himself with a bloody cloth pressed to his cut head. First thing a fighter needs to know is when to stop fighting.

'Get 'em to sound the horn. We'll do no more good today.'

Ripjack nodded, and waved the signal, and the blast of the horn echoed out as Pale-as-Snow turned away from the skirmish and crept off through the bushes, bent double, slowly shaking his head.

One day. One day he'd mount that perfect raid.

Pendel heard the faint sound of a horn. Peering out between the spokes of the cartwheel he saw men running back towards the trees. The Northmen, and in retreat. The wave of relief was almost strong enough to make him spontaneously finish the business he had begun in the woods. But he had no time, for relief or other business. Captain Bronkenhorm would no doubt even now be wheezing up with more guards, and it wouldn't do for him to find Pendel hiding behind a cartwheel. Pendel had already been drummed out of the marshal's headquarters. He wasn't sure where you ended up when you were drummed out of the baggage guard, but he had no wish to find out.

He took a look both ways to check he was unobserved, dragged his trousers up once more, still cursing the broken buckle, then slipped out from under the wagon. He gasped as he nearly tripped over the body of a dead Union soldier, a bloodstained sword lying near one hand. Then he smiled. Serendipity. He snatched up the blade and stood tall, affecting a bellicose expression and striding boldly through the ruined crops, waving his stolen weapon towards the woods.

'Come back here, you bastards! I'll show you a fight! Get back here, damn you!'

Once he was confident there were plenty of men looking at him, he flung down his sword in a fury.

'Cowards!' he roared at the trees.

Someone was shouting, but Gorst wasn't listening. He was looking down at one of the corpses. A young Union officer with a split head, one half of the face beyond recognition, the other blood-spotted, wearing the tongue-out leer of a man who has just made a revoltingly lewd suggestion.

What did he say his name was? Gorst crushed up his face as though that might somehow squeeze the answer out, but it was gone. *Let us be honest, I was not listening.* He had been married, Gorst remembered him saying that. And something about a child. *Berns, was it? Ferns?* Gorst remembered the feeling of his long steel crunching into something. *For me, a moment barely registered. For him, the end of everything.* Not that Gorst was entirely sure. It might have been his blade that did it. It might have been another.

There was no shortage of hard-swung steel here a few moments ago, and certainties are sadly rare in combat.

Gorst sighed. *What difference does it really make, anyway? Would he be any less dead if it had been a Northern sword that split his head?* He found himself reaching out, pressing at the dead man's face, trying to make it register a more dignified expression, but however he kneaded the flesh it returned to that red-speckled leer.

Should I not be choked with guilt? The little fatherless boy? The penniless widow? The family all clustered around to hear happy news from the front, then weeping over the letter? Howling and beating their breasts! Verns, Perns, Smerns, will never come back for the winter festival! Gorst puffed out his cheeks. He felt nothing but mild annoyance, the constant background hum of his own disappointment and some slight uncomfortable sweatiness beneath his armour. *What kind of monster am I, that a little sweat upsets me more than a murder?*

Gorst frowned at the last few fleeing Northmen disappearing into the woods. He frowned at the men desperately trying to beat out the flames now wreathing several of the wagons. He frowned at a Union officer, belt hanging undone and trousers sagging, brandishing one bloody fist. He frowned more deeply still, over towards the small house near the top of the field, and its slightly open door. He stood, worked his fist around the grip of his long steel and started to trudge towards it.

Looked like the fight was done, best Tinder could tell from peering around the doorframe. Who'd won, it was hard to say. In his experience, and he'd more'n enough to tell, rare were the fights after which it was easy to say who'd won. Reasonably rare were the fights anyone in particular did actually win, for that matter. There were a few dead men around, he could see that, and quite a few more wounded, he could hear them. Dying horses, too. More than one of the wagons was on fire, burning hay-stalks fluttering down all around. The Northmen were driven off, the last of 'em shooting a lazy arrow or two from the treeline. But it seemed Tinder had come through it without anyone burning his house down—

'Shit,' he hissed between his teeth. The big Union man was walking towards the house. The one with the silly voice. The one called Gorst. Striding towards the house with his head down, heavy sword still held in one fist, heavy jaw clenched like a man with some black work in mind. 'Shit.'

A thing like this turned men mean. Even men who might be decent under decent circumstances. Thing like this made men look for someone to blame, and Tinder knew there was no one better placed for that than him. Him and his children.

'What's happening?'

Tinder caught his daughter's arm and started to guide her towards the back, only just forcing words out through the fear clamping his throat up. 'Listen to me, Riam. You get by the back door, and ready to open it. You hear me shout, run. You run, d'you understand? Just like we talked about. You run over to Old Nairn's house, and I'll join up with you later.'

His daughter's eyes were wide in her pale face. 'Will you?' By the dead, how much she looked like her mother.

'Course I will!' he said, touching her cheek. 'I said it, didn't I? Don't cry, you got Cowan looking to you.'

She caught a hold of him, and he felt tears coming, too, as he pushed her off and towards the back door, and she clung to him and wouldn't let him free, and he had to start prising her fingers away but couldn't bring himself to do it.

'You got to go,' he whispered at her, 'you got to go right—'

The door was flung open, banging hard against the wall and sending a shower of dust down from the rafters. The Union man was there, a great shadow framed in the bright square of the doorway. He took a quick step into the house and Tinder was facing him, jaw clenched and axe in one hand, Riam held back behind his body with the other. Gorst stopped still, face in shadow, brightness down the edge of his heavy jaw, and his armour, and his sword, spots of blood gleaming on all three.

There was a long, still silence. Tinder could hear Riam's breathing, fast and scared, and Cowan's, faintest edge of a whimper in it, and his own, growling in his throat, and he wondered with each one whether it would be his last.

Felt like an age they stood there, then finally the Union man spoke, that strange high voice again, horribly shrill in the silence. 'Are you . . . all right?'

A pause. Then Tinder gave the slightest nod. 'All fine,' he said, surprised how firm his voice sounded with his heart going like a busy smithy.

'I'm . . . very sorry.' Gorst looked down, seemed to realise he had a sword in his hand, moved to sheathe it, then, maybe seeing it was bloody as a slaughterman's knife, didn't. He stood, posed awkwardly, sideways on. 'About . . . *this.*'

Tinder swallowed. The axe-handle felt slippery with sweat in his palm. 'Sorry about what?'

Gorst shrugged. 'Everything.' He took a step back then, just as Tinder was allowing himself to relax, stopped in the doorway, reached out and put something down on the corner of the table. 'For the milk.' Then he ducked under the low lintel and hurried down Tinder's creaking steps.

Tinder closed his eyes and breathed for a moment, revelling in the feeling of having no fatal wounds. Then he stole over to the door, easing it nearly closed with his fingertips. He picked up the coin the Southerner had left. A disc of silver, edge gleaming in the shadows, heavy in his palm. A hundred times what that cup of milk had been worth. A thousand times. Enough to replace all Tinder's lost chickens and maybe even some of his lost crops into the bargain. He slowly closed his fist around it, hardly able to stop himself from trembling now, then wiped his eyes on the back of his sleeve.

He turned to his children, both staring at him from the shadows. 'You'd best get in the back,' he said softly. 'And stay out of sight.'

He narrowed his eyes against the brightness as he peered around the doorframe again. The big Union man was walking away, head down, trying to wipe his sword clean with a rag much too small for the task. Beyond him it looked like they'd already started digging graves. Digging 'em right in the middle of Tinder's field, of course, and ripping up what was left of his barley doing it. Tinder set his axe gently down on the table, and shook his head, and spat.

Then he stood in his doorway, and watched the Union ruin his crop.

THREE'S
A CROWD

Talins, Autumn 587

S hev propped her elbows on the parapet, shoulders hunched around her ears and her fingers dangling, and gave a soft whistle. 'You've got quite an audience for it, anyway.'

She was about as well travelled as any woman in the Circle of the World. As well travelled as only a woman who'd spent half her life running can be. But even she'd rarely seen such a crowd. Maybe in Adua, at the presentation of the firstborn son and heir of the King of the Union, though her mind had been more on her empty belly than his full streets. Maybe at the execution of Cabrian when she passed through Darmium, though she'd passed through in too much pain and far too much haste to be sure. Definitely at the Great Temple in Shaffa, when the Prophet Khalul himself had come down from the mountains to speak the prayers at the new year pilgrimage, and even Shev had felt just the tiniest bit pious, if only for a moment.

But she'd certainly seen nothing like it in Styria.

The whole of Talins was down there and plenty more besides, a multitude so vast and so tight-pressed it hardly looked as if it could be made up of individuals, but had become a single form-less, mindless infestation. The steps of the ancient Senate House seethed and the great square boiled over into the adjoining streets, every window packed with faces, every roof lined with onlookers.

On the Ringing Bridge, and the Bridge of Gulls, and the Bridge of Kisses, and the Bridge of Six Promises, you couldn't have fitted one more person without squeezing another off into the water. A couple had dropped in already, only to drag themselves out downstream and force their dripping way back to a spot where they could witness the ceremony.

It wasn't every day you witnessed a ceremony like this, after all.

'Let's hope it turns out better than the last time we crowned a King of Styria,' said Shev.

Vitari ducked out onto the balcony with a glass of wine in one hand. 'Oh, I think that turned out well enough.'

'The five most powerful nobles in the land lying dead on the stage?'

'Nothing could be better. If you backed the sixth.' And Vitari grinned down at her employer, the Grand Duchess Monzcarro Murcatto. The most powerful woman in the world stood rigidly erect in the centre of the great platform below, still as the statues of her that were springing up across Styria, while her two chancellors – Scavier and Grulo – competed with each other to wail out the most overblown praise to her stewardship of the nation.

Her tailors and armourers must have been working towards this joyous moment as hard as her soldiers and spies. She wore something that neatly split the difference between queen's gown and general's armour, breastplate twinkling in the sunlight, long train stitched with gilded serpents snaking behind her and a bright sword at her side. She went nowhere without a sword. Shev had heard she slept with one. Used one for a lover, some said. They didn't say it to her face, though.

Wise people took great care over what they said to the face of the Serpent of Talins.

Shev sighed. 'It's a dark tide that lifts no boats at all.'

'I've made my living picking through the flotsam left behind by other people's dark tides,' said Vitari. 'But I'm confident this crowning will go smoothly.'

'No doubt you've made sure of it.' There were soldiers down there, with burnished armour and ceremonial weapons, but few of them, and purely for show. A naïve viewer might have supposed the Grand Duchess Monzcarro and her son needed no shield beyond the love of her people. Shev was not naïve.

Not in this, anyway.

From up here she could pick out the agents in the crowd around the platform, in the windows with the best views, at choke points and on corners. There a sharp-eyed boy waving a little flag of Talins. There a woman offering pastries with less enthusiasm than you might expect. There a man whose coat did not quite fit. Something in their watchful attitude. In their ready stance.

No doubt there were others that even Shev's eyes, filed sharp as needles by years of constant danger, could never have picked out.

Yes, Shylo Vitari left as little to chance as anyone Shev had ever met.

'You should be down there.' She nodded at the triple row of soldiers and sailors, bankers and bureaucrats, leading citizens and smirking aristocrats at the back of the platform, basking in the warmth of the grand duchess's power. 'No one's done more than you to make this happen.'

'She who takes the credit also takes the blame.' Vitari glanced sideways at Shev, and hers was about as sideways a glance as you could find. 'Those of us who work in the shadows are better off staying there. Windbags like these can strut about in the light.'

Scavier and Grulo were finally reaching the end of their address, both sweating through their cloth of gold from their oratorical efforts. A somewhat tedious double-act, in Shev's opinion, a reshuffled deck of the usual quarter-truths about loyalty, justice, leadership and standing united. Folk stood united precisely as long as it suited them, in her experience, and not one instant longer.

The restless crowd stilled as they stepped back. The boy rose from his gilded chair, dressed all in pure and simple white, and strolled with utter confidence to the front of the platform. His mother followed him, close as a long shadow, a crown of golden leaves in her gloved right fist.

While her son smiled beneficently upon the crowd she swept them with a chilling glare, as if determined to pick out any one person among those thousands who might dare to meet her eye. Might dare to challenge her. Might dare to raise the slightest objection to what was coming.

Grand Duke Orso would no doubt have raised objections if he'd been in attendance, but Murcatto had killed him, and both his sons, and both his generals, and his bodyguard and his banker for good measure, and taken his city for herself.

The great noblemen of Etrisani and Sipani, Nicante and Affoia, Visserine and Westport had objected, and one by one she had bribed them, cowed them or crushed them beneath her armoured boot.

Several leading citizens of Ospria had aired doubts that Murcatto's child really was the son of their dear departed King Rogont, and their flyblown heads had ended up spiked above the city gates, where now they aired the much more eloquent stink of rot.

His August Majesty the King of the Union had objected most of all, but Murcatto had outmanoeuvred him politically and militarily, stripped away his allies one by one, then beaten him three times in the field and proved herself the greatest general of the age.

So it was far from surprising that no one chose to object today.

Satisfied by the utter silence that only abject fear can produce, the grand duchess raised the crown high over her son's head in both hands. 'You are crowned Jappo mon Rogont Murcatto!' she called out as she slowly lowered it, her voice ringing from the faces of the buildings around the square, picked up as an echo by announcers scattered through the crowd. 'Grand Duke of Ospria and Visserine, Protector of Puranti, Nicante, Borletta and Affoia, and King of Styria!' And she settled the crown among her son's brown curls.

'King of Styria!' chorused the crowd with one thunderous voice, and there was a mighty rustling, a ripple through the press of bodies as every man and woman knelt, Murcatto stepping back and sinking stiffly herself. Evidently those clothes had not been cut for kneeling in.

Shev's eyes picked out only one figure who did not kneel. An unremarkable man in unremarkable clothes, standing beside a pillar on the steps of the Senate House, arms folded. It looked as if he glanced up towards Vitari and gave a nod, and she gave the slightest nod in return.

King Jappo himself stood and smiled. Seven years old, and already as calm and controlled before that mighty audience as Juvens himself might have been.

'Oh, do get up!' he shouted in a piping voice.

Laughter rippled out through the throng, turning quickly to a thunderous cheer. Startled birds showered up from the roofs as every bell in the city began to toll in celebration of the joyous event. Vitari raised her glass in a silent toast and Shev knocked her ring against it with a gentle ping. Down on the platform, the grand duchess embraced her son, and she was smiling. A sight only slightly less rare than the crowning of a King of Styria. Still, one could hardly begrudge her a grin.

'She has done what couldn't be done!' Shev had to lean close and shout over the noise.

'She has united Styria!' Vitari drained her glass in one long swallow.

'Most of it, at least.'

'For now.'

Shev slowly shook her head as she watched the leading citizens of Styria file past King Jappo to offer their obsequious congratulations under the hawklike glare of his mother. 'How many people had to die to give that boy a golden hat?'

'Exactly the necessary number. Console yourself with the thought that the war might have been a great deal bloodier without your work.'

Shev winced. 'It was more than bloody enough for my taste. I'm glad it's done.'

'The swords may be sheathed but the war goes on. We will move to darker battlefields now, and subtler weapons, and the Union's general will show far less mercy.'

'The Cripple?' muttered Shev.

Vitari's jaw muscles worked as she frowned down towards the new King of Styria. 'His hidden legions are already on the move.'

Shev cleared her throat at that. 'Before they get here . . . might I ask if her Grace has prepared something for me?'

'Oh, her Grace has quite the memory for debts, as Duke Orso and his sons would testify, if they were able.' Vitari slid out a rolled-up paper. 'Murcatto always pays in full.'

Now the moment was on her, Shev found herself suddenly, absurdly nervous. She plucked the scroll from Vitari's fingers with feigned confidence, ducked out of the sunlight and into the gilded shadows of the chamber and unrolled it on the table, revealing several blocks of densely written script.

'On this the third day of blah, blah, blah ... witnessed by blah, blah ... I, Horald Gasta, also known as Horald the Finger, of Westport, do hereby extend my full forgiveness to the thief Shevedieh ul Kanan mut Mayr—' She looked up. 'Thief?'

Vitari cocked an orange eyebrow as she stepped from the balcony. 'Would you prefer spy?'

'I would prefer ...' What would she prefer? 'Acquisitions specialist, maybe?'

Vitari snorted. 'I would prefer that my arse was as tight as it was twenty years ago. We must tackle the world as it is.'

'Your arse looks excellent if you ... ask ...' Shev cleared her throat as Vitari narrowed her eyes. 'Thief will do, I suppose.' She began reading again. 'For any and all offences towards me, including but not limited to the cowardly murder of my son Crandall ... Cowardly? The only bloody cowardly thing about it was him turning up with four men to kill me! I axed him in the front, which was better than he bloody deserved, I can—'

'Wording, Shevedieh, let the man have his wording.' Vitari waved it away, heavy-lidded. 'It doesn't do to get worked up over trifles.'

'Fair point.' Shev took a breath as she looked back to the document. 'I hereby give up any right to vengeance or recrimination and do solemnly swear, in the absence of any further significant offence, not to cause personal harm to the aforementioned Shevedieh or any of her associates.' She scanned down to the bottom, peered closely and gave a snort. 'The awe-inspiring Horald the Finger makes a mark?'

'Awe-inspiring or not, that bastard can't write any more than I can sing.'

'You can't sing?'

'I used to torture people for a living, but I'd never be heartless enough to sing to them.'

'And this is binding?'

'This is flimflam. But Horald gave his word to the grand duchess. That is binding, or he will become another debt to be paid. He's no fool. He understands.'

Shev closed her eyes, and took a long breath, and felt herself smiling. 'I'm free,' she whispered. Could it be? After all these years? 'I'm free,' she said, blinking back tears, and she felt her knees weaken and had to flop down in the nearest chair. She just sat, eyes shut, thinking about how she could just sit, eyes shut, not glancing over her shoulder, not startling at every noise, not picking over the routes of escape, not planning where she'd run to next.

God, she was free.

'So . . .' She opened her eyes. 'That's it?'

Vitari was pouring another glass of wine. 'Unless you don't want that to be it? I can always find work for the best . . . *acquisitions specialist* in Styria.'

'Oh, no,' said Shev, rolling up the scroll and turning for the door. 'From here on, it's the quiet life for me.'

'I tried the quiet life.' Vitari held her wine up to the light, a splash of blood-red across her frown as the sun shone through it. 'For about a week. I was bored as hell.'

'God, to be bored!' Shev had to shout over another world-shaking wave of applause for the young King Jappo. 'I can't wait!'

*

She took the steps two at a time, footfalls clattering in the echoing, flaking, mould-stained stairwell. She clutched the paper with
Horald's mark at the bottom as if it was a pass to a brave new
life – which indeed it was – smiling so wide her face hurt as she
wove pleasing fantasies of all the fine things that'd happen when
she burst through the door and Carcolf looked up.

'I'm done,' Shev would cry, breathless and appealingly tousled.

One of those golden brows would arch, just so. 'Done with
this job?'

'Done with all of them. Horald the Finger gave his word. I'm
out. I'm free.' She'd saunter over, their eyes never leaving each
other. '*We're* free.'

She thought of the happy lines around Carcolf's eyes when
she smiled, the creases at the corners of her mouth. The pattern
of them, each one scored into her memory like a prayer learned
by heart.

'We're free.'

Carcolf would plant her hands on her hips, her tongue in her
cheek, and beckon Shev over with a flick of her head, and they'd
fall into each other's arms, Shev's face full of that scent – loitering
on the edge of too sour but somehow all the better for it. God,
Shev could almost smell it now, tickling at her nose. Maybe they'd
tickle their noses with some pearl dust and dance together, Shev
leading even if she was half a head shorter, both laughing at the
melancholy sawing of that violinist playing for coppers in the
square outside.

Maybe there'd be a serious moment as they looked into each
other's eyes, and Shev would coax her out with just the right
soft words like you coax a nervous cat through a gap in a fence.
Carcolf would tell her stories of who she really was, and what she

really felt, and she'd let that smirking mask slip and give a glimpse of the beautiful, vulnerable secret self that Shev had always been sure was in there. Maybe she'd even whisper her first name. A special name, which only Shev would get to use. Didn't seem likely, but what's the point of likely fantasies?

Then they'd kiss, of course, nudging to begin with, nuzzling, nipping, feeling each other out like a pair of master swordsmen fencing. Then hungrily, messily, tongues and teeth, Shev tangling her fingers in Carcolf's hair and dragging her face down to hers. She was getting pleasantly warm in the trousers thinking about it. The kissing would lead to fumbling, and the fumbling would lead by a trail of shed clothes to the bed, and they'd stay in the bed until the room smelled of fucking, making up for all those wasted years, only getting up for a pinch more dust and maybe to make tea naked with Shev's very fine tea set, and in the morning…

Her eager hand froze halfway to the doorknob, smile slowly fading and the warmth in her trousers with it.

In the morning, the grey, early morning, while Shev was still sprawled snoozing in the sticky sheets, Carcolf would slip out, pulling the hood down over her smile, probably with Shev's very fine tea set in a bag over her shoulder – along with any other easily transported valuables – and vanish into the mists, never to be heard from again. Until she needed something.

Shev didn't much like to be honest with herself. Who does? But if she accepted the pain of it for a moment, that was how things had gone between them down the years. Carcolf had jumped into her arms often enough but just as quickly slipped through her fingers. Usually leaving Shev with a hell of a mess to run away from or, on one memorable occasion, swim away from as a medium-sized merchant vessel capsized behind her.

She swallowed as she frowned down at the doorknob.

This wasn't fantasies, it was life. And life had a habit of kicking her in the cunt.

But what were her choices? If you want to be a fine new person with a fine new life you've got to put the person you were behind you, like a snake sheds its skin. You've got to stop picking through your hoard of hurts and grievances like a miser through his coins, set 'em down and allow yourself to go free. You've got to forgive and you've got to trust, not because anyone else deserves it, but because you do.

So Shev took a deep breath, and forced a smile over her nerves, and shoved the door wide.

'I'm—'

Her place was a ruin.

The furniture was shattered and axe-hacked, the hangings torn-down and knife-slashed. The shelves had been tipped over, scattering the lovely books that Shev hadn't read but which made her look quite cultured. Lumps had been knocked from the marble fireplace with a hammer. Carolf had always insisted that painting of the smirking woman with the ample bosom she'd hung over it was an original Aropella. Shev had always harboured considerable doubts. It was a moot point now, though, as someone had slashed it to flapping shreds, bosom and all.

They hadn't just flipped the tea set over, they'd made sure every cup was individually broken, every spoon individually bent. Someone had smashed the spout and the handle off the pot and then, it appeared, pissed in it.

Shev's skin prickled with horror as she walked across the room, splinters crunching under her boots, and pushed back the gouged bedroom door.

Carolf lay slumped on the floor.

Shev gave a whooping gasp, dashing to her, dropping on her knees—

Just her clothes. Just her clothes dragged from her broken chest, tipped over on its side with the contents spilling out like the offal from a gutted corpse. The false bottom was smashed open, and the false bottom in the false bottom ripped out, forged documents scattered, fake jewels gleaming darkly in the shadows.

The room stank, but not of fucking. Carcolf's scent bottle had been shattered across the wall, the smell of her almost suffocating, a haunting insult to go with the injury of her absence. The fine mattress Shev had congratulated herself on being worth every stolen copper as she stretched out on it each night was slashed, stabbed, its feathery guts in heaps, flecks of down floating about the room as the breeze stirred the ripped hangings.

Perched on the slaughtered pillows, a sheet of paper. A letter.

Shev scrambled over and snatched it up in trembling fingers. It was written in a sharply slanted hand:

Shev
Been a long time.
Carcolf's with me, at Burroia's Fort on Carp Island. Better come quick, before I tire of her conversation. Better come alone, cause I get shy in crowds.
Just want a chat.
To begin with.
Horald

And then that mark. That same bloody idiot's mark she'd somehow tricked herself into thinking would protect her from all this.

She stood still for a long while. She did not speak, she did not move, she barely even breathed. The loss was like a blade through her guts. The loss of her lover, the loss of her place, the loss of the life of freedom and laughter that'd felt so close she could still almost taste it.

Her worst case had been Carcolf deciding she didn't want her. Carcolf feeling this was a trap shutting on her rather than a trap finally springing open for both of them. Carcolf running away again. She should've known.

There's always a worse case than your worst case, and more often than not, it happens.

She realised she'd clenched her fingers, crushing the worthless document she'd risked her life for in her fist. She flung it into the ash-scattered fireplace and set her jaw aching tight.

None of it was lost. It was stolen. And Horald the Finger should've known better than to steal from the best thief in Styria.

She stalked to the wall beside the chimney breast, picked up the broken bust of Bayaz, hefted it high, and with a shriek smashed his bald head into the plaster.

The wall folded in like cheap board – which indeed it was – leaving a ragged hole. She knocked a few splinters away with Bayaz's nose, then reached inside, grabbed the rope and dragged it out. Her black bag was on the end, reassuringly weighty, metal clattering as she tossed it down.

Everything she really needed was in that bag. In case she had to run. But Shev had been running half her life, and she was done.

Some things are only ever going to end one way.

It was time to fight.

Oh, yes, Shevedieh had moved among the lost and the fallen.

She'd cut purses in the cheapest brothels of Sipani, anthills of vice where the marsh the city was built on endlessly oozed back into the cellars, where no word for innocence was known, let alone spoken. She'd clawed a living among the beggars in Ul-Khatif, and among the beggars who stole from the beggars, and conned the beggars, and even the ones who begged from beggars more fortunate than they. She'd burrowed out temporary homes in the thieves' pits, gambling pits and charnel pits in Nicante, in Puranti, in Affoia, in Musselia, and always left with a heavier purse than she'd arrived with. She'd bribed corrupt scum on behalf of corrupt scum on the rotting docks of Visserine, when Nicomo Cosca had seized the grand dukedom of the city and there'd been less law than no law. She'd turned out dead men's pockets with the bonepickers in war-torn Darmium, in plague-riddled Calcis, in famine-ravaged Daleppa, in fire-swept Dagoska. She'd felt so much at home among the low-rent Smoke Houses of Westport, where the weak came to forget their weakness, that her highest ambition had been to open one herself.

Oh, yes, Shevedieh had moved among the lost and the fallen, but she wasn't sure she'd ever borne witness to so base a place as when she stepped through the decaying portal of the Duke's Repose in Talins.

'Did he repose of the pox?' she croaked, clapping a hand over her mouth.

It was the stench of bodies unwashed for centuries, or perhaps washed daily but in shit and vinegar. As Shev's eyes gradually adjusted to the hellish gloom, she saw cursed figures of in-determinate race or gender sprawled punch-drunk, blood-drunk, sorrow-drunk, and simply drunk. Folk tortured each other. Folk tortured themselves. Folk dragged their way towards the release of death with both hands. One lay in their own sick, blowing bubbles with every wet snore while a little dog, or perhaps a large rat, lapped hungrily at the far edge of the puddle. The sound which Shev had assumed was a long drink being poured was in fact a man with trousers around ankles, pissing, apparently endlessly, into a filthy tin bucket while he picked his crooked nose with a crooked finger. In a shadowy corner, two, or perhaps three, others grunted softly under a regularly shifting coat. Shev hoped they were doing nothing worse than fucking, but she would not have liked to bet on it.

It was a long time since she'd entertained high hopes for humanity, but had they still stood intact, they would have crumbled in that instant.

'God has abandoned us,' she whispered, narrowing her eyes in the vain hope she might prevent the unholy sights imprinting themselves for ever on her vision.

The prize exhibit in this museum of filth, the chief mourner at this funeral of all that was decent, the High Priestess of this final shrine on a lifelong pilgrimage of self-pity, self-neglect and self-destruction, was none other than Shev's long-standing best friend and worst enemy: Javre, Lioness of Hoskopp.

She sat at a rickety table infested with empty jugs, half-full bottles, slimy cups and greasy glasses, with coins and counters and overflowing ash-bowls, with several chagga and at least one husk pipe, creased and filthied cards scattered like demented confetti. Opposite her sprawled three Union soldiers, one with a beard and a scar, one with a face almost as trustworthy as the vomit-supping rat's, and one with his head tipped far, far over the back of his chair, mouth wide open, knobble on his skinny neck standing out painfully sharp and shifting gently as he snored.

Javre's red hair was a snarled-up tangle, matted with ash, with slime, with food, with things that could not be identified. That should not be identified, lest they offend God to the extent that he felt obliged to end creation. By the look of things she had been fighting in the pit again. Her knuckles flapped with bloodstained bandages, her bare shoulder – for the indescribably stained shirt she wore had lost a sleeve somewhere – was grazed and scabbed, the side of her face smeared with bruises.

Shev hardly knew how she felt to see her. Relieved that she hadn't left the city. Guilty at the state she'd made of herself. Ashamed to be asking for her help. Angry at she hardly knew what any more. A slow accumulation of years of hurts and frustrations, little things added up day after day to a burden she could not stand to carry. But, as always, she had no other choices. She peeled the hand from her mouth and padded over.

Javre stank. Even worse than she had the first time they met, in the door of Shev's Smoke House. Not long before it burned down, along with her past life. Shev wouldn't see another life burned down. She couldn't see it.

'You stink, Javre,' she said.

Javre didn't bother to look around. However carefully you crept up on her, somehow she always knew who was there. 'Have not washed lately.'

Her words came slurred and Shev's heart sank. It took days of drinking for Javre to show the slightest sign of being drunk. By then she was colossally, toweringly, heroically drunk. There was nothing Javre did by halves.

'I have been entirely busy drinking, fucking and fighting.' She cleared her throat, turned her head and spat noisily and bloodily at Shev's feet, half of it dangling from her split lip and soaking into her shirt as she turned back to the game. 'I have been drunk for . . .' She raised a bandaged hand, squinting as she clumsily stuck the fingers up one by one. When she stuck the thumb up, her cards fluttered to the floor. Javre frowned at them. 'I cannot even count any more.' She started to fish them clumsily up between scabbed fingers, one by one. 'Drinking, fucking, fighting and losing at cards. Days since I won a hand.' She burped. Even from this distance, Shev shuddered at the smell of it. 'Weeks. I hardly know which side up the cards go.'

'Javre, I need to talk to you—'

'Let me introduce you!' Javre swept a loose arm at the Union soldiers and very nearly took the sleeping man's head off with a backhand. 'This little beauty is my good old friend Shevedieh! Used to be a henchman of mine.'

'Javre.'

'Sidekick, then. Whatever. We travelled half the Circle of the World together! All kinds of adventures.'

'Javre.'

'Disasters, then. Whatever. These shits are among the finest soldiers of His August Majesty the High King of the Union. The beardy bastard is Lieutenant Forest.' He nodded to Shev with a good-natured grin. 'This stringy one is Lance Corporal Yolk.' The sleeping man stirred faintly, tongue moving against his cracked lips with vague squelching sounds. 'And this lucky fucker—'

'Skilful fucker,' grunted the ratty man around a chagga pipe gripped in his yellowed teeth.

'Is Sergeant Tunny.'

'Corporal,' he said, peering through his haze of smoke at the cards.

'Got himself demoted again,' said Forest. 'Over a goose and a whore, would you believe.'

'She was worth it,' said Tunny. 'And the whore wasn't bad, either. Fire, by the way.' And he laid his cards down with a snap.

'Tits of the Mother!' snarled Javre. 'Again?'

'There's a certain spot ...' muttered Tunny, pipe waggling between his teeth, 'between too drunk and not drunk enough ...' as he scooped up scattered winnings in a dozen different currencies, 'where I'm a hell of a card player. The trick, as with so much in life, is keeping the balance *just* right.'

'Luck,' mused Javre as she watched him gather the harvest through narrowed, red-rimmed, absurdly bloodshot eyes, 'has always been the one thing missing from my life.'

'Javre—'

'Let me guess!' Bandages trailed through spilled beer as she flung up a hand. 'You are dunked to your scrawny neck in some species of shit and have run straight back to me to fetch the shovel.'

Shevedieh opened her mouth to make an elaborate retort, thought a moment, and decided against. 'Basically, yes. Horald's taken Carcolf. Now he wants me out on Carp Island.' She forced the words through clenched teeth. 'I could really use your help—'

Javre gave a snort so explosive snot spattered down her chapped top lip. She did not appear to notice. 'See, boys? You give them everything!' And she beat her chest with a fist so hard it left a great pink mark. 'You give them your heart and they spit it in your face!'

'How can you spit a heart?' asked Shev, but Javre was not interested in unmixing her metaphors.

'The moment they get in trouble, oh, the fucking moment? Straight back to Mummy!' She glared unsteadily at Shev. 'Well, Mummy is fucking busy!'

'Mummy is fucking embarrassing herself.'

'That is Mummy's *fucking* prerogative. Shuffle those cards, Tunny, you cunny.' He did no more than raise a brow as he set to shuffling. 'I thought you were all done with me and had fine new friends. What of the grand duchess, the Snake of Talins, the Butcher of Caprile? Mother to a king, I hear.'

'Bless his eternal Majesty,' grunted Tunny out of the corner of his mouth, flicking cards to each of the four players, conscious and otherwise.

'I only met the woman twice,' said Shev. 'I doubt she knows my name.'

'But her all-powerful Minister of Whispers, Shylo Vitari, surely does. Can she not reach from the shadows and pluck your lover from danger?'

'She's on her way south to Sipani.'

'What of your grinning merchant friend, Majud? He has deep pockets.'

'It's getting him to reach into them that's the problem.'

'That Northman you were working with, then? The one with the eye. Or... without it.' Javre accidentally poked herself while waving at her face with her cards, had to clap a hand over her running eye, but at least she accidentally wiped the snot from her lip, too. 'Trembles?'

'Shivers.' Shev gave a little shiver of her own at the memory of that scarred face, the expression on it as he killed those three Sipanese who'd been chasing her. Or the terrible lack of expression. 'Some help it's better to do without,' she muttered.

'You can do without mine, then.' Javre raised the glass towards her mouth in a wobbly hand, face fixed in concentration. Shev slapped it from her fingers and it shattered in the corner.

'I need you sober.'

Javre gave a snort. 'That is never going to happen, Shevedieh. If I get my way, that is never going to happen again.'

'Here,' said Tunny, holding out his own glass, 'have mine—'

Shev slapped it from his hand and it shattered in almost exactly the same spot as the last one. He frowned, slowly removing the pipe from his mouth for the first time. 'Bloody hell, girl, I wish you wouldn't—'

Javre shoved her fist under his nose, cards crushed in it, red eyes bulging, lips curling back and spraying spit. 'Talk to my friend like that again, you fucking cocksucker, you will be picking your teeth from my knuckles!'

Tunny peered down at that great, scarred hand, one of his eyebrows going up, ever so slowly. 'Madam, I'm a soldier. The last thing I want is a fight.'

Forest cleared his wet throat and somewhat unsteadily rose. 'Ladies, with great respect, I think that puts an end to the evening. We've an early start tomorrow. Back to Midderland after our defeat, you know.' He jabbed Yolk with his elbow and the little man started awake.

'I raise!' he shouted, staring wildly about. 'I raise!' Then he flopped from his chair onto hands and knees and was sick on the floor.

Tunny was already sweeping his winnings into a battered hat. Forest caught Yolk by the belt and began to drag him away, still desperately trying to raise.

'An honour,' said Tunny as he backed towards the door through the pool of puke, almost falling over the snoring figure. 'An absolute fucking *honour*.'

'I will see you on the battlefield!' shouted Javre.

Tunny winced and waved one finger round and round. 'Let's say nearby!' And he was gone into the smoky murk.

'You have spoiled my fun, Shevedieh, as always.' Javre uncurled her fingers. A couple of the ruined cards dropped out. A couple of others were stuck to her palm and she had to shake them off. 'I trust you are bloody well pleased with yourself.'

'You've spoiled your own fun, as always, and I'm about as far from pleased as it's possible to be, since you ask.' She slid into Yolk's chair. 'No one else is going to help me, Javre. They don't trust Carcolf. They don't want Horald to kill them.'

Javre gave another snort and had to wipe more snot from under her scabbed nose with her scabbed knuckles. 'On the Great Leveller I am ambivalent, as you know, but if you think I trust that wiggling snake any more than the plague—'

'I don't think we're ever going to see eye to eye on her, do you?'

'It is hard to see eye to eye with someone a foot shorter than you. She looks like a snake, moves like a snake, thinks like a snake. She saw you coming, Shevedieh, just like she always does, and she thought *dinner*. In spite of all the wrongs she has made you lick up down the years, she only had to swagger that round arse past you once and you were hooked all over again. She sank that ship with you on it, lest we forget!'

'It's different this time,' muttered Shev, not sure whether the words hurt so much because they were false, or because they were true.

'It is never different. Nothing ever is. How can a woman as clever as you not see it?'

'I *do* fucking see it!' screamed Shev, thumping the table and making the bottles rattle. 'But I don't care any more! I have to make the best of it. I have to have ... *something*, before it's too late!' She felt tears stinging her eyes, her voice going high and warbly, but she couldn't stop it. 'I can't run any more, Javre! I can't run. I'm tired, and I need your help. Please. Help me.'

Javre stared at her for a long moment. Then she jerked up,

barging the table over and sending its cargo of glasses, pots, bottles, pipes scattering, shattering, clattering across the filthy floor.

'Cunt of the Goddess, Shevedieh, you know you only had to ask!' She stabbed Shev painfully in the tit with one inept finger. 'My sword is yours, always!' Her brow knitted with puzzlement, then she stared wildly around. 'Where *is* my sword?'

Shev sighed and nudged it from under Javre's chair with the toe of her boot.

It was dark, down on this quietest part of the docks. The sea flapped and slopped at the mossy stones of the quay, and the warped supports of the wharves, and the slimy flanks of the moored boats. The reflections of the few lamps, torches and candles that still burned danced and broke in the restless water.

A gust of wind fluttered the ragged papers on the warehouse wall. Bills celebrating young King Jappo's coronation pasted over bills celebrating the victory at Sweet Pines pasted over bills condemning Union aggression pasted over bills revelling in the ascension of Monzcarro Murcatto pasted over bills announcing the death of Monzcarro Murcatto pasted over bills trumpeting victories and defeats of enemies and rulers long forgotten. Probably it was only the ancient crust of bills that kept the warehouse standing.

Shev frowned out across the bay. In the distance she could just see a few faint points of light, flickering ghostly.

'Carp Island,' muttered Javre, planting a hand on her hip and nearly missing, she was that drunk.

Shev puffed out her cheeks. 'And on Carp Island, Burroia's Fort.'

'And in Burroia's Fort, Horald the Finger.'

'And with Horald the Finger...' Shev trailed off. God, she hoped Carcolf was still alive.

'Once we are there,' murmured Javre, leaning close enough that Shev almost gagged on the boozy reek of her breath, 'what's your plan?'

She wished she had time to get Javre sober. Or at least clean. But she did not. 'Rescue Carcolf. Kill Horald. Don't get killed ourselves.'

A pause, while Javre pushed the greasy hair out of her face then flicked something that had been stuck in it off her fingers. 'I think you will agree that it is lacking detail.'

Shev took a glance up and down the quay. The thief's glance, which looks without seeming to look. 'You never complained about charging into the jaws of death before. Without plans, without weapons... without clothes, on more than one occasion.'

'On clothes I am ambivalent, as you know, but I have *always* hated plans.'

'Then why are you worried now?'

'Because I always knew *you* would have one.'

'Welcome to my life of constant doubt, anxiety and occasional sudden and unpredictable horror, Javre. I hope you enjoy your *fucking* visit.' And she walked across the empty quay and down the steps to the nearest wharf. The thief's walk, neither striding boldly nor scurrying crouched. The walk of someone forgettable going about their boring business. A walk that raises no eyebrows and no alarms.

A good thief goes unseen. A truly great one merely goes unnoticed.

She stopped by a boat that suited, checked the oars were in the bottom, then winced at a loud clatter, turned to see that Javre had stumbled into a set of fishing nets on a frame and was now tangled with them, desperately trying to stop them falling. She finally got them settled, shrugged at Shev, then strode down the wharf towards her, about the most conspicuous woman who ever drew breath.

'Could you be any louder?' hissed Shev.

'Undoubtedly,' said Javre, turning back towards the nets. 'Shall I demonstrate?'

'No, no, that's fine!' With some effort Shev steered her towards the boat, unshouldered her bag and tossed it in, then followed it silently across the flapping water.

'You will simply steal it?'

'The one upside of being a thief,' Shev muttered through tight lips, 'is that you can make free with things that don't belong to you. It's practically a requirement of the job.'

'I understand the principle, but this is some poor bastard's livelihood. Some family of righteous, honourable, hardworking bastards, maybe. There might be a dozen little weeping children depending on it.'

'Better to rob the righteous,' muttered Shev as she slipped the oars silently through the rowlocks. 'Evil people tend to be suspicious and vengeful.'

Javre made her voice go piping high. 'Oh, Daddy, whatever shall the twelve of us eat now that the boat is gone?'

'For God's sake, Javre, do I tell you how to start fights, suck cocks, destroy my property or ruin my life? No! I trust to your unchallengeable fucking expertise! Now let me steal the boat I judge appropriate! We can bring it back when we're done!'

'When do we ever do that? At the very least we bring it back smashed.'

'*You* bring it back smashed!'

Javre snorted. 'You remember that cart we borrowed in—'

'Might I remind you we have something of a demanding schedule?' Shev pressed her fingers to her temples and gave a growl of frustration. 'All the bloody arguing over every little bloody thing, it's exhausting!' She stabbed at the rower's seat with a finger. 'Just get in the fucking boat!'

'Could you be any louder?' Javre grumbled as she tossed the mooring rope in, followed it with the ragged bundle that contained her sword and clambered unsteadily after, the whole thing rocking alarmingly under her considerable weight. 'You are the one always telling me I should give more thought to consequences,'

'The consequence that's preying on my mind is the love of my life with her fucking throat cut!'

Javre blinked as she dropped heavily between the oars. 'Love of your life?'

'Well, I mean . . .' Shev hadn't meant to say that. Hadn't meant to admit it, even to herself. 'You know what I mean! Exaggerating, for effect.'

'I have heard you exaggerate a hundred million times, Shev-edieh. I know how it sounds. That was the much rarer sound of you letting slip the truth.'

'Shut up and row,' grumbled Shev as she shoved the boat away from the slimy wharf.

Javre leaned to the oars, great muscles in her bare arms twitching and bulging with each stroke, the boat sliding smoothly out onto the calm, dark waters of the harbour. Shev undid the buckles on her bag and unrolled it, metal rattling.

Javre whistled softly as she peered down at all those gleaming tools. 'Going to war?'

'If need be.' Shev buckled the sword-eater onto her thigh. 'A wise man once told me you can never have too many knives.'

'Sure you'll be able to climb with all that weight of steel?'

'We're not all built like bulls.' Shev slid the throwing blades one by one into the strapping inside her coat. 'Some of us need an edge.'

'Be careful the edge does not cut your head off, Shevedieh.' She watched as, ever so gently, Shev slid a little vial of green liquid from her bag and into the fleece-lined loop on her belt. 'Is that what I think it is?'

'Depends what you think it is.'

'I think it is as likely to blow she who throws it to hell as to blow those it's thrown at to heaven.'

'Fancy that, you're not the only one who can go down in a fireball.'

'You are more or less the only friend I have not been obliged to kill. I am concerned for your welfare.'

'If you're such a good friend you could try being happy for me.'

'Happy to see you strung along by that golden-haired siren?'

'Happy that I've found some little respite from the endless tide of *shit* my life has been!' Shev winced, trying to find some position where her blowpipe wasn't jabbing her in the armpit. 'Did I complain when you were noisily enjoying your frequent dalliances?'

'Did you complain?' Javre snorted. 'You, the baroness of bitching? The countess of carping? The princess of prating? The ... er ... the grand duchess of ... of ...'

'I get the idea,' snapped Shev, checking the trigger of her crossbow before she slid it into the holster under her coat.

'Good, because apparently your memory is almost as short as you are. Complain, Shevedieh? You made my life a misery day in and day out for the past ...' Javre frowned up at the starry sky, moonlit lips moving as she counted. 'Thirteen ... no fourteen!'

She gave a long pause before her bleary eyes settled on Shev, then added in a weary drawl, '*Fourteen fucking years.*'

'Fourteen years,' muttered Shev. 'Half my life, near as damn it.' And she felt the back of her nose aching with the need to cry. For all those years wasted. For the ruin of their friendship, which for so long had been all she had. For the fact that it had still been there when she needed it. For the fact that it was still all she had.

Javre puffed out her scarred cheeks. 'Small wonder we are ... somewhat wearied.'

The blades of the oars feathered the water, trails of sparkling drops falling from their ends, then cut silently into the surface. The rowlocks creaked. The wind picked up and stirred Javre's dirty hair.

'I am happy for you,' she said, softly. 'I try to be, anyway.'

'Well, I'm happy you're happy.'

'Good.'

'Good.'

Another slow silence. 'I am just sad for myself.'

Shev looked up, caught Javre's eye. A wet gleam in the darkness. 'I'm sorry you're sad,' she said.

'Good.'

'Good.'

'Shit,' mouthed Shev as she scrabbled about in the dark for a reliable toehold on that crumbling wall. Burroia's damn fort was falling apart. But then it was a ruin. Bit like Shev's hopes in that regard. 'Bloody, bloody *shit*.'

Javre might've had a point about all the hardware. It was a hell of a weight for someone who'd built their reputation on a light tread. There were a couple of buckles she'd dragged too tight now threatening to cut off the blood to her legs, and a couple she hadn't dragged tight enough, loose metal clinking and the garrotte knocking distractingly against her arse crack every time she pulled herself up.

What was she doing with a damn garrotte anyway? She'd never used a garrotte in her life, except once to cut a cheese and that was for a joke and hadn't even ended up that funny. You can make an argument for a knife. Sometimes people just need a knifing. Like Crandall had. She shed no tears for him. But once you start garrotting people you can't claim to stand with the righteous.

Garrottes simply are not part of God's chosen path and although, through a combination of personal weakness, evil acquaintance and plain bad luck, Shev had to admit her feet had often left the chosen path behind, she liked to imagine she could at least still see it, in the distance, if she squinted.

She froze at a noise above, the latest of a volley of curses stopped cold on her lips.

Footsteps scraping. The tuneless humming of a person deeply bored and with no musical aptitude. Shev's eyes went wide. A guard, on patrol. She wondered what the chances were of his not noticing the grapple wedged against the parapet. Not good, was her guess. She clung tight to the rope with one hand, jerked a dart out with the other and shoved it between her teeth.

It would've been the perfect end to her career of misadventures if she'd pricked herself in the cheek, lost consciousness and dropped off the rope into the sea. But Shev was blessed with a nimble tongue. Probably that was what Carcolf saw in her. God knows, there had to be something.

The humming stopped. Footsteps scuffed closer. She snatched out her blowpipe, raising it to her lips. Sadly, at that moment, her fingers were less nimble than her mouth. The blowpipe caught on a jutting stone, she fumbled it, juggled it desperately, almost let go of the rope in her confusion, then gave a despairing gasp of, 'Thuck!' around the dart in her teeth as she watched it tumble away.

Javre caught it, then peered up, puzzled. 'What is this?' she hissed.

Shev looked back to the parapet, helpless panic settling on her like snow on a sleeping tramp. A face suddenly appeared. The face of a big man with curly hair. His thick brows went sharply up when he saw her clinging to the rope with her feet against the wall, close enough to reach out and touch.

Her first bizarre instinct was to give him a hopeful smile, but with the dart between her teeth it was impossible.

'Bloody hell,' he said, and leaned out, lifting a spear.

Lucky that Shev had always been a quick thinker in a tight spot. Years of practice, maybe. She jerked herself up as if over-powered by a desire to kiss him and stuck him in the neck with the dart.

'Bloody hell,' he said again, but less angry this time, and more surprised. He tried to stab her but she was too close, his elbow caught on the battlements and the spear slid from his slack grip, dropping over Shev's shoulder.

Fast-acting, that toxin. He flopped limp over the parapet with a sigh and Shev grabbed his belt and dragged herself up by it, rolling silently across his back and onto the walkway.

With rare good fortune, she found it empty. A stretch of stone maybe two strides wide, crumbling battlements to either side, a door leading into an ivy-throttled turret at the far end, faint torchlight showing around its edge. More lights twinkled further off in the windows of the old fortress. The place might be a ruin, but it was evidently far from abandoned.

She leaned over the slumbering guard to hiss at Javre. 'Planning to fucking join me?'

The Lioness of Hoskopp was still fumbling drunkenly with the rope, her boots scuffing the wall no more than a stride above the boat. 'Yes I am fucking planning on it!' she hissed back.

Shev shook her head and padded on towards the door, allowing herself the slightest smile. Considering the mess with the blowpipe, that really couldn't have gone much—

She frowned as she heard faint laughter, then the door flew open and a man walked out, holding a lamp high and chuckling over his shoulder to another. There were more behind them. At least two more. 'We'll finish that hand when Big Lom gets back and I'll—' His head turned and he saw her frozen with her mouth an apologetic O of surprise. He had a bent nose and absurd hair cut in a straight line across his forehead.

'Horald told us to expect you.' And he grinned as he drew his sword.

Shev had always hated fighting. She'd hidden from it, talked her way free of it, bought her way out of it. She'd dodged it, she'd ducked it and, with shameful frequency, she'd watched Javre do it for her.

But Horald the Finger had pushed her over the line, and she would be pushed no further.

She whipped out the little crossbow and levelled it. The eyes of Horald's bent-nosed man went wide.

'He tell you to expect this?' she asked, and squeezed the trigger.

The string snapped with a ping and the bolt went twittering end-over-end sideways and was lost in the darkness above the water, leaving them staring at one another, all somewhat surprised.

'Huh.' Bent Nose cleared his throat. 'I'm thinking—'

If she'd learned one thing from Javre, it was that when it came to fighting, the less thinking the better. She flung the crossbow at his head and it hit him just above the eye. He gasped, stumbling back into the man behind him, his lamp dropping to the stones and spraying burning oil across the walkway.

'Shit!' another shouted, slapping at the flames that had suddenly sprung up his trouser leg.

Shev charged, popping the thong from the hilt of her sword-eater as Bent Nose righted himself, whipping it from the sheath as his hard eyes focused on her, jerking it up just as he flailed his sword down. Steel squealed as blade slid into serrated jaws and she snarled, twisting her wrist. Bent Nose's outraged bellow turned to a squawk of shock as his sword snapped just above the hilt and left him staggering forwards. He did not have to stagger far, however, before Shev's fist thudded into his gut and doubled him up, wheezing. She clubbed him on the back of the head with the pommel of the sword-eater so hard it went flying out of her hand and skittered down the walkway.

She saw a heavy mace swinging at her, ducked it on an instinct, the wind of it tearing at her hair, spun away as it whipped past and crashed into the parapet, kept spinning, giving a scream, lifting her leg in a raking kick. Her heel could not have connected more sweetly with the fat man's head if they'd rehearsed the whole thing. It snatched him off his feet, blood and teeth spraying spectacularly from his face, turned him over in the air and sent him tumbling from the walkway, a satisfying series of crashes below strongly suggesting that he had fallen onto, then through, the fragile roof of a lean-to in the yard.

A flash of metal and Shev jerked back. A skinny man with a birthmark around one eye stabbed at her and she dodged again. He was wearing a ridiculous swashbuckler's three-cornered hat, no doubt reckoning himself quite the master swordsman now he'd slapped out the flames on his leg. Shev thought it always wise to play to the pretensions of an opponent, so as he brought his sword whistling over she shrank into a crouch, the helpless victim, thrusting her fist into a pouch at her belt, lifting her other arm despairingly as if to block the blow. She saw his rotten teeth as he smiled, sure the blade would strike her hand straight off. It was most satisfying to see him grimace as it clanged instead against the steel rods under her sleeve and scraped clear. She stepped past him as he lurched off balance, ripped her fist free, opened her palm and blew the dust in his face.

He squealed, reeling about, swatting blindly with sword and knife, trampling through the still-burning oil and setting his trousers on fire again. She ducked under his whistling blades, slipped silently behind him, grabbed the back of his coat as he spun around and gently but firmly assisted him over the parapet. A moment later, Shev heard the sweet sound of him hitting water.

Not much time to celebrate, though, as Shev was already wrestling with the last of the four. A little fellow, he was, but slippery as a fish and she was tired now, slow. An elbow in the gut brought vomit to the back of her throat, then a fist above the eye only half-blocked snapped her head back and made her ears ring. He forced her against the parapet. She fumbled for a gas bomb but her straining fingers couldn't quite get there. Tried to reach her poisoned needle but he caught her wrist first. She growled through gritted teeth as he bent her back, crumbling stones grinding into her shoulders.

'Quiet, now,' he hissed, forcing her wrist around. His thumb must have caught the mechanism by accident. The spring twanged, the knife shot out of her sleeve and jabbed him in the throat. He retched, she butted him in the face, then as his head snapped back twisted her hips and kneed him full in the fruits.

He gave a breathy gasp, tried to clutch at her, but she slid around him, caught his hair and mashed his face into the battlements, loosing a shower of crumbled mortar and leaving him floppy as new washing. She jerked out the first thing her free hand closed around.

The garrotte.

God, but no one had ever been in a better position for a garrotting. Easiest thing in the world to jerk the wire across his throat, screw her knee into his back and garrotte the merry hell out of him. Probably he deserved it. Wasn't as if he'd been taking much pity on her until the knife went off in his face.

But you do right for your own sake. Shev just wasn't a garrotting sort of girl.

'God damn it,' she grunted, clubbing him across the back of the head with the handles and knocking him senseless, then tossing the garrotte over the wall into the sea.

'What the—'

A great, slow, grinding voice, and Shev turned. A man had ducked out onto the walkway from a door at the other end. He had been obliged to duck because he stood considerably taller than the lintel. The Big Lom mentioned earlier, she guessed, and the name had evidently been bestowed without irony. They hadn't struck her as a particularly ironic crowd, in truth. His head was immense, with a tiny prim little mouth, hard little eyes, a pimple of a nose all lost in the trackless, doughy expanse of his face. A shield the size of a tabletop was strapped to one trunk of an arm, and as his diminutive features crept together first in puzzlement, then anger, he jerked an enormous hammer from his belt as if it were a child's toy.

'Ha!' Shev whipped her coat open, throwing knives jingling

in a gleaming line. Fast as a woodpecker strikes she sent them spinning down the walkway, her hand a blur.

Her accuracy, it had to be admitted, was less impressive than her speed. Several missed entirely, clattering from the walls or twittering off into the night. Three others thudded into Big Lom's shield and a fourth hit his shoulder handle-first and dropped off.

'Huh,' he grunted, peering over the rim with angry little eyes. 'That your best?'

'No,' said Shev. 'That is.' And she pointed towards the one knife that had found its mark, lodged in his thigh just below the hem of his studded jacket.

He snorted as he plucked it out and tossed it away, a few specks of blood along with it. 'If you think that'll stop me you're even sillier'n Horald said.'

'The knife? No.'

Lom roared as he charged, shield up ahead of him like the end of a battering ram. Shev merely planted her hands on her hips and raised her brows. Halfway down the walkway, his great steps went a little unsteady. Above his shield, his hard eyes went a little crossed, then a little wide, and his furious roar turned to a hurt bellow and finally a brainless gurgle.

He was tottering towards her like a drunkard now, carried forward only by his considerable momentum, shield wobbling sideways, the great hammer dropping from his nerveless hand and bouncing into the yard below.

Shev nudged the door to the guardroom open and politely stood aside, pausing only to stick one delicately upturned foot into Lom's path.

He blundered past, eyes already rolling back in his huge head. She hooked one of his great boots with hers and he tripped, slobbered, drool dangling from his clumsy lips. He bounced from the doorframe, spun wildly, knees drunkenly knocking, arms flung wide, then one foot caught the other and he crashed straight through the midst of a set of chairs and tables sending plates, pots and half-eaten dinner flying. He lay in the wreckage, face in a puddle of spilled stew, breath slurping, about as unconscious as it was possible to be.

'But the poison's another matter,' said Shev, feeling intensely pleased with herself. Hannakar had told her that toxin could knock out an elephant, and for once he hadn't exaggerated, apparently.

'Ha!' came a shout from behind and Shev spun about, rolled neatly, grabbing the sword-eater as she came up in a ready crouch.

It was Javre, dragging herself over the still-slumbering guard on the parapet, catching her foot on his head, tripping, stumbling up bleary-eyed and breathing hard, rag-wrapped sword clutched in one hand.

'Huh.' She stared at the crumpled bodies and slowly straightened. 'What did you need me for?'

'Someone had to row me out here.' Shev slid her sword-eater back into the sheath, stepping over Big Lom's slumbering form and towards the steps. 'Let's go.'

'Here!' hissed Shev, leaning close to the door and beckoning Javre up behind her.

Voices burbled on the far side, suddenly clear as she pressed her ear to the lock.

'She won't come for me. You're wasting your time!'

'Oh, I've got time.'

The voice might've been soft, cheerful, even, but it sent the chills prickling down Shev's sweaty back regardless. The voice of a man who'd order a family murdered as easily as wiping his arse. A man ruthless as the plague and with a conscience no bigger than a speck of salt. The voice of Horald the Finger.

'Don't underestimate your charms, Carcolf. Shev will be along, I'm sure of it, and her friend, too. In the meantime, here, have some more!'

'No!'

Harsh, ugly laughter, and a clinking that sounded like chains. 'You'll take some more if I say you'll take some more!'

'No!' Carcolf's voice, gone shrill now, agonised. 'No more, you evil bastard! No more, please!'

Shev raised her boot and kicked the door open with a scream. It flew back, almost as if it wasn't locked at all, bounced from the wall beyond and gave her a jarring blow in the shoulder as she dived through, spinning her around and almost knocking the sword-eater from her hand. She struggled to keep her balance while giving a war cry that ended up more than half a howl of pain and—

She tottered to an uncertain stop in the middle of a ruined courtyard, its crumbling walls coated with dead creeper.

Carcolf sat in a chair. Horald the Finger leaned over her.

But the terrifying scourge of Styria's underworld held no hideous instrument of torture. Only a bottle of wine, tipped as if to pour. His smile, far from being a twisted murderer's leer, was good-natured and fatherly. Carcolf, meanwhile, sat apparently unmolested and unrestrained, her usual sleek and beautiful self, legs calmly crossed with one pointed boot swinging comfortably back and forth, holding her hand over a glass.

As if to say *no more*.

'See?' Horald positively beamed as he threw up his free hand in delight. 'She *did* come!'

Carcolf sprang up. She walked to Shev, their eyes never leaving each other. That walk she had, that Shev couldn't look away from, even now. Shock, anger, fear, all swept aside by a heady wave of relief so strong her knees almost buckled from it.

'You're hurt.' Carcolf winced as she pressed Shev's cut eyebrow with her thumb. 'Are you all right?'

'Ow! About as good as you could hope for, considering I just fought five thugs!'

'Don't worry about it.' Horald shrugged as he sat, charging his own glass. He was a good deal older than when Shev last saw him, of course, but a good deal more prosperous-looking, too. You could have taken him for a well-heeled merchant if it wasn't for the tattoos on his neck, the scars on his knuckles and a certain flinty hardness about the eyes. 'If I've discovered one thing during my career, it's that there are always more thugs.'

'You came for me.' If Shev hadn't known better she might've fancied there was a little torchlit shimmer at the corners of Carcolf's eyes.

Shev snapped out the letter and flung it at Horald, and it fluttered to the worn flagstones between them. 'I was rather under the impression you were about to be *murdered if I didn't*.'

'I must admit,' and Javre nudged the door open and stepped through, 'that was my understanding, too.'

Carcolf nervously cleared her throat, edging slightly closer to Shev. 'Javre.'

Javre narrowed her eyes. 'Carcolf. Horald.'

'Javre!' He grinned as he raised his glass. 'The Lioness of Hoskopp, who walks where she pleases! Now we've got a party.'

'Party?' snapped Shev, shaking her sword-eater at him. 'I should bloody kill you!' It was hard to maintain her fury with Carcolf standing uninjured beside her, still smelling as wonderfully sharp and sweet as ever, but she took her best stab at it. 'You gave your word, Horald!'

'Imagine that,' said Javre as she took a cautious circuit of the yard, kicking loose stones out of her way. 'Styria's most infamous criminal mastermind being untrustworthy.'

'Now hold on just a moment,' said Horald, all offended innocence. 'I haven't broken my word in thirty years and I'm not about to start. I said neither you nor your associates would be harmed and neither you nor your associates have been. As you can see, Carcolf is in fine, if not to say superb, fettle. I'd never hurt her. Not after she saved my life that time in Affoia.'

'Saved your . . .' Shev stared at Carcolf. 'You never told me about that.'

'What kind of a mysterious beauty would I be without any mysteries?' Carcolf tipped Shev's head back and started dabbing the blood from her cut head with a handkerchief. 'It was nothing heroic. Just the right word in the right ear.'

'Right words in right ears change the world! They're the only things that can.' Horald held up the bottle. 'You're sure you won't have some more?'

Carcolf sighed. 'Oh, go on then, you evil bastard!'

'You killed my place!' snapped Shev.

'Your place?' Horald shook his head as he poured. 'Come now, Shevedieh, it's just things. You can always get new ones. Had to make it look good, didn't I? I mean, you'd hardly have come if I just asked. And there was nothing in that paper about tea sets.' He twisted the bottle to let the drips fall just the way an Osprian cellar-master might've. 'I made sure of it. Checked the wording.'

'You and your bloody wording,' muttered Shev.

'It pains me to say it,' said Horald, 'but my son Crandall was a nasty fucking idiot. Had my doubts over his parentage, if I'm honest. Want a glass of wine, Shev? It's the good stuff. Osprian. Older than you are.'

Shev felt like she was drunk already. Waved it away.

'I will take one,' said Javre, plucking the bottle from Horald's hand and peering down at him as she upended it in her bandaged fist, thick throat shifting as she swallowed, a little running down her neck and into her filthy collar.

'By all means,' he said, holding up his palms in a peaceable gesture. 'Look, I've no doubt it all happened the way Carcolf always said. You defending yourself against some undeserved meanness on Crandall's part.'

'The way you always said?' muttered Shev, peering sideways at Carcolf.

'I've been pleading your case for years.' And, evidently satisfied with her doctoring, she tucked the handkerchief into Shev's pocket and gave it a pat.

'I'm no fool,' said Horald. 'I always knew Crandall would make things difficult for me, sooner or later. More than likely you spared me the trouble of killing him myself.'

Shev stared. 'Eh?'

'I've got eleven other children, after all. You ever meet my eldest daughter, Leanda?'

'Don't believe I've had the pleasure.'

'Oh, you'd like her. Got her running things in Westport now and she's ten times the man Crandall ever was. When you're in my position, you have to maintain an implacable image.' His stare went so hard for a moment that Shev took a little shuffling step back. Then he broke out in a smile again. 'But between you and me, I forgave you for killing him years ago.'

'You might have fucking said so!'

'Had to get something out of it, didn't I? And, more importantly, had to be *seen* to get something out of it. Reputation's everything in our game, Shev. Who'd know that better than the best bloody thief in Styria?'

'Then . . .' She stared from Horald, to Carcolf, and back, sluggish mind only now starting to grope past the present moment. 'What the hell is this about?'

'Oh. Yes. Sorry. This isn't about you at all, Shev. Nor Carcolf, neither, much though it's been a pleasure to see you again, my dear.' And he and Carcolf gave each other a respectful little nod, as of two champion squares players just fought a testing game to a draw. 'The two of you are incidental in all this. As am I, really.' Horald grinned up at Javre, who was looking back at him with a sad little smile on her bruised face.

She tossed the empty wine bottle away and it clattered across the courtyard and into a corner. 'It is about me.'

Horald spread his palms. 'A man simply can't prosper in business without owing debts to someone.'

Shev felt her relief being overcome by an uneasy queasiness. 'Who do you owe?'

'Among other people . . .' Horald licked his teeth as though he was far from happy about it. 'The High Priestess of the Great Temple of Thond.'

Shev's eyes went wide. 'Javre, get—' She spun towards the door they had come through, but there was a woman standing there. A tall, lean woman with a hard face and a shaved head and a long sword in her tattooed fist. Another woman, huge as a house, was already ducking under the lintel to join her. Shev caught Carcolf's sleeve and took a step towards a door at the far side of the yard. It swung gently open and a heavy-muscled woman stepped through, her thumbs tucked in a great belt from which two curved swords hung. Another with her white hair gathered into a hundred tiny braids followed grinning after, arms folded across her chest.

A shrill whistle came from above and a figure flashed down from the top of the wall, turning over, landing with hardly a sound in a ready crouch and standing tall, taller even than Javre, fine blonde hair shifting in the breeze across her face, so all Shev could see was the gleam of one eye and the glisten of her perfect teeth as she smiled. She plucked a spear from the air as it was tossed down to her without even looking, its long blade shining, blinding, mirror-bright.

Shev swallowed as she glanced about, trying to make it the thief's glance that hardly seems to look at all but probably failing. She usually did fail, when it came down to it, for all her boasting. Some best bloody thief in Styria, while she was playing at the hero she'd blundered straight into a trap and dragged the one real friend she had into it with her.

There were two more women on the walls above, a pair of twins with great bows draped across their shoulders like milk-maids' yokes, wrists hooked over them as they smiled blandly down. Seven in all, and each, Shev had no doubt, a Templar of the Golden Order, and far beyond her fighting skills even if she hadn't used half her tricks on those fools upstairs.

'Fuck,' she said, simply. Sometimes no other word will cover it.

Horald shifted somewhat nervously as he glanced at the scarred, sinewy, tattooed, heavily armed women now surrounding him on every side. They looked deadly, and Shev knew they were a lot deadlier than they looked. 'Have to say I feel a little outnumbered,' he muttered.

Javre gave a weary nod, ran her tongue around her mouth and spat. 'I, too.'

'Javre,' came a deep voice.

As if it was a spoken command, the Templars all bowed their heads as one. Another woman stepped through the door. A big, broad-shouldered woman in a sleeveless white robe, moving with such wonderful poise she appeared to glide more than walk. 'It has been too long.'

A great string of beads was looped around and around her thick neck until it covered half her chest. Grey showed in the orange stubble on her shaved scalp, her sharp-boned face with deep lines in the cheeks and about the eyes. And what eyes they were. Calm and blue as deep water. Bright as stars. Hard as hammered iron. And ruthless as a backstreet knifing.

Javre watched her sit at the table opposite Horald. 'Never would have been too soon for me, Mother.'

Shev cleared her throat. 'I'm guessing "mother" in this case is a term of respect due to the High Priestess of—'

'Javre is my daughter.' The woman raised one brow. 'And she has never been all that interested in terms of respect.'

Shev stared. She found herself doing that a lot, lately. There was indeed a strong resemblance, if only in the muscle that squirmed in the woman's arms as she crossed them over those rattling beads. 'So we've been chased across the breadth of the Circle of the World for fourteen years by . . . your mother?'

'She can be extremely stubborn,' said Javre.

'So that's where you get it from,' murmured Shev. 'I finally see the upside of being an orphan.'

There was a tense, quiet moment, then. A couple of dry leaves chased each other across the cracked flagstones as the wind swirled around the yard. The High Priestess pursed her lips as she looked her wayward daughter up and down. Fourteen years, Shev and Javre had been running, and now they stood before the two people who had done the chasing. After that long, it was bound to be something of an anticlimax.

'You look...'

'Like shit?' ventured Javre.

'I would have tried to be more diplomatic.'

'I fear the time for diplomacy between us is long past, Mother.'

'Like *shit*, then. Never was a woman more blessed by the Goddess than you. It grieves me to see you treat her gifts with such scant respect. Did you really run away from me... for this?'

'I left so I could choose my own path.'

Javre's mother slowly shook her head. 'And you chose to wallow in your own filth?'

'Having murderers chasing you every hour of your life does rather limit your options,' snapped Shev.

She felt Carcolf's hand on her shoulder, gently drawing her back into the shadows. She shook her off, moved instead to stand beside Javre. If she was about to die, that was where she chose to do it.

The blue, blue eyes of the High Priestess slid over to her. 'Who is this... person?'

Javre drew herself up to her full height then, puffing up her chest, and put her hand on Shev's shoulder. 'She is Shevedieh, the greatest thief in Styria.'

Shev might have had a foot less height and about a quarter of the chest that Javre did, but she drew up and puffed out what she had. 'And I am proud to be Javre's sidekick.'

'Partner,' said Javre, and gently guided her back. 'But leave her out of it.'

The eyes of the High Priestess drifted towards her daughter. 'Believe it or not, and in spite of all the pointless bloodshed between us, I have never wished to harm anyone.'

Javre stretched her neck out one way and the other, then put her bandaged hand on the rag-wrapped grip of her sword. 'I will tell you what I told Hanama, and Birke, and Weylen, and Golyin, and all your other lapdogs. I will be no one's slave. Not even yours.' She narrowed her eyes. 'Especially not yours. I would sooner die than go back with you.'

'I know.' Javre's mother wearily puffed out her cheeks in just the way Javre did when she and Shev had their endless theological debates. 'If the last fourteen years have taught me anything, it is that. Even as a girl you were stubborn beyond belief. All my efforts to make you bend, with smiles, with entreaties, with threats, with blows, and finally with blades, have done nothing but temper you. There are some wearying patterns to life that, try as we might, we never can seem to escape.'

Shev could hardly deny that. Here she was, outnumbered and facing death once again. How many bloody times now? She made a show of holding up one hand, as if to check her fingernails, and slipped the other towards that vial at her belt. One lucky throw might blow two of those Templars to the hereafter they were so fond of and maybe bring one of the towers down to boot. A spectacular note to end on, if nothing else . . .

'The Goddess teaches us to embrace them.' The High Priestess glanced towards Shev. 'You can leave that vial alone, my child. I have another choice for your partner. There is something that I need.'

Javre snorted. 'You have never been one to bridle at taking what you want.'

'This thing is not easily taken. It is in the possession of . . .' And Javre's mother worked her mouth as though there was a sour taste there. 'A wizard. A Magus of the Old Time.'

Shev leaned close to Javre. 'I don't much like the sound of—'

'Shush,' she said.

'Deliver this thing to me, Javre, and you are free. I, and the guards of my temple, will pursue you no longer.'

'That is all?' asked Javre.

'That is all.'

Shev caught her by her big bare arm. 'Javre! We don't know what this thing is, or where it's kept, and I really don't like the sound of this whole Magus of the Old Time business—'

'Shevedieh.' Javre patted her hand and gently peeled her fingers away. 'When you have only one choice, there is no purpose waiting to make it. I accept.'

'Well, then.' Shev glanced over at Carcolf and gave a long, shuddering, painful sigh, her puffed chest rapidly collapsing. 'Guess I'll be stealing a thing off a wizard.'

Javre had a little smile at the corner of her mouth as she glanced down at her. 'You and I, side by side?'

'That's where a sidekick belongs, no? You can do the fighting, I can do the complaining.'

'Just the way it has always been.'

'How else would it be?'

Javre's smile curled up a little further. 'I appreciate the offer, Shevedieh. It means ... more than you can know. But you have earned the chance at something better. Some things one has to do alone.'

'Javre—'

'If I die, drowned in some bog, or spitted by some guard, or roasted by some wizard's Art, well, it will be some consolation to know that my partner lived to be old and shrivelled, still telling tall tales of our high adventures together.'

Shev blinked. Strange, how a day before all she could think of were the bad times. The thousand hurts, the million arguments, the nights spent on the stony ground. Now all the good came up at once and choked her. The laughter, the songs, the knowing there was always, always someone at her back. She tried to smile but her sight was swimming. 'It's been something, though, hasn't it?'

'It has,' said Javre, glancing over to Carcolf. 'Look after her.'

Carcolf swallowed. 'I'll try.'

'Fail, and there will be no place in the Circle of the World where you will be safe from me.' She laid that great, heavy, comforting hand on Shev's shoulder one more time. 'Fare you well, my friend.' And she turned away, towards her mother.

'Fare you well,' whispered Shev, wiping her eyes.

Carcolf took her gently by the shoulders from behind and drew her close. 'Let's go home.'

'You should come talk to me!' called Horald after her. 'I can always find work for the best thief in—'

'Go fuck yourself, Horald,' said Shev.

When they got back there, her place was still killed.

'Nothing broken that can't be fixed.' Carcolf righted Shev's ruined table and brushed some broken plaster off it with the back of her hand. 'We'll get it all put right in no time. I know people.'

'Seems you know everyone,' muttered Shev, numbly, tossing down her bag.

'We'll take a trip. Just you and me. Change of scene.' Carcolf had hardly stopped talking since they rowed away from Carp Island. As if she was worried by what might be said if she left a gap. 'Jacra, maybe. Or the Thousand Isles? I've never been. You always said the Isles are beautiful.'

'Javre thought so,' muttered Shev.

Carcolf paused, then pressed on as if the name hadn't been

mentioned at all. 'When we get back it'll all be so much better. You'll see. Let me change. Then we'll go out. We'll do something fun.'

'Fun.' Shev flopped onto the one intact chair. She was the one who really needed to change but she couldn't be bothered. She hardly had the strength to stand.

'You remember what it is?'

Shev forced out a weak grin. 'Maybe you can remind me.'

'Of course I can.' Carcolf smiled. 'Fun's my middle name.'

'Oh? So it's just your first name I'm missing.'

'What kind of a mysterious beauty would I be without any mysteries?' And Carcolf consummately acted the part of a mysterious beauty over her shoulder as the bedroom door swung shut.

Shev winced, bruised side aching as she squirmed out of her coat, tools clattering as it dropped to the floor, a loose smoke bomb rolling free through the mess. She slumped down, elbows on her knees, chin on her hands.

Javre was out of her life. Carcolf was in it. She was square with Horald the Finger. Everything she'd wanted, wasn't it?

So why did she feel so bloody miserable?

There was a soft knock at the door and Shev frowned as she looked up. Another knock. She slid out her sword-eater, held it down by her right side as she stood, and with her left hand nudged the door open a crack.

There was a twitchy youth out in the stairwell with big ears and a rash of spots around his mouth.

'You Carcolf?' He squinted through the gap. 'You're shorter than I thought you'd be.'

'I'm shorter than I hoped I'd be,' snapped Shev. 'Reckon my height's a disappointment to us both.'

The lad shrugged. 'Disappointment's part of life.' And he held out a folded paper between two fingers.

'Everyone's a fucking philosopher.' Shev opened the door wide enough to pluck it free, then shouldered it shut and turned the key. A letter, with *Carcolf* written on the front in a slanted hand. Something familiar about the writing. Something that picked at her.

She tossed it down on the scarred tabletop and frowned at it while Carcolf started singing in the bedroom. Bloody hell, she even sang well.

If you want to be a fine new person with a fine new life you've got to put the person you were behind you, like a snake sheds its skin. You've got to stop picking through your hoard of hurts and grievances like a miser with his coins, set 'em down and allow yourself to go free. You've got to forgive and you've got to trust, not because anyone else deserves it, but because you do.

Shev took a hard breath and turned away from the letter.

Then she turned back, snatched it up and slashed it wide open with the sword-eater.

No one changes that much. Not all at once.

She knew the hand, now she saw more of it. The same one that had written the note Horald the Finger had put his mark to. The note that had been left here in her ruined place. The note that had drawn her and Javre out to Burroia's Fort.

Carcolf, my old friend
Just wanted to thank you again for your help. No one spins
a story like you. Pleasure to watch you work, as always. If
you come through Westport again I'll have more for you, and
well paid. I've always got things that need taking from here
to there.

Hope it all went well with my father in Talins. I swear,
you're the one woman he holds in higher regard than me.
Stay careful,
Leanda

Shev's eyes went wider and wider as she read, the cogs upstairs
spinning at triple speed.

Leanda. Horald's oh-so-competent daughter running things
in Westport.

My old friend. Carcolf might know everyone, but these were
tighter ties than she'd ever given a hint of.

Hope it all went well with my father in Talins. Shev looked
up and saw Carcolf standing in the doorway in her underwear.
A sight she would've swum oceans for once. It gave her scant
happiness now.

Carcolf blinked from Shev's stricken face to the letter, and
back, and slowly held up a calming palm, as if Shev was a skittish
pony that a sudden move might startle. 'Now, listen to me. This
isn't what it looks like.'

'No?' Shev slowly turned the letter around. 'Because it looks
like you're about as tight as can be with Horald and his family,
and this whole fucking business was your idea!'

Carcolf gave a guilty little grin. A toddler caught with stolen
jam all around her face. 'Then, maybe . . . it is what it looks like.'

Shev just stood and stared. Again. The old violinist chose that
moment to strike up in the square outside, overplaying the hell
out of a plaintive little piece, but Shev didn't feel like dancing to
it, and like laughing at it even less. Seemed a fitting accompani-
ment to the collapse of her pathetic little self-deceptions. God,
why did she insist on demanding from people what she knew

they could never give her? Why did she insist on making the same mistakes over and over? Why was she fooled so easily, every time?

Because she wanted to be fooled.

You've got to be realistic, that old Northman on the farm near Squaredeal used to tell her. Got to be realistic. And she'd leaned on the fence with a stalk of grass in her teeth and nodded sagely along. And yet, in spite of all she'd seen and all she'd suffered, she was still the least realistic fool in the Circle of the World.

'Look, Shevedieh . . .' Carcolf's voice was smooth and calm and reasonable, a politician explaining their great plans for the nation. 'I can see how you might feel . . . a *little* bit deceived.'

'A little bit?' squeaked Shev, her voice going high with disbelief.

'I just wanted . . .' Carcolf looked down, prodding at a bent teaspoon with one pointed toe, and glanced up shyly under her lashes, trying on the innocent new bride for size, '. . . to know that you *cared*.'

Shev's eyes went even wider. She positively goggled. 'So . . . it was all a fucking *test*?'

'No! Well, yes. I wanted to know we've got something . . . that can *last*, is all. That didn't come out right!'

'How could *that* come out *right*?'

'Because you passed! You passed and then some!' Carcolf padded towards her. That walk she had. God, that walk. 'You came for me. I never thought you would. My hero, eh? Heroine. Whichever.'

'You could've just asked me!'

Carcolf crushed her face up as she came closer. 'But . . . you know . . . people say all kinds of things in bed that it's probably not best to put to too hard a test later on—'

'So I'm beginning to fucking see!'

Carcolf's brows drew in a touch. An impatient mother,

frustrated that her daughter's tantrum won't subside. 'Look. I know it's been a hard night for everyone but it all turned out for the best. Now you're square with Horald, and I'm square with Horald, and we can—'

Shev felt a sudden cold twinge in her stomach. 'What do you mean, you're square with Horald?'

'Well . . .' A flicker of annoyance across Carcolf's face that she'd let something slip, then she started flapping her hands around like a circus magician disguising a trick. 'I had a little debt of my own, as it happens, and he had the debt to the High Priestess, so, you know, favours for favours, we could help each other out. It's the Styrian way, Shev, isn't it? But that's not the point—'

'So you sold my friend to settle your debt?'

If Shev had been hoping Carcolf would sag like a punctured wineskin with the weight of her shame, she was disappointed. 'Javre's a fucking menace!' Carcolf stepped closer with a stabbing finger. 'As long as she was here you'd just have got sucked back into her madness like you always do! You had to get free of her. *We* had to get free of her. You told me so, in this room!'

Shev winced. 'But I didn't mean it! I mean, I *did* mean it but . . . not this way—'

'What way, then?' asked Carcolf. 'You were never going to do it. You know it now. You knew it then. That's why you said it. I had to do it for you.'

'So . . . you've done me a favour?'

'I think so.' Carcolf stepped closer. Fair now, humble, a merchant offering the deal of a lifetime. 'And I think . . . when you've had time to think about it . . . you'll think so, too.'

She smiled down, taller than Shev even without her shoes. A winning smile. Point proved. Argument won.

She took horrified silence for agreement, reached out and

cupped Shev's face in her hands. The sensitive lover, whose only joy was her partner's happiness.

'Just us,' she whispered, leaning close. 'Better than ever.'

Carcolf sucked at Shev's top lip. Then she nipped the bottom one with her teeth, pulled it back, almost painful, and let it go with the faintest flapping sound. Shev's head was full of that scent, but there was no sweetness in it any more. It was just sour. Gaudy. Sickening.

'Now let me get dressed, and we'll go have fun.'

'Fun's your middle name,' whispered Shev, wanting to shove her off. To shove her off and punch her in the face besides.

Shev didn't much like to be honest with herself. Who does? But if she accepted the pain of it for just a moment, it wasn't Carcolf's treachery that truly hurt. You can't bed a snake then complain when you get bit. It was that Shev had suddenly realised there was no secret self hidden under Carcolf's smirking mask. There was just another mask, and another. Whatever role it suited her to play. Whatever got her what she wanted. If Carcolf had anything underneath, it was hard and shiny as a flint.

She had no first name to learn.

A few hours ago Shev had been willing to kill for this woman. Willing to die for her. Now she didn't feel love, or lust, or even much anger. She just felt sad. Sad and bruised and so, so disappointed.

She made herself smile. 'All right.' She made herself put her hand on Carcolf's cheek, brush a strand of golden hair back behind her ear. 'You get dressed. But I promise you it won't be for long.'

'Oh, promises make me nervous.' Carcolf brushed the tip of Shev's nose with her fingertip as she let her go. 'I never know whether to trust them.'

'You're the one who lies for a living. I just steal for one.'

Carcolf grinned back at her from the bedroom doorway, calm and beautiful as ever. 'True enough.'

The moment she was gone, Shev snatched up her bag and walked out.

She didn't even shut the door.

FAR
COUNTRY

Aulcus

Calcis

Darmium

Hastum

Gordius

OLD EMPIRE

SHABULYAN

Isparda

BR
SE

SHA

FREEDOM!

A note from the publisher

Following his death at the age of ninety-five, this fragment was discovered, crumpled, stained and almost worn through, plugging a hole in the sole of an ancient boot belonging to Spillion Sworbreck, the noted biographer, epicurean and poet widely known for, among a bibliography of daunting scale, his eighteen-volume The Life of Dab Sweet, Scourge of the Wild Frontier, *and* The Grand Duchess of Villainy, *his romantic reimagining of the career of Monzcarro Murcatto presented in epic verse.*

Fact? Whimsy? Satire? The origins and purpose of the writing remain entirely a mystery, but it is now published for the first time, along with its peculiar footnote, written in a different hand from the author's, florid and sharply angled. A reader's observation? A critic's opinion? An editor's verdict? Only you, dear reader, can be the judge . . .

Being an absolutely true account of the liberation of the town of Averstock from the grip of the incorrigible rebel menace by the Company of the Gracious Hand under the Famous Nicomo Cosca penned by your humble servant Spillion Sworbreck.

Averstock, Summer 590

What can my unworthy pen set down upon the subject of that great heart, that good friend, that magnificent presence, that dauntless explorer, proud statesman, peerless swordsman, accomplished lover, occasional sea captain, amateur sculptor of renown, noted connoisseur, champion short-distance swimmer and warrior poet, the famous soldier of fortune, Nicomo Cosca?

He was a man of great parts, of extraordinary abilities both mental and physical, of a keen mind and a quickness to action characteristic of the fox, but with a sensitivity and mercy of which the gentlest dove would have been envious. He was a giving friend, quick to laugh and generous to a fault, but an implacable enemy, loved and feared equally across the Circle of the World, none of the diverse lands of which were unknown to him. And yet, in spite of grand achievements at his back to fill five famous lifetimes, he held not a trace of arrogance or vanity, was always challenging himself to do better, to reach further, to aim higher, and, though his conduct had in the main, across his dozens of successful campaigns, been unimpeachable, was frequently troubled by what he saw as the regrets and disappointments of the past. 'Regrets,' as he once told this unworthy reporter, with a boundless sadness plainly stamped into that noble visage, 'are the cost of the business.'

Though he was, at the time I was fortunate enough to make his acquaintance, approaching a full sixty years of age, he showed no sign of infirmity. A lifetime in the saddle, breathing the clean air and living a life free of low habits made him appear no older than a hale and athletic thirty-seven, with as full and lustrous a raven-black head of hair as any boy of sixteen could boast. According to the reports of womenfolk, who – gentle creatures! – must be taken as better judges of such matters than your humble servant, he was possessed of an extremely handsome face and a goodly frame entirely undiminished by the years in power and muscularity. He took drink but rarely and only in the strictest moderation, for the awful depravities he had seen visited by drunken soldiers upon an innocent populace during his long career were terrible, and, as he once told me, 'No devil is more dangerous to a soldier than that which occupies the bottle.'

On the occasion the details of which I am about to relate, and which well illustrates the character of the man, Nicomo Cosca and his Company of the Gracious Hand had been employed by that noted servant of His August Majesty, Superior Pike, to root out the ringleaders of the vile rebellion in Starikland which culminated in the horrifying massacre at Rostod. To this righteous purpose, the Company, numbering some five hundred brave souls, was now sworn, and, having sworn, they would achieve or die in the attempt. Perhaps you have heard lurid tales of the faithlessness of the mercenary kind? Banish such thoughts from your minds, dear readers, at least in so far as they bear upon the happy brotherhood presided over by the famous Nicomo Cosca! For these men, though born under diverse skies, speaking diverse tongues, coming from high and low, near and far, representing every colour and creed to be found within the Circle of the World, were as faithful and loyal to one another, and to their employers, as any tight-knit band of countrymen. Once their notary had prepared a paper of engagement and the noble Cosca set his flourishing signature upon it, they put aside by one accord all other considerations and were bound to the mission as staunchly as the Knights of the Body are bound to the defence of His August Majesty's royal person, and no entreaty, no offers of golden hoard, land or title, no rewards earthly or divine could persuade them to deviate from their promised purpose.

The town of Averstock was one of those pioneer settlements that, like a seed taken root in stony ground, was at that time flourishing in the lawless land of the Near Country, close to the civilising border of the Union. It was well built of firm timber and, though simple and lacking any ornament, was cunningly situated, clean and orderly, pleasing to the eye, and ringed by a stout palisade constructed by the good townsfolk as protection against the dread Ghosts, who had for some years previous visited terrible slaughter upon the defenceless settlers.

It was towards this fair and previously peaceable settlement that Cosca now piercingly gazed, his manly brow furrowed by deep concern and righteous outrage.

'The rebels are in the town, at least a hundred strong,' said Captain Dimbik, springing down from his lathered charger, his golden locks bouncing upon his broad shoulders. He had been an officer of the King's Own, but so singularly attached to adventure that, when peace with the fell Northman was declared, he instantly resigned his commission to seek new dangers in the unmapped West. 'They have, through base treachery, taken the townsfolk hostage, are perpetrating hourly outrages upon their innocent persons, and threaten to kill the women and defenceless babes should any man attempt to deliver the settlement from their tyranny.'

'Are these men or monsters?' spoke Captain Brachio, a cultured Styrian gentleman of the highest breeding, slender and well formed, and sporting an old wound beneath the eye which lent a rugged flare to his goodly countenance.

'I must go down there myself, curse them!' Cosca's lustrous moustaches trembled with fair indignation as his bright eye directed its perilous fire toward the infested settlement. 'And negotiate the release of the hostages. I can allow no possibility of failure. If one innocent man, woman or child were to be harmed . . .' And here, friends, I must report that the general dashed a manly tear from his cheek at the very thought of injury to the minor. 'My fragile conscience could not bear the weight of it. I will warn these rebels in no uncertain terms that—'

'No!' spoke Inquisitor Lorsen, representative of the general's employer and custodian of the mission for which the brave Company were engaged. 'Your keenness to spare bloodshed does you much credit, General Cosca, but the dread rebel cannot be trusted to behave according to the rules of war. They lack your unimpeachable good character and I will not hear of you placing yourself in their power. I, the Union and indeed the world cannot afford to lose so useful a servant as you have proved, and daily continue to prove, yourself to be. You have a company of bold and righteous men all eager to carry out your order, any one of whom, I cannot doubt, would be more than willing to risk their lives if it might spare those of the defenceless. Let one of them be sent to this admirable purpose. I, my master Superior Pike, his master the Arch Lector, and indeed *his* master His August Majesty the High King of the Union,' and here the men, though not all natives of that great nation, bowed their heads in deep respect, 'would, I am sure, though carrying many great cares, no less deeply regret a single life wasted.'

Following this exhaustive speech, volunteers stepped forward instantly to lend their strong arms to the noble project. Cosca wiped aside a second manly tear, holding out his arms towards them and speaking, 'My boys! My brave boys!' and pressing his strong hands to his noble breast in gratitude to them, and to the Fates, for furnishing him with such men.

It was one Sufeen on whom the great man's eye now alighted, a scout of long experience and Kantic extraction but tall and of a noble bearing, no doubt one among those people who had rather fled their homeland than submit to the tyranny of the Gurkish Emperor, a man who laughed at fear almost as loudly as the captain general himself.

'Offer the rebels fair treatment if they abandon their cowardly kidnap and surrender themselves to his Majesty's justice,' said Inquisitor Lorsen.

'And warn them they shall taste the full measure of my wrath should they harm a hair upon the heads of their hostages,' said Cosca. 'Do this for me, Sufeen, and you will be rewarded.'

'Sir, your respect is all the reward I could desire,' answered the scout, and the two men embraced. Taking the notary of the Company with him to arrange the terms of the rebels' surrender, brave Sufeen began the long and lonely walk down the grassy hillside towards the bastion of the enemy and, presently, was seen to be admitted and the tall gates of the settlement firmly shut behind him.

An eerie silence now ensued while the Company awaited the result of Sufeen's negotiations, hoping for a happy outcome and yet prepared entirely for the bloody alternative. It was as tense a passage of time as your abject reporter has ever borne witness to. The wind still whispered through the trees and across the grass, the careless birds still warbled their morning song from the branches, but every man gathered there surely occupied the very extremities of nervous anxiety.

Every man, that is, save one!

'Ah, that moment before battle is joined!' spoke Cosca, prostrate in the long grass above the town like a lion waiting to spring, his eye glittering and his great fists clenched in anticipation of the work that was to come. 'The delicious calm before the storm of steel! Perhaps a man should not be keen to engage in such bloody business as ours, but the excitement! It has always set my veins to thrill! Does it not yours, Sworbreck?'

Your humble servant must at this juncture confess a touch of understandable reticence, and could answer only in the negative. I, after all, had not the long experience, the consummate skill at arms, nor the natural immunity to fear with which the captain general was furnished. He, after all, was Nicomo Cosca. He laughed in the face of fear!

But no laughter escaped those well-formed lips now. 'Something is amiss,' he murmured as the time dragged out, and the men immediately stiffened for action. They knew from long experience that Nicomo Cosca was possessed of a special sense for danger almost magical, a sixth sense if you will, beyond the range of perception of the common man. Whether this was a thing learned by long and painful trials or an inborn talent I cannot say, but this humble reporter observed its operation on several occasions and its efficacy was not to be denied. Springing to his feet with the agility of an acrobat, and an instant later into his gilded saddle – a gift, as I understand it, from the Grand Duchess Sefeline of Ospria following his great victory on her behalf at the Battle of the Isles – the captain general roared, 'To arms!'

Freedom!

Within a twinkling, several score men were mounted and pouring down the hillside towards Averstock, their deep and passionate war cries resounding across the picturesque valley. A timely signal given by mirror induced another detachment, carefully sited in trees on the far side of the settlement, to begin their attack at the same moment, such that not one rebel could possibly escape this deadly pincer. In battle the Company worked with the smoothness, precision and perfect accuracy of a priceless watch, with Cosca the master watchmaker, each of five hundred men giving himself utterly to his place in the grand machine.

How many heartbeats did it take for the speeding horses to reach the fence of the town? I cannot categorically state the number, but inconceivably few! How many more for the dauntless men of the Company to swarm over the defences, crushing the cowardly resistance at the walkways? But a handful more! I will not enter too deeply into the sordid details of the combat that ensued, in part because your humble observer, fearing for his very life, was kept at some remove from the hottest fighting, in part to spare the delicate sensibilities of my female readers, and in part because to describe such animal actions blow by blow ill befits a cultured readership.

Let me only note that I observed the captain general in combat himself and, though kitten in the company of his friends, he was a tiger and more in the presence of his enemies! Never has such wondrous dexterity with a throwing knife been seen, nor such deadly facility with a blade! At one stage this reporter witnessed, with his own two eyes, the remarkable sight of two men killed with one thrust of Cosca's flashing blade! Run through. Nay! Impaled. Nay! Spitted, I say, like two writhing cubes of meat upon a Gurkish skewer. The gushing blood watered the windblown grit of the street, the quivering innards of the rebels laid open to the skies, with blood-curdling shrieks and womanly wails for mercy not given. Their intestines were unwound, eyes punctured, brains dashed upon the wattle walls of the settlement to be left as food for the flies. Fleshy bodies were savagely ripped asunder by unforgiving steel to divulge their vermilion cargoes of still-writhing offal upon the merciless dust! Oh, such the ugly truth of war, which we, the civilised, must not flinch from a full description of!

'We must protect the townsfolk!' bellowed Captain Jubair over the noise of combat, who, though born in Gurkhul and displaying all the superstition natural to his kind, had learned from Cosca a mercy and respect for the weak entirely foreign to his dusky race. At most times a gentle giant, the ire of his simple mind was fully inflamed by the possibility of injury to the helpless and now he fought like an enraged elephant.

Though it felt an age to this reporter, such was the righteous ferocity of the Company that the combat was finished in but a few savage moments, the cowardly rebels utterly routed, destroyed and put to the sword, without – oh, happy chance and vindication of their cause by fate – a single injury to the Company. Cosca had let fall retribution upon the base curs with such terrible speed – no more slowly than does the brooding storm smite the earth with blinding lightning – that they had not time to visit the promised massacre upon the townsfolk, and each and every precious hostage was released smiling from bondage to be happily reunited with their tearful families.

Here was a dangerous moment, for, the blood of the men being fully inflamed, there was the chance that some among them, gentle and forbearing as lambs though they might be under gentler circumstances, might forget themselves and stoop to plunder. But Cosca sprang now upon a wagon and, spreading his arms, called in such ringing tones and in such gentle terms for calm that his Company was instantly brought under control and returned to the proper discipline of civilised men.

'I would rather we go hungry,' the good general exhorted them, 'than that there should be any loss of property to these good people, who may in future times call themselves subjects of His August Majesty the High King of the Union!'

And the Company sent up as one man a rousing cheer. One humble member, overcome by guilt, returned a clutch of eggs to the goodwife from whose coops he had removed them, muttering his most profuse apologies and weeping tears of deepest regret, but she begged him to keep them, and implored besides the grateful and hungry men of the Company to take all the eggs she had, and sent up in a higher pitch, frail hands pressed together, her own thanks to the king and his faithful and diligent servant his Eminence the Arch Lector for delivering she and her neighbours from the tyranny and foul depredations of the dread rebel.

At this moment, and your humble servant must admit he brushes away a tear of his own at the recollection, the corpse of noble Sufeen was discovered among the dead. His companions, with many expressions of manly sorrow and remembrances of his high qualities, let fall a river of tears. Nicomo Cosca, as in all things, was first among their number.

'Oh, good Sufeen!' The general beat upon his blood-spattered breastplate. 'Oh, great heart and worthy friend! The regret of this sacrifice shall bear upon me until my dying day!'

The brave scout had fought like a champion, surrounded by craven enemies who had fallen upon him under flag of parley, and killed more than a dozen filthy rebels before they cut him down. A satchel of ancient coins was found near his mutilated body and instantly surrendered to the captain general.

'Take an inventory of this money, Sergeant Friendly,' spoke Cosca.

'I shall count it,' said Cosca's faithful henchman, nodding his assent.

'It shall be distributed according to our Rule of Quarters! Let one quarter be divided among the men in recognition of their brave work today! Let another be used to commission a competent stonecutter to produce a timeless monument to brave Sufeen! Let the third be spent in the purchase of supplies from the townsfolk, and let the final quarter be given to them for the repair of damage done by the rebels, and the founding of a hospital for the orphan children of those who have stood martyr to the cause!'

Another rousing cheer went up from the throats of the mercenaries for, though many were men of low origins, they all were men of high character, and base greed was foreign to their giving natures, gain always the very least of their motivations. They instantly began the work of returning the settlement to its original fine condition, extinguishing a fire the rebels had set in their extremity, and putting right the uncouth damage wrought upon the buildings and public spaces during the occupation.

I reported earlier that Cosca was the best friend to have, but he was also the worst enemy, and implacable in his punishment of wrongdoers. It gives me no pride, but at the same time no shame, to report that the severed heads of several of the rebel ringleaders were left mounted above the gates of the town as a dread warning to others. No one took the least pleasure in this awful operation, but this was the Near Country, far beyond the borders of civilisation, and outside the jurisdiction of Union, or even of Imperial justice, if there is any such thing in that benighted nation. Cosca, in the light of his vast experience, judged that strong lessons now might spare much bloodshed later. Such is the terrible arithmetic of warfare.

'We must be merciful whenever possible,' said the fair-minded general. 'We must!' And he struck one solid palm with one strong fist. 'But, sad to say, one cannot afford to indulge oneself with too much mercy.' He looked now towards those grisly warnings mounted, with expressions horribly vacant, and already attracting avian attentions, upon the town's palisade. 'Heads on spikes,' he said, shaking his own. 'A most terrible and regrettable necessity.'

'Your forbearance does you much credit, General,' spoke the good Inquisitor Lorsen. 'His Majesty's Inquisition demands that the guilty be sternly punished and the innocent protected.'

The townsfolk implored Cosca to remain, and offered him flowers and, indeed, gold to stay within their settlement, but he demurred. 'Other towns of the Near Country yet chafe under the rebel yoke,' he said. 'I can have no rest until Superior Pike's noble mission is fulfilled and the treacherous leader of the rebels, foul Conthus, is delivered in chains into the hands of the Inquisition to await the king's justice.'

'But will you and your men not take your ease for just one night, General Cosca?' the town's headman enquired. 'For but one happy hour? With the triumphant liberation of our humble burg your labours have surely for the time being reached their end?'

'My thanks,' replied the great man, laying a heavy hand upon his shoulder, 'but I have taken my ease too long already.' That famous soldier of fortune, Nicomo Cosca, now worked the waxed tips of his proud black moustaches to deadly points between finger and thumb and directed his piercing gaze towards the western horizon. 'If I have learned one thing in forty years of warfare, it is that doing right . . . has no end.'

⚔

All well enough, I suppose, but I was hoping for more. It's dowdy. It's bland. I'm all for realism in its place, report the facts and so forth, but you can't expect to make the readers gasp with this manner of understatement. Did I not tell you it hasn't been boring?

For pity's sake, Sworbreck, work it up! More heroism, more dazzle, more blood in the action there, a larger-than-life quality! More villainous, the fiendish rebels! A rescued maiden or two? Put your back into it! Give it a bit more zing!

Then strip out any mention of that bloody notary, if you please. Expunge that treacherous bastard from the record!

And capitalise Captain General.

TOUGH TIMES
ALL OVER

Sipani, Spring 592

D amn, but she hated Sipani.

The bloody blinding fogs and the bloody slapping water and the bloody universal sickening stink of rot. The bloody parties and masques and revels. Fun, everyone having bloody fun, or at least pretending to. The bloody people were worst of all. Rogues, every man, woman and child. Liars and fools, the lot of them.

Carcolf hated Sipani. Yet here she was again. Who, then, she was forced to wonder, was the fool?

Braying laughter echoed from the mist ahead and she slipped into the shadows of a doorway, one hand tickling the grip of her sword. A good courier trusts no one, and Carcolf was the very best, but in Sipani she trusted . . . less than no one.

Another gang of pleasure-seekers blundered from the murk, a man with a mask like a moon pointing at a woman who was so drunk she kept falling over on her high shoes. All of them laughing, one of them flapping his lace cuffs as though there never was a thing so funny as drinking so much you couldn't stand up. Carcolf rolled her eyes skyward and consoled herself with the thought that behind the masks they were hating it as much as she always did when she tried to have fun.

In the solitude of her doorway, Carcolf winced. Damn, but she needed a holiday. Fun used to be her middle name. Now look. She was becoming a sour arse. Or, indeed, had become one and was getting worse. One of those people who held the entire world in contempt. Was she turning into her bloody father?

'Anything but that,' she muttered.

The moment the revellers tottered off into the night she ducked from her doorway and pressed on, neither too fast nor too slow, soft boot heels silent on the dewy cobbles, her unexceptional hood drawn down to an inconspicuous degree, the very image of a person with just the average amount to hide. Which in Sipani was quite a bit.

Over to the west somewhere, her armoured carriage would be speeding down the wide lanes, wheels striking sparks as they clattered over the bridges, stunned bystanders leaping aside, driver's whip lashing at the foaming flanks of the horses, the dozen hired guards thundering after, streetlamps gleaming upon their dewy armour. Unless the Quarryman's people had already made their move, of course: the flutter of arrows, the scream of beasts and men, the crash of the wagon leaving the road, the clash of steel, and finally the great padlock blown from the strongbox with blasting powder, the choking smoke wafted aside by eager hands and the lid flung back to reveal . . . nothing.

Carcolf allowed herself the smallest smile and patted the lump against her ribs. The item, stitched up safe in the lining of her coat.

She gathered herself, took a couple of steps and sprang from the canal-side, clearing three strides of oily water to the deck of a decaying barge, timbers creaking under her as she rolled and came smoothly up. To go around by the Fintine Bridge was quite the detour, not to mention a well-travelled and well-watched way, but this boat was always tied here in the shadows, offering a short cut. She had made sure of it. Carcolf left as little to chance as possible. In her experience, chance could be a real bastard.

A wizened face peered out from the gloom of the cabin, steam issuing from a battered kettle. 'Who the hell are you?'

'Nobody.' Carcolf gave a cheery salute. 'Just passing through!' And she hopped from the rocking wood to the stones on the far side of the canal and was away into the mould-smelling mist. Just passing through. Straight to the docks to catch the tide and off on her merry way. Or her sour-arsed one, at least. Wherever Carcolf went, she was nobody. Everywhere, always passing through.

Over to the east that idiot Pombrine would be riding hard in the company of four paid retainers. He hardly looked much like her, what with the moustache and all, but swaddled in that ever-so-conspicuous embroidered cloak of hers he did well enough for a double. He was a penniless pimp who smugly believed himself to be impersonating her so she could visit a lover, a lady of means who did not want their tryst made public. Carcolf sighed. If only. She consoled herself with the thought of Pombrine's shock when those bastards Deep and Shallow shot him from his saddle, expressed considerable surprise at the moustache, then rooted through his clothes with increasing frustration and finally no doubt gutted his corpse only to find . . . nothing.

Carcolf patted that lump once again and pressed on with a spring in her step. Here went she, down the middle course, alone and on foot, along a carefully prepared route of back streets, of narrow ways, of unregarded short cuts and forgotten stairs, through crumbling palaces and rotting tenements, gates left open by surreptitious arrangement and, later on, a short stretch of sewer which would bring her out right by the docks with an hour or two to spare.

After this job she really had to take a holiday. She tongued at the inside of her lip where a small but unreasonably painful ulcer had lately developed. All she did was work. A trip to Adua, maybe? Visit her brother, see her nieces? How old would they be now? Ugh. No. She remembered what a judgemental bitch her sister-in-law was. One of those people who met everything with a sneer. She reminded Carcolf of her father. Probably why her brother had married the bloody woman...

Music was drifting from somewhere as she ducked beneath a flaking archway. A violinist either tuning up or of execrable quality. Neither would have surprised her. Papers flapped and rustled on a wall sprouting with moss, ill-printed bills exhorting the faithful citizenry to rise up against the tyranny of the Snake of Talins. Carcolf snorted. Most of Sipani's citizens were more interested in falling over than rising up, and the rest were anything but faithful.

She twisted about to tug at the seat of her trousers, but it was hopeless. How much did you have to pay for a new suit of clothes before you avoid a chafing seam in the very worst place? She hopped along a narrow way beside a stagnant section of canal, long out of use, gloopy with algae and bobbing rubbish, plucking the offending fabric this way and that to no effect. Damn this fashion for tight trousers! Perhaps it was some kind of cosmic punishment for her paying the tailor with forged coins. But then Carcolf was considerably more moved by the concept of local profit than that of cosmic punishment, and therefore strove to avoid paying for anything wherever possible. It was practically a principle with her, and her father always said that a person should stick to their principles—

Bloody hell, she really was turning into her father.

'Ha!'

A ragged figure sprang from an archway, the faintest glimmer of steel showing. With an instinctive whimper Carcolf stumbled back, fumbling her coat aside and drawing her own blade, sure that death had found her at last. The Quarryman one step ahead? Or was it Deep and Shallow, or Kurrikan's hirelings ... but no one else showed themselves. Only this one man, swathed in a stained cloak, unkempt hair stuck to pale skin by the damp, a mildewed scarf masking the bottom part of his face, bloodshot eyes round and scared above.

'Stand and deliver!' he boomed, somewhat muffled by the scarf.

Carcolf raised her brows. 'Who even says that?'

A slight pause, while the rotten waters slapped the stones beside them. 'You're a woman?' There was an almost apologetic turn to the would-be robber's voice.

'If I am, will you not rob me?'

'Well ... er ...' The thief deflated somewhat, then drew himself up again. 'Stand and deliver anyway!'

'Why?' asked Carcolf.

The point of the robber's sword drifted uncertainly. 'Because I have a considerable debt to ... that's none of your business!'

'No, I mean, why not just stab me and strip my corpse of valuables, rather than giving me the warning?'

Another pause. 'I suppose ... I hope to avoid violence? But I warn you I am entirely prepared for it!'

He was a bloody civilian. A mugger who had blundered upon her. A random encounter. Talk about chance being a bastard. For him, at least. 'You, sir,' she said, 'are a shitty thief.'

'I, madam, am a gentleman.'

'You, sir, are a dead gentleman.' Carcolf stepped forward, weighing her blade, a stride-length of razor steel lent a ruthless gleam by a lamp in a window somewhere above. She could never be bothered to practise, but nonetheless she was beyond passable with a sword. It would take a great deal more than this stick of gutter trash to get the better of her. 'I will carve you like—'

The man darted forward with astonishing speed, there was a scrape of steel and before Carcolf even thought of moving, the sword was twitched from her fingers and skittered across the greasy cobbles to plop into the canal.

'Ah,' she said. That changed things. Plainly her attacker was not the bumpkin he appeared to be, at least when it came to swordplay. She should have known. Nothing in Sipani is ever quite as it appears.

'Hand over the money,' he said.

'Delighted.' Carcolf plucked out her purse and tossed it against the wall, hoping to slip past while he was distracted. Alas, he pricked it from the air with impressive dexterity and whisked his sword-point back to prevent her escape. It tapped gently at the lump in her coat.

'What have you got . . . just there?'

From bad to much, much worse. 'Nothing, nothing at all.' Carcolf attempted to pass it off with a false chuckle but that ship had sailed and she, sadly, was not aboard, any more than she was aboard the damn ship still rocking at the wharf for the voyage to Thond. She steered the glinting point away with one finger. 'Now, I have an extremely pressing engagement, so if—' There was a faint hiss as the sword slit her coat open.

Carcolf blinked. 'Ow.' There was a burning pain down her ribs. The sword had slit her open, too. 'Ow!' She subsided to her knees, deeply aggrieved, blood oozing between her fingers as she clutched them to her side.

'Oh . . . oh no. Sorry. I really . . . really didn't mean to cut you. Just wanted, you know . . .'

'Ow.' The item, now slightly smeared with Carcolf's blood,

dropped from the gashed pocket and tumbled across the cobbles. A slender package perhaps a foot long, wrapped in stained leather.

'I need a surgeon,' gasped Carcolf, in her best I-am-a-helpless-woman voice. The grand duchess had always accused her of being overdramatic, but if you can't be dramatic at a time like this, when can you? It was likely she really did need a surgeon, after all, and there was a chance the robber would lean down to help her and she could stab the bastard in the face with her knife. 'Please, I beg you!'

He loitered, eyes wide, the whole thing plainly gone further than he had intended. But he edged closer only to reach for the package, the glinting point of his sword still levelled at her.

A different and even more desperate tack, then. She strove to keep the panic out of her voice. 'Look, take the money, I wish you joy of it.' Carcolf did not, in fact, wish him joy, she wished him rotten in his grave. 'But we will both be far better off if you leave that package!'

His hand hovered. 'Why, what's in it?'

'I don't know. I'm under orders not to open it!'

'Orders from who?'

Carcolf winced. 'I don't know that either, but—'

Kurtis took the packet. Of course he did. He was an idiot, but not so much of an idiot as that. He snatched up the packet and ran. Of course he ran. When didn't he?

He tore down the alleyway, heart in mouth, jumped a burst barrel, caught his foot and went sprawling, almost impaled himself on his own drawn sword, slithered on his face through a slick of rubbish, scooping a mouthful of something faintly sweet before staggering up, spitting and cursing, snatching a scared glance over his shoulder—

There was no sign of pursuit. Only the mist, the endless mist, whipping and curling like a thing alive.

He slipped the packet, now somewhat slimy, into his ragged cloak and limped on, clutching at his bruised buttock and still struggling to spit that rotten-sweet taste from his mouth. Not that it was any worse than his breakfast had been. Better, if anything. You know a man by his breakfast, his fencing master always used to tell him.

He pulled up his damp hood with its faint smell of onions and despair, plucked the purse from his sword and slid blade back into sheath as he slipped from the alley and insinuated himself among the crowds, that faint snap of hilt meeting clasp bringing back so many memories. Of training and tournaments, of bright futures and the adulation of the crowds. Fencing, my boy, that's the way to advance! Such knowledgeable audiences in Styria, they love their swordsmen there, you'll make a fortune! Better times, when he had not dressed in rags, or been thankful for the butcher's leftovers, or robbed people for a living. He grimaced. Robbed *women*. If you could call it a living. He stole another furtive glance over his shoulder. Could he have killed her? His skin prickled with horror. Just a scratch. Just a scratch, surely? But he had seen blood. Please, let it have been a scratch! He rubbed his face as though he could rub the memory away, but it was stuck fast. One by one, things he had never imagined, then told himself he would never do, then that he would never do again, had become his daily routine.

He checked once more that he wasn't followed then slipped from the street and across the rotting courtyard, the faded faces of yesterday's heroes peering down at him from the newsbills. Up the piss-smelling stairway and around the dead plant. Out with his key and he wrestled with the sticky lock.

'Damn it, fuck it, shit it— Gah!' The door came suddenly open and he blundered into the room, nearly fell again, turned and pushed it shut, and stood a moment in the smelly darkness, breathing hard.

Who would now believe he'd once fenced with the king? He'd lost. Of course he had. Lost everything, hadn't he? He'd lost two touches to nothing and been personally insulted while he lay in the dust, but still, he'd measured steels with His August Majesty. This very steel, he realised, as he set it against the wall beside the door. Notched, and tarnished, and even slightly bent towards the tip. The last twenty years had been almost as unkind to his sword as they had been to him. But perhaps today marked the turn in his fortunes.

He whipped his cloak off and tossed it into a corner, took out the packet to unwrap it and see what he had come by. He fumbled with the lamp in the darkness and finally produced some light, almost wincing as his miserable rooms came into view. The cracked glazing, the blistering plaster speckled with damp, the burst mattress spilling foul straw where he slept, the few sticks of warped furniture—

There was a man sitting in the only chair, at the only table. A big man in a big coat, skull shaved to greying stubble. He took a slow breath through his blunt nose and let a pair of dice tumble from his fist and across the stained tabletop.

'Six and two,' he said. 'Eight.'

'Who the hell are you?' Kurtis's voice was squeaky with shock.

'The Quarryman sent me.' He let the dice roll again. 'Six and five.'

'Does that mean I lose?' Kurtis glanced over towards his sword, trying and failing to look nonchalant, wondering how fast he could get to it, draw it, strike—

'You lost already,' said the big man, gently collecting the dice with the side of his hand. He finally looked up. His eyes were flat as those of a dead fish. Like the fishes on the stalls at the market. Dead and dark and sadly glistening. 'Do you want to know what happens if you go for that sword?'

Kurtis wasn't a brave man. He never had been. It had taken all his courage to work up to surprising someone else, and being surprised himself had knocked the fight right out of him. 'No,' he muttered, his shoulders sagging.

'Toss me that package,' said the big man, and Kurtis did so. 'And the purse.'

It was as if all resistance had drained away. Kurtis had not the strength to attempt a ruse. He scarcely had the strength to stand. He tossed the stolen purse onto the table, and the big man worked it open with his fingertips and peered inside.

Kurtis gave a helpless, floppy motion of his hands. 'I have nothing else worth taking.'

'I know,' the man said as he stood. 'I have checked.' He stepped around the table and Kurtis cringed away, steadying himself against his cupboard. A cupboard containing nothing but cobwebs, as it went.

'Is the debt paid?' he asked in a very small voice.

'Do you think the debt is paid?'

They stood looking at one another. Kurtis swallowed. 'When will the debt be paid?'

The big man shrugged his shoulders, which were almost one with his head. 'When do you think the debt will be paid?'

Kurtis swallowed again, and he found his lip was trembling. 'When the Quarryman says so?'

The big man raised one heavy brow a fraction, the hairless

sliver of a scar through it. 'Have you any questions... to which you do not know the answers?'

Kurtis dropped to his knees, his hands clasped, the big man's face faintly swimming through the tears in his aching eyes. He did not care about the shame of it. The Quarryman had taken the last of his pride many visits before. 'Just leave me something,' he whispered. 'Just... something.'

The man stared back at him with his dead-fish eyes. 'Why?'

Friendly took the sword, too, but there was nothing else of value. 'I will come back next week,' he said.

It had not been meant as a threat, merely a statement of fact, and an obvious one at that since it had always been the arrangement, but Kurtis dan Broya's head slowly dropped, and he began to shudder with sobs.

Friendly considered whether to try and comfort him, but decided not to. He was often misinterpreted.

'You should, perhaps, not have borrowed the money.' Then he left.

It always surprised him that people did not do the sums when they took a loan. Proportions, and time, and the action of interest, it was not so very difficult to fathom. But perhaps they were prone always to overestimate their income, to poison themselves by looking on the bright side. Happy chances would occur, and things would improve, and everything would turn out well, because they were special. Friendly had no illusions. He knew he was but one unexceptional cog in the elaborate workings of life. To him, facts were facts.

He walked, counting off the paces to the Quarryman's place. One hundred and five, one hundred and four, one hundred and three...

Strange how small the city was when you measured it out. All those people, and all their desires, and scores, and debts, packed into this narrow stretch of reclaimed swamp. By Friendly's reckoning, the swamp was well on the way to taking large sections of it back. He wondered if the world would be better when it did.

. . . seventy-six, seventy-five, seventy-four . . .

Friendly had an extra shadow. Pickpocket, maybe. He took a careless look at a stall by the way and caught her out of the corner of his eye. A girl with dark hair gathered into a cap and a jacket too big for her. Hardly more than a child. Friendly took a few steps down a narrow snicket and turned, blocking the way, pushing back his coat to show the grips of four of his six weapons. His shadow rounded the corner, and he looked at her. Just looked. First she froze, then swallowed, then turned one way, then the other, then backed off and lost herself in the crowds. So that was the end of that episode.

. . . thirty-one, thirty, twenty-nine . . .

Sipani, and most especially its moist and fragrant Old Quarter, was full of thieves. They were a constant annoyance, like midges in summer. Also muggers, robbers, burglars, cutpurses, cutthroats, thugs, murderers, strong-arm men, swindlers, gamblers, fences, moneylenders, rakes, beggars, tricksters, pimps, pawnshop owners, crooked merchants, not to mention accountants and lawyers. Lawyers were the worst of the crowd, as far as Friendly was concerned. Sometimes it seemed that no one in Sipani made anything, exactly. They were all working their hardest to rip it from someone else.

But then Friendly supposed he was no better.

. . . four, three, two, one, and down the twelve steps, past the three guards, and through the double doors into the Quarryman's place.

Tough Times All Over

It was hazy with smoke inside, confusing with the light of coloured lamps, hot with breath and chafing skin, thick with the babble of hushed conversation, of secrets traded, reputations ruined, confidences betrayed. It was as all such places always are.

Two Northmen were wedged behind a table in the corner. One, with sharp teeth and long, lank hair, had tipped his chair all the way back and was slumped in it, smoking. The other had a bottle in one hand and a tiny book in the other, staring at it with brow well furrowed.

Most of the patrons Friendly knew by sight. Regulars. Some come to drink. Some to eat. Most of them fixed on the games of chance. The clatter of dice, the twitch and flap of the playing cards, the eyes of the hopeless glittering as the lucky wheel spun.

The games were not really the Quarryman's business, but the games made debts, and debts were the Quarryman's business. Up the twenty-three steps to the raised area, the guard with the tattoo on his face waving Friendly past.

Three of the other collectors were seated there, sharing a bottle. The smallest grinned at him, and nodded, perhaps trying to plant the seeds of an alliance. The biggest puffed himself up and bristled, sensing competition. Friendly ignored them equally. He had long ago given up trying even to understand the unsolvable mathematics of human relationships, let alone to participate. Should that man do more than bristle, Friendly's cleaver would speak for him. That was a voice that cut short even the most tedious of arguments.

Mistress Borfero was a fleshy woman with dark curls spilling from beneath a purple cap, small eyeglasses that made her eyes look large, and a smell about her of lamp oil. She haunted the anteroom before the Quarryman's office at a low desk stacked with ledgers. On Friendly's first day she had gestured towards the ornate door behind her and said, 'I am the Quarryman's right hand. He is never to be disturbed. *Never*. You speak to me.'

Friendly, of course, knew as soon as he saw her mastery of the numbers in those books that there was no one in the office and that Borfero was the Quarryman, but she seemed so pleased with the deception that he was happy to play along. Friendly had never liked to rock boats unnecessarily. That's how people ended up drowned. Besides, it somehow helped to imagine that the orders came from somewhere else, somewhere unknowable and irresistible. It was nice to have an attic in which to stack the blame. Friendly looked at the door of the Quarryman's office, wondering if there even was an office, or if it opened on blank stones.

'What was today's take?' she asked, flipping open a ledger and dipping her pen. Straight to business without so much as a how do you do. He greatly liked and admired that about her, though he would never have said so. His compliments had a way of causing offence.

Friendly slipped the coins out in stacks, then let them drop, one by one, in rattling rows by debtor and denomination. Mostly base metals, leavened with a sprinkling of silver.

Borfero sat forward, wrinkling her nose and pushing her eyeglasses up onto her forehead, eyes looking now extra small without them.

'A sword, as well,' said Friendly, leaning it up against the side of the desk.

'A disappointing harvest,' she murmured.

'The soil is stony hereabouts.'

'Too true.' She dropped the eyeglasses back and started to scratch orderly figures in her ledger. 'Tough times all over.' She often said that. As though it stood as explanation and excuse for anything and everything.

'Kurtis dan Broya asked me when the debt would be paid.'

She peered up, surprised by the question. 'When the Quarryman says it's paid.'

'That's what I told him.'

'Good.'

'You asked me to be on the lookout for . . . a package.' Friendly placed it on the desk before her. 'Broya had it.'

It did not seem so very important. It was less than a foot long, wrapped in very ancient stained and balding animal skin, and with a letter, or perhaps a number, burned into it with a brand. But not a number that Friendly recognised.

Mistress Borfero snatched up the package, then immediately cursed herself for looking too eager. She knew no one could be trusted in this business. That brought a rush of questions to her mind. Suspicions. How could that worthless Broya possibly have come by it? Was this some ruse? Was Friendly a plant of the Gurkish? Or perhaps of Carcolf's? A double bluff? There was no end to the webs that smug bitch spun. A triple bluff? But where was the angle? Where the advantage?

A quadruple bluff?

Friendly's face betrayed no trace of greed, no trace of ambition, no trace of anything. He was without doubt a strange fellow but came highly recommended. He was all business, and she liked that in a man, though she would never have said so. A manager must maintain a certain detachment.

Sometimes things are just what they appear to be. Borfero had seen strange chances enough in her life.

'This could be it,' she mused, though in fact she was

immediately sure. She was not a woman to waste time on possibilities.

Friendly nodded.

'You have done well,' she said.

He nodded again.

'The Quarryman will want you to have a bonus.' Be generous
with your own people, she had always said, or others will be.

But generosity brought no response from Friendly.

'A woman, perhaps?'

He looked a little pained by that suggestion. 'No.'

'A man?'

And that one. 'No.'

'Husk? A bottle of—'

'No.'

'There must be something.'

He shrugged.

Mistress Borfero puffed out her cheeks. Everything she had
she'd made by tickling out people's desires. She was not sure
what to do with a person who had none. 'Well, why don't you
think about it?'

Friendly slowly nodded. 'I will think.'

'Did you see two Northmen drinking on your way in?'

'I saw two Northmen. One was reading a book.'

'Really? A book?'

Friendly shrugged. 'There are readers everywhere.'

She swept through the place, noting the disappointing lack
of wealthy custom and estimating just how dismal this evening's profits were like to be. If one of the Northmen had been
reading, he had given up. Deep was drinking some of her best
wine straight from the bottle. Three others lay scattered, empty,
beneath the table. Shallow was smoking a chagga pipe, the air

thick with the stink of it. Borfero did not allow it normally, but she was obliged to make an exception for these two. Why the bank chose to employ such repugnant specimens she had not the slightest notion. But she supposed rich people need not explain themselves.

'Gentlemen,' she said, insinuating herself into a chair.

'Where?' Shallow gave a croaky laugh. Deep slowly tipped his bottle up and eyed his brother over the neck with sour distain.

Borfero continued in her business voice, soft and reasonable. 'You said your ... *employers* would be *most grateful* if I came upon ... *that certain item* you mentioned.'

The two Northmen perked up, both leaning forward as though drawn by the same string, Shallow's boot catching an empty bottle and sending it rolling in an arc across the floor.

'Greatly grateful,' said Deep.

'And how much of my debt would their gratitude stretch around?'

'All of it.'

Borfero felt her skin tingling. Freedom. Could it really be? In her pocket, even now? But she must not let the size of the stakes make her careless. The greater the pay-off, the greater the caution. 'My debt would be finished?'

Shallow leaned close, drawing the stem of his pipe across his stubbled throat. 'Killed,' he said.

'Murdered,' growled his brother, suddenly no further off on the other side.

She in no way enjoyed having those scarred and lumpen killers' physiognomies so near. Another few moments of their breath alone might have done for her. 'Excellent,' she squeaked, and slipped the package onto the table. 'Then I shall cancel the interest payments forthwith. Do please convey my regards to . . . your employers.'

'Course.' Shallow did not so much smile as show his sharp teeth. 'Don't reckon your regards'll mean much to them, though.'

'Don't take it personally, eh?' Deep did not smile. 'Our employers just don't care much for regards.'

Borfero took a sharp breath. 'Tough times all over.'

'Ain't they, though?' And Deep stood, and swept the package up in one big paw.

The cool air caught Deep like a slap as they stepped out into the evening. Sipani, none too pleasant when it was still, had a decided spin to it of a sudden.

'I have to confess,' he said, clearing his throat and spitting, 'to being somewhat on the drunk side of drunk.'

'Aye,' said Shallow, burping as he squinted into the mist. At least that was clearing somewhat. As clear as it got in this murky hell of a place, anyway. 'Probably not the bestest notion while at work, mind you.'

'You're right.' Deep held the baggage up to such light as there was. 'But who expected this to just drop in our laps?'

'Not I, for one.' Shallow frowned. 'Or for . . . not one?'

'It was meant to be just a tipple,' said Deep.

'One tipple does have a habit of making itself into several.' Shallow wedged on that stupid bloody hat. 'A little stroll over to the bank, then?'

'That hat makes you look a fucking dunce.'

'You, brother, are obsessed with appearances.'

Deep passed that off with a long hiss.

'They really going to score out that woman's debts, d'you think?'

'For now, maybe. But you know how they are. Once you owe, you always owe.' Deep spat again and, now the alley was a tad steadier, tottered off with the baggage clutched tight in his hand. No chance he was putting it in a pocket where some little scab could lift it. Sipani was full of thieving bastards. He'd had his good socks stolen last time he was here and worked up an unpleasant pair of blisters on the trip home. Who steals socks? Styrian bastards. He'd keep a good firm grip on it. Let the little fuckers try to take it *then*.

'Now who's the dunce?' Shallow called after him. 'The bank's this way.'

'Only we ain't going to the bank, *dunce*,' snapped Deep over his shoulder. 'We're to toss it down a well in an old court just around the corner here.'

Shallow hurried to catch up. 'We are?'

'No, I just said it for the laugh, y'idiot.'

'Why down a well?'

'Because that's how he wanted it done.'

'Who wanted it done?'

'The boss.'

'The little boss, or the big boss?'

Even drunk as Deep was, he felt the need to lower his voice. 'The bald boss.'

'Shit,' breathed Shallow. 'In person?'

'In person.'

A short pause. 'How was that?'

'It was even more than usually terrifying, thanks for reminding me.'

A long pause, with just the sound of their boots on the wet cobbles. Then Shallow said, 'We better hadn't do no fucking up of this.'

'My heartfelt thanks,' said Deep, 'for that piercing insight. Fucking up is always to be avoided when and wherever possible, wouldn't you say?'

'Y'always aim to avoid it, of course you do, but sometimes you run into it anyway. What I'm saying here is we'd best not run into it.' Shallow dropped his voice to a whisper. 'You know what the bald boss said last time.'

'You don't have to whisper. He ain't here, is he?'

Shallow looked wildly around. 'I don't know. Is he?'

'No, he ain't.' Deep rubbed at his temples. One day he'd kill his brother, that was a foregone conclusion. 'That's what I'm saying.'

'What if he was, though? Best to always act like he might be.'

'Can you shut your mouth just for a fucking *instant*?' Deep caught Shallow by the arm and stabbed the baggage in his face. 'It's like talking to a bloody—'

He was greatly surprised when a dark shape whisked between them and he found his hand was suddenly empty.

Kiam ran like her life depended on it. Which it did, o' course.

'Get after him, damn it!'

And she heard the two Northmen flapping and crashing and blundering down the alley behind, and nowhere near far enough behind for her taste.

'It's a girl, y'idiot!'

Big and clumsy but fast they were coming, boots hammering and hands clutching and if they once caught a hold of her . . .

'Who fucking cares? Get the thing back!'

And her breath hissing and her heart pounding and her muscles burning as she ran.

She skittered around a corner, rag-wrapped feet sticking to the damp cobbles, the way wider here, lamps and torches making muddy smears in the mist and people busy everywhere. She ducked and wove, around them, between them, faces looming up and gone. The Blackside night-market, stalls and shoppers and the cries of the traders, full of noise and smells and tight with bustle. Kiam wriggled under a wagon limber as a ferret, plunged between buyer and seller in a shower of fruit then slithered over a stall laden with slimy fish while the trader shouted and snatched at her, caught nothing but air, and she stuck one foot in a basket and was off, kicking cockles across the street. Still she heard the yells and growls as the Northmen knocked folk flying in her wake, crashes as they flung the carts aside, as though a mindless storm was ripping apart the market behind her. She dived between the legs of a big man, rounded another corner and took the greasy steps two at a time, along the narrow path by the slopping water, rats squeaking in the rubbish and the sounds of the Northmen now loud, louder, cursing her and each other. Her breath whooping and cutting in her chest and running desperate, water spattering and spraying around her with every echoing footfall.

'We've got her!' The voice so close at her heels. 'Come here!'

She darted through that little hole in the rusted grate, a sharp tooth of metal leaving a burning cut down her arm, and for once she was plenty glad that Old Green never gave her enough to eat. She kicked her way back into the darkness, keeping low, lay there clutching the package and struggling to catch her breath. Then they were there, one of the Northmen dragging at the grating, knuckles white with force, flecks of rust showering down as it shifted, and Kiam stared and wondered what those hands would do to her if they got their dirty nails into her skin.

The other one shoved his bearded face in the gap, a wicked-looking knife in his hand, not that someone you just robbed ever has a nice-looking knife. His eyes popped out at her and his

SHARP ENDS ‡ Joe Abercrombie

scabbed lips curled back and he snarled, 'Chuck us that baggage and we'll forget all about it. Chuck us it now!'

Kiam kicked away, the grate squealing as it bent.

'You're fucking dead, you little piss! We'll find you, don't worry about that!'

She slithered off, through the dust and rot, wriggled through a crack between crumbling walls.

'We'll be coming for you!' echoed from behind her.

Maybe they would as well, but a thief can't spend too much time worrying about tomorrow. Today's shitty enough. She whipped her coat off and pulled it inside out to show the faded green lining, stuffed her cap in her pocket and shook her hair out long, then slipped onto the walkway beside the Fifth Canal, walking fast, head down.

A pleasure boat drifted past, all chatter and laughter and clinking of glass, people moving tall and lazy on board, strange as ghosts seen through that mist, and Kiam wondered what they'd done to deserve that life and what she'd done to deserve this, but there never were no easy answers to that question. As it took its pink lights away into the fog she heard the music of Hove's violin. Stood a moment in the shadows, listening, thinking how beautiful it sounded. She looked down at the package. Didn't look much for all this trouble. Didn't weigh much, even. But it weren't up to her what Old Green put a price on. She wiped her nose and walked along close to the wall, music getting louder, then she saw Hove's back and his bow moving, and she slipped behind him and let the package fall into his gaping pocket.

Hove didn't feel the drop, but he felt the three little taps on his back, and he felt the weight in his coat as he moved. He didn't see who made the drop and he didn't look. He just carried on fiddling, that Union march with which he'd opened every show during his time on the stage in Adua, or under the stage, at any rate, warming up the crowd for Lestek's big entrance. Before his wife died and everything went to shit. Those jaunty notes reminded him of times past, and he felt tears prickling in his sore eyes, so he switched to a melancholy minuet more suited to his mood, not that most folk around here could've told the difference. Sipani liked to present itself as a place of culture but the majority were drunks and cheats and boorish thugs, or varying combinations thereof.

How had it come to this, eh? The usual refrain. He drifted across the street like he'd nothing in mind but a coin for his music, letting the notes spill out into the murk. Across past the pie stall, the fragrance of cheap meat making his stomach grumble, and he stopped playing to offer out his cap to the queue. There were no takers, no surprise, so he headed on down the road to Verscetti's, dancing in and out of the tables on the street and sawing out an Osprian waltz, grinning at the patrons who lounged there with a pipe or a bottle, twiddling thin glass-stems between gloved fingertips, eyes leaking contempt through the slots in their mirror-crusted masks. Jervi was sat near the wall, as always, a woman in the chair opposite, hair piled high.

'A little music, darling?' Hove croaked out, leaning over her and letting his coat dangle near Jervi's lap.

Jervi slid something out of Hove's pocket, wrinkling his nose at the smell of the old soak, and said, 'Fuck off, why don't you?' Hove moved on, and took his horrible music with him, thank the Fates.

'What's going on down there?' Riseld lifted her mask for a

moment to show that soft, round face well powdered and fashion-
ably bored.

There did indeed appear to be some manner of commotion up
the street. Crashing, banging, shouting in Northern.

'Damn Northmen,' he murmured. 'Always causing trouble,
they really should be kept on leads like dogs.' Jervi removed
his hat and tossed it on the table, the usual signal, then leaned
back in his chair to hold the package inconspicuously low to the
ground beside him. A distasteful business, but a man has to work.
'Nothing you need concern yourself about, my dear.'

She smiled at him in that unamused, uninterested way which
for some reason he found irresistible.

'Shall we go to bed?' he asked, tossing a couple of coins down
for the wine.

She sighed. 'If we must.'

And Jervi felt the package spirited away.

Sifkiss wriggled out from under the tables and strutted along,
letting his stick rattle against the bars of the fence beside him,
package swinging loose in the other. Maybe Old Green had said
stay stealthy but that weren't Sifkiss's way any more. A man has to
work out his own style of doing things and he was a full thirteen,
weren't he? Soon enough now he'd be passing on to higher things.
Working for Kurrikan, maybe. Anyone could tell he was marked
out special – he'd stole himself a tall hat that made him look
quite the gent about town – and if they were dull enough to be
entertaining any doubts, which some folk sadly were, he'd perched
it at quite the jaunty angle besides. Jaunty as all hell.

Yes, everyone had their eyes on Sifkiss.

He checked he weren't the slightest bit observed then slipped
through the dewy bushes and the crack in the wall behind, which

honestly was getting to be a bit of a squeeze, into the basement of the old temple, a little light filtering down from upstairs.

Most of the children were out working. Just a couple of the younger lads playing with dice and a girl gnawing on a bone and Pens having a smoke and not even looking over and that new one curled up in the corner and coughing. Sifkiss didn't like the sound o' those coughs. More'n likely he'd be dumping her off in the sewers a day or two hence but, hey, that meant a bit more corpse money for him, didn't it? Most folk didn't like handling a corpse but it didn't bother Sifkiss none. It's a hard rain don't wash someone a favour, as Old Green was always saying. She was way up there at the back, hunched over her old desk with one lamp burning, her long grey hair all greasy-slicked and her tongue pressed into her empty gums as she watched Sifkiss come up. Some smart-looking fellow was with her, had a waistcoat all silver leaves stitched fancy, and Sifkiss put a jaunt on, thinking to impress.

'Get it, did yer?' asked Old Green.

'Course,' said Sifkiss with a toss of his head, knocked his hat against a low beam and cursed as he fumbled it back into place. He tossed the package sourly down on the tabletop.

'Get you gone, then,' snapped Green.

Sifkiss looked surly, like he'd a mind to answer back. He was getting altogether too much mind, that boy, and Green had to show him the knobby-knuckled back of her hand 'fore he sloped off.

'So here you have it, as promised.' She pointed to that leather bundle in the pool of lamplight on her ancient table, its top cracked and stained and its gilt all peeling but still a fine piece of furniture with plenty of years left. Like to Old Green in that respect, if she did think so herself.

'Seems a little thing for such a lot of fuss,' said Fallow, wrinkling his nose, and he tossed a purse onto the table with that lovely clink of money. Old Green clawed it up and clawed it open and straight off set to counting it.

'Where's your girl Kiam?' asked Fallow. 'Where's little Kiam, eh?'

Old Green's shoulders stiffened but she kept counting. She could've counted through a storm at sea. 'Out working.'

'When's she getting back? I like her.' Fallow came a bit closer, voice going hushed. 'I could get a damn fine price for her.'

'But she's my best earner!' said Green. 'There's others you could take off my hands. How's about that lad Sifkiss?'

'What, the sour-face brought the luggage?'

'He's a good worker. Strong lad. Lots of grit. He'd pull a good oar on a galley, I'd say. Maybe a fighter, even.'

Fallow snorted. 'In a pit? That little shit? I don't think so. And he'd need some whipping to pull an oar, I reckon.'

'Well? They got whips, don't they?'

'Suppose they do. I'll take him if I must. Him and three others. I'm off to the market in Westport tomorrow week. You pick, but don't give me none o' your dross.'

'I don't keep no dross,' said Old Green.

'You got nothing but dross, you bloody swindler. And what'll you tell the rest o' your brood, eh?' Fallow put on a silly la-di-da voice. 'That they've gone off to be servants to gentry, or to live with the horses on a farm, or adopted by the fucking Emperor of Gurkhul or some such, eh?' Fallow chuckled, and Old Green had a sudden urge to make that knife of hers available, but she'd better sense these days, all learned the hard way.

'I tell 'em what I need to,' she grunted, still working her fingers around the coins. Bloody fingers weren't half as quick as they once were.

'You do that, and I'll come back for Kiam another day, eh?' And Fallow winked at her.

'Whatever you want,' said Green, 'whatever you say.' She was bloody well keeping Kiam, though. She couldn't save many, she wasn't fool enough to think that, but maybe she could save one, and on her dying day she could say she done that much. Probably no one would be listening, but she'd know. 'It's all there. Package is yours.'

Fallow picked up the luggage and was out of that stinking fucking place. Reminded him too much of prison. The smell of it. And the eyes of the children, all big and damp. He didn't mind buying and selling 'em, but he didn't want to see their eyes. Does the slaughterman want to look at the sheep's eyes? Maybe the slaughterman don't care. Maybe he gets used to it. Fallow cared too much, that's what it was. Too much heart.

His guards were lounging by the front door and he waved them over and set off, walking in the middle of the square they made.

'Successful meeting?' Grenti tossed over his shoulder.

'Not bad,' grunted Fallow, in such a way as to discourage further conversation. *Do you want friends or money?* he'd once heard Kurrikan say and the phrase had stuck with him.

Sadly, Grenti was by no means discouraged. 'Going straight over to Kurrikan's?'

'Yes,' said Fallow, sharply as he could.

But Grenti loved to flap his mouth. Most thugs do, in the end. All that time spent doing nothing, maybe. 'Lovely house, though, ain't it, Kurrikan's? What do you call those columns on the front of it?'

'Pilasters,' grunted one of the other thugs.

'No, no, I know pilasters, no. I mean to say the name given to that particular style of architecture, with the vine-leaves about the head there?'

'Rusticated?'

'No, no, that's the masonry work, all dimpled with the chisel, it's the overall design I'm discussing— Hold up.'

For a moment, Fallow was mightily relieved at the interruption. Then he was concerned. A figure was occupying the fog just ahead. Occupying the hell out of it. The beggars and revellers and scum scattered around these parts had all slipped out of their way like soil around the plough 'til now. This one didn't move. He was a tall bastard, tall as Fallow's tallest guard, with a white coat on, hood up. Well, it weren't white no more. Nothing stayed white long in Sipani. It was grey with damp and black-spattered about the hem.

'Get him out of the way,' he snapped.

'Get out of the fucking way!' roared Grenti.

'You are Fallow?' The man pulled his hood back.

'It's a woman,' said Grenti. And indeed it was, for all her neck was thickly muscled, her jaw angular and her red hair clipped close to her skull.

'I am Javre,' she said, raising her chin and smiling at them. 'Lioness of Hoskopp.'

'Maybe she's a mental,' said Grenti.

'Escaped from that madhouse up the way.'

'I did once escape from a madhouse,' said the woman. She had a weird accent, Fallow couldn't place it. 'Well . . . it was a prison for wizards. But some of them had gone mad. A fine distinction, most wizards are at least eccentric. That is beside the point, though. You have something I need.'

'That so?' said Fallow, starting to grin. He was less worried now. One, she was a woman, two, she obviously was a mental.

'I know not how to convince you for I lack the sweet words – it is a long-standing deficiency. But it would be best for us all if you give it to me willingly.'

'I'll give you something willingly,' said Fallow, to sniggers from the others.

The woman didn't snigger. 'It is a parcel, wrapped in leather, about . . .' She held up one big hand, thumb and forefinger stretched out. 'Five times the length of your cock.'

If she knew about the luggage, she was trouble. And Fallow had no sense of humour about his cock, to which none of the ointments had made the slightest difference. He stopped grinning. 'Kill her.'

She struck Grenti somewhere around the chest, or maybe she did, it was all a blur. His eyes popped wide and he made a strange whooping sound and stood there frozen, quivering on his tiptoes, sword halfway drawn.

The second guard – a Union man big as a house – swung his mace at her but it just caught her flapping coat. An instant later there was a surprised yelp and he was flying across the street upside down and crashing into the wall, tumbling to the ground in a shower of dust, sheets of broken plaster dropping from the shattered brickwork on top of his limp body.

The third guard – a nimble-fingered Osprian – whipped out a throwing knife but before he could loose it, the mace twittered through the air and bounced from his head. He dropped soundlessly, arms outstretched.

'They are called Anthiric columns.' The woman put her

forefinger against Grenti's forehead and gently pushed him over. He toppled and lay there on his side in the muck, still stiff, still trembling, still with eyes bulgingly focused on nothing.

'That was with one hand.' She held up the other big fist, and had produced from somewhere a sheathed sword, gold glittering on the hilt. 'Next I draw this sword, forged in the Old Time from the metal of a fallen star. Only six living people have seen the blade. You would find it extremely beautiful. Then I would kill you with it.'

The last of the guards exchanged a brief glance with Fallow, then tossed his axe away and sprinted off.

'Huh,' said the woman, with a slight wrinkling of disappointment about her red brows. 'Just so you know, if you run I will catch you in . . .' She narrowed her eyes and pushed out her lips, looking Fallow appraisingly up and down. The way he might have appraised the children. He found he didn't like being looked at that way. 'About four strides.'

He ran.

She caught him in three and he was suddenly on his face with a mouthful of dirty cobblestone and his arm twisted sharply behind his back.

'You've no idea who you're dealing with, you stupid bitch!' He struggled but her grip was iron, and he squealed with pain as his arm was twisted even more sharply.

'It is true I am no high-thinker.' Her voice showed not the slightest strain. 'I like simple things well done and have no time to philosophise. Would you like to tell me where the parcel is, or shall I beat you until it falls out?'

'I work for Kurrikan!' he gasped.

'I am new in town. Names work no magic on me.'

'We'll find you!'

She laughed. 'Of course. I am no hider. I am Javre, First of the Fifteen. Javre, Knight Templar of the Golden Order. Javre, Breaker of Chains, Breaker of Oaths, Breaker of Faces.' And here she gave him a blinding blow on the back of the head which, he was pretty sure, broke his nose against the cobbles and filled the back of his mouth with the salt taste of blood. 'To find me, you need only ask for Javre.' She leaned over him, breath tickling at his ear. 'It is once you find me that your difficulties begin. Now, where is that parcel?'

A pinching sensation began in Fallow's hand. Mildly painful to begin with, then more, and more, a white-hot burning up his arm that made him whimper like a dog. 'Ah, ah, ah, inside pocket, inside pocket!'

'Very good.' He felt hands rifling through his clothes but could only lie limp, moaning as the jangling of his nerves gradually subsided. He craned his neck around to look up at her and curled back his lips. 'I swear on my fucking front teeth—'

'Do you?' As her fingers found the hidden pocket and slid the package free. 'That's rash.'

Javre pressed finger against thumb and flicked Fallow's two front teeth out. A trick she had learned from an old man in Suljuk and, as with so many things in life, all in the wrist. She left him hunched in the road struggling to cough them up.

'The next time we meet I will have to show you the sword!' she called out as she strode away, wedging the package down behind her belt. Goddess, these Sipanese were weaklings. Was there no one to test her any more?

She shook her sore hand out. Probably her fingernail would turn black and drop off, but it would grow back. Unlike Fallow's teeth. And it was scarcely the first fingernail she had lost.

Including that memorable time she had lost the lot and toenails, too, in the tender care of the Prophet Khalul. Now *there* had been a test. For a moment, she almost felt nostalgic for her interrogators. Certainly she felt nostalgic for the pleasure of shoving their chief's face into his own brazier when she escaped. What a sizzle he had made!

But perhaps this Kurrikan would be outraged enough to send a decent class of killer after her. Then she could go after him. Hardly the great battles of yesteryear, but something to wile away the evenings.

Until then Javre walked, swift and steady with her shoulders back. She loved to walk. With every stride she felt her own strength. Every muscle utterly relaxed yet ready to turn the next step in a split instant into mighty spring, sprightly roll, deadly strike. Without needing to look she felt each person about her, judged their threat, predicted their attack, imagined her response, the air around her alive with calculated possibilities, the surroundings mapped, the distances known, all things of use noted. The sternest tests are those you do not see coming, so Javre was the weapon always sharpened, the weapon never sheathed, the answer to every question.

But no blade came darting from the dark. No arrow, no flash of fire, no squirt of poison. No pack of assassins burst from the shadows.

Sadly.

Only a pair of drunk Northmen wrestling outside Pombrine's place, one of them snarling something about the bald boss. She paid them no mind as she trotted up the steps, ignoring the several frowning guards, who were of a quality inferior even to Fallow's men, down the hallway and into the central salon, complete with fake marble, cheap chandelier and profoundly unarousing mosaic of a lumpy couple fucking horse-style. Evidently the evening rush had yet to begin. Whores of both sexes and one Javre was still not entirely sure about lounged bored upon the overwrought furniture.

Pombrine was busy admonishing one of his flock for over-dressing, but looked up startled when she entered. 'You're back already? What went wrong?'

Javre laughed full loud. 'Everything.' His eyes widened, and she laughed louder yet. 'For them.' And she took his wrist and pressed the parcel into his hand.

Pombrine gazed down at that unassuming lump of animal skin. 'You did it?'

The woman thumped one heavy arm about his shoulders and gave them a squeeze. He gasped as his bones creaked. Without doubt she was of exceptional size, but even so the casual strength of it was hardly to be believed. 'You do not know me. Yet. I am Javre, Lioness of Hoskopp.' She looked down at him and he had an unpleasant and unfamiliar sensation of being a naughty child helpless in his mother's grasp. 'When I agree to a challenge I do not shirk it. But you will learn.'

'I keenly anticipate my education.' Pombrine wriggled free of the crushing weight of her arm. 'You did not . . . open it?'

'You told me not to.'

'Good. Good.' He stared down, the smile half-formed on his face, hardly able to believe it could have been this easy.

'My payment, then.'

'Of course.' He reached for the purse.

She held up one calloused hand. 'I will take half in flesh.'

'In flesh?'

'Isn't that what you peddle here?'

329

He raised his brows. 'Half would be a great quantity of flesh.'

'I get through it. And I mean to stay a while.'

'Lucky us,' he muttered.

'I'll take him.'

'An excellent choice, I—'

'And him. And him. And her.' Javre rubbed her rough palms together. 'She can get the lads warmed up, I am not paying to wank anyone off myself.'

'Naturally not.'

'I am a woman of Thond and have grand appetites.'

'So I begin to see.'

'And for the sun's sake someone draw me a bath. I smell like a heated bitch already, I dread to imagine the stink afterward. I will have every tomcat in the city pursuing me!' And she burst out laughing again.

One of the men swallowed. The other looked at Pombrine with an expression faintly desperate as Javre herded them into the nearest room.

'. . . you, remove your trousers. You, get the bandages off my tits. You would scarcely credit how tightly I have to strap this lot down to get anything done . . .'

The door snapped mercifully shut.

Pombrine seized Scalacay, his most trusted servant, by the shoulder and drew him close.

'Go to the Gurkish temple off the Third Canal with all haste, the one with the green marble pillars. Do you know it?'

'I do, Master.'

'Tell the priest who chants in the doorway that you have a message for Ishri. That Master Pombrine has the item she was asking after. For Ishri, do you understand?'

'For Ishri. Master Pombrine has the item.'

'Then run to it!'

Scalacay dashed away leaving Pombrine to hurry to his office with hardly less haste, the package clutched in one sweaty hand. He fumbled the door shut and turned the key, the five locks closing with a reassuring metallic clatter.

Only then did he allow himself to breathe. He placed the package reverently upon his desk. Now he had it, he felt the need to stretch out the moment of triumph. To weigh it down with the proper gravitas. He went to his drinks cabinet and unlocked it, took his grandfather's bottle of Shiznadze from the place of honour. That man had lived his whole life waiting for a moment worthy of opening that bottle. Pombrine smiled as he reached for the corkscrew, trimming away the lead from the neck.

How long had he worked to secure that cursed package? Circulating rumours of his business failings when in fact he had never been so successful. Placing himself in Carcolf's way again and again until finally they appeared to happen upon each other by chance. Wriggling himself into a position of trust while the idiot courier thought him a brainless stooge, clambering by minuscule degrees to a perch from which he could get his eager hands around the package, and then ... unhappy fate! Carcolf had slipped free, the cursed bitch, leaving Pombrine with nothing but ruined hopes. But now ... happy fate! The thuggery of that loathsome woman Javre had by some fumbling miracle succeeded where his genius had been so unfairly thwarted.

What did it matter how he had come by it, though? His smile grew wider as he eased the cork free. He had the package. He turned to gaze upon his prize again.

Pop! An arc of fizzy wine missed his glass and spurted across his Kadiri carpet. He stared open-mouthed. The package was hanging in the air from a hook. Attached to the hook was a gossamer thread. The thread disappeared through a hole in the glass roof high above where he now saw a black shape spreadeagled.

Pombrine made a despairing lunge, bottle and glass tumbling to the floor and spraying wine, but the package slipped through his clutching fingers and was whisked smoothly upwards out of his reach.

'Guards!' he roared, shaking his fist. 'Thief!'

A moment later he realised, and his rage turned in a flash to withering horror.

Ishri would soon be on her way.

With a practised jerk of her wrist, Shev twitched the parcel up and into her waiting glove.

'What an angler,' she whispered as she thrust it into her pocket and was away across the steeply pitched roof, knee pads sticky with tar doing most of the work. Astride the ridge and she scuttled to the chimney, flicked the rope into the street below, was over the edge in a twinkling and swarming down. Don't think about the ground, never think about the ground. It's a nice place to be but you wouldn't want to get there too quickly . . .

'What a climber,' she whispered as she passed a large window, a garishly decorated and gloomily lit salon coming into view, and—

She gripped tight to the rope and stopped dead, gently swinging.

She really did have a pressing engagement with not being caught by Pombrine's guards, but inside the room was one of those sights one couldn't simply slide past. Four, possibly five or even six naked bodies had formed, with most impressive athleticism, a kind of human sculpture – a grunting tangle of gently shifting limbs. While she was turning her head sideways on to make sense of it, the lynchpin of the arrangement, who Shev took at first glance for a red-haired strongman, looked straight at her.

'Shevedieh?'

Decidedly not a man, but very definitely strong. Even with hair clipped close there was no mistaking her.

'Javre? What the hell are you doing here?'

She raised a brow at the naked bodies entwined about her. 'Is that not obvious?'

Shev was brought to her senses by the rattle of guards in the street below. 'You never saw me!' And she slid down the rope, hemp hissing through her gloves, hit the ground hard and sprinted off just as a group of men with weapons drawn came barrelling around the corner.

'Stop, thief!'

'Get him!'

And, particularly shrill, Pombrine desperately wailing, 'My package!'

Shev jerked the cord at the small of her back and felt the pouch split, the caltrops scattering in her wake, heard the shrieks as a couple of the guards went tumbling. Sore feet they'd have in the morning. But there were still more following.

'Cut him off!'

'Shoot him!'

She took a sharp left, heard the flatbow string an instant later, the twitter as the bolt glanced from the wall beside her and away into the night. She peeled off her gloves as she ran, one smoking from the friction, and flung them over her shoulder. A quick right, the route well planned in advance, of course, and she sprang up onto the tables outside Verscetti's, bounding from one to the next with great strides, sending cutlery and glassware flying, the patrons floundering up, tumbling in their shock, a ragged violinist flinging himself for cover.

'What a runner,' she whispered, and leaped from the last table, over the clutching hands of a guard diving from her left and a reveller from her right, catching the little cord behind the sign that said *Verscetti's* as she fell and giving it a good tug.

There was a flash like lightning as she rolled, an almighty bang as she came up, the murky night at once illuminated, the frontages of the buildings ahead picked out white. There were screams and squeals and a volley of detonations. Behind her, she knew, blossoms of purple fire would be shooting across the street, showers of golden sparks, a display suitable for a baron's wedding.

'That Qohdam certainly can make fireworks,' she whispered, resisting the temptation to stop and watch the show and instead slipping down a shadowy snicket, shooing away a mangy cat, scurrying on low for three-dozen strides and ducking into the narrow garden, struggling to keep her quick breath quiet. She ripped open the packet she'd secured among the roots of the dead willow, unfurling the white robe and wriggling into it, pulling up the cowl and waiting in the shadows, the big votive candle in one hand, ears sifting at the night.

'Shit,' she muttered. As the last echoes of her fiery diversion faded she could hear, faintly but coming closer, the calls of Pombrine's searching guards, doors rattling as they tried them one by one.

'Where did he go?'

'I think this way!'

'Bloody firework burned my hand! I'm really burned, you know!'

'My package!'

'Come on, come on,' she muttered. To be caught by these idiots would be among the most embarrassing moments of her career. That time she'd been stuck in a marriage gown halfway up the side of the Mercers' guildhall in Adua with flowers in her hair but no underwear and a steadily growing crowd of onlookers below would take some beating, but still. 'Come on, come on, come—'

Now, from the other direction, she heard the chanting and grinned. The Sisters were always on time. She heard their feet now, the regular tramping blotting out the shouting of Pombrine's guards and the wailing of a woman temporarily deafened by the fireworks. Louder the feet, louder the heavenly song, and the procession passed the garden, the women all in white, all hooded, lit candles held stiffly before them, ghostly in the gloom as they marched by in unison.

'What a priestess,' Shev whispered to herself, and threaded from the garden, jostling her way into the midst of the procession. She tipped her candle to the left so its wick touched that of her neighbour. The woman frowned across and Shev winked back.

'Give a girl a light, would you?'

With a fizzle it caught and she fell into step, adding her own joyous note to the chant as they processed down Caldiche Street and over the Fintine Bridge, the masked revellers parting respectfully to let them through. Pombrine's place, and the increasingly frantic searching of his guards, and the furious growling of a pair of savagely arguing Northmen dwindled sedately into the mists behind.

It was dark by the time she slipped silently through her own open window, past the stirring drapes, and crept around her comfortable chair. Carcolf was asleep in it, one strand of yellow hair fluttering around her mouth as she breathed. She looked young with eyes closed and face relaxed, shorn of that habitual sneer she had for everything. Young, and very beautiful. Bless this fashion for tight trousers! The candle cast a faint glow in the downy hairs on her cheek, and Shev felt a need to reach up and lay her palm upon that face, and stroke her lips with her thumb—

But, lover of risks though she was, that would've been too great a gamble. So instead she shouted, 'Boo!'

Carcolf leaped up like a frog from boiling water, crashed into a table and nearly fell, lurched around, eyes wide. 'Bloody hell,' she muttered, taking a shuddering breath. 'Do you have to do that?'

'Have to? No.'

Carcolf pressed one hand to her chest. 'I think you might have opened the stitches.'

'You unbelievable baby.' Shev pulled the robe over her head and tossed it away. 'It barely broke the skin.'

'The loss of your good opinion wounds me more deeply than any blade.'

Shev unhooked the belts that held her thief's tools, unbuckled her climbing pads and started to peel off her black clothes, acting as if it was nothing to her whether Carcolf watched or not. But she noted with some satisfaction that it was not until she was slipping on a clean gown that Carcolf finally spoke, and in a voice slightly hoarse besides.

'Well?'

'Well what?'

'It has always been a dream of mine to see a Sister of the White disrobe before my eyes, but I was rather wondering whether you found the—'

Shev tossed over the package and Carcolf snatched it smartly from the air.

'I knew I could rely on you.' Carcolf felt a little dizzy with relief, not to mention more than a little tingly with desire. She'd always had a weakness for dangerous women.

Bloody hell, she really was turning into her father . . .

'You were right,' said Shev, dropping into the chair she had so recently frightened Carcolf out of. 'Pombrine had it.'

'I bloody knew it! That slime! So hard to find a good expendable decoy these days.'

'It's as if you can't trust anyone.'

'Still. No harm done, eh?' And Carcolf lifted up her shirt and ever so carefully slid the package into the uppermost of her two cash belts.

It was Shev's turn to watch, pretending not to as she poured herself a glass of wine. 'What's in the parcel?' she asked.

'It's safer if I don't tell you.'

'You've no idea, have you?'

'I'm under orders not to look,' Carcolf was forced to admit.

'Don't you ever wonder, though? I mean, the more I'm ordered not to look, the more I want to.' Shev sat forward, dark eyes glimmering in a profoundly bewitching way, and for an instant Carcolf's head was filled with an image of the pair of them rolling across the carpet together, laughing as they ripped the package apart between them.

She dismissed it with difficulty. 'A thief can wonder. A courier cannot.'

'Could you be any more pompous?'

'It would require an effort.'

Shev slurped at her wine. 'Well, it's your package. I suppose.'

'No, it isn't. That's the whole point.'

'I think I preferred you when you were a criminal.'

'Lies. You relish the opportunity to corrupt me.'

'True enough.' Shev wriggled down the chair so her long, brown legs slid out from the hem of her gown. 'Why don't you stay a while?' One searching foot found Carcolf's ankle, and slid gently up the inside of her leg, and down, and up. 'And be corrupted?'

Carcolf took an almost painful breath. 'Damn, but I'd love to.' The strength of the feeling surprised her, and caught in her throat, and for the briefest moment she almost choked on it. For the briefest moment, she almost tossed the package out of the window, and sank down before the chair, and took Shev's hand and shared tales she had never told from when she was a girl. For the briefest moment. Then she was Carcolf again, and she stepped smartly away and let Shev's foot clomp down on the boards. 'But you know how it is, in my business. Have to catch the tide.' And she snatched up her new coat and turned as she pulled it on, giving herself time to blink back any hint of tears.

'You should take a holiday.'

'With every job I say so, and when every job ends, I find I get . . . twitchy.' Carcolf sighed as she fastened the buttons. 'I'm just not made for sitting still.'

'Huh.'

'Let's not pretend you're any different.'

'Let's not pretend. I've been considering a move myself. Adua, perhaps, or back to the South—'

'I'd much rather you stayed here,' Carcolf found she had said, then tried to pass it off with a carefree wave. 'Who else would get me out of messes when I visit? You're the one person in this whole damn city I trust.' That was a complete lie, of course, she didn't trust Shev in the least. A good courier trusts no one, and Carcolf was the very best. But she was a great deal more comfortable with lies than with truth.

She could see in Shev's smile that she understood the whole situation perfectly. 'So sweet.' She caught Carcolf's wrist as she turned to leave with a grip that was not to be ignored. 'My money?'

'How silly of me.' Carcolf handed her the purse.

Without even looking inside, Shev said, 'And the rest.'

Carcolf sighed once more and tossed the other purse on the bed, gold flashing in the lamplight as coins spilled across the white sheet. 'You'd be upset if I didn't try.'

'Your care for my delicate feelings is touching. I daresay I'll see you next time you're here?' she asked as Carcolf put her hand on the lock.

'I shall count the moments.'

Just then she wanted a kiss more than anything, but she was not sure her resolve was strong enough for only one, so though it was a wrench she blew a kiss instead and pulled the door to behind her. She slipped swiftly across the shadowed court and out through the heavy gate onto the street, hoping it would be a while before Shevedieh took a closer look at the coins inside the first purse. Perhaps a cosmic punishment was thus incurred, but it was worth it just for the thought of the look on her face.

The day had been a bloody fiasco, but she supposed it could have been a great deal worse. She still had ample time to make it to the ship before they lost the tide. Carcolf pulled up her hood, wincing at the pain from that freshly stitched scratch, and from that entirely unreasonable ulcer, and from that cursed chafing seam, then strode off through the misty night, neither too fast nor too slow, entirely inconspicuous.

Damn, but she hated Sipani.

THE MIDDLE

WHITE SEA

ANGLAND

Osten

FAR
COUNTRY

Neworja   New
           Keln   Rostod   STARKLAND

Aulcus   ·Epedra

Ros   Calcis

OLD EMPIRE   ·Darmium

Avstom·   Starkhea

(Gordius)   MIDDE

CIRCL

Dag

Isparda

KADIR   Daleppo

Ul-Khalif   GU

OF

BRIGHT   GURK
SEA   Alubat·
       Shaffa

Bizurt

SHAMIR   GURK

MADE
A MONSTER

Carleon, Summer 570

'What's peace, Father?'

Bethod blinked down at his older son. Eleven years, and Scale had scarcely seen peace in his lifetime. Moments of it, maybe. Glimpses through a haze of blood. As he struggled to answer, Bethod realised he hardly remembered what peace felt like himself any more.

How long had he been living in fear?

He squatted before Scale and thought of his own father squatting before him, twisted with sickness and old beyond his years. 'Some men will break a thing just because they can,' he had whispered. 'But war must be a leader's last resort. Fight a war, you've lost already.'

In spite of all his victories, all the odds beaten and the enemies put in the mud, all the ransoms claimed and the land taken, Bethod had been losing for years. He saw that now.

'Peace,' he said, 'is when the feuds are all settled, and the blood debts are paid, and everyone is content with how things are. More or less content, anyway. Peace is when ... when no one's fighting any more.'

Scale thought about that, frowning. Bethod loved him, of course he did, but even he had to admit the boy wasn't the quickest. 'Then ... who wins?'

'Everyone,' said Calder.

Bethod raised his brows. His younger son was as quick as his older was slow. 'That's right. Peace means everyone wins.'

'But Rattleneck's sworn there'll be no peace 'til you're dead,' said Scale.

'He has. But Rattleneck is one of those men who swears oaths quickly. Given time he may think better of it. Especially since I have his son in chains downstairs.'

'*You* have him?' snapped out Ursi from the corner of the room, stopping brushing her hair long enough to train one eye on him. 'I thought he was Ninefingers' prisoner?'

'Ninefingers will give him to me.' Bethod tossed that breezily to his wife as if it was a thing done with a snap of his fingers, rather than a trial he was having to scrape together the courage for. What kind of a Chieftain feared to ask a favour of his own champion?

'Order him to do it.' The man's words sounded strange in Calder's high child's voice. 'Make him do it.'

'I cannot order him in this. Rattleneck's son is Ninefingers' prisoner. He was taken in battle, and Named Men have their ways.' Not to mention that Bethod wasn't sure Ninefingers would obey, or what to do if he refused, and the thought of putting it to the test sank him in dread. 'There are rules.'

'Rules are for those who follow,' said Calder.

'Rules must be for all, and for those who lead most of all. Without rules, every man stands alone, owning only what he can tear from the world with one hand and grip with the other. Chaos.'

Calder nodded. 'I see.' And Bethod knew he did. So little alike, his two sons. Scale sturdy, blond and bullish. Calder slight, dark and cunning. Each so like their mothers, Bethod sometimes wondered whether there was anything of him in them.

'What'll we do with peace?' asked Scale.

'Build.' Bethod smiled as he thought about his plans, turned over so often he could see them like things already done. 'We'll send the men back to their land, back to their trades, back to their families in time for the harvest. Then we'll set them to pay us taxes.'

'Taxes?'

'They're a Southern thing,' said Calder. 'Money.'

'Each man gives his Chieftain some of what he has,' said Bethod. 'And we'll use that money to clear forests, and dig mines, and put walls about our towns. Then we'll build a great road from Carleon to Uffrith.'

'A road?' muttered Scale, not seeing the glamour in packed earth.

'Men can travel twice as fast on it,' snapped Calder, starting to lose patience.

'Fighting men?' asked Scale, hopefully.

'If need be,' said Bethod. 'But also carts and goods, livestock and messages.' He pointed towards the window, bright in the darkness, as though they might all glimpse a better future through it. 'That road will be the spine of the nation we'll build. That road will knit the North together. I might have won battles, but it's that road I'll be remembered for. It's that road that will change the world.'

'How can you change the world with a road?' asked Scale.

'You're an idiot,' said Calder.

Scale hit him on the side of the head and knocked him over, thus demonstrating the limits of cleverness. Bethod heard Ursi gasp, and he hit Scale in much the same way and knocked him over, too, thus demonstrating the limits of brute force. An ugly pattern, often acted out between the four of them.

'Up, the pair of you,' Bethod snapped.

Calder glared darkly at his brother as he stood, one hand to his bloody mouth, while Scale glared darkly back, one hand to his. Bethod took them each by one arm and drew them close with a grip not to be resisted.

'We are family,' he said. 'If we're not always for each other, who will be? Scale, one day you'll be Chieftain. You must control your temper. Calder, one day you'll be your brother's right hand, and first councillor, and most trusted adviser. You must control your tongue. Between the two of you, you have all the best of me and plenty more besides. Between the two of you, you could make our clan the greatest in the North. Alone, you're nothing. Remember that.'

'Yes, Father,' muttered Calder.

'Yes, Father,' grunted Scale.

'Now go, and if I hear of more fighting, let it be of how the two of you beat someone else together.' He stood with his hands on his hips as they barged each other in the doorway then tumbled out into the corridor, the door swinging shut behind them. 'I can scarcely keep the peace between my own sons,' he muttered, shaking his head. 'How will I do it between the leaders of the North?'

'One might hope the leaders of the North will act more like grown men' said Ursi, her dress swishing against the floor as she walked up behind him, her hands slipping gently around his ribs.

Bethod snorted as he held her arms against his heart. 'I fear that would be a rash hope. They like great warriors in the North, and great warriors rarely make great leaders. Men without fear are men without imagination. Men who use their heads for smashing through things rather than thinking. They celebrate spiteful, prideful, wrathful men here, and pick the most childish of the crowd for leaders.'

'They've found a different kind of leader in you.'

'I've made them listen. And I will make Rattleneck listen. And I will make Ninefingers listen, too.' Though Bethod wondered whether it was his wife or himself he was trying to convince. 'He can be a reasonable man.'

'Perhaps he used to be.' Ursi's breath tickled his neck as she spoke softly in his ear. 'But Ninefingers is blood-drunk. Murder-proud. Every day he is less your friend, less to be trusted, less a man at all and more an animal. Every day he is less Logen and more the Bloody-Nine.'

Bethod winced. He knew she had the right of it. 'Some days he's calm enough.'

'And the others? Last week he killed a whole pen full of sheep, did you know that?'

Bethod's wince twisted into a grimace. 'I heard.'

'Because their bleating bothered him, he said. He killed them with his hands, one by one, so calmly the others didn't even stir.'

'I heard.'

'And when the sheepdog barked he crushed her head, and they found him sound asleep and snoring among the corpses. He is made of death, and he brings death wherever he goes. He scares me.'

Bethod turned in her arms to look down at her, laid one hand gently on her cheek. 'You need never be scared. Not you.' Though the dead knew, he was scared enough himself. How long had he been living in fear?

She put her hand on his. 'I'm not scared of him. I'm scared of the trouble he might bring you. *Will* bring you.' Her voice dropped to a whisper as she looked into his eyes. 'You know I'm right. What if you can stitch a peace together? Ninefingers is not a sword you can hang over the fireplace and tell fond tales of after supper. He is the Bloody-Nine. If you stop finding fights for him, do you think he'll stop fighting? No. He will find his own, and with whoever's nearest. That's what he is. Sooner or later he will find a fight with you.'

'But I owe him,' he muttered. 'Without him, we never—'

'The Great Leveller pays all debts,' she said.

'There are rules.' But his voice was weak now, so weak he could hardly meet her dark eyes.

'Tell that to the children, by all means,' she whispered. 'But we know otherwise. There are only judgements – what is better, what is worse.'

'I'll talk to him,' he said again, knowing how feeble it sounded even in his own ear. He broke free of her and strode to the window. 'He'll give up Rattleneck's son. He will see the sense of it. He *must*.' He planted his fists on the sill and hung his head. 'By the dead, I'm sick of this. So sick of the blood.'

She came close again, kneading at his shoulder, at the back of his neck, and he heaved a sigh at her touch. 'You never looked for blood.'

He had to laugh at that, though there was little joy in it. 'I did. I demanded it. Not this much, I never thought it could be this much, but that's the trouble with blood. Wounds are so easy to open, so difficult to close. And I opened them eagerly. I needed a man to fight for me. I needed a man who'd stop at nothing. I needed a monster.'

'And you found one.'

'No,' he whispered, shrugging off her hand. 'I made one.'

*

It was one of those days at the very start of summer when, like a clever general, the warm sun draws you out then catches you unawares with a downpour of sudden violence. The straw eaves of the buildings dripped with the latest shower, the yard of the holdfast churned to slop and pocked with glistening puddles.

'A bad day for attacking,' said Craw, following watchfully at Bethod's shoulder with one hand slack on his sword's pommel. 'A good day for holding a good position.'

'There are no bad days for holding good positions,' said Bethod as he squelched across the yard, trying and failing to find firm ground to step on.

'A good leader holds positions whenever he can, I reckon. Lets less prudent men do the attacking.'

'So he does,' said Bethod. 'How good is my position, do you think?'

Craw scratched at his brown beard. 'Couldn't say, Chief.'

A quarter of Bethod's army was camped outside the gates. Men sat clustered around their tents, cooking and drinking, picking scabs and dicing for trophies from yesterday's battle, lazing in the sunshine. They took up notched weapons to clash on their battered shields as he passed and roared out praise.

'The Chief! It's the Chief!'

'Bethod!'

'One more victory!'

He wondered how long the cheers would keep flowing if they went on fighting but the victories dried up. Not long, was his guess. He shook his head at the thought. By the dead, was there no success he couldn't look at like it was a failure?

Logen's tent was at a distance from the others. Whether he chose to pitch it away from them, or he pitched it where he pleased and everyone else chose to keep away, it was hard to say.

But it was at a distance, anyway. Nothing from the outside said it belonged to the most feared man in the North. A big, shapeless, stained thing, mildewed canvas flapping with the breeze.

The Dogman sat at a dead fire near the stirring flap, trimming flights for arrows. Sitting as faithfully as any dog at his master's doorway. Bethod had pity in him, whatever men might say, and he felt a touch of pity then. He was bound tight to Ninefingers, surely, but nowhere near as tight as this poor fool.

'Where's the rest of the flotsam?' asked Bethod.

'Threetrees took 'em out scouting.' said the Dogman.

'Took them where they didn't have to face their shame, you mean.'

The Dogman looked up for a moment, not awed in the least. 'Maybe, Chief. We all got our shame, I reckon.'

'Wait here,' Bethod grunted at Craw, wishing he was staying with him as he stooped towards the tent's flap.

'I wouldn't go in there right now,' said the Dogman, starting to get up.

'You don't have to,' snapped Bethod, with no intention of working up the courage to squelch all the way over here again later. He was the master, and he would act like it. He ripped back the tent's flap, shouting, 'Ninefingers!'

It took a moment for his eyes to get used to the fusty dimness. A moment in which he smelled the sharp stink of unwashed bodies, and heard a scuffling and a grunting and a slapping of skin.

Then he saw Ninefingers, naked on his knees on a heap of bald old furs, muscles knotted in his back, head twisted to glare over his great slab of a shoulder. There was a new scar on his cheek, glistening black in a track of twisted stitches. His eyes were starting wide and his teeth bared in an animal snarl and for a moment Bethod thought he'd come flying at him with murder in mind.

Then his fresh-scarred face broke out in a jaunty smile. 'Well, either come in or go out, Chief, but don't loiter, there's a breeze on my arse.'

Bethod saw the woman then, on her knees beyond Ninefingers, the daylight harsh on her greasy hair and the sweaty side of her face.

For a thousand reasons, Bethod would have very much liked to leave. But Rattleneck was on his way. It had to be done, and done now.

'Get out,' said Bethod to the woman. Instead of leaping to obey, she twisted about for Ninefingers's say.

He shrugged. 'You heard the Chief.'

Bethod might have been Chieftain of Carleon and Uffrith both, winner of two dozen battles, acknowledged by all the greatest war leader since Skarling Hoodless. But Logen Ninefingers had gathered an aura of fear about him the past few years. An aura of death. Like the one Shama Heartless used to have, but worse, and with every duel won and every man killed, it grew worse yet.

Within reach of his hand, the Bloody-Nine was master.

The woman wriggled up and hurried past Bethod, snatching her clothes on the way and not even bothering to put them on. The dead knew the relief she felt. Bethod only had to talk to Ninefingers and his bowels felt weak. He dreaded to imagine what having to fuck him might be like. He took one last, longing glance into the daylight and let the flap drop, sealing him in the darkness with his old friend. His old enemy.

Ninefingers had rolled onto his back on the greasy furs, fully as careless as if he was alone, legs and arms wide and his half-hard cock flopped over to one side.

'Nothing like a fuck in the afternoon, is there?' he asked the tent's ceiling.

'What?' Bethod prided himself on never being taken by surprise. These days Ninefingers's every utterance seemed to catch him off balance.

'A fuck.' He propped himself up on his elbows. 'You been fucking, Chief?'

'I've been laying plans.'

Ninefingers wrinkled his nose. 'Well, it smells like fucking.'

'That's you.'

'Uh.' Ninefingers sniffed at one armpit and raised a scarred brow in acknowledgement. 'Well, you should fuck. Afternoon. Whenever. You look worried.'

'I'm worried because half the North wants me dead.'

Logen grinned. 'All the North wants me dead. Don't see me frowning, do you? Say one thing for Logen Ninefingers, say he looks on the sunny side o' the case.' Bethod ground his teeth. If he never heard that phrase again it would be too damn soon. 'Your wife looked worried, too, when I saw her t'other day. Was it yesterday? Day before? Marriage won't come to nothing without fucking, will it? Whole point o' the exercise.'

Bethod hardly knew what to say. The smell of the place was chasing out his wits. 'You're teaching me about marriage now? You?'

'Wisdom's wisdom, ain't it, no matter the source? I mean, if a man's a fucker or a fighter then I'm more of a fighter. Say one thing for Logen Ninefingers, say he's a fighter, but a fuck just soothes all those—'

'Rattleneck's coming,' said Bethod.

'Here?'

'Yes.'

352

Ninefingers frowned. 'Might be I should get dressed.'

'That's one idea.'

But, sadly, he didn't. He brought his knees up to his face and, with snakelike speed, sprang onto his feet in one motion, drew himself to his full height, stretching his arms out wide and wriggling his fingers. His nine fingers and his stump, anyway.

Bethod swallowed. He swore the bastard kept getting bigger. He was no small man but Ninefingers stood half a head taller, a twisted mass of scar and muscle and woody sinew, like a machine made for killing with no thought spared by the engineers on the looks of it. The way he held himself was all pride, and hate, and contempt at the world and everyone in it. Contempt for Bethod, too, who was meant to be his Chief.

Bethod wondered again if he should do what Ursi wanted. Kill Ninefingers. He had been wondering about it ever since Heonan, when Logen climbed the cliffs and spilled the Hillmen's blood in spite of his orders. While the rash fools cheered his audacity and made up bad songs about his skill, Bethod had been turning over how to kill the bloodthirsty fool. Who he could send to do it, and when. Knives in the night, how hard could it be? Put the mad dog down before he bit his master's hand. Or perhaps cut off his master's head.

And yet... and yet... they were friends, were they not? Bethod owed him, did he not? There were rules, were there not? A man should pay his dues, his father had always said.

And then there was the doubt niggling at the back of Bethod's neck. What if something went wrong? What if the Bloody-Nine survived, and came for him?

'So Rattleneck's coming?' Ninefingers strutted to a table made from an old door, his fruits slapping against his bare thighs with each step. 'What's that old bastard after?'

'I asked him to come.'

Ninefingers paused with his left hand halfway towards the table. 'You did?' There was a wine jug there, and some cups. And there was a huge knife, too, only just this side of a sword, buried in the scarred tabletop close to Logen's three reaching fingertips, its blade glittering cold in the chinks of daylight leaking into the tent.

Bethod realised then the place couldn't have held more weapons had it been an armoury. A sheathed sword lay on the ground with its belt in a tangle, an unsheathed one on top of it. Nearby was an axe with a heavy head stained brown, Bethod hoped with rust but rather feared it wasn't. There was a shield so hacked and dented and crossed with scars there was no telling what had once been painted on the face. And knives. Knives everywhere, the telltale glints of their blades and pommels among the furs, stabbed into the tent poles, buried to their crosspieces in the dirt. You can never have too many knives, Ninefingers was always saying.

Bethod wondered how many men he had killed. Wondered if anyone could put a count on it now. Named Men, and champions, and famed warriors, and Thralls, and Shanka, and peasants, and women, and children. Everything that breathed he'd stopped the breath of. For him to kill Bethod would be nothing. Every moment they stood together was a moment in which he chose not to do it. And Bethod felt again, as he did ten times a day, how weak a thing was power. How flimsy an illusion. A lie that everyone, for some unknown reason, agreed to treat as truth. And that blade in the table could, in an instant, be the ending of it, and the ending of Bethod, too, and all he had worked for. All he wanted to pass on to his sons.

Ninefingers grinned, a hungry grin, a wolf grin, as though he brushed aside the tissue of Bethod's authority and saw into his thoughts. Then he wrapped his three fingers around the handle of the wine jug. 'You want me to kill him?'

'Rattleneck?'

'Aye.'

'No.'

'Oh.' Ninefingers looked a little crestfallen, then started sloshing wine into a cup. 'Right.'

'I want to make peace with him.'

'Peace, you're saying?' Ninefingers paused, cup halfway to his mouth. 'Peace?' He rolled the word around in his mouth as if it was a strange new dish. As if it was a word in a foreign tongue. 'Why?'

Bethod blinked. 'What do you mean, why?'

'I can take that fucker, Chief, believe me! I can take him like *that*.' And the cup burst apart in his hand, spraying wine and bits of pot across the furs on the floor of the tent. Ninefingers blinked at his bleeding fist, as though he'd no idea how that happened. 'Uh. Shit.' He looked for something to wipe it on, then gave up and wiped it on his chest.

Bethod stepped towards him. The dead knew he did not want to. The dead knew his heart was pounding. But he stepped towards him anyway, and fixed him with his eye, and said, 'You can't kill the whole world, Logen.'

Ninefingers grinned as he reached for another cup. 'Folk are always telling me who I can't kill. But strong men, weak men, big names, little names, they all die once you cut 'em enough. Shama Heartless, you remember him? Everyone told me not to fight him.'

'I told you not to fight him.'

'Only 'cause you were scared I'd lose. But when I fought him, and when I looked set to win... did you ask me to stop?'

Bethod swallowed, mouth dry. He remembered the day well enough. The snow on the trees, and the smoke of breath as the crowd roared, and the clashing of steel, and both his fists clenched painfully tight as he willed Ninefingers on. Willed him on desperately, every hope hanging on him.

'No,' he said.

'No. And once I spilled his guts with his own sword... did you ask me to stop?'

'No,' said Bethod. He remembered the steam from them, remembered the smell of them, remembered the gurgling moan Shama Heartless made as he died, the great roar of triumph that had burst from his own throat. 'I cheered you on.'

'Yes. You called for no peace then, if I remember right. You felt...' Ninefingers's eyes were fever-bright, his hands clutching at the air as he searched for the word. 'You felt... the *joy* of it, didn't you! Better'n love. Better'n fucking. Better'n anything. Don't deny it!'

Bethod swallowed. 'Yes.' He could still feel the joy of it.

'You showed me the way.' And Ninefingers raised his forefinger and touched it gently to Bethod's chest. So gentle a touch, but his whole body turned cold at it. 'You. And I've walked the path you pointed, haven't I? Wherever it led. No matter how far or how dark or how long the odds, I've walked your path. Now let me show *you* the way.'

'And where will you lead us?'

Ninefingers raised his arms and tipped his head back towards the stained canvas above them, flapping gently with the breeze. 'The whole North! The whole world!'

'I don't want the whole North. I want peace.'

'What does peace mean?'

'Anything you want it to.'

'What if what I want is to kill Rattleneck's son?'

By the dead, it was worse than speaking to Scale. It was like speaking to an infant. A terribly dangerous infant standing four-square in the way of everything Bethod wanted. 'Listen to me, Logen.' Carefully. Patiently. 'If you kill Rattleneck's son, there'll be no end to the feuds. No end to the blood. Everyone in the North will be against us.'

'What do I care to that? Let 'em come! He's my prisoner. I took him, and I'll say what's done with him.' His voice grew louder, wilder, more cracked. 'I'll say! I'll decide!' He stabbed at his chest with a finger, spit flecking from his teeth and his eyes popping. 'Easier to stop the Whiteflow than to stop the Bloody-Nine!'

Bethod stood staring. Blood-drunk and murder-proud, just like Ursi had said. The selfishness of a baby, the savagery of a wolf, the vanity of a hero. Could this truly be the same man he once counted his closest friend? Who he used to ride beside, laughing, for hours at a time? Pointing at the landscape and saying how they'd site an army on it. How they'd make fortresses, or traps, or weapons from the ground. He hardly recognised him any more.

For a moment, he wanted to ask, *What happened to you?*

But Bethod knew what had happened. He'd been there, hadn't he? He'd pointed the way, just like Ninefingers said. He'd been a willing companion on the road. He'd swept up the rewards and smiled while he did it. He'd made a monster, and he had to make things right. Had to try, at least. For everyone's sake. For Logen's. For his own.

He lowered his voice and spoke softly, calmly. He did not attack, but he did not retreat. He was a rock.

'He's your prisoner. Of course he is. You'll decide. Of course you will. But I'm asking you, Logen. As your Chief. As your friend. Let me use him. Do you know what my father used to say?'

Logen blinked, frowning like a spiteful child now. And like a spiteful child, his curiosity won out. 'What did he say?'

And Bethod tried to pour all his conviction into the words. The way his father had, each one heavy as a mountain. 'Before you make a man into mud, make sure he's no use to you alive. Some men will smash a thing just because they can. They're too stupid to see that nothing shows more power than mercy.'

Ninefingers frowned. 'You saying I'm stupid?'

Bethod looked into the black pits of his eyes, the faintest reflection of his own face at the corners, and said, 'Prove you're not.'

They stared at each other then, for what felt like an age, close enough that Bethod could feel Ninefingers's breath on his face. He did not know what would happen. Did not know whether Ninefingers would agree. Did not know whether he would kill him where he stood. Did not know anything.

Then, like a leaf of steel bent and suddenly released, Logen's mouth snapped into a grin. 'You're right. Course you're right. I'm just funning.' And he slapped Bethod on the arm with the back of his hand.

Bethod wasn't sure he'd ever had less fun than in the last few moments.

'Peace is what we need now.' Logen capered to the table, all good humour, and sloshed out more wine, spilling some down his leg and barely noticing. 'I mean, I've no use for the bastard's corpse, have I? What good is he dead? Just meat. Just mud. Give him back to Rattleneck. Send him back to Daddy. Best all round. Let's get done with this and go home. Breed some fucking pigs or some shit. He's yours.'

'Thank the dead,' muttered Bethod, hardly able to speak for his hammering heart. 'You've made the right choice. Trust me.' He took a long breath, then walked on wobbly legs to the tent-flap. But he stopped before he got there and turned back.

A man should pay his dues, his father always told him.

'Thanks, Logen,' he said. 'Truly. I couldn't have got here without you. That much I know.'

Logen laughed. 'That's what friends are for, ain't it?' And he smiled that easy smile he used to have – the smile of a man who'd never entertained a dark purpose – and the fresh cut on his cheek twisted, and the stitches wept a streak of blood. 'Now where'd that girl get to?'

It was bright outside, and Bethod closed his eyes and took a steadying breath, wiped his sweating forehead on the back of his hand.

He could do it. He could taste it.

Freedom.

Peace.

The scythes in the fields, the men building instead of breaking, the forest cleared for his great road, and a nation rising from the dust and ashes. A nation that would make all the sacrifices worthwhile...

And all he had to do was make a man who hated him beyond all else see things his way. He took another breath and puffed out his cheeks.

'He giving up Rattleneck's son?' asked Craw, taking a pause from nibbling at his thumbnail to spit out the bitings.

'He is.'

The Dogman closed his eyes and gave his own sigh of relief. 'Thank the dead. I tried to tell him. Tried to, but...'

'He's not an easy man to talk to, these days.'

'No, he isn't.'

'Just keep him here until Rattleneck's gone,' said Bethod. 'The last thing I need is the Bloody-Nine wandering into my negotiations with his wet cock hanging out. And by the dead, make sure he does nothing stupid!'

'He's not stupid.'

Bethod looked back to the shadowy mouth of the tent, Logen's happy humming floating from it. 'Then make sure he does nothing mad.'

'You can stop right there,' said Craw, putting his shoulder in front of Bethod and drawing a length of steel as a warning.

'Of course.' The stranger didn't look much of a threat, even to Bethod, who was well used to seeing threats everywhere. He was an unassuming little fellow in travel-stained clothes, leaning on a staff. 'I only want a moment of your time, Lord Bethod.'

'I'm no lord,' said Bethod.

The man just smiled. There was something odd about him. A knowing glint in his eyes. Different-coloured eyes, Bethod noticed. 'Treat every man like an emperor, you'll offend no one.'

'Walk with me, then.' Bethod set off through the tents and the mud towards the holdfast. 'And I can spare you a moment.'

'Sulfur is my name.' And the man bowed humbly, even while hurrying after. A touch of fancy Southern manners, which Bethod quite liked to see. 'I am an emissary.'

Bethod snorted. Emissaries rarely brought good news. New challenges, new insults, new threats, new feuds, but rarely good news. 'From what clan?'

'From no clan, my Lord. I come from Bayaz, the First of the Magi.'

'Huh,' grunted Craw, unhappily, sword still halfway drawn.

And Bethod realised what most bothered him about this man.

He carried no weapon. As strange as to be travelling without a head in these bloody times.

'What does a wizard want with me?' asked Bethod, frowning. He did not care for magic in the least. He liked what could be touched, and predicted, and relied upon.

'It is not what he wants that he wishes to discuss, but what *you* want. My master is a most wise and powerful man. The wisest and most powerful who yet lives in these latter days, perhaps. Doubtless he can help you, with your...' Sulfur waved one long-fingered hand about as he sought the word. 'Difficulties.'

'I appreciate all offers of help, of course.' They squelched between the guards and back through the gate of the holdfast. 'But my difficulties end today.'

'My master will be overjoyed to learn it. But, if I may, the trouble with difficulties solved is that, so often, new difficulties present themselves soon after.'

Bethod snorted at that, too, as he took up a place on the steps, frowning towards the gate, Craw at his shoulder. 'That much is true enough.'

Sulfur continued to talk in his ear, voice soft and subtle. 'Should your difficulties ever weigh too heavy to bear alone, my master's door is always open. You may pay him a visit whenever you wish, at the Great Northern Library.'

'Thank your master for me, but tell him I have no need of—' Bethod turned, but the man was gone.

'Rattleneck's on his way, Chief.' Pale-as-Snow was hurrying across the yard, cloak spattered with mud from hard riding. 'You've got his son, aye?'

'I do.'

'Ninefingers agreed to give him up?'

'He did.'

Pale-as-Snow raised his white brows. 'Well done.'

'Why wouldn't he? I'm his Chief.'

'Of course. And mine. But it's getting how I don't know what that mad bastard'll do one day to the next. Sometimes I look at him and . . .' He shivered. 'I think he might kill me out of pure meanness.'

'Hard times call for hard men,' said Craw.

'That they do, Craw,' said Pale-as-Snow, 'and no doubt these times qualify. The dead know I've faced some hard men. Fought beside 'em, fought against 'em. Big names. Dangerous bastards.' He leaned forward, white hair stirred in the breeze, and spat. 'I never met one scared me like the Bloody-Nine, though. Have you?'

Craw swallowed, and said nothing.

'Do you trust him?'

'With my life,' said Bethod. 'We all have, haven't we? More than once. And each time he's come through.'

'Aye, and I guess he came through again taking Rattleneck's son.' Pale-as-Snow gave a grin. 'Peace, eh, Chief?'

'Peace,' said Bethod, rolling the word around his mouth and savouring the taste of it.

'Peace,' muttered Craw. 'Think I'll go back to carpentry.'

'Peace,' said Pale-as-Snow, shaking his head like he could hardly believe such a thing might happen. 'Shall I tell Littlebone and Whitesides to stand down, then?'

'Tell them to stand up,' said Bethod. He thought he could hear the sound of hooves outside the gates. 'Get their men ready to fight. All their men.'

'But—'

'The wise leader hopes he won't need his sword. But he keeps it sharp even so.'

Made A Monster

Pale-as-Snow smiled. 'So he does, Chief. Ain't no point in a blunt one.'

Riders came thundering through the gate. Battle-worn men on battle-ready horses. Men with well-used armour and weapons. Men who wore their frowns like swords. Rattleneck was at the front, balding and running to fat but a big man still, with gold links in his chain-mail shirt and gold rings in his hair and gold at the hilt of his heavy sword.

He spattered mud across the yard and everyone in it as he pulled his horse up savagely and glowered down at Bethod, teeth bared.

Bethod only smiled. He held the upper hand after all. He could afford to. 'Well met, Rattleneck—'

'I don't think so,' he snapped. 'Shitly met, I'd say. Shitly fucking met! Curnden bloody Craw, is that you?'

'Aye,' said Craw, mildly, hands folded over his sword-belt.

Rattleneck shook his head. 'Never expected a good man like you to stand for the likes of this.'

Craw only shrugged. 'There's always good men on both sides of a good fight.' Bethod was starting to like him more and more. A reassuring presence. A straight edge in a crooked time. If there'd ever been an opposite of the Bloody-Nine, there he stood.

'I don't see too many good men here,' snapped Rattleneck.

Bethod had told his wife they liked spiteful, prideful, wrathful men in the North, and picked the most childish of the crowd for leaders, and here was the best example one could have asked for, or perhaps the worst, booming away with nostrils flaring wider than his blown horse's.

Bethod amused himself with the thought but filled his tone to the brim with deep respect. 'You honour my holdfast with your presence, Rattleneck.'

'*Your* holdfast?' he frothed. 'Last winter it was Hallum Brown-staff's!'

'Yes. But Hallum was rash and he lost it to me, along with his life. I'm glad you came to it, anyway.'

'Only for my son. Where's my son?'

'He's here.'

The old man worked his mouth. 'I heard he fought the Bloody-Nine.'

'And lost.' Bethod saw the flicker of fear across Rattleneck's lined face. 'The folly of youth, to think you'll win where a hundred better men have gone in the mud.' He let that hang for a moment. 'But Ninefingers only knocked him on the head and that's your family's least vulnerable spot, eh? He hardly got worse than a scratch. We aren't the blood-mad bastards you may think.' Not all of them, anyway. 'He's safe. He's well treated. A perfect guest. He's down below us now, in my cellar.' And because it would not do to give him things all his own way, Bethod added, 'In chains.'

'I want him back,' said Rattleneck, and his voice was rough, and his cheek trembled.

'So would I, in your position. I have sons myself. Get down from your horse, and let's talk about it.'

They stared at each other across the table. Rattleneck and his Named Men on one side, glaring as if they were about to start a battle rather than make a peace. Bethod on the other, with Pale-as-Snow and Curnden Craw beside him.

'Will you have wine?' asked Bethod, gesturing to the jug.

'Fuck your wine!' shouted Rattleneck, slapping the cup away so it skittered down the table and shattered against the wall. 'And fuck your maps, and fuck your talk! I want my son!'

Bethod took a long breath and sighed. How much time did he waste sighing? 'You can have him.'

As he had hoped, that caught Rattleneck and his men well and truly off guard. They blinked at each other, frowned and grumbled, cast him dark glances, trying to work out the ruse.

'Eh?' was the best Rattleneck could manage.

'What use is he to me? Take him, with my blessing.'

'And what do you want in return?'

'Nothing.' Bethod sat forward, staring into Rattleneck's grizzled face. 'I want peace, Rattleneck. That's all I've ever wanted.' That was a lie, he knew, he'd sought more battles than any man alive, but a good lie's better than a bad truth, his mother always used to tell him.

'Peace?' snorted Blacktoe, one of Rattleneck's Named Men and a fierce one at that. 'Did you give peace to them five villages you burned up the valley?'

Bethod met his bright eye, calm and even. He was a rock. 'We've had a war, and in a war folk do things they regret. Folk on both sides. I want no more regrets. So yes, Blacktoe, I want peace, whatever you believe. That's all I want.'

'Peace,' murmured Rattleneck. Bethod was watching his scarred face, and caught it. That twitch of need. That softening of his mouth. That misting of his eye. He recognised it from his own face and knew Rattleneck wanted peace, too. After the blood that had been spilled these last few years, what sane man wouldn't?

Bethod clasped his hands on the table. 'Peace now, and the Thralls can go back to their farms, the Carls to their halls. Peace now, and their wives and mothers and children need not struggle with the harvest alone. Peace now, and let us *build* something.' And Bethod thumped the table. 'I've seen enough waste, how about you?'

'I never wanted this,' snapped Rattleneck.

'Believe it or not, nor did I. So let us end the fighting. Here. Now. We have the power.'

'You listening to this?' Blacktoe asked his Chief, voice squealing up high with disbelief. 'Old Man Yawl won't have no peace, not ever, and nor will I!'

'Shut your mouth!' snarled Rattleneck, glaring Blacktoe into a sullen silence then glancing back to Bethod, combing thoughtfully at his beard. Most of his other men had softened up, too. Thinking it over. Thinking what peace might mean. 'Blacktoe's got a point, though,' said Rattleneck. 'Old Man Yawl won't have it, and there's Black Dow to think on, too, and plenty of others on my side with scores to settle. They might not take to peace.'

'Most will. For the others, it's our job to make them take to it.'

'They won't let go their hate of you,' said Blacktoe.

Bethod shrugged. 'That they can keep. As long as they hate me in peace.' He leaned forward and put the iron into his voice. 'But if they fight me, I'll crush them. Like I did Threetrees, and Beyr, and all the rest.'

'What about the Bloody-Nine?' asked Rattleneck. 'You'll be making a farmer of that animal, will you?'

Bethod gave away no hint of his doubts in that direction. 'Maybe I will. My man. My business.'

'He'll just do what you tell him, will he?' sneered Blacktoe.

'This is bigger than one man,' said Bethod, holding Rattleneck's eye. 'This is bigger than you, or me, or your son, or the Bloody-Nine. This is something we owe our people. Talk to the other clans. Call off your dogs. Tell them the land I've taken in battle belongs to me and my sons and their sons. What you still hold is yours. Yours and your sons'. I don't want it.' He stood and held out his hand, making sure it was neither palm up nor palm down, but perfectly level. Perfectly fair. A hand that took no liberties and gave no favours. A hand that could be trusted. 'Take my hand, Rattleneck. Let's end this.'

Rattleneck's shoulders slumped. He looked a tired man as he slowly rose. An old man. A man with no fight left in him.

'All I want is my son,' he croaked, and he reached out and took Bethod's hand, and by the dead his grip felt fine. 'Give me my son, you can have a thousand years of peace, far as I care.'

Bethod walked with a spring in his step and an unfamiliar joy in his heart. As though a great weight had been lifted from his shoulders, and why not? How many enemies made, how much blood spilled, how many times had he beaten impossible odds, just to survive? How long had he been living in fear?

Peace. They had told him he would never have peace.

But it was as his father had always said. Swords are well enough, but the only true victories are won with words. Now he would set to building. Building something to be proud of. Something his father would have been proud of. Something his sons—

And then he saw the Dogman, lurking at the head of the steps with the strangest guilty look on his pointed face, and Bethod felt a horror flood up in him, cold as ice, and freeze all his dreams dead.

'What are you doing here?' he managed to whisper.

The Dogman only shook his head, tangle of long hair swaying across his face.

'Is Ninefingers down there?'

The Dogman's eyes were wide and wet, and his mouth opened, but he said nothing.

'I told you not to let him do anything stupid,' Bethod forced through his gritted teeth.

'You didn't tell me how.'

'You want me to come down there with you?' But Craw looked far from keen, and Bethod hardly blamed him.

'Best I go alone,' he whispered.

Reluctantly as a man digging his own grave, Bethod edged sideways down the steps, one at a time into the buried dark. The tunnel stretched away, torchlight shining on the damp rock at the far end, shadows shifting across the moss-streaked wall as something moved.

He wanted only to run, but he forced himself towards it, step by reluctant step, breath by wheezing breath. He started to hear strange noises over the thudding of his heart. A squelching and a crunching. A humming and a whistling. Growling and grunting and occasionally full-sung phrases, and badly sung at that.

The breath crawled in Bethod's throat as he forced himself around the corner, and looked through the wide-open door and into the cell, and he went cold from the tips of his toes to the roots of his hair. Cold as the dead.

Ninefingers stood, naked still, lips pursed as he tunelessly whistled, twisted muscles knotting and flexing as he worked, eyes shining with happiness, skin dashed and spattered black from head to toe.

There was something hanging all around the cell, glistening rope in swags and festoons like decorations for some mad festival. Guts, Bethod realised. Guts, unwound and nailed up.

'By the dead,' he whispered, putting one hand across his mouth at the stink.

'That's got it!' And Ninefingers buried the big knife in the table and held the head dangling by one ear, blood still trickling from the hacked-off neck and spattering the floor. The head of Rattleneck's son. He grabbed the slack jaw with his other hand

and moved it clumsily up and down while he spoke through his clenched teeth in a piping mockery of a voice.

'I want to go back to my daddy.' And Ninefingers laughed. 'Take me back to Daddy.' And he chuckled. 'I'm scared.' And he sighed, and tossed the head away, and frowned at it as it rolled into the corner.

'Thought that'd be funnier.' And he looked around for something to wipe his hands on, blood-slick to the elbows, but couldn't find anything. 'You reckon Rattleneck'll still want him?'

'What have you done?' whispered Bethod, staring at the thing on the table that hardly looked like it had ever been a man.

And Logen smiled that easy smile he used to have – the smile of a man who'd never entertained a dark purpose – and shrugged.

'Changed my mind.'

Acknowledgements

As always, four people without whom:

Bren Abercrombie, whose eyes are sore from reading it.
Nick Abercrombie, whose ears are sore from hearing about it.
Rob Abercrombie, whose fingers are sore from turning the pages.
Lou Abercrombie, whose arms are sore from holding me up.

Then, my heartfelt thanks:

To the editors of anthologies who, unbelievably, paid me to write some of these stories in the first place: Lou Anders, Jonathan Strahan, George R. R. Martin, Gardner Dozois and Shawn Speakman.

To all the lovely and talented folks at my UK Publisher, Gollancz, and their parent Orion, particularly Simon Spanton, Sophie Calder, Jen McMenemy, Mark Stay and Jon Wood. Then, of course, to all those who've helped make, publish, publicise, translate and above all *sell* my books wherever they may be around the world.

To the artists responsible for somehow continuing to make me look classy: Dave Senior and Laura Brett.

For keeping the wolf on the right side of the door: Robert Kirby.

To all the writers whose paths have crossed mine on the Internet, at the bar, or in some cases around the D&D table and in the fencing hall, and who've provided help, support, laughs and plenty of ideas worth the stealing. You know who you are.
And lastly, yet firstly:

My partner in crimes against fantasy fiction, Gillian Redfearn. There is no end sharper than the point of her pencil...

ABOUT GOLLANCZ

Gollancz is the oldest SF publishing imprint in the world. Since being founded in 1927 Gollancz has continued to publish a focused selection of bestselling and award-winning authors. The front-list includes **Ben Aaronovitch**, **Joe Abercrombie**, **Charlaine Harris**, **Joanne Harris**, **Joe Hill**, **Alastair Reynolds**, **Patrick Rothfuss**, **Nalini Singh** and **Brandon Sanderson**.

As one of the largest Science Fiction and Fantasy imprints in the UK it is no surprise we have one of the most extensive backlists in the world. Find high quality SF on Gateway written by such authors as **Philip K. Dick**, **Ursula Le Guin**, **Connie Willis**, **Sir Arthur C. Clarke**, **Pat Cadigan**, **Michael Moorcock** and **George R.R. Martin**.

We also have a strand of publishing in translation, which includes French, Polish and Russian authors. Gollancz is home to more award-winning authors than any other imprint, with names including **Aliette de Bodard**, **M. John Harrison**, **Paul McAuley**, **Sarah Pinborough**, **Pierre Pevel**, **Justina Robson** and many more.

The SF Gateway
More than 3,000 classic, rare and previously out-of-print SF novels at your fingertips.
www.sfgateway.com

The Gollancz Blog
Bringing you news from our worlds to yours. Stories, interviews, articles and exclusive extracts just for you!
www.gollancz.co.uk

GOLLANCZ
LONDON